CW01184166

N-WORD

KIEREN-PAUL BROWN

For permission requests, write to the author at: info@kierenpaulbrown.com

ISBN: 9798345910511
Printed Globally
First Edition

Trigger Warning

This novel contains depictions of violence, sex. racism, and themes that may be distressing to some readers. Reader discretion is advised.

Author's Note

This story is an exploration of identity, resilience, and love in the face of adversity. While it draws on real-world issues, it remains a work of fiction. It is my hope that readers find both discomfort and hope in these pages; discomfort that prompts reflection, and hope that inspires action.

DEDICATIONS

To Antonia, the woman this novel's protagonist is named after, thank you for being a part of my life. The time we shared was special, and I'll never forget you. You've been there for me when I needed you, and all I can say is thank you for existing and being the ray of sunshine you are.

To the person reading, Antonia's a gifted singer who's just moved to Dubai to chase her dreams. Please support her on IG @nellimondo.

To my mother and biggest fan, thanks for teaching me how to read and indirectly making all of this possible. I've told a few people this, but the reason I love writing so much is because of the fond memories I have of reading with you when I was a boy.

If you didn't make those experiences so fun for me, this book wouldn't exist, so thanks, Mom. But that said, I feel bad that I've written a book this dark because I know it makes you uncomfortable. I honestly want to write stories that make you proud, Mom, so I promise you I'll never write anything this dark ever again. :)

To Rama, thank you for being a sounding board of ideas. Thank you for spending hours and hours listening to me read chapters of N-Word before giving me feedback when you could have been doing anything else with your time. I appreciate the advice you gave me about this book. And I'll never forget you telling me it was a masterpiece when I lacked confidence. I want you to know you're amazing, and I greatly care about you.

Rama's one of the best female coaches in the world and can be followed on IG @ramandala.

And finally, to the special soul I met in 2022, I still have the memories of the unforgettable time we spent together, and I'll keep them close forever. I mean that; I'll treasure them until the very day my heart stops beating.

Who knows? Maybe one day, we'll share those moments with the world.

EPIGRAPH

"By Any Means Necessary."

—Malcolm X

CONTENTS

01 | WELCOME TO YOUR DOOM

ANTONIA | The Hoell Residence: Moss Bluff: Present Day

Antonia Hoell hated every single thing about her body. She hated the disgusting wrinkles which oozed from her haggard skin like molten candle wax. She hated the withered breasts which hung from her equally withered chest like spent balloons. Breasts which had entirely and utterly yielded to gravity's whims the way her withered spirit had yielded to life.

But most importantly, Antonia hated herself, her own self, and everything about the worthless ancient fuck in the mirror. The ancient fuck she could never escape, no matter how much she wished she could. Day after miserable day and decade after miserable decade she stood by helplessly as her body became even more pathetic, broken, and ugly than before.

She was decrepit.

Spent.

Worthless.

Old.

Antonia moved through her house with the grace of a rampaging rhinoceros, the power of a field mouse, and the coordination of a woman three times her 85 years of age.

As she yet again smashed her knee against the sharp corner of her oak coffee table and yet again felt that stabbing jolt of pain shoot from the point of impact up to her brain and then all the way back down, she even despised her own nervous system.

Antonia's body didn't just look and feel repugnant, it was broken. Truly broken.

No.

Scratch that.

It was fucked.

Absolutely. Positively. Fucked.

Just moving was an effort. Just the simple act of putting one fucking foot in front of the other, something even the dumbest of three-year-olds has mastered, something which literally is child's play, was a strenuous effort for Antonia. Her feet had all the coordination of a palsy sufferer on LSD, and her perpetually aching legs had to dig deep into their strength reserves to keep her haggard form upright.

She felt pain everywhere. Literally everywhere. There wasn't a single part of her body which was connected to her nervous system that didn't suffer from moderate to severe discomfort. It circulated throughout the cells of her gaunt frame at all times, regardless of what she was or wasn't doing.

However, despite all the above, somehow, some way, she forced herself to her desk. Dragging one withered foot after the other, she shambled to her chair and collapsed her bony backside on its wooden exterior with a pained groan. After that, she switched on her iPad, and once that was done, she started up Instagram.

You see, Antonia had created an anonymous account for what she was about to do. No name, no profile picture, no posts, and certainly no followers. She'd never have dreamed of using her public account for what was about to transpire.

No chance in hell.

She'd rather have died than have the world know this element of her personality. She'd rather have burned in hell than let society voyage that far into the depths of her psyche. She couldn't let them know what she truly yearned for. What she so dearly craved. A woman her age caught looking at such content would suffer more humiliation than her poor soul could bear.

Antonia detested the shame she felt at safeguarding that secret. She abhorred the way it made her view herself and wished she could be free from its grip. But alas, Antonia sadly knew freedom simply wasn't a possibility.

Such was her life.

After she logged into her anonymous Instagram account, she scrolled to her discovery page. And, as her feed quickly populated with content she'd have been mortified for anyone to see her looking at, her dry eyes bore witness to a sight as painful as it was intoxicating to behold.

Scores and scores of gorgeous, sexy, and young black women.

Women who lived lives Antonia could never hope to live in bodies she could never hope to have while wearing clothes she could never dream of having the confidence to wear.

The pupils of her eyes dilated with wonder as they took in the sight before her, all while the whites of those same eyes now became lubricated with wet tears.

Seeing such a never-ending array of gorgeous, young, and adorable bodies was both excruciating and bewitching. Both a temporary reprieve from her eternal prison and a stark reminder of the outer confines of its unbreakable walls.

Antonia tapped on the profile of her favourite model, a woman called Kara Fit, and was as anguished by pain as she was aroused by fantasy.

Why can't I be like her? She thought.

Why the fuck couldn't Antonia be Kara Fit? Her skin was smooth like butter made silk and those breasts.

Good God, her breasts!

They were thick, full, heaving, gravity-defying, and breathtakingly sensual. Her body was solid and powerful, yet feminine, and she knew it.

She knows it.

She clearly knew it.

Kara had a presence about her, a power, an energy. An air of feminine confidence in who she was and what she was about. She didn't just look at the camera; she looked straight through it with intensity burning from her eyes and the poise of a sexual goddess.

She has zero doubts about the effect she has on people. She knows it.

Men wanted her.

Women wanted to be her.

And to her, it just was what it was.

Kara's shapely and thick thighs were supple, strong, and seductive. They twisted and snaked around her environment in a manner as poetic as it was erotic. Her body wasn't just sexy.

It wasn't just sensual.

It was art.

Her body was a living, breathing work of art. Da Vinci himself couldn't have improved it.

The way her thick butt stretched the tight fabric of her skirt and how the muscles of her shapely calves flexed so elegantly as they shone in the dim moonlight was enchanting.

It was art.

Kara was art.

But she was also trauma.

Deep, unavoidable, psychological trauma.

Why?

Because no matter how much Antonia wanted to be Kara, it never would be. No matter how vividly she imagined Kara's life to be hers, such fantasies would never materialise.

Antonia could lock her eyes shut and picture everything, the colours, the smells, the sounds, the millions of likes and thousands of comments on her posts, but it would all be for nought.

She would never be the woman over whom millions worldwide fantasised.

She would never have handsome, confident, successful men courting her.

She would never have that validation.

Antonia would never again be young, and she would never know what it was like to be beautiful. She would die without ever having known the thrill of being appreciated, and nothing would change that.

That fact crushed her spirit. It ripped her soul in two.

For that reason, Antonia found herself once again sliding her wrinkled fingers underneath the hemline of her skirt and pulling her uninspiring old granny underwear to one side. For that reason, Antonia once again found herself probing and twisting the dilapidated ruins of her clitoris, trying in vain to stimulate it to life.

Antonia needed to feel something.

Anything.

Anything to save her mind from the growing sea of regret which threatened to drown her in its wake.

And she could feel it.

I can feel it.

She could feel it once again.

Yet again.

It was the pain. The pain which grew with every extra miserable year she spent sucking oxygen. The pain which never went away and only ever lowered in volume.

It was back and significantly louder than before.

Like a python slivering out from a dark rock to devour its unsuspecting prey, said pain had reemerged slowly but with sinister intent.

Antonia felt a tightness in her chest. A dull ache pulsed from her heart and across her bloodstream to infect the cells of her body. Her brain bled with a trauma that was as emotional as it was physical as it was psychic.

And, as her trembling thumb continued to scroll through Kara Fit's gorgeous pictures and videos, Antonia screamed a quarter of a cup's worth of saliva onto her iPad screen.

Don't think about it! Don't think about it! You old fuck!

Those posts were both a breathtaking mixture of erotic sensuality and a testament to Kara's peerless dedication to her craft of yoga. The way she moved, the way she contorted her body, she wasn't just gorgeous; she was also skilled in a way that Antonia wasn't.

She could put her body into positions that made you gasp. Antonia had to deal with the reality that someone about a quarter of her age had achieved a level of mastery she'd never reached in 85 fucking years.

Why isn't it doing anything?! Why isn't it doing anything?!

Nothing was happening. Nothing. She couldn't feel anything. Her broken clitoris wasn't working. But then again, it never did. Not since they cut most of it off all those years ago. Since then, it just felt numb year after year, but still. But still.

She needed something.

Anything!

Still obsessing over Kara's updates through a screen now coated with her own sticky saliva, Antonia slammed her fist onto her wooden oak desk in frustration. Unsurprisingly, doing so ruptured several blood vessels in her pale hand, bringing with it a significant degree of trauma.

Shards of electrical agony erupted within said fist as her iPad fell to the floor. Undeterred, however, she picked it back up and carried on regardless.

Antonia had to keep looking.

In her latest post, Kara wore nothing but black boots with matching stockings, panties, and a bra, all while gracefully swinging on a steel pole.

Jesus Christ, her strength is incredible.

It was out of this world. She could actually hang horizontally and support her entire body weight with just her arms.

Just her fucking arms.

Antonia's atrophied legs could barely walk 15 feet without buckling, let alone perform so athletic a feat.

However, this was the moment when she finally felt something. The moment when the powers that be finally decided to stop shitting on her and give her a fucking break.

Why?

Because somewhere within the dark recesses of her gaunt frame's dilapidated nervous system, Antonia actually felt something.

Something small, yes.

Minute, yes.

But real nonetheless.

It wasn't much.

No.

Not much at all. In fact, it was more akin to a flicker. An ember. A muted and distant echo of the long extinguished flame that Antonia once knew to be the molten inferno of sexual desire.

But said ember was something no matter how slight. Said ember was hope. Said ember caused the pupils of Antonia's pale eyes to dilate with pleasure.

Said ember caused drips of contentment to flow through her brittle bones, making her physical and mental torment almost three percent more bearable than before.

Said ember made Antonia finally feel alive once more as moisture slowly returned to a realm from which it had remained barren for decades.

As intermittent flickers of euphoria pulsed from her brain to her breasts, down to her toes, and all the back up to her vagina, Antonia moaned.

As all of this happened, Antonia sighed.

As she continued to scroll through Kara Fit's Instagram page, keeping her eyes locked on every minute detail of that gorgeous woman's life, she bit her lip with pleasure.

Hard.

The expensive cars, the 5-star hotels, the designer clothes, her beautiful afro, and that breathtaking physique. As she slowly forgot her troubles, Antonia's heartbeat intensified to levels not reached since before Nixon was impeached.

Slowly, she lost all concept of who she was. Slowly, she began to believe she wasn't actually herself. No. She wasn't old, withered, spent, and drained of life.

She was Kara Fit.

She was young, gorgeous, smothered in delicious caramel brown skin with millions in the bank and the whole world at her oyster. She turned heads wherever she went just by her mere existence.

Just by her mere existence.

Women envied her.

Men craved her.

Antonia was someone.

Someone important.

Someone who mattered.

And so, as those flickering and spasming shards of ecstasy perforated her bloodstream, Antonia continued to stroke what little remained of her body's primary pleasure organ until another moan escaped her lips.

For the second time in so long, a deep and guttural moan forced its way from her ribcage, up her throat, and out through the gaps in her teething.

"Uhhhh!"

And then another.

"Guhhhhhh!"

And another.

"Nnhhhhhh!"

And another. Still, she kept scrolling through Kara's pictures and pouring over her gushing comments.

"Hey, cutie, let me know when you're in Vegas, and I'll take you out sometime."

"OMG HUN YOUR BODY IS GOALS!"

"Soooo sexy!"

Nobody ever spoke to Antonia like that, even when she was young. Those compliments were all she ever wanted. They were everything. But she never got them. She never fucking got them. Even when she was young.

Only from Winston, rest in peace.

Only from her father, rot in fucking pieces.

Those words filled her jackhammer-beating heart with joy and made her think for even the slightest second that maybe, just maybe, she actually deserved to love herself.

But then, Antonia felt that long-forgotten feeling. The feeling she didn't think she'd ever know again in this lifetime. The flowing, pulsing, and unavoidable feeling which let her know an orgasm was en route.

Churning.

Imminent.

The sweet, exquisite, and agonising buildup of emotion which threatened to burst within her being and merge her essence with a life force greater than her own.

Antonia's eyes wanted to scrunch shut in submission to such sweet misery. Still, she kept them prised open in total defiance of her body's natural instincts. Her gaunt fingers wanted to shake and tremble, but she ordered them to stroke what remained of her clitoris like a matter of life and death.

She did all this while forcing the fingers of her left hand to scroll through that IG page like nothing else mattered because nothing else did, in fact, matter.

Antonia's body tingled all over. Lost in the intensity of multiple eruptions of cascading energy perforating her soul and snaring her body in delirious pleasure like a Venus fly trap of seduction.

Yet again, she moaned.

"Ahh."

"It felt good. Blissful. So deliciously exquisitely blissful. It felt right. And as Antonia's chest began to rise and fall in a sensual rhythm akin to an Egyptian belly dancer, those moans kept coming.

"Mmmmmmmhhhhh."

It was coming. It was coming. Her orgasm was coming. Antonia was cumming. She could feel it. She could feel it. There was nothing else she could do. Nothing else she wanted to do.

"AHHHRRGGGHHHH!"

She was melting. Merging. Blending. Losing herself in sexual pleasure the way a single droplet of water loses itself in the Atlantic. Antonia was becoming one. Antonia was transcending her body, transcending her mind, flowing into all there is, was, and ever could be. She was almost there; she was almost there!

"OHHHH GOOOOODDDD!"

Her first orgasm in decades. Her first orgasm in countless numbers of years was here, and she'd forgotten how glorious it felt. How overwhelming. How deliriously elastic it felt to be reunited with eternity!

To feel that divine spark of ecstatic agony tear through her being and, in its wake, turn what once was a barren wasteland into a gushing river getting drenched amid a tropical rainstorm.

"OHHHHHHHH!"

It was finally here.

"OHHHHHHHHHHHH!"

Antonia's orgasm was finally here.

"OHHHHHHHHHHHHHHHH!"

And it was more than worth the wait.

"OHHHHHHHHHHHHHHHHHHHH!"

But then, just like that, it dissipated.

“WHAT?”

It vanished.

“WHAT?!”

The arousal vanished even quicker than it had arrived. The sweet misery of delirious ecstasy was gone.

“WHAT?!”

Antonia was no longer teetering on the brink of toe-curling rapture. In fact, she didn’t feel anything. She was just normal. Completely normal. Somehow, back to being just her.

Back to just being Antonia.

“WHAT? WHAT HAPPENED!?”

She didn’t know what happened.

“WHAT THE HELL HAPPENED?!”

She didn’t know what happened.

Where did it go? What happened to her orgasm? What happened to that beautifully imminently pre-explosive bubble of passion?

“NO!”

She hadn’t felt that feeling for decades. Whole fucking decades.

“I HAVE TO HAVE IT AGAIN!”

She had to have it again.

“I HAVE TO!”

She had to.

“I HAVE TO!”

She just had to. So she wasn't going to stop. Not when she was so close. Antonia was going to have her orgasm if it killed her.

And so, with an intensity they'd long forgotten they possessed, her ancient fingers resumed their task of stimulating her clitoral ruins. Antonia felt her heart rate continue to quicken, but that didn't matter.

She also felt beads of sweat build upon her brow and arms, but they didn't matter. She even felt her thoughts become cloudy, disjointed, and confused, but again, none of that mattered. Antonia had to do it. Antonia had to have her orgasm. Antonia had to forget who she truly was.

But nothing would work. Nothing was happening.

No matter how hard she stared at that Instagram feed, her body wouldn't respond. In fact, she felt it calling out in pain, crying out in anguish, and screaming out in misery. Antonia may not have felt sexual delight, but she certainly felt something. She was straining her ancient form far beyond its comfort zone, and she knew it.

Her heart rate had accelerated way past the safe zone for a woman of her advanced years, and she felt fresh pain slicing through it. She felt her fingers begin to cramp from overuse. She felt her lungs working overtime in a desperate attempt to take oxygen into a body that was fast losing the necessary strength to convert said oxygen into usable energy.

Antonia had lived with pain for over half of her life. This was nothing new. But that pain was a low-level background hum, which, with the right amount of mental focus, could be ignored to a degree. The pain she felt at this moment was anything but, and what's more, it was growing.

Crying. Shouting. Screaming.

It was pain which served to remind her of the futility of her goal. Pain which served to taunt her with the fact that try as she might, she would never be the woman she desired to be.

But Antonia couldn't stop. She just couldn't. She couldn't face what she'd see on the other side if she did. No amount of physical pain would be worse than the existential agony of facing another moment in the nightmare hellscape of a reality that was her life.

She couldn't bear to see it. She couldn't bear to experience that existence. So she had to keep going. She had to be Kara Fit.

But it hurt. It hurt so much. What's more, her body, wracked with pain, was starting to convulse. Second, after second, it took more of what precious little strength she still retained to stimulate the rotten remains of the clitoris she no longer possessed.

"You're going to die today, Antonia."

Who the fuck was that?!

She didn't know, and nor did she care. All Antonia knew was that she still felt nothing.

Still.

Still, after so much hard work. Still, after her fingers worked themselves into frenzies to stimulate herself, she felt nothing. No arousal, no orgasmic feeling. Just pain. Just growing convulsions. A growing white light in the centre of her field of sight. A light that started out as a tiny dot but slowly stretched to encompass 25% of her vision.

Antonia couldn't breathe.

Her lungs wouldn't work.

She sucked with everything she had to take in oxygen but, in doing so, felt like she might swallow her tongue.

"You're going to die today, Antonia."

Something was wrong.

Her body convulsed and spasmed badly. Her determined eyes strained to focus on Kara Fit's feed through an increasingly impenetrable field of white static as her fingers twitched erratically, seemingly unable to obey her mental commands.

Something was wrong.

Antonia had felt pain before, but not like this.

Never like this.

"You're dying, Antonia."

Not like this.

She didn't want that to be true. She wanted nothing more than for that to be a lie but she was losing the ability to see and had already lost the ability to move. Her arms and legs jerked on the spot, her fingers twisting violently in random directions like a scene from The Exorcist.

Something was wrong. Very wrong.

Now she couldn't see. Now she couldn't think. Now she couldn't breathe. Her lungs heaved but could only take in a few jerky puffs of air at a time.

It just wasn't enough.

The pain was everywhere. Screaming in her ears. Millions and billions of bright white dots turning her vision into a flickering, pulsating field of white static. And, as fresh warm saliva began to burst from her lips, Antonia felt unbearable agony shoot from her brain and heart at precisely the same time.

Something was wrong. Very wrong.

And so, with what little of her strength remained, Antonia groaned in agony as her frail and ancient body finally succumbed to defeat. She collapsed onto her desk right on top of her iPad as it played one of Kara Fit's Instagram videos on a loop, all while her hand rested against her exposed nether regions.

And with that, her entire world went black.

"Welcome to your doom."

02 |
EMBRACE THE DARK GODDESS

ANTONIA | The Timeless Place

She didn't know where she was, but she didn't even know she was a she because she had lost all concept of space, identity, and reality. All she knew was that she was floating in a void devoid of sight, an endless black expanse that felt both lonely and inviting at the same time.

She couldn't feel her arms or legs; in fact, she couldn't feel her body at all. She was merely a disembodied soul floating through eternity like a single water molecule adrift atop an ocean's wave.

But then, she began to hear something. She heard echoes, both muted and morphing. She heard obscured sounds emanating from unknown locations of that endless black expanse. Sounds that were transcendent, like a dolphin's underwater song, yet ominous, like the dark wail of a fallen soul.

And then she remembered her identity. Her name was Antonia Hoell, an 85-year-old American white woman who had been masturbating to young black Instagram models in a futile attempt to forget her pathetic life.

A woman whose existence was as much of a joke as any of Chappelle's finest material. A woman who now realised that the sounds she could hear, those which echoed all around, were voices.

Male and female voices emanated from that void, and the voices knew her.

"Excuse me?? What was she doing?"

"You heard me, Claire."

"Oh my God, Peter, that's so pathetic."

The voices knew Antonia.

"Tell me about it."

"No, but that's a next level of pathetic. That's honestly what she was doing?"

They were laughing.

"No matter how many times you ask me, the answer isn't going to change."

"Jesus H Christ. How fucking embarrassing."

The voices were laughing at Antonia.

"At this point, we'd just be doing her a favour."

"Exactly."

They were doctors.

"If I found myself in even half as worthless a state as that at her age, I'd just fucking end it."

"Exactly."

She was at a hospital. Antonia was in a hospital, and the doctors were talking about her.

"She's so fucking worthless."

"I know."

"But I'm serious, Peter. Like if I ever stoop so low, just put a knife in my throat. My fucking throat. You'd think a woman from her generation would know better than to be a fucking nigger lover."

Within the dark depths of that sightless void, a disembodied Antonia was consumed by the blistering inferno of rage.

How dare they say those things?!

They were talking about her like she wasn't even there.

Like she didn't have worth.

"She's worthless."

How dare they?!

Antonia tried to scream, but she had no lips to scream. All she could do was howl a psychic cry of rage into that black expanse. A psychic cry of rage which nobody heard.

"We hear you, Antonia."

There was another voice, a group of voices. A cluster of voices which were feminine, dark, soothing and mysterious. But who were they?

"You need not know our name.

Your life will end today."

Who are you!?

"Your existence ends today."

"Why bother even trying to save her life?"

"Exactly."

"We break our backs to keep her heart beating at the expense of more deserving patients, so what? So she can have another 6 months of precious life to waste masturbating to ebony porn?"

STOP TALKING ABOUT ME LIKE I'M NOT HERE!

"They cannot hear you, Antonia."

WHO ARE YOU?!

"Your life will end today."

"Let's do it. Let's switch off the life support."

NO! NO, I REFUSE TO DIE! I REFUSE TO FUCKING DIE!

"Your life will end today."

"We're doing her a favour. There's no way she'd want to continue living in that state. She was seriously compromised before, but she'll be a vegetable after this."

DON'T KILL ME!

"There is nothing you can do, Antonia."

I DON'T WANT TO DIE!

"Repeat it."

I DON'T WANT TO DIE!

"Repeat it."

I REFUSE TO FUCKING DIE!

"We have more important patients to attend to."

I'M GOING TO KILL YOU! I'M GOING TO FUCKING KILL YOU!

"You are at the terminus of this phase of existence.

Your expiration is imminent."

WHO ARE YOU?!

"We are the star that shines to bring light to the darkest sky.

We are the blood that spills when one is killed.

We are the thrill you crave from that stiff, penetrating drill.

We are pain.

We are strain.

The personification of shame.

We are endless regret.

We are aeons of stress.

Yet you may not know our name."

I DON'T WANT TO DIE!

"You are about to expire."

I DON'T WANT TO DIE!

"What would you give in order to live?"

ANYTHING!

"What would you give in order to be young again?"

ANYTHING!

"What would you give in order to be beautiful?"

ANYTHING!

"What would you give in order to finally receive everything you have ever wanted, Antonia?"

ANYTHING... OH, OH MY. WHAT IS THAT?

Antonia felt like she was drowning. Slowly but surely, being smothered by sexual desire. It was so warm yet slowly increasing in temperature. Every single cell of the body she could no longer feel was ensnared by a venomous embrace like vines of delicious ecstasy which constricted her soul.

Vines that choked the misery out of her non-existent neck and penetrated it with delirious pleasure. Pythonic vines that would have her eyes bulging with pupils the size of the fucking moon if she knew where her eyes even were.

WHAT IS THAT?!

"This is but a mere sample of our gift."

The level of arousal Antonia felt was out of this world. It was breathtaking. Awe inspiring, crippling.

Antonia was liquid in form. Moist to the touch. She was connected to everything there is, was, and ever will be on a level as primal as it was eternal.

Antonia was little more than pure, unadulterated, dripping wet satisfaction.

Utterly powerful yet completely powerless. The helplessly divine goddess. Ravenously insatiable while insatiably ravenous. She was smothered, ensconced, enveloped, and overwhelmed by dark waves of femininity.

The spark of creation.

The alpha and the omega.

The seed of life, which was, in turn, the focal point of death. It called to her. It called out to Antonia. It begged her to yield to its dark embrace in sweet submission and dominate it with her omnipotent power.

She felt a spark which flowed through her like electrical passion. One which linked her to the non-existent ground like only a dominant warrior could. Like only a real man could to a real woman.

And that real woman was Antonia.

Antonia was a real woman.

"No. Not yet, but you will be. You will be."

Oh my God.

"We are not gods. We are goddesses."

Oh my God.

If Antonia had lungs to breathe, they would have been paralysed by delight. If she had breasts to squeeze, their nipples would be thick with pleasure. And, if she had a yoni to enjoy, it would have been swollen and fully engorged with blood.

Somehow, Antonia heard the long and drawn-out sound of a sine wave. It was an EKG machine. The hospital's EKG machine. The one which was connected to her heart.

She was dying.

But an orgasm was imminent.

But her heart wasn't beating.

But still, the buildup continued. Somehow and someway, that intoxicating sensual euphoria continued to coalesce.

And it was too much. Too powerful. Too strong.

But Antonia's heart had stopped.

"This is but a taste of the delights we have to share. All of this and more will be yours if you dare."

I want it. I want it, please.

Antonia's non-existent lips let out deep and guttural moans of erotica into the surrounding ether. They did this, all while that EKG machine's slow, drawn-out, and consistent screech grew louder and louder.

"Do you really want it? Are you sure?"

Ohhhhh.... ohhhhh.. I want it... give it to me... give it to me!

"As you wish. Welcome to the next stage of your existence."

Antonia's disembodied soul moaned and howled with delight as an earth-shattering orgasm caused what once was a void of pure black to explode into a kaleidoscope of colours, shapes, and sounds.

Here it was. Her first orgasm in decades was finally here, and it was more than worth the wait.

It was so explosive, so nourishing, she would have happily waited five times as long.

Antonia's heart had stopped.

Antonia was dying.

Antonia was a dead woman.

But she didn't give a fuck.

It mattered for nought.

Because her orgasm was finally here, and it was more than worth the wait.

Fuck her heart. She didn't need it anymore.

Her orgasm was finally here.

And it was more than worth the wait.

Even if she had to die to get it.

03 | ECSTASY IN A FOREIGN BODY

ANTONIA | New York: Present Day

Antonia screamed louder than she'd ever thought possible. Bolts of force rocked her body from her neck down to her toes, sending her into a convulsing heap on that bed. A series of concussive blasts struck her body as a ball of eternal flame detonated deep within her pussy.

It was a chaotic dichotomy of sensations. Utterly mind-blowing and yet relaxing to the spirit. Totally devastating and yet nurturing to the soul. Agonisingly explosive and yet soothing to the core.

Antonia didn't know what to do.

She'd never before experienced such delicious torture, and as such, every muscle in her body was taut to near paralysis. Her entire body was erect with pleasure. Her once barren pussy was now akin to Niagara Falls as a river of pleasure flowed forth from the portal to ecstasy that had materialised between her legs.

Antonia had never been a squirter; however, now she couldn't stop as bursts of hot juices shot from her pussy against the leg of the woman beside her.

One might expect a woman to be offended at being smothered by another's vaginal secretions sans consent, but she didn't even notice. This wasn't shocking, however, because, from the looks of things, this chick had her own set of problems with which to contend.

Why?

Because she was also neck-deep within the throes of her own orgasm.

They were both cumming. She and Antonia. Right at the same time. Both were locked in the grip of thunderous sexual explosions.

And as that beautiful woman slid her wet tongue against Antonia's own, they both felt their firm breasts pressed together. Antonia felt shivers of excitement as that girl's erect nipples began to glide against hers, all while a third and previously unseen woman planted soft kisses against her neck while stroking her butt with her caramel fingers.

If this was what dying felt like, Antonia could get used to this. She was in heaven.

No, I'm not!

That's right, she was not. In fact, not only was Antonia not in heaven, Antonia wasn't even dead.

Where the fuck am I?!

Still somewhat gripped in the throes of orgasm, she looked around to see she was in a room. A beautiful hotel room. An opulent sanctuary adorned with plush velvet drapes and shimmering gold glowing accents. One with a king-sized bed stood in the centre, draped in silk sheets. A bed on which Antonia lay with those women.

Those women!?

This was when Antonia truly processed the fact that she wasn't alone. Somehow, there were two women right beside her. Two women pressed right against her. One was white and blonde with long, thick curls and a slim body covered in animal tattoos.

The other was mixed race with skin like pistachio milk chocolate and a body that was nothing short of curvaceous. Both had to be no older than 25.

Where the fuck was she?

"Where the fuck am I?!" she cried.

"Kara, what's wrong?" the white one asked.

"Where the fuck am I?!"

Where the fuck was she?

Confused and terrified, without a clue what to think, Antonia sat quivering like a leaf in a hurricane until the white girl placed a delicate young hand on her cheek.

"Nu badda touch mi!" Antonia screamed in what sounded like Jamaican patois, swatting her hand away.

However, as she did so, she caught a glimpse of something.

Something on her arm.

Something that wasn't supposed to be there.

Something that shocked her more than anything ever had in her miserable 85 years of existence.

Something that couldn't possibly have been real.

Still feeling the afterglow of that orgasm and with legs that were every bit as strong as wet linguine, Antonia jumped out of that bed and painfully crumpled to the cold marble floor when she realised they didn't work.

Ignoring said pain, she pulled herself along that cold marble floor until a young, portly, ginger-haired man wielding a digital camera reached down and grabbed her arm.

"Kara, what the fuck?!" he asked, confused.

"Move di rass offa mi!" she screamed, once again, in Jamaican patois.

Antonia sank her teeth into his shin like a woman possessed, leaving him howling like a stuck pig. Immediately after, she crawled into what looked like a bathroom, closed the door, clumsily staggered to her feet, awkwardly fumbled for the lock, and eventually locked the door.

However, as she did all of the above, her mind was awash with one simple yet overwhelming question.

"Why the fuck do I have so much energy?!"

04 | YOUNG, BEAUTIFUL & BLACK

ANTONIA | New York: Present Day

With said bathroom door now locked, Antonia finally looked in the opposite mirror and had the single greatest shock of her existence.

She was Kara Fit.

That wasn't a joke or a euphemism; she literally inhabited Kara Fit's body. Antonia wasn't old anymore, frail anymore, ugly or disgusting anymore. She wasn't even white anymore! She was young, beautiful, positively brimming with life, and black!

Antonia was black!

No longer a collection of wrinkled heaps of discoloured beige, her skin was now a gorgeous shade of caramelised honey brown and smooth like butter-made silk. Adorned with multicoloured tattoos of stars, planets, Egyptian deities, and inspirational quotes, Antonia marvelled at its form from head to painted toe.

Atop her head sat a gravity-defying jet black Afro with interspersed streaks of light blue highlights, and her legs!

Good Lord, my legs!

Thick yet muscular like an Olympic sprinter's, her legs were strong yet deeply feminine as only those of a sensual seductress could be.

Antonia Hoell was no longer an old and decrepit white woman. She was now young, absolutely breathtaking, and black.

She was Kara Fit.

What the fuck!?

"As you asked, so have we delivered."

What the fuck!?

"Enjoy."

"Kara, what's wrong!?"

"Kara!?"

"Kara, are you OK?!"

That was the young cameraman and two girls standing outside the bathroom, clearly worried. Like Antonia, they obviously had no idea what was happening, but she was blind to their concerns.

They barely registered because, at that moment, she quickly realised how glorious she felt. She began to fully appreciate how magnificent this body was not only to behold but to inhabit.

Now Antonia felt no discomfort.

No stiffness.

No pain.

None of the existential horror of being trapped within a dilapidated frame anxiously waiting to return to the earth from whence it came.

No.

Unstoppable energy coursed throughout the cells of Antonia's newly acquired seductive frame. This body's heart beat strong and steady. This body's lungs breathed slowly but deeply, thoroughly energising every last cell with each intake of breath. And its muscles, its muscles were supple yet taut.

Functionally robust yet sensually feminine.

Sensually feminine yet vibrantly alive.

Vibrantly alive and capable of doing anything.

Her new body was capable.

Her new body was alive.

Antonia was finally alive.

The unimportant sheep outside were frantically banging on that door, but Antonia was fresh out of fucks to give. They didn't matter. They were nothing. Little more than flies splattering against the steel hull of a speeding train.

What did matter was the reflected vision of perfection Antonia now saw staring back at her in that mirror.

What did matter was the growing sexual delight she felt trickling its way from her toes to her calves, and then all the way to the blossoming flower of rapture which resided between her now perfectly shaped thighs.

Led as much by a sincere desire to explore this body's sublime form as undeniable arousal, Antonia lightly slid a caramel-coated finger against its clitoris and bit her lip as billions of shooting stars scorched a flaming path across its surface.

Her now young eyes became lubricated with fresh tears as waves of delight poured from her heart.

She couldn't believe it.

"I CAN'T FUCKING BELIEVE IT!"

She looked at the floor, overwhelmed with emotion and operating on pure instinct rather than rational thought. She saw a pale blue pair of booty shorts and a matching sports bra there.

Within seconds, she was wearing both and was awestruck not only at how perfectly they caressed the contours of her new physique but also at how the hell she was able to move so gracefully. It had been half a century since

Antonia possessed even half of the degree of mobile fluidity her new body had in spades.

Soon after that, she opened the bathroom door, barged right past the three confused souls outside, and sprinted right out of the front door of that hotel room entirely barefoot. However, as she ran, Antonia somehow realised she knew those people.

Their names are Greg, Daniela, and Juliette, but how the hell do I know that?

How the hell did she know that?

But still, Antonia ran and ran through the corridor, out of the hotel, and beyond, not knowing where the hell she was going and also not caring. She just couldn't stop! This body was so fit, so capable, it was intoxicating!

No matter how hard she pushed, no matter how much force she applied, no matter how intensely she would thrust herself further, this body always had more gas in the tank!

It was so athletic! So energetic! Antonia could touch her toes again! She could jump again! She was fast again! She was young again!

However, as strong and fit as her new body was, it didn't quite have the insatiable gas tank she'd first imagined, and eventually, Antonia did find herself entirely out of energy. When that happened, she collapsed to her knees from both exhaustion and delight, heaving in a sweat-ridden state in what she now realised was a large park.

Now, as for what park? That was anybody's guess. She didn't know where she was, nor did she care.

Still, Antonia realised something as she kneeled on that grass on that bright summer's afternoon.

Everyone was staring at her.

Everyone.

Men and women alike looked in her direction, but she didn't know what to make of it.

Why are they staring?

What could they see?

What are they looking at?

But then she noticed men averting their gazes as she looked back.

But then she saw a young Chinese man checking out her ass before being slapped hard in the face by his wife.

But then she saw a middle-aged white man awkwardly covering the obvious tent in his shorts.

But then she saw a young black woman staring with what could only be described as the molten inferno of lust leaking like lava from her eyes.

And this was the moment when Antonia got it. This is when she truly understood.

They wanted her.

They craved her.

She was beautiful.

She was fucking beautiful!

She was fucking beautiful!

An uncontainable emotion flowed from her soul right through her heart, making her body shiver from head to toe.

Antonia leaned back on her knees and soaked up every last drop of that moment. Her now young arms thrust to the skies, beautiful head rocked back, and every muscle taut with unstoppable strength. She could feel it. It was overwhelming.

Overpowering.

Energy was building inside her. Raw, intense, penetrating, undeniable energy. It was coming, swelling, and growing, and there was nothing she could do to contain it. Nothing she could do to abate it. Antonia was receiving a download from the heavens.

And so she began to scream. Antonia screamed wildly and with reckless abandon. Antonia screamed passionately and with zero fucks for the opinions of all present. Antonia screamed ecstatically but without an ounce of anger or aggression.

Antonia just started screaming.

All of the energy. All of the emotion. All of the pain from all of the years spent trapped in that dilapidated prison and the joy of having finally escaped. It all erupted from her neck in the form of a roar so primal it would have intimidated an alpha male lion.

Antonia kneeled on that grass with a jaguar's seductive poise, howling passionately into the heavens while utterly oblivious to the multitudes of passers-by who passed her by. She didn't even have her eyes open; Antonia's eyes were tightly shut because, at that moment, she simply didn't need them.

Antonia didn't need eyes to see.

There she kneeled with her eyes wide shut, screaming into the heavens above for a length of time she wouldn't have been able to guess and didn't care to try. However, by the time she was done, when she finally saw fit to reopen said eyes, Antonia saw a strange black man standing in front and looking directly at her.

She didn't know what on earth he wanted.

05 |
EVERY QUEEN NEEDS A KING

ANTONIA | New York: Present Day

Sweaty, heaving, and nearly hoarse, Antonia knelt before what might have been the second most beautiful man she'd ever seen. His energy was electric, intoxicating, compelling, mesmerising, and somehow comforting all at the same time. In fact, her new heart skipped several beats as she bore witness to his perfection.

Coated from head to toe in rich chocolate skin and blessed with a beautifully masculine face, thick lips, and a strong jawline, he truly was breathtaking.

And his eyes, his blue eyes, were so mesmerising. Antonia hadn't seen eyes like that in decades. They gazed through her brain and into her soul.

The strange man had to be at least six feet tall and was coated from head to toe in solid muscle. And, like Antonia, he too was sweating as he'd clearly also been running through that park. He wore a baggy blue vest, which perfectly accentuated the contours of his muscular frame, matching shorts, and white running sneakers.

Oddly enough, he also wore a backpack from which the head of a cute white puppy stuck out. The adorable little tyke looked around in all directions, its tongue wagging excitedly.

Antonia lost herself in his piercing blue eyes until he finally spoke.

"Look, I know this is totally random, but I had to come and speak to you. Your energy is incredible."

The shock was so immense that she barely registered his words. In no reality were men who looked like him interested in someone like her. They'd never been another since Winston. In fact, this man might have been the second most good-looking man she'd met since Winston, rest in peace.

"The way you're so in touch with your primal self is incredible. You let out so much emotion and didn't give a fuck who saw," he continued, still exploring her very soul with his blue eyes.

"Thanks," Antonia replied, smiling, starting to return to this earthly plane of existence.

"I sense such a wild and chaotic energy in you. You're like an untamed beast."

"You didn't think that was weird?" she asked, smiling genuinely but with more than a tinge of nervous energy.

"Hell no. Most people are nothing more than NPCs who do what they're told when they're told to do it, but that's not you. You're a queen."

"You think so?"

"100%. You're a leader."

"Really?"

"You take what's yours and don't give a fuck about what society thinks."

Antonia didn't know what to say to that. She couldn't remember the last time anyone had spoken to her this way, and now her heart floated in a blissful expanse of freedom. She felt like a giddy schoolgirl and probably looked like one too.

The gorgeous black man noticed this and shot her a sly but supportive smile.

"Has my queen gone shy on me?"

"Your queen doesn't know what to say," Antonia replied, realising that her cheeks would have been redder than a stop sign if she were still in her white body.

He was so beautiful, so sweet, and so confident. Second only to Winston, God rest his soul.

"Why?" he asked.

Because you look like you're almost my dream man. Because less than 20 minutes ago, I was an 85-year-old wrinkly white woman who you wouldn't have looked twice at, and I can't believe for a second that you're attracted to me.

Antonia thought all the above but, unsurprisingly, opted to keep it to herself.

"I guess your queen is tired from all that screaming," came her eventual reply.

"I see that. My queen clearly needs a smooth beverage to soothe her tired throat."

Does he want to take me out??!

"And what would my king recommend?"

"So I'm your king now?"

"Every queen needs a king."

"And every parched throat needs an oat milk latte with sugar-free hazelnut syrup to soothe it," he continued.

My God, he does! But can I do this?! Will I be safe!? Would I even know what to say?!

"That does sound delicious," she replied, somewhat hesitantly.

"Indeed it is, but the latte itself is a distant second to the company with whom it's imbibed."

"That's a bold claim."

"That's a factual statement. As my queen is about to discover."

Can I do this?! What if I make a fool of myself?! What if I embarrass myself and say something stupid that lets him know I'm really a white woman?! What if he's actually an axe murderer or a rapist?!

"Right now?"

"Right now."

"But I don't know you," she replied, tentatively.

His eyes widened with genuine empathy as his face softened into a supportive smile.

"Yeah, that's true. You definitely don't know me and I guess I could be anyone. Don't worry my queen, I'm sorry to bother you and didn't mean to scare you. Please have a lovely day, and know I was truly taken aback by your energy."

With that, he gave Antonia a polite yet masculine handshake, rubbed her palm softly, turned around, and started to walk away. However, the further away he got, the more she was overwhelmed by an ever-deepening sense of loss.

I've already died once today. What are the odds it'll happen twice?

"Are you sure you're not an axe murderer?!" She cried. He stopped, turned around, and smiled before replying.

"I'm a reformed axe murderer," he said, making her giggle. "My hacking and slashing days are behind me, I assure you."

"When's the last time you hacked and slashed anyone?"

"Thirty-one years ago."

"And how old are you?"

"Thirty-two."

"So that would have been when you were a baby?"

"Indeed, but the son of a bitch had it coming, trust me."

Antonia laughed and then walked up to the gorgeous black man who had stuck his arm out to link with hers. She obliged, and they started walking together.

"Does my king have a name?" she asked curiously.

"His name is Blake. And my queen?"

"Her name is Kara," she replied, feeling an uncomfortable lump in her throat from the lie.

"Kara, it's a pleasure. Let's go."

Blake oozed passion, confidence, poise, and sexual energy, but something else, too. She just felt comfortable in his presence. Something about his vibe, how he carried himself, and those beautiful eyes told her she could trust him. She somehow knew there was nothing to fear.

But she couldn't help being intoxicated by the way he looked at her. It was with a true passion no man had ever had for her since Winston, some 70 years before, God rest his soul. She didn't know if Winston was dead, but by this point, he had to be.

'Intoxicating' didn't even do him justice; no word in English could genuinely convey how he made her feel.

Alive? Yes.

Desired? Absolutely

Adored? Oui.

He made her feel all the above and more, and Antonia never wanted that feeling to end.

As they walked out of that park, Blake unlinked his muscular arm from hers and wrapped it softly around her neck and shoulders with his hand hanging dangerously close to her right breast.

She held it without a second thought as the scent of his sandalwood body lotion, and Jean Paul Gaultier aftershave began to permeate her senses.

He was leading her somewhere, but she didn't know where.

And neither did she care.

As they walked to a destination only Blake knew, with his little white puppy still excitedly looking in all directions from his backpack, he finally looked down at Antonia's feet and asked why the hell she wasn't wearing any shoes.

She simply didn't have a good answer for him.

06 | PASSION IN THE PUBLIC EYE

ANTONIA | New York City Bar: Present Day

As it turned out, Blake was taking Antonia for coffee. However, while she assumed that meant they were heading to Starbucks, she couldn't have been any further from the truth. He, in fact, took her to a lavish and stunning bar, one which exuded an aura of opulence and sophistication.

One where sleek, black marble countertops reflected the ambient glow of strategically placed LED lights, casting an ethereal shimmer across the meticulously polished surfaces.

One where the walls, adorned with abstract art pieces and backlit shelves, showcased an extensive collection of premium spirits, framing the space in a chic, contemporary style.

One where plush, velvet bar stools lined the counter, their rich burgundy hue adding a touch of elegance. At the same time, the soft hum of carefully curated music created an atmosphere of relaxed exclusivity.

It seemed like an overly elaborate spot for coffee; honestly, Antonia didn't feel worthy of being there.

The doorman had eagerly greeted Blake on the way in, and the gorgeous blonde on the bar was about as excited to see him as Antonia had ever seen anyone be to see anyone. She even tried to flirt with Blake right in front of Antonia before he made his excuses and took her to an upstairs window-side cubicle.

She was pretty surprised that such an upmarket venue swould let Blake enter with Jasper, his small puppy, in his backpack, but they didn't seem to mind one bit. In fact, the blonde even petted him, so either Antonia was wrong about those sorts of venues, or Blake was clearly a very important man.

Probably a bit of both.

Anyway, the view from their cubicle was exquisite, to say the least. A panoramic view of what Antonia now realised to be New York. A city she'd visited many times with Brother Malcolm and even after his passing to see his wife, too, before her passing. So much about it had changed, yet so much was exactly the same. In some ways, Antonia felt at home.

She sat in her seat, still barefoot but with the sweat now largely evaporated from her booty shorts and sports bra. Her eyes were transfixed on the man in front as his were transfixed right back.

Apparently, Blake made his living as a photographer and men's dating coach, which Antonia didn't even realise was a thing. According to him, there were scores of lonely men worldwide for whom meeting women was nearly impossible. Hence, they needed help finding love.

Who knew?

Blake also showed her his impressive photography portfolio. Scores and scores of beautiful women of all races, one of whom was the blonde from downstairs, wearing all manner of colourful and creative ensembles in several compelling locations from woodland jungles to arctic snowscapes, Bali beaches, and everything else in between.

Blake was 32, single, and came from a small yet close family that he absolutely adored, most notably his six-year-old niece, Cherise, with whom he had a weekly ice cream and movie date, and his grandfather, who lived in a care home.

He showed her a video of him and Cherise on his phone, which was nothing less than touching. It was clear how much she loved him and how much he loved her back. In fact, as Antonia watched it, she had to wonder:

Where the hell was this kind of supportive masculine love when I was growing up?

Where was the strong, nurturing father figure in her childhood? She had absolutely no love from her abusive family and father especially.

None.

Something that had to be said about Blake was that while he radiated self-assuredness and poise, he apparently wasn't always like this. Apparently, he wasn't always physically beautiful and brimming with self-belief, so he had taken a somewhat arduous journey to reach that point.

Antonia asked him to elaborate, but he clearly didn't want to and thus kept his answer vague. In fact, if she was correct, she saw just the tiniest tinge of pain streak, a flaming trail behind his piercing blue eyes.

Wanting to change the subject, she asked to see a photo of his grandfather just as a waiter came and asked if they wanted more drinks. Feeling brave and having now graduated beyond the mere desire for caffeine, she asked for a bottle of Dom Perignon champagne, something Blake's unmistakable smirk indicated he was happy with.

He then asked questions about Kara's life, which, surprisingly, Antonia had in-depth answers to. Her name was Kara Clark, and she was a 23-year-old Instagram model who also did some work for TV and magazines.

Moreover, she even had an Onlyfans account where she posted pictures and videos of her feet and the occasional piece of girl/girl content, which Blake found hilarious.

Laughing, he whipped out his phone, took a pic of her grubby bare feet, and asked what the going rate would be, to which Antonia replied:

"More than you realise," without a shred of irony.

"Nice work if you can get it!" he added.

Kara Clark was passionate about yoga, reading, and music and had apparently reached something called Warlord rank on a videogame called Street Fighter 6. Blake played that game, too, and was beyond impressed by that. Apparently, he was only at Platinum rank, whatever that meant.

Still, the more Antonia talked to Blake, the more uncomfortable her mind became. Locked between the sincere desire to lose itself within his endless blue eyes and the stark awareness of the dry, pungent sweat which coated every inch of her new perfect form.

"You don't look comfortable," Blake added, seemingly reading her mind.

"I'm not dressed for a place like this, and I feel sticky from all that running."

"I hear that," he said thoughtfully. "OK, how about this? Let's go back to my penthouse, and you can change there. It's really close by, and I've got lots of women's clothes you can slip into."

"What are you, a cross-dresser?" Antonia asked cheekily.

"Yeah, that a problem?"

"Really?!"

"No, silly. And even if I was, we're not even close to being the same size."

"So they are your ex-girlfriend's clothes?"

"They're my models' clothes," Blake replied with a sly smirk.

"Oh. OK, but I just need to use the restroom first."

Antonia stood up and squeezed past Blake to get out of the cubicle. However, as she pressed by, she tripped, slipped, and reached for something to steady herself against. That thing happened to be Blake's muscular thigh, on which she felt the tip of her pinky finger graze against something thick and hard.

Something that twitched.

Something that caused his face to momentarily contort with shock and pleasure.

Something that caused her own crotch to lubricate.

Saying nothing, Antonia proceeded to the bathroom, where she used the toilet, washed her hands, and then spent precisely five minutes marvelling at the exquisite beauty of her new body in the mirror. By the time she returned, Blake's face was the picture of confusion.

"Where has my queen been for so long?" he asked.

Antonia then told a both barefaced and barefooted lie about a massive queue for the ladies' room, which she wasn't sure he had bought. After that, he took her by the hand and led her and Jasper out of the bar.

On the way out, she took a few sly glances at his crotch and was happy to see that the stiffness she grazed with her fingertip was still bulging in his shorts.

Also, on that topic, he didn't even make the slightest effort to hide his erection. He just owned his desires in a way she couldn't help but respect and be somewhat turned on by.

It was hot.

It was sexy.

And it aroused her.

Now, Antonia expected the journey to Blake's penthouse to be relatively long. Still, as fate decreed, he lived directly above that bar, and unsurprisingly, his home was every bit as opulent.

In fact, it was the embodiment of modern luxury. Its open-plan living space boasted floor-to-ceiling windows that framed panoramic views of the city, flooding the apartment with natural light.

Blake's aesthetic leaned towards minimalism, with a palette dominated by cool greys and whites, accented by bold splashes of colour in his curated art collection. The furnishings were as stylish as they were functional, featuring a mix of mid-century modern pieces and contemporary design, each carefully chosen to reflect his artistic sensibilities.

A state-of-the-art kitchen gleamed with stainless steel appliances. At the same time, the adjoining living area housed a plush sectional, perfect for entertaining. His personal touch was evident in the carefully displayed photography and his own work, which captured intimate moments and stunning landscapes, adding a deeply personal layer to the otherwise polished space.

This wasn't just a home but a gallery of his life and passions, meticulously curated and effortlessly chic.

Once inside, Blake handed Antonia a clean towel, a red, tight-fitting cocktail dress with matching bra and panties and pointed her in the direction of the restroom.

Once inside his lavish white marble bathroom, she peeled off her sweaty clothes and stepped into his walk-through shower, taking a moment to truly savour the breathtaking cityscape view from the window. The water was heated to absolute perfection and as it rained down over every inch of her caramel chocolate skin, she tilted her head back and sighed in satisfaction as that warm liquid washed away her cares.

Thousands of droplets of liquid all caressing, kissing, and licking her neck, breasts, back, arms, and butt. Tens of thousands of droplets of liquid combined with eucalyptus-scented oil to lubricate her hands, allowing them to glide effortlessly across every curve of her perfect form. And as she bathed, her nipples slowly began to fill with blood and stiffen to the touch.

And Antonia moaned with pleasure.

Once finished, she stepped out of that shower with her new young body feeling and smelling as clean as it was beautiful. She looked at the cocktail dress that hung up against the door, then the lingerie, and then a bathrobe. Half a minute later, she wore the lingerie, and the experience was glorious.

It was so form-fitting, so tight, and yet so soft against her skin at the same time. It accentuated her voluptuous hips, full breasts and thick yet muscular thighs so seductively that she wished she had a camera on hand to capture how perfect she looked.

Never in her past life would she have dared to wear something so unashamedly feminine and sexy. Never had she felt worthy of the honour. Deserving of the privilege. She felt so empowered, so liberated, so beautiful.

This is what it feels like! This is how it feels to be sexy! She thought.

She was so happy she could almost cry, so elated she could hardly draw breath, so confident she decided she didn't need the cocktail dress. It just wasn't relevant. There was no need to mask her body's awe-inspiring beauty. She had nothing to fear.

Nothing to be ashamed of.

She wouldn't hide away under the presumption that her new form was inherently wicked, distasteful, or unseemly to the eye. Not anymore. Antonia would wear that lingerie, put on that bathrobe, make sure it was untied, and head out with her head held high.

However, as soon as she opened the door, Blake was right there, staring deep into her soul with those piercing blue eyes while presenting her with another glass of Dom Perignon. Unlike Antonia, he had seen fit to ensure his exquisite frame was fully clothed and was wearing a navy blue silk shirt with gold cufflinks and matching trousers. He was also clearly surprised that she wasn't wearing the cocktail dress.

"Your queen wanted to make herself comfortable," she said with a smirk, slowly growing into her confidence.

"Your king humbly respects his queen's decision. But now he feels somewhat overdressed for the occasion," Blake replied, still looking her directly in the eyes before slowly removing his shirt, trousers, and socks right before her.

Soon, he was completely naked save for the small gold chain hanging around his neck and tight pair of red boxer shorts, which did precious little to hide the mild swelling between his legs.

He took a step towards her and stopped, his chest grazing her thick breasts as she gasped in shock. Smiling, he grabbed her by the arms, guided her from the doorway, and pressed her against the wall with his chest now wedged tight against hers. Her thigh was trapped tight against the growing rock that was sadly confined to his tight boxers.

Still peering through her eyes and into the heart of her essence itself, Blake held her right hand above her head with his left as his right hand cradled her cheek.

Her body became awash with submissive bliss as her pupils dilated so wide she looked like she was on hard drugs. Her trembling fingers struggled to hold onto that champagne glass, spilling expensive Dom Perignon all over her painted toenails.

With that, Blake leaned in, let his lips graze against Antonia's neck and ear and said.

"Excuse me."

Before walking right into the bathroom leaving her completely breathless and able to do nought but pull her trembling hand to her lips to down what was left of her champagne. Seconds later, he returned wearing a white bathrobe of his own, took a look at her empty champagne glass, smirked, and said:

"My queen needs another drink."

All Antonia's young body had the strength to do was nod meekly before he took her by the hand and led her through his beautiful living room onto his balcony, which overlooked the expansive cityscape.

It was now dark, dusk, and yet tranquil still.

Calm, safe, and seemingly nurturing in a way one wouldn't imagine a city at night to appear. Thousands of stars twinkled brightly in the night sky as the moon shot a constant luminant beam like a lighthouse guiding lost ships at sea to safety.

As the quiet hum of city life and traffic penetrated and caressed Antonia's eardrums, Blake poured her another glass of champagne.

Neither spoke another word, but then again, no words were needed. Side by side, they stood in perfect silence, the all-encompassing background hum of New York City massaging their senses and blending seamlessly with the thousands of soft, fizzing pops of carbonated bubbles that escaped their champagne flutes.

Blake positioned himself directly behind Antonia with his arms surrounding her on the railing from either side but still said nothing. A whole minute passed, but still, he said nothing.

Slowly, Antonia continued to grow in confidence. Slowly, she earned the courage to back her butt up ever so slightly in search of his dick. And eventually, she found exactly what she was looking for. There it was, trapped within the confines of his blood-red boxer shorts and her bathrobe; her thick and ample butt found the thick cock which strained to press against it.

Both searching for the same thing. Both yearning to be pressed against each other skin to skin but both restrained by torturous prisons of cloth and fabric.

It had been years since Antonia felt anything remotely so exhilarating.

So erotic.

So sensual.

His cock felt so big but so fucking hard that her mind began to drown in a sea of carnal fantasy. Yes, her eyes were locked onto the city's lights, and yes, her tongue was savouring the sweet taste of that expensive champagne, but her mind was somewhere else entirely.

Antonia's mind had become a lifelong artist passionately painting its magnum opus on a blank canvas, frantically cross-referencing the data her butt gave her about the rock-hard tool that pressed against it to construct a mental image of exactly how it looked.

How it felt.

How it smelled.

How it tasted.

"You won't have to think so hard if you get out of that," Blake whispered into her ear. His chocolate hands slowly pulled her bathrobe from her trembling body and dropped it to his balcony's cold, hard marble floor.

As Antonia felt the chill of the New York City air rush across almost every inch of her near-naked skin, the fine hairs on her arms quickly became as erect as Blake's cock.

She was flowing further into sensual ecstasy, standing against that balcony wearing nothing but lingerie with that agonisingly sexy black man standing right behind.

She needed to touch him, kiss him, press herself against him, and she tried to make that happen. She craved the feeling of his flesh coming into contact with hers, and again, she tried. She tried to turn around, but he held her in place. She tried yet again, even harder still, but still couldn't budge an inch. He was just too strong. She tried with everything she had, but she was helpless.

Physically helpless.

She couldn't move.

Suddenly, she felt his bathrobe hit the floor and graze her ankles. And seconds after that, she got the shock of her life as his big, thick, and fully engorged black tool wedged itself between her butt cheeks and right against her the thong line of her panties.

It was no longer constrained by his underwear.

Now, Antonia could experience every last millimetre of its twitching length. Now, she could feel the coursing blood pumping through the veins that pulsated along its surface. Now she could feel it bulging from base to tip, each minor spasm making her ass convulse in responsive arousal, and each convulsion causing that cock to twitch even harder in frustration.

"Uuuhhhh." she moaned. It was guttural and primal. A moan which erupted from deep within her chest. A moan which wasn't even finished before Blake's lips once again found their way to her ears and said:

"Your body feels so soft, so smooth. It's incredible."

"You're so hard," she replied. Not knowing if she was talking about his muscular body or dick.

"It's such a beautiful night. The stars are out, and the city is alive in the distance. We're surrounded by hundreds of thousands, maybe even millions of people who have no idea what we're doing," he continued, his lips kissing her ears. At the same time, his left hand traced a line from her shoulder down to her smooth and tight stomach.

"Wives watching TV with their husbands, mothers feeding their children. All those people living all those lives, and then there is us."

"Us," Antonia replied breathlessly.

He took a step closer. Now she could feel his swollen testicles bulging against her butt as the fingers of his left hand briefly ran underneath her panties before resting on her hip.

Antonia moaned again, this time even more guttural than before, deeper than before. And this time, he smothered her mouth with his hand to stifle her noise.

"Shhh. Focus, my queen. You can handle this."

His cock was so hot it was almost boiling against her skin. She wanted to touch it. She needed to experience it. She tried to grab it and managed to graze a fingertip against its head before he grabbed her hand and held her in place.

"My queen, you need to focus. I want you to do that for me. Will you do that for me?"

"I don't know if I can!" she moaned.

"Yes, you can, but you're letting your thoughts run away. Your mind is losing itself to the moment, and you're letting it win. But you're better than that. Focus."

"Yes, Daddy."

"Do you feel it?"

"I feel it."

"What do you feel?"

"Your wet tongue is on my neck."

"My wet tongue is licking your neck."

"I'm wet. Oh fuck, I'm so wet. I haven't felt like this in decades."

"Decades? OK, maybe you've had enough alcohol."

"No. I want more."

"Do you now?"

"And I want you inside me."

"You want to feel me inside you?"

"Yes."

"My hard cock?"

"Yes."

"My hard, 9-inch cock? You want to feel it deep inside your pussy?"

"Fuck me."

"What about my tongue?"

"Fuck me, please."

"What if my wet tongue licked, flicked, and teased your dripping pussy? Would you like that?"

Antonia let out another guttural moan, one which was yet again stifled by Blake's strong hand as it smothered her spasming mouth.

"My queen, you need to do better. You need to exercise restraint."

"Fuck me, please."

Blake pulled her thong to the right, eased his hard, pulsating dick exactly one inch into her quivering pussy, and just left it there. In place. Wedged tightly inside the opening.

The tease was merciless.

Antonia wanted more. Craved more. Feeling that one single inch of his massive tool penetrated her walls was turning her brain to mist. A dominant enchantment that she was powerless to resist. It swelled inside her, threatening to stretch her beyond control and cast her adrift in the tides of willing surrender.

Antonia was a vulnerable lamb, and Blake was her stalking predator.

But she wouldn't have had it any other way.

She wanted to be overwhelmed by his energy, enveloped in it, drowned in it. She tried to drink the wet juices of his dominant sexual force until her body burst into orgasmic psychopathy.

She wanted to scream his name into the high heavens as he rammed her tight pussy into submission like the horny little slut she always knew she really was.

"Say my name," he commanded forcefully as if reading her mind.

"Please fuck me."

"Say my name."

"Please fuck me."

Blake eased that single inch of penis out of Antonia's wet pussy, causing a significant amount of her juices to spill forth. She then gasped in a mixture of deep pleasure and stark regret.

"Put it in, please."

"I've told you to say my name three times now. Don't make me repeat myself."

"Blake."

"What is my name?"

"Your name is Blake."

With that, Blake took the head of his granite member and pressed it against the moist opening of her pussy.

"Do you deserve this dick?"

"No, but I need it, Dad..."

Before Antonia could even finish, Blake thrust the entire length of his nine-inch penis into her vulva. She needed less than a second to succumb to its form as it forced its way through its tight confines. It took less than a second for her legs to buckle under the weight of such unbearable sexual overwhelm.

As she fell, she dropped her champagne glass to the hard marble floor before it rolled off the side of Blake's balcony and tumbled to the ground below, causing a barely audible shatter seconds later.

So there Antonia hung, dangling from the steel tool between Blake's legs. At the same time, he forcefully tilted her head back with his left hand and poured champagne directly into her gaping mouth with his right.

Blake just kept pouring, and Antonia kept drinking, opening her mouth and throat as wide as both could possibly go until she'd consumed three glasses of champagne.

She craved that man like a starving child craves water. That much couldn't be denied. But now she was also drunk, incredibly so, in fact, and with a face and brain that felt warm, soft and wet.

Smiling, Blake once again leaned against her ear as she steadied her feet and tried to methodically impale herself on his manhood.

"MY THROAT! MY ACTUAL FUCKING THROAT!"

That wasn't Antonia, nor was it Blake. That was a flashback. A vivid flashback of an all too recent and all too humiliating memory. One that made her fists clench as her throat wanted to scream with rage.

However, before she could even draw her next breath, Blake pinned her down, clamped a hand around her neck and methodically began choking the oxygen out of her lungs.

"Stop acting out of turn. It isn't time for that, and if you do this again, I will punish you."

As Blake's hand continued to press against Antonia's neck, her new body's self-preservation response had her thrashing on the spot. Her mind wanted to obey, of course. Her mind desperately wanted to do everything Blake commanded, but her body wouldn't.

Her body couldn't.

Her body needed oxygen.

Her body needed to breathe, and the more he squeezed her throat, the more that new, beautiful, gorgeous body of hers began to panic.

However, none of this meant Antonia couldn't feel how wet she was. Her juices oozed out of her new young pussy and slid right down her new thick caramel thighs.

And she needed to taste them.

She had to.

It wasn't a want.

It was a need.

But her new fingers were seemingly no longer hers to command. Her new nervous system was so wracked by suffocation that it found it impossible to carry commands from the mind to its extremities.

And then Antonia's vision went white.

Slowly but surely, thousands of near-microscopic balls of luminance began to burst into her field of vision.

She still couldn't breathe.

She couldn't.

Her body thrashed like it needed an exorcism, but the more it thrashed, the weaker she felt, and the weaker she felt, the hornier she became.

Antonia couldn't breathe.

I CAN'T BREATHE!

She needed to feel his cock inside her.

But Antonia couldn't breathe.

I CAN'T BREATHE!

She just needed to feel his cock deep inside the walls of her pussy one more time.

But still, she couldn't breathe.

I CAN'T BREATHE!

Until she could.

Without warning, Blake's hand released its grip on Antonia's neck, and she collapsed against the balcony railing, filling her lungs with several massive intakes of air.

"You did amazingly well, my queen. I'm so proud of you."

Blake's right hand caressed Antonia's breasts, running circles over their fleshy mounds and stimulating her engorged nipples. At the same time, his left poured sparkling champagne over her neck and shoulders before his lips and tongue began to drink them off the soft contours of her chocolate skin.

He was worshipping her. Adoring her.

"Your body is incredible."

"I fucking want you! Blake!" she gasped breathlessly.

"Oh my God. Your skin is so smooth, so soft. I want to lose myself in you."

"I want you to fuck me."

"Say, please."

"Please fuck me."

"How badly do you want it?"

"More than anything."

"Whose pussy is this?"

"Your pussy, Daddy."

And that was the moment when Blake finally gave Antonia exactly what she craved. Precisely what she needed. After all of the teasing, the taunting, the unbearably delightful torture, he eased his thick, stiff weapon into her wet vulva and slowly began to rock back and forth, allowing its entire length to penetrate her in totality.

Oh fuck it's so big!

So fucking big. The feeling was exquisite, and now more moans erupted from Antonia's lips. She already knew she could barely handle Blake at this speed. If he fucked her any harder, she was done for.

"Bend over the railing and stick your butt out."

She did exactly as she was told and let him have his way with her new young body as he held her left hand with his own and gripped her right hip with his right.

Her gasps continued. Quiet moans of pain mixed with loud groans of pleasure. This was, without doubt, the most enormous cock she'd ever felt. With every thrust, Blake went deeper and deeper, reaching places inside Antonia that had never known a man's touch. And so, as her juices gushed all over it and down to her legs and feet, she felt the intensity of his ramming increase.

Each thrust more brutal than the last.

Each thrust more penetrative than the last.

Each thrust made Antonia sacrifice just a little bit more of her precious sanity. Each thrust made her lose herself in the pain. Lose herself in the ecstatic joy of being fucked like never before by such a gorgeously dominant man.

Antonia's horse cries of subservient ecstasy circulated like floating flower petals throughout the cold New York City night sky as Blake continued to drill her mercilessly.

I NEED MORE! She thought.

"I NEED MORE!" she screamed.

And she did. Antonia needed more. She craved more. More pain and especially more cock. She couldn't take what was happening but knew she needed more. She knew she needed to be broken. She knew she needed to be penetrated.

Perforated. Obliterated.

Dominated. Annihilated.

She yearned for it.

Even though the unrelenting force of every thrust turned her brain to jelly. Even though she was already losing her grip on reality and didn't know how much more she could take. And even though those hoarse moans of pleasure were turning into rapturous screams of sexual euphoria.

Screams which synchronised with the relentless pounding of Blake's tool and the electrical seizures of her malfunctioning brain which turned her sexy arms and legs into a spasming mess of limbs.

Blake gave Antonia a single last powerful pump. One so hard she felt both of his testicles slam hard into her bulbous ass cheeks and compress themselves deep into their form. One so hard she let out a scream of decadent pleasure as her legs once again turned to linguini, and he once again had to steady her with his powerful arms.

"I CAN'T TAKE THIS!!" she cried breathlessly as he turned her around, picked her up, wrapped her thick and smooth legs around his ripped midsection, and kissed her with passionate revelry.

His kiss was so soft, so tender, so entirely at odds with how aggressively he'd fucked her only seconds before. His full lips lovingly caressed the contours of her own before he pulled away and connected with her soul via the medium of his oceanic blue eyes.

His gaze was so intense, so commanding, so nurturing, so supporting, so loving, and yet so protecting. She knew she was his. At that moment, Antonia was his queen.

"You are my queen," he said breathlessly, reading her mind.

Blake's eyes weren't just mere tools for vision but a portal to another universe. One in which Antonia and he were not two separate people but one unified entity. One in which she realised this had always been so. She and Blake had been one since the beginning of creation, simply waiting for this precise moment to remember who and what they truly were.

"OH MY GOD!"

The more she looked into his eyes, the more she merged with his essence. The more she flowed into him. The more two separate entities ceased to be as they surrendered to the overwhelming force of all there is, was, and ever will be.

"OH FUCK!! OH FUCKKK!"

Blake kissed Antonia once more as flustered gasps left her lips and flowed straight into his lungs. All the while, she helplessly dangled her arms around his shoulders, and he pressed her against the railing to penetrate her once more.

This time, looking her deep into her eyes with each sadistic stroke. He rocked his hips back and forth with rhythmical force as, for the second time in one day, after so many barren decades of sexual starvation, Antonia once again felt an orgasm beginning to build.

"OH SHITTT!"

Her body vibrated as every cell became alive and cried with passion.

Her mind felt traversed universes, seemingly connected to every blade of grass, ray of sunshine, and all other molecules in between.

"OH GOODD!"

Her pussy was scorching hot, like a nuclear inferno, and that heat was going to consume her. It was going to devour her. She couldn't take it.

“I CAN’T TAKE IT!”

Antonia couldn't fucking bear it!

"FUCKKKK!"

That heat smeared across her entire body, and she couldn't take it! She just couldn't take it, but there was nowhere else she wanted to be! Nowhere else she needed to be!

"I'M CUMMING!" she screamed. "I'M CUMMING!"

"YOU'RE GOING TO CUM FOR THIS DICK."

"AAAAHHHHHH"

"THIS DICK IS GOING TO MAKE YOU CUM HARD."

"YES! YES! FUCK!"

"YOU CAN'T TAKE IT. CAN YOU?"

"OHHHH GODDDD!"

"YOU CAN'T TAKE IT. CAN YOU?"

"NO! NO! MI CYAAN TEK IT!"

Blake pulled his rock-hard dick out of Antonia's dripping pussy, placed her down on the ground, turned her around, bent her over the railing, rammed it back inside her and once again brought his thick lips to her ears.

"It's time for you to cum," he whispered.

Antonia had just enough oxygen to scream:

"I'M GONNA CUM SO FUCKING HARD!"

She was delirious.

"OHHHH SHIIIIT!"

Gurgling with orgasmic panic.

"I'm going to fuck you with all my strength, my queen. I'm not going to hold back. You'll be fucked like you've never been fucked in your life."

"PLEASE! PLEASE FUCK ME!"

"Hold on for as long as you can."

Blake was not joking.

True to his word, he drilled Antonia like nothing else mattered. Hard, deep, fast and with impossible force.

She was lost. Confused. Flabbergasted. Perplexed. Defeated. She was able to do nought but hold onto that railing and scream from the very top of her lungs. In fact, Antonia screamed louder and longer than most would ever think possible as Blake mercilessly violated her with his mammoth manhood.

And it was so hard. So stiff. A sexual weapon of granite-made steel built solely for the purpose of obliterating her new young pussy.

Antonia moaned so hard and screamed so wildly. Blake grabbed her hand, placed it on her wet clit, and then moved it back to her lips.

"Taste it."

She did as she was told, but before she could even finish, he'd already returned her hand to her wet pussy.

"Touch yourself. Now."

And she did just that. Antonia's young caramel fingers explored the outer edges of her new body's engorged clitoris. At the same time, that swollen python between her legs sadistically abused her insides. All the while, she let out an earth-shattering scream. All while she howled in an erotic frenzy.

All while she cried in submissive victory. All while she moaned in delicious agony. All the while, she let out a primal roar of sexual conquest, the likes of which she didn't know she was capable. All while her legs buckled and her arms twisted and distorted like she'd received the lethal injection.

"OHHH GODDDDDD!"

"CUM. CUM FOR THIS DICK."

"OH FUCK!! FUCK FUCK, FUCK ME!"

"CUM ALL OVER YOURSELF."

"I'M COMING! OH FUCK I'M COMING!"

"CUM ALL OVER YOURSELF."

“OHHHH MYYYY GODDDDD!”

"WHO DO YOU FUCKING CUM FOR?"

"I CUM FOR YOU DADDY! I CUM FOR YOU!"

"TAKE IT. TAKE THIS FUCKING DICK."

"FUCK MI! FUCK MI LIKE A RAAS CLAAT SLUT!"

"CUM LIKE A FUCKING SLUT!"

"AHHHHHHHHH! NGHHHHHHHHH!"

Antonia did precisely as she was told and had an earth-rupturing orgasm.

One that caused the moon's gravitational pull to increase beyond rhyme or reason, sending all the water in all seven seas hurtling into the vast vacuum of space.

One that caused the sun to detonate, launching millions, billions and trillions of balls of lava into the cosmos in every conceivable direction.

One that turned Antonia into nothing less than a howling banshee of perversion.

Inside was left, and outside was right. She'd lost all concept of concepts. She didn't know if she was going or coming, but she did know she was cumming. For a single yet indescribable moment, reality collapsed into a single point as Antonia's soul experienced realities unknown to her human mind.

"AHHHHHHHHH! NGHHHHHHHHH!"

She screamed like a wild beast of rapturous femininity. She screamed like a divine goddess of universal lust. She screamed like the devilishly angelic succubus of creation, bucking and rocking against the rock-hard cock and body of the muscular chocolate-skinned god who fucked her into eternity.

As she wailed and thrashed against that New York balcony, Blake continued to assault her pussy like a black jackhammer until she squirted all over her own stockinged legs and feet.

How long that orgasm lasted is up for debate; it was definitely over a minute, but the exact length of time will remain a mystery. However, it did eventually subside. It did ultimately abate, and once that happened, Antonia found Blake's strong arms wrapped around her supportively.

In stark contrast to the dominant sexual assault he'd waged on her only seconds before, he now held her in a soft and tender embrace. As throes upon throes of pulsating rapture slowly left her body, Blake cradled Antonia close and kissed her softly, whispering sweet nothings into her ear.

Again, Antonia had no idea how much time had passed, nor did she care. All she knew, all that mattered was that she had collapsed against that railing with a feeling of contentment never before known in her 85 years of existence. At that moment, Antonia felt a sense of happiness she'd only known in her old white body with Winston, God rest his soul.

With a tired and heaving Blake pressed against her from behind and still planting soft kisses against the back of her neck, she stayed exactly where she was. At that moment, Antonia was content.

Complete. Whole. There was nowhere she needed to go, and there was nothing or no one she needed to be.

Antonia was complete.

Antonia was whole.

Utterly rejuvenated at both the cellular and spiritual levels.

Antonia was an honoured queen being tended to by her loving king, and that was all that mattered.

Nothing else was of consequence.

Nothing else held value.

The deep relaxation and effortless ease she felt at that moment would have taken her breath away if there were any left in her lungs to take.

But Antonia didn't need oxygen because Antonia didn't need to breathe. Antonia was immortal. Omnipotent. A goddess. Ever-present and never-ending. The alpha and the omega. Death and rebirth.

And she was content. She was whole.

Now and forevermore.

There it was. It had finally happened. The orgasmic delight she had been denied for decades had finally arrived.

And it was more than worth the wait.

However, as her vision and senses slowly returned to normal, as Antonia eventually fell out of sync with that spiritual realm of godhood and returned to the earthly plane from whence she came, she felt Blake urgently tapping her shoulder.

"I haven't been fucked like that since before Nixon was in office," she panted breathlessly.

"Oh fuck. Oh fuck, oh fuck!" he exclaimed nervously.

"What's wrong?" Antonia asked.

"Look," he replied.

And so she did. Antonia looked down and out across the way from Blake's apartment balcony and saw scores of people gazing up at them with varying degrees of shock, wonder, disgust, and arousal on their faces.

Every single last one was filming her on their phones.

"Oh fuck."

07 | WHEN I'M WITH YOU, I CAN'T REMEMBER PAIN

ANTONIA | Hoell Residence, Moss Bluff: June 8, 1957

"Stop crying, or I'll give you something to cry about!" Jonathan screamed as he punched Antonia square in the jaw.

It was a good punch, to be fair. Strong. Stiff. Clean. Solid. Definitely one of his best, as seen by the fact that he knocked one of her front teeth loose.

The funny thing, however, was that Antonia wasn't even crying.

Yes, she'd have been in floods of tears when she was younger, but not today. Yes, this latest ass whoopin' was a real doozy, a real humdinger, if you will, and sure, it hurt like a female dog, but it was nothing she couldn't handle.

Intentionally or not, Antonia's dear-old, ever-loving Daddy dearest had calloused her body and mind to physical pain and thus imbued her with a mentality that didn't sweat the small stuff.

And his latest fist to the jaw was exactly that.

The small stuff.

She wouldn't do him that courtesy of crying. No chance in hell. No fucking way.

Still, putting hands on his daughter wasn't the worst way Jonathan Hoell abused her because there were worse ways he often violated her person.

Ways that didn't involve his fists and only sometimes involved physical pain.

Ways that left her feeling confused, filthy, and disgusted.

Ways she was ashamed to say were the only times he ever showed her any genuine affection.

Ways she was ashamed to say were the only times he ever made her feel like she had value.

Ways he repeatedly enforced upon her with zero regard for her consent.

The sad fact is that Antonia had spent her entire childhood being violated in ways no little girl should, which, as just stated, had imbued her with a mindset which saw a single solitary punch as a fucking picnic.

As for her father, however? As for Jonathan? He was indeed an ugly man in mind, body, spirit, and soul. Coated from head to toe in sweaty, useless, disgusting flab and cursed with a perpetual state of intense perspiration, his trademark stained wife beater and grey stinking slacks were usually littered with damp patches of stinking sweat.

To be honest, the word stinking doesn't quite do his odour justice, as his stench was pungent at best and sickening at worst. A truly bespoke combination of secretions from Jonathan's ripe sweat glands and reeking stink intermixed with gin, whiskey, bourbon, and whatever liquor he'd been able to chug down his fat neck that day.

From the way Jonathan Hoell smelled, you'd think asking him to take a bath was akin to telling a devout Muslim to worship Satan, and today, he was especially ripe. Today, he was blessed with a rare breed of stink that would have given flies and maggots pause to enter his airspace.

However, it must be said that Jonathan Hoell wasn't any more horrific of a parent than his wife aka, Antonia's mother, Margaret. One could be forgiven for expecting a woman to be horrified at the sight of her husband brutalising the child she carried to term and gave birth to. But, one would also be mistaken because dear Margaret simply didn't give a solitary shit.

Rather than rush in all teary-eyed and drag Jonathan away from her teenage daughter, Dear Margaret stood leaning against that kitchen door, nodding her head in silent support of her husband's heinous deeds.

"Stop crying, or I'll give you something to cry about!"

There was that threat again, the same one Antonia had heard thousands of times in the short number of laps she'd completed around that nuclear explosion in the sky.

It was so weird.

So strange.

Despite the fact she wasn't even crying, if Daddy dearest didn't want her to do so, then why the fuck was he punching her? If the point wasn't to make her cry, then what the fuck was it?

Why do something that's designed to make someone howl in agony only to get angry when they do exactly that?

Fucking idiot.

Antonia had put up with this for her whole entire life. She'd spent all of her 18 fucking years with that dickhead and had given up on trying to work out how his brain worked. But still, one thing which was deathly for sure was why he was punching her and why dear Margaret was in complete agreement.

Both of them wanted her to:

"Stop fraternisin' with that fuckin nigger scum!"

And they weren't wrong. Well, yes, they clearly were wrong for referring to African Americans as 'nigger scum', but Antonia had indeed been fraternising with them and certainly had no intention of stopping.

In fact, Antonia had secretly been fraternising with 'nigger scum' for many years but didn't think the dumb fucks who gave her life had a clue. She thought she'd been careful.

Obviously not careful enough.

"Stop calling them that!" she screamed.

Despite the flippant tone of the writing in this chapter, it must be said that Antonia loved her black family very much and was violently offended by the disgusting hardships they faced in white America.

Her black family were better people than any of the racist crackers she'd ever known, and the abuse they endured was horrible. They were people, not animals. Good, clean, honest and God-fearing people who 'didn't do no harm to nobody'. They didn't deserve to be treated the way they were. It wasn't fair.

But sadly, morality was not reality. In fact, all of the inherent morality in the world couldn't do a damn thing to change said reality. The simple fact was that for a white teenage girl like Antonia in 1950s America, fraternising with 'nigger scum' was a cardinal sin.

In her parents' eyes, there wasn't much worse she could do.

"The town's starting to talk, Antonia."

It would honestly have been better if she'd killed someone.

"About what?! I ain't do nothin'!"

"Antonia, honey, there's something you need to hear," said her mother, aka dear Margaret, looking all sad, pensive, and reflective.

"What?!"

"Just because you built like a nigger woman, don't mean you gots to act like a nigger woman."

"WHAT?!"

"It means stop hangin' with those filthy fuckin niggers!" said Jonathan, aka dearest Daddy, before once again seeing fit to rock her jaw with a devastating right hook.

This particular blow, charged by the righteous fury of Caucasian racial superiority, sent Jonathan's daughter to the floor, finally bringing with it the tears he loved to pretend he didn't so desperately crave.

"See?! You see!? That's what you get for not following the rules!"

"It don't gots to be like this, Antonia."

"I been giving you my fists, Antonia. Don't make me take it to step two and give you my belt!"

"I HATE YOU!! I HATE YOU!!"

"GO TO YOUR FUCKING ROOM & DON'T COME OUT TILL THE MORNING!"

Antonia did go straight to her room but certainly didn't stop there. Not for a second. Once inside, she climbed right out of her window and ran 20 minutes through the woods to see her black family.

Her real family.

The drunken, hate-filled idiots who had the audacity to call themselves her parents wouldn't check on her that night. They'd be too busy getting plastered off whiskey and gin to remember she existed until the morning.

However, if they did check in on her, she wouldn't be there. And if that bothered them, they could stick those whiskey bottles right up their assholes and sit on them.

Antonia was ready to face the consequences. She just didn't give a fuck.

Anyway, 20 minutes later, she was finally at her destination and so excited she'd forgotten all about the pain that had begun to spread across her cheeks.

She was exhausted, yes. Covered in sweat, yes, but ecstatic nonetheless.

Antonia knocked on the door and within seconds was standing green to blue eyes with Winston, aka the love of her life. Winston was an 18-year-old black boy from her town of Moss Bluff, Louisiana, and the kindest, sweetest, and most honourable human being she'd ever met.

Antonia didn't just love him with all her heart; she loved him with every inch of her body, mind, and soul and knew he felt exactly the same way.

Unlike her birth family, who abused, ignored, ridiculed and neglected her, Just being in Winston's presence was enough to make her feel like a princess. He didn't even need to speak; he would gaze into her being with those oceanic eyes of his and melt all of her troubles.

He would wrap her up in his strong and nurturing arms and that would be all she'd need to know everything would be ok.

Antonia loved Winston more than words could say.

And he felt exactly the same way.

Winston Poole came from a great family. His mother, father, and two sisters treated each other with love, care, and respect. They didn't have much, but they had each other, and that was all they needed.

Even though they knew the white world didn't care for black folk, they were always good to Antonia. They were always nice to her. Always affectionate. They saw and treated her as one of their own even though she came from a world that hated and feared them.

And she loved them almost as much as she loved Winston.

Speaking of Winston, he took one look at Antonia's face and was crestfallen. Clearly, she was beginning to sport a new bruise.

"Again?" he asked, stroking what felt like a lump on her cheek.

She nodded sadly, tears forming in her eyes. With that, he took her by the hand and led her through the woods to their favourite cypress tree. Once there, they climbed it and sat huddled together on a branch as she sobbed quietly onto his shoulder.

The woods of Moss Bluff, Louisiana, were an enchanting realm seemingly untouched by time. Towering cypress trees with their thick, gnarled trunks and Spanish moss draped like ghostly veils, swaying gently in the humid breeze. The air was thick with the scent of earth and decaying leaves, mingling with the sweet aroma of wild magnolias.

Dappled sunlight filtered through the dense canopy, casting ethereal patterns on the forest floor, a tapestry of shadows that danced with the rustling leaves. Nearby, a slow-moving creek meandered through the woods, its waters whispering softly over smooth stones, harmonising with the distant calls of songbirds and the occasional croak of a hidden bullfrog.

Those woods were a sacred haven for Antonia and Winston, a world away from the harsh reality that lurked beyond the trees.

"You know what you need, Tiger?" Wilson asked, smiling sweetly.

Tiger was his nickname for Antonia, and he said it perfectly summarised her character.

He had a point.

"What?" she asked.

"A circular back rub," he replied before continually rubbing her back in a soft and circular motion.

Winston's circular back rubs weren't romantic or sexual in any way. They were simply his way of giving love and support to the women closest to him. As he always loved to say, only 4 women on the planet were worthy of receiving circular back rubs: his mother, his two sisters, and, of course, Antonia.

They weren't bad, not by a long shot; in fact, Antonia rather enjoyed them. But, from the way Winston spoke, you'd have thought these massages were imbued with the divine touch of Christ himself.

He would always ramble on about how lucky she was to be a member of such an elite yet small circle of humans who were worthy enough to get them, which, in honesty, she secretly agreed with.

As Antonia sat in that tree in the dead of night with the moon shining in the distance, insects chirping all around, and the love of her life right by her side, She knew nothing else mattered. And, as they continued to sit high in that tree together in absolute silence, she felt a wave of emotion build and swell from deep within.

Within moments, she was in floods of tears.

"My family don't love me," she sobbed.

"They not your real family," Winston replied, smiling. "We are, and we love you to death."

"Why? I'm ugly."

"Don't be silly."

"Everybody says I am. Everybody hates on me for my big butt, and now, my Daddy knocked my tooth loose, so I'm gonna be even more ugly."

"Don't do that."

"Do what?"

"You so much more than how beautiful you are."

"Like what?"

"It means it don't matter what your butt or tooth look like."

"So you don't like my butt?"

"I'm sayin' you got so much more goin' for you."

"Like what?"

"Antonia, you the bravest and most intelligent person I ever met."

"For real?"

"For real. The fam always talk about it."

"I love you, Winston. I love all you guys."

"We love you too."

"Nobody ever told me that."

"I'm tellin' you now. You worth so much more than your looks."

"It feels like I ain't nothin' if I ain't pretty."

"That's stupid."

"But it's the only time anybody's nice to me."

She then broke down into a flood of even deeper tears.

“It's the only time my Daddy's nice to me."

Antonia looked deep into Winston's oceanic blue eyes as she spoke, noticing him wincing angrily at the realisation of what she'd said.

A maelstrom of turbulent emotions flashed through him. He wanted to defend her, clearly that was true. He wanted to protect her, clearly that was true. In fact, Antonia suspected he wanted to do more than that, but he was powerless.

The world wasn't on his side. The law wasn't on his side.

If Winston, a black man, did anything to a white man, he'd be lynched by the entire town, castrated at best and murdered at worst. That wasn't an exaggeration, mind you. That was precisely what would have happened, and they both knew it.

As they both sat in silence, Antonia striving to forget her troubles within Winston's strong arms and him striving to overcome the impotence of his societal standing, he slowly began to sing.

There was a particular song he always sang to her, one that never failed to imbue her heart with more love and support than it could handle. One which made her feel like she was the only girl in the world and that he was the only boy.

And, as she hung her head in a fresh flood of tears, he wrapped his arms even tighter around her waist and sang from the heart.

"I am for you, and you are for me."

"When we are together, our souls they are free."

"Free as the stars, as free as the seas."

"Free as the eagles, and free to just be."

"You're never alone; I'm right by your side."

"Always I'll love you till after I die."

"So please stop your crying,"

"And lose all your fear."

"And enjoy your back rub."

"Cause Winston is here."

Antonia sat still at that moment, lost in blissful silence with the boy she loved. Elated to the core of her being as, what once were tears of sadness now became tears of joy. Eventually, she finally spoke.

"I wish I was black," she said honestly.

"Nigga, you always say that."

"And I always mean it too, nigga."

"You must be out your cotton-pickin' mind."

"Why? Black people are nice to me, and y'all families love each other and, and you have beautiful skin."

"You lucky to be white."

"Why?"

"White people can be and do whatever they want."

"I don't wanna be or do nothin that don't involve you."

"Ain't that the truth? It's like I can't get rid of you."

"No, Turtle, I'm serious. I don't want nothin' that don't got nothin' to do with you."

Turtle was Antonia's nickname for Winston, inspired by his strong yet slow and calming energy.

"Why?"

"I don't know how to say it."

"Try."

"I'm shy."

"Just say it, baby."

"I'm always sad. Always. I ain't never happy. Never. Only time I ever feel somethin' is when I'm touchin' myself, or, or when I'm with you. When I touch myself, it's like I can handle the pain, but when I'm with you, I can't remember what pain is. I love you, Winston. Even listenin' to your heartbeat makes me happy. I love everythin' about you, and I want to be with you forever."

"I don't know how I feel 'bout that."

"Why?"

"It's lovely what you sayin' and all, and I want to be with you forever, too. But I don't want to be the only thing that makes you happy. I want you to always be happy, not just when you with me."

"I understand."

"And I noticed somethin' about you."

"What?"

"I think you use sex like medicine."

Another thing Antonia loved about Winston was just how bright he was. He was easily the most insightful person she'd ever met and would constantly say things that blew her mind. She couldn't even imagine the heights he could have soared to if he were allowed to get a good education at a school like Harvard or Princeton.

"I think you're right," she replied.

Winston truly was one of a kind.

Rest in peace?

08 | THE WHORE OF NEW YORK

ANTONIA | Kara's Apartment: Present Day

Sure, Antonia had heard of going viral. In her first existence, she'd spent countless hours scrolling through social media, studying the trends of the youth. This meant that she was one of, if not the most informed old person on the planet and that meant the idea of going viral was nothing new.

But still, knowing something as a concept and experiencing it first-hand are two very different things. And so, as the World Wide Web went absolutely apeshit over her sex tape, she simply didn't know what to think.

Dozens of people saw her getting fucked by Blake on that balcony, and every last one of them had shared their clips online. That meant there were scores of alternate angles of Antonia screaming her lungs out, all being shared like crazy.

Sure, hers wasn't the first sex tape known to man, and definitely wouldn't be the last. Still, something about that particular moment resonated with the masses like never before. Her encounter with Blake was extraordinary and activated something deep and primal in people's hearts.

She wasn't having sex for the sake of it. She relished the exquisite beauty of every last drop of her femininity.

And everyone felt it.

She became one with the goddess within. She surrendered to the universal power of lust and transcendence as guided by Blake's massive cock.

And the entire world watched.

But then again, it wasn't really Antonia that they saw, was it? It was Kara. Antonia's soul in Kara's body. Nobody would have given a single solitary fuck if she were in her own body.

Then again, they probably would have.

Except it would have been sad and pitiful instead of erotic and daring.

Unsurprisingly, different people had different things to say about Antonia's viral act of debauchery. Many called her a menace, a whore, both a tragic symptom and evil symbol of the moral decay of society.

In fact, some religious thought leader by the name of Adrian Phillips had made several popular videos literally denouncing Kara (Antonia?) as a demonic succubus. According to Phillips, she was little more than a whore with no moral compass. One who was deliberately dragging Western civilisation head first into the lake of fire.

Now, if that seems a touch extreme, you're in damn good company because it seemed extreme to Antonia too. All she'd done was have sex on Blake's balcony. It wasn't like she'd killed an old man or a small girl.

She wasn't a monster.

Phillips was a man with many fanatical acolytes. Sycophants from across all four corners of the globe who supported his vision wholeheartedly. Many of whom saw it as their divine mission to attack Kara (Antonia?) from pillar to post and all the way back.

However, even though such souls were as plentiful as ants in the Amazon, they didn't speak for everybody because Antonia (Kara?) also had her own legion of supporters.

Many were inspired by her attitude and saw her as the ultimate expression of feminist liberation. Such souls heralded her as a 'badass boss bitch goddess' who did exactly who and what she pleased unapologetically.

To her newfound devotees, Kara (Antonia?) was a true lioness who didn't concern herself with the opinions of sheep. They waged digital war with her haters from dawn until dusk and she'd have been lying if she said it wasn't touching to see.

Antonia (Kara?) was positioned as either a champion of femininity or a succubus from hell but absolutely nothing in between.

However, what was crazy was that both groups had utterly missed the point.

She wasn't crusading for good or evil, nor was she trying to make a political statement.

She just happened to be captured having mind-blowing, out-of-this-world, earth-shattering sex. She didn't know those people were there, and neither did Blake. That could have happened to anybody, so why the world acted like she was crusading for an agenda was beyond her.

Also, on that topic, why the hell was all the focus on Kara? Blake was there too, and he was the one fucking her senseless. Why did nobody care about him? What kind of weird sexist hypocrisy was that?

Still, it was crazy. The situation was ludicrous. Everyone was talking about Kara (Antonia?) no matter where she went, and she hadn't seen anything like it since that little British Indian girl went apeshit at the Prime Minister of England.

But still, all the virality in the world was nothing compared to what really detonated her brain cells. Somehow, some way, Antonia Hoell actually was Kara Clark. Somehow, and some way, she was actually living in the body of a gorgeous 23-year-old black Instagram model.

The heart that wasn't truly hers seized every time she caught a glimpse of herself in a mirror. She didn't know how to process it but knew she couldn't possibly have been happier.

Antonia was genuinely scared to sleep. Genuinely terrified to even blink in case it all turned out to be a sadistic trick. She was petrified that if she did, she'd wake up back in her original 85-year-old decrepit body, but somehow, that never happened.

This was real.

No matter how long Antonia held out, her eyes eventually blinked, but nothing changed. No matter how long she tried to stay up, Antonia eventually fell asleep, only to wake up the very next morning, still in Kara's body.

This was very real.

Antonia Hoell's body died in that hospital. She knew that for certain because a quick Google search had easily turned up her death records. But that said, clearly, her soul hadn't died with it.

This was mind-blowing.

Everywhere she went, people treated her reverentially. Men gasped as she sauntered by swaying her voluptuous hips from right to left. At the same time, women were jealous and angry from a distance but insecure and shy in person.

This was glorious.

Absolutely, positively, fucking glorious. Antonia loved every second of it.

She just couldn't stop looking at herself.

Whether in lingerie, smart dresses, casual outfits, or just stark naked, no matter what she wore, she always looked incredible. No matter what angle she took pictures of herself in, they always looked sensational.

She'd never have had the courage to post selfies of her decrepit, front tooth missing, 85-year-old self online. She'd have struggled to do it if social media existed when she was younger.

If the 20-year-old version of Antonia had access to that kind of technology, she would have spent half an hour taking 30 different variations of the same picture before running it through all manner of filters and face-tuning apps to get it just right before daring to share it online.

In Kara Clark's body, however, that simply wasn't necessary. Literally, every picture she took was fucking exquisite. She could just take a shot, post it immediately, and have supreme confidence that the masses would go bonkers.

But even more unbelievable was Antonia's innate knowledge about her new life. She didn't know how she knew, but she knew everything about Kara. She knew her bank details, phone passwords, home address, friends, everything. She somehow intuitively knew everything she needed to slot perfectly into this new existence.

As for Kara Clark, she was an intriguing entity, to say the least. Born in a village called Hillside in St Thomas, Jamaica, she emigrated to New York when she was four but still had family back in Hillside. Humorously, she would occasionally drop into a Jamaican patois accent when drunk, angry, or otherwise emotionally stimulated.

Kara had studied Molecular Biology and Neuroscience at college and actually graduated with an A and Summa Cum Laude honours.

However, her inability to repay her student loans and cover her living expenses with her meagre entry-level salary led her to start an Instagram and OnlyFans to make ends meet. As fate would have it, said OnlyFans blew up more than she ever thought possible and unsurprisingly relieved Kara of the inclination to work a 9-5.

Kara Clark now made 50K per month modelling on IG and other websites. Also, amusingly enough, she made another monthly 75K by selling pictures and videos of her feet on Onlyfans with the occasional girl/girl scene whenever she felt particularly frisky.

This is all after tax, mind you. Kara Clark literally made 125K per month after tax from modelling.

Anyway, she spent at least three hours working on her body per day, with an hour and a half dedicated to building muscle, strength, and endurance at the gym and another hour and a half dedicated to flexibility and mindset through yoga.

She was also religious about following a strict ketogenic diet both to keep her body fat low and to optimise her mental performance.

You see, Kara's keen interest in biology and neuroscience had instilled within her the importance of honing her body's functionality as much as its appearance. As such, she considered her health to be a top priority.

In her spare time, she streamed herself playing a videogame called Street Fighter on a website called Twitch. Also, she put considerable effort into raising awareness for black charities.

Also, and somewhat surprisingly, Kara Clark was a firm proponent of using psychedelics as a means of achieving mastery over the self. Because of this, she would regularly sit in abject solitude, consume psilocybin mushrooms, and journey to the deepest reaches of her consciousness.

Those trips were as varied as the species of fauna in the Amazon. Some were glorious and ecstatic, in which she'd giggle hysterically and traverse the multiverse. Still, others were dark, malevolent, and sinister. In those, she would bravely attempt to face, accept, and overcome the darkness deep within her psyche. Sometimes, she succeeded, and others, she failed.

Kara Clark had about 750,000 IG followers when Antonia stalked her profile, but since that sex tape went viral, she now had 1.2 million and counting. All within a few days.

Needless to say, Antonia (Kara?) was inundated with interview requests, most notably from that Adrian Phillips douchebag. From his correspondence, it was clear he had a massive problem with her existence and badly wanted to have a sit down to hash it out.

Sadly for Mr Phillips, however, he would have to compete with the dizzying array of newspapers, talk shows, magazines, and podcasts that vied for Kara's (Antonia's?) attention. It wasn't even a slight exaggeration to say that her social media was going bonkers, and all eyes were on her.

Comments, tags, likes, and DMs bombarded her page faster than she could count. Seeing that never-ending stream of notifications flooding her phone hurt her new eyes. The constant noise and animations from all those alerts murdered her battery, so she had to switch her notifications off to bring back a semblance of sanity.

Kara Clark was in serious demand, so Adrian Phillips would simply have to sit down, fall back, and wait his turn like a good little boy.

But still, words could not describe how much Antonia loved the attention she was getting.

Everybody wanted to be around her.

Everybody craved her energy.

Kara was a drug.

Heroin laced with crack and with a splash of ecstasy thrown in for good measure.

And that feeling was intoxicating.

It was everything.

Whenever she posted pictures or videos, the praise she received was absurd.

A multi-millionaire businessman begged for her hand in marriage.

Blue-collar men left breathless voice notes about how they couldn't believe how hard they came just from seeing a picture of her ass in a tight pair of shorts.

Women worldwide said hers was the body they coveted and quizzed her on her fitness and eating habits.

But of course, being a prominent figure on the World Wide Web meant Antonia didn't only receive praise. Many of the comments she received showed a degree of racism she hadn't seen since Winston was ripped from her life. Rest in peace.

She'd been called a filthy nigger so many times she'd lost count.

And a jungle bunny.

And a coon.

And a monkey.

And so much more.

But, disgusting pre-civil rights era racism aside, she wondered why those idiots couldn't realise she didn't choose this. She didn't make that tape, and it wasn't her who posted it online. She literally had a private moment invaded by strangers sans consent yet was being attacked by slack-jawed, buck-toothed numbskulls who saw her as the second coming of Diddy.

Drooling, brain-dead mouth breathers who ranted and raved like she was the reincarnation of Epstein.

Malformed halfwits who acted like she was the leading student of the Weinstein school of sexual predation, having graduated with first-class honours.

Still, one thing these dickheads clearly didn't know was how little their insults bothered her. Sure, she'd seen Winston and her black family be called niggers on countless occasions and been forced to curtail the urge to commit violent acts every single time.

In fact, whenever she heard a white person use that word, it wasn't an exaggeration to say she had to suppress the urge to cut their throats.

The n-word was systematically used to dehumanise black folk for hundreds of years, and Antonia couldn't stand it.

She hated everything it represented and always had.

However, for some reason, when people now called her a nigger it just hit different.

They meant it to be an insult, but to her, it was high praise.

She'd always wanted to be a black woman, and now she was. So, whenever they tried to hurt her feelings, they only made her happier. She took pride in it.

Every single last iteration of the n-word Antonia saw directed at her was simply another reminder of the fact that her life's greatest dream was now its most vivid reality. Now, that word served as a beautiful representation of the fact that she had finally become exactly who she'd always wanted to be.

Antonia revelled in the insults, both for that reason and because she knew who they were coming from. Sad, lonely, miserable people with no lives who wanted to take out their frustrations on her instead of doing whatever they could to make their own situations better.

So, with that in mind, she often made a point of responding with sincere thanks to those who hurled such racist abuse her way. She wouldn't give them the satisfaction of getting upset.

No.

She'd deny them what they truly craved.

Instead, Antonia would thank them sincerely, laughing at the thought of them frantically searching for new ways to provoke her.

You see, Antonia was deeply acquainted with how it felt to be a pathetic and depressed loser and, as such, was deeply in tune with the inner machinations of said pathetic and depressed losers.

However, at least she had the decency to take ownership of her own reality and realise nobody was to blame for who and what she was but her. She used her fake accounts to follow people she wanted to be like, not to denigrate and try to bring them down to her own level of misery.

At least she had the ovarian fortitude to look in the fucking mirror and see herself as she truly was.

And so, it seemed that as low and pathetic as she thought herself to be in her prior incarnation, there were indeed forms of life even lower than she.

Curiouser and curiouser.

But there was indeed one troglodyte for whom Antonia held particular disdain. An anonymous white nationalist prick called HippocraticOath22. A self-proclaimed genetically pure Aryan who saw it as his duty to harass her day and night for being a 'filthy nigger.'

As expected, his profile was anonymous, and there was no profile picture or followers. Created solely to allow him to anally spray his frustrations across cyberspace like digital diarrhoea.

Antonia had contemplated sending a biting put down his way when BlueEyedBlake, aka Blake, aka the sexy black man from the park, sent her a DM.

BlueEyedBlake: Hey, Queen. How are you?

Her eyes lit up as she read the message before eagerly responding.

KaraClarkHadoken: My King! I can't believe what's happening!

BlueEyedBlake: I know, it's insane. It's like the whole world's talking about you.

KaraClarkHadoken: I know, I can't believe it! I've gained like half a million followers!

BlueEyedBlake: Yeah, because people love you :)

KaraClarkHadoken: Some do, but most of them hate me! They're acting like I'm some kind of seductress from hell!

BlueEyedBlake: Well, they're half right.

KaraClarkHadoken: Blake, I don't know what to do!

BlueEyedBlake: Just keep doing you and let people say whatever they want.

KaraClarkHadoken: But so many people hate me!

BlueEyedBlake: Fuck em. Fuck em right in the ear.

KaraClarkHadoken: You're amazing, Blake. Thank you.

BlueEyedBlake: You're very welcome, my Queen.

KaraClarkHadoken: I want to tell you something.

BlueEyedBlake: What?

KaraClarkHadoken: I just want to tell you that that night was amazing, and I really appreciated meeting you. You're an amazing person, inside as well as on the outside, and I want you to have a great life, Blake.

BlueEyedBlake: Why are you acting like this is the end?

KaraClarkHadoken: Isn't it?

BlueEyedBlake: Why would it be?

KaraClarkHadoken: They're calling me the whore of New York.

BlueEyedBlake: And?

KaraClarkHadoken: You're happy being associated with someone like that?

BlueEyedBlake: Kara, I don't give a flying fuck what anyone says about you.

KaraClarkHadoken: No?

BlueEyedBlake: No. Firstly, I was there too, and it's fucking weird that all the focus is on you. It's not like you were on your own; I was with you, and I don't know why everyone's ignoring that.

Secondly, you know why that video's gone viral?

KaraClarkHadoken: Why?

BlueEyedBlake: For the same reason, I was so drawn to you in the park.

KaraClarkHadoken: What do you mean?

BlueEyedBlake: You have a raw, powerful, and primal energy. It bleeds through into everything you do, and it's captivating. I felt it when we first met, and you expressed it to its fullest when we had sex on my balcony. That fire you have, it's unbelievable. You're like a phoenix of pure desire, and you know what?

KaraClarkHadoken: What?

BlueEyedBlake: On some level, everybody wishes they could be like that. Men want to be with a woman like you, and women wish they were you, but not everyone's in touch with how they feel. Not everyone's willing to connect with that part of themselves.

A lot of people have shame, guilt, and God knows what else attached to their sexualities. When they see someone like you fully embodying something about themselves that they can't fully own, they make you the problem.

But you're not the problem. You're not bad, you're not wicked, you're not a demon, a whore or anything those idiots are calling you. What you are is an incredible fucking human being, and I'm really glad I met you.

KaraClarkHadoken: Oh my God, Blake. Thank you.

BlueEyedBlake: You don't need to thank me. I wanted to get to know you from the moment I laid eyes on you and nothing's changed. As far as I'm concerned, we're in this together, and any idiots who have a problem with that can go eat a plate of dicks because I don't give the tiniest fuck about what they have to say.

KaraClarkHadoken: I don't know what to say.

BlueEyedBlake: Say you'll come to a party with me this Saturday.

KaraClarkHadoken: What party?

BlueEyedBlake: You know 50 Cent?

KaraClarkHadoken: What kind of question is that?

BlueEyedBlake: Well, he's having a mansion party on Saturday, and he asked me to invite you.

KaraClarkHadoken: Hold up, you know 50 Cent?

BlueEyedBlake: Yeah, but that's not the point. Are you coming?

KaraClarkHadoken: Of course. I'm already there!

BlueEyedBlake: Excellent.

It was at this moment when Antonia realised just how incredible of a man Blake was. Beneath those smouldering good looks and devilish charm lay a true heart of gold that belonged to a warm and loving soul. If he still wanted to get to know her, she sure as hell wanted to get to know him.

09 | I BELONG TO THE ORGASM

ANTONIA | Woods of Moss Bluff: October 1 1957

18-year-old Antonia was with Winston at their secret woodland spot laughing her ass off until her head felt faint. As usual, she felt happier with him than at any other moment, but something was getting her down today. Something made her worry.

She tried to take her mind off it by discussing her favourite topic, science fiction and the various high-tech gadgets that would exist by the time they were old, but none of it worked.

Still, she felt down.

Still, she felt depressed.

Having just finished administering an epic, 10-minute, circular back rub, Winston noticed something was up.

"What's wrong?" he asked curiously.

"Do you love me?" she asked in response.

"Nigga, you always ask this same question," he replied, exasperated.

"And you always react like this."

"How many times I gotta tell you the same thing?"

"I don't know, nigga, damn," she replied. "Sometimes I just need to hear it."

"You shouldn't even need to ask."

"I'm askin'."

"I love you more than life itself."

"Really?"

"Yeah."

"I want to be with you forever, Antonia. I want you to have my babies."

"Really?!"

"Of course."

"Really? Are you sure?? You want babies with me?"

"More sure than I've ever been about anythin'."

"Winston, are you sure?"

"Yeah, nigga damn. How many times I gots to say it?"

"I'm just makin' sure."

"Why?"

"Cause I ain't bleed in 2 months."

"What?"

"I think I'm pregnant, Winston."

"What?"

"I'm pregnant, Winston."

"What?!"

"We gonna have a baby."

"What?!"

"You gonna be a father again."

"Oh, thank you! Thank you!"

"You ain't mad?"

"Thank you, Jesus!"

"You ain't mad?"

"Mad?! This is the best news I ever heard!"

"But what are we gonna do?!"

"About what?!"

"I'm white, and you black! What we gonna do?!"

"I don't know!"

"Nobody knows I'm your lady!"

"Well, now they'll know!"

"Winston, what if someone tries to take our baby?"

"That ain't never gonna happen."

"How you know?"

"Because that ain't never gonna happen."

"How you know, Winston?"

"Anyone tries to take our baby away, that gon' be the last thing they ever do."

"I'm scared."

"Don't be."

"I'm scared about my family. I'm, I'm scared about this town. You know what Moss Bluff is like."

"I'll protect you, no matter what."

"How?"

"We'll leave."

"But what about your family?"

"I love my family to death but if you pregnant with my baby, you my priority."

"I love you, Winston."

"I love you more."

"Not possible,"

"Possible and true."

"You so silly."

"I'm glad you like it."

Antonia giggled playfully for a few seconds before resting her head against Winston's broad shoulder. Together, they shared a peaceful silence as birds chirped and crickets sang all around.

Winston had said all of the right things. He'd said everything she wanted to hear, and she could tell he meant it. He wanted to stay with her no matter what. He was going to find a way to make this work, and Antonia loved him. She loved him so much. But could they do it?

Could they make it work?

"So what we gonna do?" she asked.

"Head up north. I hear the northern states are kinder to black and white folk being together so I'm thinking we go to New York."

"Ain't that where your first baby was taken?"

"Yeah. Be real good if I could find her."

"You really think we can do this?"

"We will do this. I know it. I love you, Tiger. I always have, and I always will. I want to be with you forever. I want us to have lots of babies with your looks and my brain!"

"Hey, why I gots to be the dumb one? Why can't I be smart?" she asked teasingly.

"OK, lots of babies with your brains and my looks!"

"Hey, why I gots to be the smart and ugly one?!"

"Lots of babies with your brains, your looks, and my eyebrows!"

"Deal!" she laughed.

"I'm serious," Winston added. "We gonna make this work. I'm never going to leave your side, Tiger. You my lady, and I'm your man and ain't nothin' ever gonna come between us. I love you more than I know how to say, and I'm gonna be by your side until the day I die. Even after I die, too."

"You the reason I wake up in the mornin', and you the last thing on my mind before I sleep at night. If I ain't with you, I'm thinkin' about you and what you're doin', and when I'm with you, it's like nothin' else matters," Antonia replied.

"Me too," said Winston.

"Let's run away. Together. Me and you. Let's build a life and start a family. We'll have two children first!" Antonia added.

"A girl called Winnie and a boy called Antonio!" Winston exclaimed.

"That's exactly what I was gonna say!" she said excitedly.

"Nothin' gonna stop us from being together. Not even death. We'll always be together."

Antonia began to feel a lightness growing, flowing and easing its way across her being. Emotional shackles she'd carried for years were being cast aside.

Shackles she'd worn for so long she'd forgotten how much they weighed her down were dematerialising, meaning she was beginning to feel as light as a feather and free as a bird.

Antonia was content, assured, protected, and safe.

Antonia felt worthy.

Antonia was enough.

The feeling was slight at first, almost imperceptible, but very real and eventually grew into a tidal wave of transformation. One that flowed from her mind to her eyes, bathing her vision in a relaxing golden hue until everything in sight sang vibrantly.

The trees, plants, insects, animals, her own arms, and even Winston's body sang a song of harmonious vibration right before Antonia's eyes.

Winston began to stroke her lightly. Tenderly. She felt his strong chocolate hand sensually caress hers from the tips of her fingers along the soft padding of her palm and up the fine hairs of her wrist. It was so soft and so smooth, like tingles of electrical joy bubbling against the pores of her pale white skin.

As she sighed softly, Winston let his nimble fingers skillfully glide from her right wrist up to her forearm without actually touching her. He just let his fingertips brush gently against the hairs of her forearm, pushing them back against her skin without coming into contact with it themselves.

"I love you, Antonia. We gon' have a life together."

She sighed from deep within her gut. She sighed with a profound sense of deep relaxation and eternal peace. Slowly, surely, Antonia felt herself becoming awash with an overwhelmingly feminine energy.

A patient, deliberate, flowing, pulsating, and rhythmic force which made her troubles fade into the ether and eased her mind into the present moment.

Colours became vivid, vibrant and teeming with a life she could never have imagined. She saw multi-coloured caterpillars adorning lush green leaves, which in turn adorned earthy brown and patterned tree trunks, those, in turn, adorning the breathtaking beauty of the all-encompassing woods.

The sounds were intense, clean, and pure. The playful songs of the millions of lifeforms that inhabited those woods swam throughout the air and penetrated her pores, ears and mind. The songs of crickets, American robins, deer, and foxes all merged in perfect harmony to become a unified hymn of nature as Antonia's nose became awash with Winston's masculine musk.

Winston was always impeccably clean and showered at least three times a day. Still, right now, he'd clearly been exercising and, as a result, had a thin layer of sweat permeating and intensifying his delicious scent.

And Antonia was intoxicated.

But then, at that moment, Winston began singing their song. Her song. The song he'd written for her so many months before and that her heart soared to hear him sing.

"I am for you, and you are for me."

"When we are together, our souls they are free."

"Free as the stars, as free as the seas."

"Free as the eagles, and free to just be."

"You're not alone. I'm right by your side."

"Always I'll love you till after I die."

"So please stop your cryin'."

"And lose all your fear."

"And enjoy your back rub."

"Cause Winston is here."

Despite Winston's wishes, Antonia had tears streaming down her pale cheeks. Tears of happiness. Tears of love. Tears of pure, indescribable joy.

His touch was so soft, gentle, and tender; it was electric. Every last syllable of every last word was a voyage to an unseen realm of delight. She could feel the resonant pulsations of his heart reverberating through his lungs, throat and lips to provide pure declarations of love that permeated her soul.

Winston whispered slowly in her ear. Constantly but softly still. Softly but deeply still. Deeply still but with a solid masculine purpose. However, at no point did he ever stop exploring her exposed skin with his chocolate fingers.

Their touch was endless.

They grazed her lips, neck, chin, and cheeks as his thick lips spoke into her ears through her blonde hair. Hair he pulled back to expose her ears and neck to the slightly cold woodland air before bringing his lips millimetres away from her tingling skin.

Just the sound of Winston's voice made Antonia's skin flush with blood. Just the sound of his voice was enough to make the fine hairs on her body stand erect as the skin in which they were embedded became as sensitive and delicate as a blossoming rose.

Just the mere sound of Winston's voice made Antonia disengage from reality.

Her entire frame had become a vessel through which he connected with her very essence. She was marooned on an island of passionate love and losing herself within him as he spoke in those soft, hushed, honeyed whispers.

The boundaries of her consciousness began to dissolve.

She merged with and flowed into a realm of oceanic unity. One where he was all that mattered. One where they were all that mattered. One where nothing else held significance.

Antonia was no longer the colour of her skin. That was a concept about which she no longer understood. Antonia wasn't even her name because that also was a concept that no longer held meaning.

Who was Antonia?

What was Antonia?

Her soul had moved beyond the need to exist with that label.

That burden.

That pain.

The shackles were gone. They no longer weighed her down. She was no longer the ugly white girl with the big butt and missing front tooth that nobody understood.

Now, she was free.

As Winston said, she was as free as an eagle soaring high through the clouds and ascending into the heavens. As free as the wind flowing blissfully through said eagle's feathers and as free as the trillions of rain droplets that fell gently in swirling m patterns to the ground below.

At that moment the soul formerly known as Antonia was free to be and do whoever and whatever it pleased.

It was held by no constraints.

No limits.

No chains.

No shackles.

Antonia was free to manifest whatever experience she wished. Whatever reality she desired.

She was pure awareness.

Eternal energy made manifest by a divine force.

Antonia was a goddess.

Antonia was the goddess.

Antonia was the source of all creation.

The divine feminine.

The spark of birth which becomes the searing fire of life before fading into the dark sleep of death, only to reawaken once more like a flaming phoenix from the ashes.

This was who she truly was.

Who was Antonia?

She didn't even exist.

What was Antonia?

She was just a story.

An idea.

A fantasy.

And with each soft touch, each tender caress, each sensation of Winston's thick lips grazing upon her cheek, the soul formerly known as Antonia felt its vibration rising, ascending, and soaring.

But this was when said soul noticed that it was indeed rising. It had left its female body and was watching it collapse into Winston's strong masculine frame against that tree. It silently observed the life force of that forest, breathing in synch with its body's lungs.

With every exhale of breath, fear, negativity, insecurity, and hatred poured out of Antonia's lungs as dark liquid gas. Gas, which was then alchemised by that forest into a bright light of devotion.

With each breath, that bright white light flowed into her body, settled in her heart, and morphed into a deep green glow. A beacon of love.

The soul formerly known as Antonia watched in awe as that beacon of love healed the cells of her body from the inside out. It watched in wonder as even the bruises and swelling on her face faded into a mist which spiralled outwardly into the forest.

It watched in amazement as said mist interacted with the surrounding flora and fauna, causing them to glow in indescribable hues of brilliance.

As all of this occurred, the soul formerly known as Antonia saw and felt her white body react to Winston's chocolate touch. It saw and felt her chest rise and fall with increasing speed. It saw and felt her temperature grow until she was almost boiling.

It saw and felt moisture collect on her skin as beads of sweat that clung to her clothes rolled down her skin and evaporated into the night's air.

But the soul formerly known as Antonia also saw and felt that feeling.

That powerful feeling.

The churning, burning, blissful feeling. The feeling that made colours coalesce into shapes and the sounds of the forest's wildlife edible. The feeling that made both soul and body once again become a vessel for a level of energy neither could begin to fathom.

The feeling which made Antonia's body grind on the spot as gasps of pleasure left her lips as blue beams of light.

The feeling which, through a kaleidoscope of scents, sounds, colours and shapes, had her body heat to an indescribable degree as steam left her skin and even deeper moans of joy escaped her lips alongside those blue beams of light.

But then, Antonia felt something overwhelming.

Something against which she couldn't even begin to fight. Something which, within seconds, had sucked her soul back into her body.

And that was when everything intensified.

That is when her already overwhelming level of sexual pleasure became a titanic overload of orgasmic destruction.

That is when her lips moaned louder still, even as Winston covered them with his strong brown hands.

In fact, Winston wasn't singing now but whispering.

He was different, but Antonia had no idea why he was different.

He was panicking, but Antonia had no idea why he was panicking.

He was terrified, but Antonia had no idea why he was terrified.

But Antonia didn't have any idea of anything anymore.

All she knew was that she was the universe, the universe was her, and all of it had collapsed into her vagina. Fantasy and reality became one as her body and soul let out screams of delight that pierced the night sky and made her toes curl hard enough to break.

She moaned, cried, screamed and thrashed for a single moment of eternity until strong hands grabbed Winston from behind, causing them both to fall to the ground below.

Antonia lay on the famous dirt, consumed by the most intense orgasm of her existence. She couldn't stop herself. It just wasn't possible. She was a conduit for forces far beyond herself, helpless to resist their power.

But still, as she cried and screamed with eyes ablaze with sexual insanity, she saw her father and other white men from the town appear and repeatedly kick Winston in his beautiful face.

She wanted to stop them, but she just couldn't.

She wanted to move her body, but she just couldn't.

Why? Because it didn't belong to her anymore.

It belonged to the orgasm.

But as her father assaulted the man she loved, she felt every strike.

Every punch.

Every kick.

Every stomp.

All while consumed by the single most powerful orgasm in her existence.

As she lay helplessly on that field, sadly unable to lift a finger to protect the man she loved, she heard someone scream the phrase, "nigger lover!"

Antonia wanted to save Winston; she wanted it more than anything, but she couldn't.

She just couldn't.

Her body wasn't her own.

It belonged to the orgasm.

Antonia belonged to the orgasm.

There was simply nothing she could do.

10 | BEAUTY IS THE ULTIMATE NARCOTIC

KARA | 50 Cent's Mansion: Present Day

Antonia arrived at 50 Cent's mansion party with blonde highlights while clad in an outfit she'd never have been seen dead wearing in her past life. It was a figure-hugging sheer black bodysuit with exposed patches over her right thigh, left shoulder, left hip, and cleavage.

Truly a feast for the eyes.

Antonia was an irresistible concoction of chocolate skin, multicoloured tattoos, and shimmering yet sheer black fabric that turned every head in the venue.

There wasn't a single soul who didn't do a double, triple, or sometimes quadruple take when they saw her and that made Antonia feel nothing less than divine.

And, as for the venue, it was as lavish as lavish could be, truly the home of a man worth hundreds of millions.

50 Cent's mansion was an opulent fortress of modern luxury, sprawling across acres of meticulously manicured grounds. The exterior, a sleek blend of glass, steel, and stone, gleamed under the carefully placed lights, a testament to his sheer power and excess.

Inside, every inch of the space was designed to impress, from the grand spiralling marble staircase to the cavernous living room in which walls of glass provided an uninterrupted view of the infinity pool and cityscape beyond.

The party oozed with energy, each room pulsating with music, laughter, and the clink of expensive champagne glasses as guests moved through spaces adorned with custom furnishings beneath ceilings that seemed to touch the sky itself. It was a palace built for a king, and tonight, it vibrated with the electricity of celebration.

All around Antonia were gorgeous women and famous celebrities. She saw music producers, movie stars, directors, comedians, and even world-class athletes all mingling while still taking conspicuous notice of her.

Is it because they've seen my video or because they just can't believe how beautiful I am?

The answer was anyone's guess; regardless, the feeling it gave her was legendary. She was at a party with America's most famous and influential people, but all were subtly bowing in deference. Every single woman in that venue was envious of her.

She felt it.

She sensed it.

She could tell.

Antonia was no fool.

Oscar-winning actresses and Grammy award-winning singers jealously side-eyed her.

Top 5 ATP-ranked tennis stars and gold medal-winning Olympic gymnasts stared at her with envy.

All wanted what she had.

All knew she was the most beautiful woman in attendance.

All wished they were her.

All wish they had what Antonia had.

And that was the moment when something clicked.

That was the moment when she stopped pretending and finally started being.

That was the moment when Antonia realised she was no longer Antonia.

Women want to be me, and men are fantasising about me.

Antonia was Kara.

Me. They're all looking at me.

Antonia wasn't Antonia anymore.

Me.

Antonia was Kara.

She wasn't old, ugly, or white anymore. Now, she was young, beautiful and black.

I'm Kara.

She wasn't watching this scene vicariously from behind her iPad screen; she was living it first-hand.

I'm Kara.

She was Kara.

I'm fucking Kara.

Everybody in that venue paid Kara her attention, and she adored it.

I'm fucking Kara.

Cherished it.

I'm fucking Kara.

Thrived on it.

Kara sucked that attention deep into her being like forbidden nectar from the phallus of Zeus himself. One which nourished her in body, mind, and soul. One Kara intimately craved as if it were her very life force. And she had zero problems taking said phallus deep into her neck to drain it dry of every last drop of its salty goodness.

None whatsoever.

Still, all the godlike phalluses in the world couldn't change the fact that Kara was there to meet Blake but had no idea where he was. Now, this wasn't particularly surprising, mind you, because not only was that mansion epic in size but also heaving with human traffic, meaning he indeed could have been anywhere.

In any event, one of its kitchens was a free bar with staff serving every possible permutation of alcoholic beverage known to man next to supple nude dancers covered in blue body paint.

Kara headed over to get a strawberry daiquiri and did just that before checking her IG and seeing, among others, a series of insulting DMs from her old friend, Mr HippocraticOath22. He'd seemingly taken severe offence to a selfie she'd posted to her story in her party outfit.

HippocraticOath22:

"My God, you'll do anything for attention, won't you? Fuck people on camera, dress like a nigger whore. You'll literally do anything, won't you, you black cunt."

Kara knew this man's deal. He was jealous and angry because not only was his life shit, but he sadly knew his tongue would never get to taste the moist delights which resided between her thighs. He was epically miserable and lashing out in frustrated rage as a result.

Yes, Kara knew all of the above, but still, at that moment, she was feeling spicy and decided to play with him a little.

KaraClarkHadoken:

"Not true, there's something I'll never do."

There was silence.

A delay.

A massive pause. The troglodyte never for a second thought she'd reply, and now she had he didn't know what to say. He spent about 60 seconds starting, deleting, and restarting new messages before he finally got it together and said:

HippocraticOath22:

"What."

Kara was floored by his impeccable wit.

KaraClarkHadoken:

“You.”

Another pause. The little numbskull didn't like that comment. It clearly hurt his poor little man-feelings.

Kara smiled inwardly.

HippocraticOath22:

"I'd never want to fuck a whore like you."

KaraClarkHadoken:

"Right."

HippocraticOath22:

"You're an ugly nigger."

KaraClarkHadoken:

"I'm sexier than any woman your microdick has ever touched and you know it."

HippocraticOath22:

"I fuck beautiful white women."

Kara then took and sent him a series of cleavage-revealing selfies posing with her cocktail at the bar, along with the caption, "Don't ya wish your girlfriend was hot like me". The little worm saw the images and took a whole two minutes and 30 seconds of starting and restarting messages just to say:

HippocraticOath22:

"You literally think you're God's gift. You're fucking pathetic."

KaraClarkHadoken:

"OK. So why are you wasting your time blessing me with your superior Aryan energy?"

HippocraticOath22:

"Because you're a fucking idiot."

KaraClarkHadoken:

"That why you're on my Onlyfans?"

Yet another pause. He didn't see that coming either. After two minutes and 37 seconds, he finally said:

HippocraticOath22:

"What."

KaraClarkHadoken:

"You paid $150 for a 5-minute video of my toes this morning. You think I don't know?"

Yet another protracted silence as Kara nodded her head and swayed her hips to the R&B music emanating from all around. Funnily enough, there didn't seem to be just one speaker or even a few visible ones dotted about. It was as though the entire venue was a speaker in and of itself. As though they were somehow built seamlessly into the furniture.

Anyway, eventually, the simpleton replied.

HippocraticOath22:

"That wasn't me."

KaraClarkHadoken:

"Just so we're clear. I'm a worthless nigger who's beneath you. One with so little self-respect that I fuck on camera and shamelessly parade on social media for attention. However, you're not only paying a monthly subscription to my content; you paid $150 just to see a video of my feet. And you say I'm the worthless one."

HippocraticOath22:

"Go back to Africa, you jungle whore."

KaraClarkHadoken:

"That's one idea, but here's another."

Kara slipped off her right shoe, made a 5-second video of her flexing and unflexing her toes, and then sent it.

KaraClarkHadoken:

"Here. Here's something for you to jerk to tonight."

HippocraticOath22:

"If we could kill every one of you black nigger cunts the world would be a much better place."

KaraClarkHadoken:

"You see, that's the difference between me and you."

HippocraticOath22:

"What?"

KaraClarkHadoken:

"I mean so much more to you than you do to me. You're sitting in your Mom's basement, and I'm at a celebrity mansion party. Talking to me is the highlight of your evening, but talking to you is literally the lowest point of mine. Once I'm done with you, I guarantee my night will only go up from here."

HippocraticOath22:

"Whore."

KaraClarkHadoken:

"I get it. Your ego hates the fact that I'm talking to you like this, but you can't deny the rock-hard erection you got from that video, can you? I know you've got it gripped tightly in your right hand right now."

HippocraticOath22:

"I'm left-handed."

KaraClarkHadoken:

"My bad. But fundamentally, it's like this, I'm at 50 Cent's mansion party, and he doesn't know it yet, but I'm gonna fuck him tonight. It's gonna be long, it's gonna be hard, and it's gonna be wild. Who I'm not gonna fuck, however, in any way, shape, or form is you with your pathetic little two-inch KKK dick.

So, with that in mind, here's what you are going to do. You, my friend, are going to sit at home stroking your little peepee all night until the early hours of the morning, thinking about me until you're swimming in your own nut butter. You're gonna cum like a fountain to the thought of what I'm going to do with him but never will do with you, and you're gonna thank me for the privilege."

HippocraticOath22:

"Fuck you. I hate you so much."

KaraClarkHadoken:

"Fuck me? I literally just told you that will never happen. Clearly, paying attention isn't your strong suit."

HippocraticOath22:

"You're gonna get yours. I promise you. You're just a dumb filthy nigger, and that's all you'll ever be."

KaraClarkHadoken:

"I wonder who's more despicable, me the dumb filthy nigger, or you the proud white man whose cock gets hard for said dumb filthy nigger? I guess it's a chicken and egg kinda scenario."

HippocraticOath22:

"Fuck you, you black cunt."

KaraClarkHadoken:

"My God, you're like a broken record. I can't tell if you're really fucking angry, really fucking horny, or just really fucking stupid, but I guess it doesn't matter.

Anyway, I'm gonna go enjoy this party, so I'll leave to tend to the bloated slug between your legs. If you're lucky, I might send you some pics of my soles to drool over while you beat it. You can imagine me stepping on your face while 50 rails me from behind. Ciao."

And with that, Kara closed the chat before he could reply, sent Blake a message asking where he was, got off her seat, and headed out into the party. As she walked by, casually sipping her daiquiri and sensually swaying her hips to the music, she noticed that everybody was staring again. However, there was a white woman standing against a wall with a man, and that bitch was looking hard.

Extra hard.

Kara felt pure animosity radiating from her. There was nothing but hatred behind her eyes. Nothing but contempt. As she walked through that mansion, minding her own fucking business, this bitch refused to take her eyes off her. She was staring like Kara had personally attacked her. Like she'd just seen the high school bully who used to slap her silly and dump her head in dirty toilet water.

What the fuck is her problem?

She looked so self-righteous. So judgemental. So holier than thou, and she refused to stop. It was like nothing else mattered. Like Kara represented some moral threat that had to be extinguished. Kara looked over and she looked right back. Daring her. Challenging her. Taunting her. For whatever reason, she hated Kara and wanted her to know it.

But why? What had she done to her? Kara hadn't done a damn thing but exist. That's all she'd ever done, just exist. Yet somehow, the mere act of her living was always enough to piss someone off.

There was always someone offended by how she chose to express herself. How dare she be a white girl with a black boyfriend? How dare she be a woman who loved technology, gadgets, and sci-fi? How dare she work with civil rights leaders to build a better and fair world for everyone, not just black folk? How dare she?

How fucking dare she?

Now, what happened next wasn't planned. Kara didn't consciously know it was going to happen. She didn't mentally rehearse what transpired; she'd simply had enough and acted impulsively.

Kara was just sick. Sick and tired. Sick and tired of having people judge her right to her face for nothing and feel like they could get away with it.

It was one thing to read social media comments made by cowards lurking behind the anonymity of their devices, but another for someone to have the audacity to let her know to her face that they thought she was lacking.

Once again, Kara had had enough, and because of that walked right up to that bitch and stood less than one foot away from her nose to nose. Their breasts literally touched, and Kara could smell the vodka tonic on the bitch's breath. They were that close.

But she didn't say a word.

Kara didn't say a thing.

She just stood there, coldly and calmly, looking right into that woman's hateful eyes with eyes of her own. Eyes that revealed precisely zero per cent of the animosity she had for Kara.

Eyes that communicated everything she needed to say in a way words never could.

Eyes that made their point.

Eyes that established dominance.

Eyes that made that bitch take a sharp intake of breath as she stood rooted to the spot trying to look confident but slowly succumbing to overwhelming intimidation.

Her pupils dilated and quivered, her breathing became shallow, and her body tremored. It was small, yes. Almost imperceptible, yes. But real nonetheless.

The bitch was scared.

She didn't know what to do. Kara could literally smell her fear, and she loved the scent. Its aroma both aroused and intoxicated her. And as she took another step even closer still and pressed her breasts right against those belonging to the now intimidated and self-conscious frump, its sweetness flooded her nostrils.

This woman had so much bravado at a safe distance but didn't know what to do when push came to shove.

So disappointing.

So sad.

All lipstick, no bite.

The poor prude was so paralysed with fear that she didn't even realise Kara had actually grabbed her boyfriend's cock through his trousers.

Right in front of her.

That cow had stared at Kara like she'd stolen her boyfriend, but that's exactly what was now happening.

Right in front of her.

While peering right through this woman's soul with emotionless eyes, Kara circled her fingers around her boyfriend's rapidly stiffening cock, literally feeling his heartbeat intensify as shockwaves of blood pumped through its veins.

Finally, after what must have felt like an eternity of intimidation for the frump, Kara spoke.

"You want it to be one way," she said coldly.

"What?" replied the frump.

"You want it to be one way," Kara repeated.

"Why do you keep saying that?"

"You want it to be one way."

"Stop saying that!"

Kara gestured down to her hand with a smirk and continued to stare right into her eyes as the frump finally saw what was happening.

She was shocked, dismayed, distraught, confused, terrified, and maybe, just maybe, even slightly excited?

As Kara brought her lips to meet those of the bitch's seemingly paralysed boyfriend, she looked through her eyes one final time and spoke.

"But it's the other way."

Less than a second later, she playfully kissed the bitch's boyfriend right on his bright red cheek. All right in front of her. All while still gripping his now pulsating and rigid member with her slender and manicured right hand.

Kara loved this power. She loved being this beautiful. It was the best drug to be found across all seven seas. More heroic than heroin, more psychedelic than psilocybin, it made her more amped than amphetamines and more ecstatic than ecstasy.

She looked back again. Taking a moment to savour the putridly sweet scent of terror and defeat emanating from the soul of the intimidated white bitch.

"But it's the other way," she repeated.

Everything she'd ever wanted was now made manifest in human form.

Everything.

Kara finally had everything.

Well, almost everything.

Why?

Because at that moment she felt a profound emptiness in her heart that she couldn't place at first but soon realised was loneliness and guilt.

As much as she wanted to, she didn't like what she'd done. On the surface, it felt great, but deep down, it violated her ethics and made her feel terrible.

Part of her wanted to be just as bad or even worse than that bitch thought she was just to prove a point, but a larger part of her just wanted to be free to live in peace.

That part of her also knew she didn't have Winston and that nothing would bring him back. That part of her sadly knew he was most likely dead.

Rest in peace.

And this was when Kara realised she definitely didn't have everything she'd ever wanted. Not by a long shot. Yes, she loved her new body. Yes, she loved her new identity, but what was it all for without Winston?

What did it all mean?

Eager to escape from the thorny vines of depression which threatened to ensnare her, Kara banished those thoughts and ventured deep into the party to look for Blake.

11 | THE DEAL SHE COULDN'T REFUSE

KARA | 50 Cent's Mansion: Present Day

Once again, Kara was trapped within a pure and pitch-black void. A void without sight nor sound. A void in which she once again was little more than a disembodied consciousness. A soul without a mind. A mind without a heart. A voice in which Kara wasn't anything in particular.

She just was.

There were no external labels placed upon her. She wasn't anything in particular.

She just was.

And along with that dark void of nothing came a silence, a stillness, a peace.

A comfort.

It nurtured her. Supported her. Relaxed and soothed her as she drank it all in through the mouth she now didn't have. Kara surrendered herself to that void. She allowed it to permeate her being as she floated through a dark cosmos of contentment.

But then she heard voices.

Screams.

Shouts.

Panicked cries could be heard all around, yet they didn't emanate from within the void; they emanated from another plane of existence. They were in the void, but somehow not of the void, and they were in terror.

Pure, unbridled, horrified shrieks of terror that pierced Kara's soul. Shrieks, which caused that black expanse to slowly become bright white as they perpetually increased in volume to create a cacophony as deafening as it was confusing.

"WHAT THE FUCK IS THAT?!"

"WHAT THE FUUUUCK?!"

"NO! NO! DON'T TOUCH IT!"

"OH MYYYY GOD!"

Suddenly, the eyes Kara forgot she possessed sprung wide open as she saw that she was on a gigantic bed with at least ten other naked people. All looked at her with a fear reserved only for one's wildest nightmares.

It was like she was a demon or worse.

She tried to speak but words couldn't come, just a gargle of warped utterances from what felt like broken vocal cords.

Kara couldn't speak.

And then she remembered where she was. She was at 50 Cent's mansion party. She'd snorted more than a fair amount of cocaine, eventually met Blake and partied with him until an orgy erupted in one of the bedrooms involving her, 50, and various celebrities and models.

She'd heard about the Freakoffs Diddy used to hold, and this had to have been what they were like.

At some point, Kara spent precisely 17 minutes laying on a bed completely naked as everyone else used her body as a table to snort coke off.

Yes, that did actually happen. In fact, she'd even sent HippocraticOath22 a video of that just to piss him off. Mission thoroughly accomplished, by the way.

Anyway, Blake had fucked her so hard and so well that night that she could now still feel pain in her nether regions before she'd somehow lost him again. After that, she put her clothes back on to play strip poker with several NBA players, lost decisively, and fell asleep.

And here Kara was.

Wide awake once more the very next morning.

What's going on? She thought. *Why are they screaming like that?*

She tried to ask them but all that came out was inaudible garbles from her throat. Something was very wrong.

Why are they so terrified?

A young and naked Japanese model backed away in abject terror. An NBA player she couldn't name but who had spent the previous night cosying up to her was screaming like an extra from the Texas Chainsaw Massacre. Even 50 was as white as a sheet, an impressive feat for a man so dark of skin.

"Whhatsyshagahhsjs?!" Kara gurgled, trying in vain to form a proper sentence.

And this was when she saw something terrifying.

Something which horrified her more than anything ever seen in both of her lives.

Something which had her running at full speed out of that bedroom and into the nearest bathroom.

Something which once in that bathroom and looking at herself in its giant mirror had her now broken voice box howling and crying as her body thrashed against all of its four walls.

Kara looked like a corpse. A literal dead body.

No, not just a corpse. She looked like she'd been dead for months, like a zombie from The Walking Dead. Her hair was patchy, grey, and singed like it'd been burned in a fire.

Her once thick lips were non-existent and bore an exposed mouth of dry yellow teeth and no tongue.

Her skin was shrivelled like a rotten prune and discoloured in the hue of green and black sewage.

This was just too much to take.

This was too much for her soul to bear. Within five seconds of seeing the hideous freak in the mirror perfectly mimic her movements, Kara fell to the ground, howling in abject misery as best as her ruptured lungs would allow.

She didn't know how long she spent on that floor, nor did she care. She was just overwhelmed with one single unifying thought.

Mi affi kill miself. She thought in Jamaican patois.

But how? How could she do it?

Kara looked high and low in that bathroom while the sounds of commotion from scared partygoers emanated from outside.

But she couldn't find anything.

She couldn't find a damn thing she could use.

Until she did.

Until she saw a sharp pair of scissors on the sink, grabbed them, put them to her throat and once again heard that familiar set of feminine voices.

"Now you know the impermanence of our gift.

If beauty you require then beauty we will give.

But the universe is balance, and energy is shared.

Grant us one favour; do this if you dare."

"What?!" she tried to scream through her obliterated voice box.

"Do you wish to be beautiful, Antonia?"

"Mshsgshsjsj!" she gurgled, trying to say that her name was Kara.

"Do you wish to be beautiful again, Antonia?"

Kara cried a cry of sweet misery.

"Do you wish to be beautiful again, Antonia?"

"YHSSS, PEEESSSHDHH!"

"End the life of the next soul to enter this space.

You have under two minutes; please make haste."

"HHSHSHSH?!"

Kara was still trying to process what was said as she heard a knock on the door.

"One minute and fifty seconds."

"Are you alright in there?! Do you need help?!"

It was a man. A concerned-sounding man.

"DON'T GO IN THERE!"

Those were the screams and shouts of others outside the bathroom.

"One minute and 40 seconds."

That was those familiar yet feminine voices.

"I'm coming in!"

That was the concerned man again.

"DSHFJFJFJNDDHH!"

That was Kara, trying in vain to tell him not to enter.

"One minute and 30 seconds."

Unable to comprehend her through the broken remains of her now decomposed neck, the man entered the bathroom and stood face to face with the living corpse known as Kara. However, as they made eye contact, she had a profoundly humiliating realisation.

This was the man she'd kissed in front of his girlfriend. The one who was literally spellbound by her only the night before. But the way he looked at her now was poles apart. Now, she wasn't a gorgeous siren of seduction in his eyes. Now, he simply felt pity for her.

He wasn't aroused by her.

He wasn't intimidated by her beauty.

He just pitied her.

Now, he thought she was beneath him.

And Kara hated that.

"He does pity you. He does not respect you. He does not desire you, Antonia."

It filled her with rage.

"He thinks you are nothing.

One minute and zero seconds."

As said rage burned a chasm of hatred into Kara's soul, she felt a splitting pain slice into what was left of her heart. A pain that sent her crashing to the floor in agony.

"Are you alright?" asked the man sympathetically.

"Kill him." said the voices. "Kill him or see how deep this rabbit hole will go."

"ARRKKHHHH!"

"What's wrong?!" he screamed.

"SSSHH MMDIDUD DHHDYIS!"

"What happened to you?!"

"You know what to do. Zero minutes and forty seconds."

Through a thunderstorm of pain, Kara once again looked into that man's eyes and felt herself becoming more and more enraged by the second.

He pitied her.

He was sorry for her. He gave her the same sad, sympathetic look people reserve for stinking paraplegic homeless bums on the street.

"WHAT HAPPENED TO YOU?!"

He was a good man. Genuinely a good man. He was trying to help, but he didn't want her anymore. He didn't desire her anymore. And she couldn't have that.

"You know what you must do, Antonia."

Not only did he not want her anymore, he didn't even recognise her.

"He doesn't even know who you are."

He doesn't know who I am.

"He doesn't recognise you."

He doesn't know who I am!

"Are you OK?"

He doesn't know who I am!

"You're nothing to him now. Zero minutes and twenty-five seconds."

That realisation was too much. Too much for her to handle. Way too much for her to bear. Kara began rocking on the spot. Bucking. Screaming. And thrashing against all four corners of that bathroom until everything in her field of vision turned a deep shade of red.

She couldn't see anything. Just an endless sea of red liquid. She couldn't hear anything. Just heavy breathing, grunting, the bubbling, churning, squelching of blood, screams, and the words:

"Good girl.Good girl."

When her vision returned to normal Kara was on the floor on top of that man. He had those scissors wedged into his neck as blood pumped out of the resulting hole like water from a hose.

A wa do rass mi do??

In panic, she pressed her hand over the wound and looked him in the eye. He looked back in pure fear as he convulsed on the spot, trying his best to breathe but failing miserably.

They shared something at that moment. Kara still didn't know his name and he didn't realise she was the woman he'd lusted over just hours before. She had no idea who this man was, but still, they shared something.

He kept his eyes locked onto hers as life slowly drained from him. Little by little, bit by bit, she felt him fade away until he was no more than a hunk of meat on that bathroom floor. A hunk of leaking meat that gazed upward behind wide open but utterly vacant eyes.

Dead eyes.

It didn't make sense.

She couldn't comprehend it. Just seconds before, that hole in his neck was the most painful thing that man had ever experienced, but now it was nothing to him. Now, he just didn't care.

Kara had never seen anyone die before. Not since Brother Malcolm, but she didn't see that directly anyway.

This man was dead.

And she'd killed him.

"What's going on in there?!"

"Everything OK?!"

"Oh no."

"Leave now," said the voices.

Kara didn't even reply. She was too shell-shocked to speak.

"Leave now."

"What's happening?!"

"Leave now or face capture."

Kara burst through the bathroom door, completely drenched in that man's blood, and ran through the corridor past dozens of confused and horrified onlookers, most notably the woman from last night.

In this instance, her hideous appearance was functional. It was a benefit.

All present were so terrified and disgusted that going near her wasn't even an option. In fact, they all ran in the opposite direction. Sadly, however, as she continued to hurtle through that mansion, she heard the very clear screams of that man's girlfriend.

But Kara wouldn't stop running.

Kara couldn't stop running.

And as such, Kara ran out of that mansion, down the street, into an alley and kept going for as far as her strong legs would carry her. Unbeknownst to her, however, with each additional step, her body slowly morphed once again into that of a beautiful young black woman.

Also, as she sped through those back alley streets, she heard something. Kara definitely heard something. Like the faint whisper of a distant feminine cry.

But she had no idea where it was coming from.

12 |
CORRUPTED BY THE N-WORD

ANTONIA | Woods of Moss Bluff: October 1, 1957

Antonia's father and several other men from the town had been beating seven shades of faeces out of Winston for ten straight minutes, and she was powerless to help. Simply able to do nought but watch while crying, screaming, and begging them to let him go.

10 straight minutes of vicious violence and panicked screaming, which had alerted most of the town, including her mother.

Antonia's parents had tears in their eyes, and everyone else saw this as a huge deal. Antonia, a white teenage girl, had been caught fornicating with a black man, and that wasn't even close to being unacceptable.

Sure, they weren't actually having sex, and sure, his penis was nowhere near her vagina. Still, nobody gave a damn about the semantics of the issue. Antonia and Winston were committing a cardinal sin, and he'd even given her an orgasm, so all bets were off.

As far as the white people of the town were concerned, he may as well have been caught having relations with a minor.

"Did he hurt you?! He hurt you, didn't he?!" screamed Antonia's father.

"No! He didn't, I love him!" she replied bravely, refusing to throw Winston under the bus.

No matter what happened next, she would be right by his side from start to finish. She was never going to abandon him.

"Antonia, you can't possibly love a nigger!"

Oh, but she did; she loved Winston more than trees love the sun or dolphins love the ocean.

"Don't call him that!"

"Antonia, he's scum!"

"You're scum!"

One of the men, the local town butcher Martin Newinski, punted Winston in the face with his steel toe-capped boot. Winston groaned in pain as an explosion of blood erupted from his nose, and his body twitched almost lifelessly on the dirt.

Antonia tried to run to him but was stopped by Gloria and Jennifer Newinski, Martin's middle-aged wife and young adult daughter.

Two solid punches later and both were sent to the dirt unconscious moments before Antonia was tackled from behind by John Ford, the local tailor. She drove the back of her skull into his nose, shattered it, broke free from his grip, and hurled herself on top of Winston's body to shield him from further harm.

Of course, they tried to pull her off him. They gave it everything they had, but she wouldn't let go. She refused to. While no less than 5 people fought to pull her off, Antonia locked her body around Winston's near-lifeless form like a crocodile death grips its jaw around a gazelle.

Eventually, they succeeded. But not without a fight.

"WINSTON!"

"He forced himself on you, didn't he?!"

"Didn't he!?"

"NO, HE DIDN'T!"

"DON'T COVER FOR HIM"

"I LOVE HIM!"

"HE'S CORRUPTED HER!"

"NO HE HASN'T!"

"YOU SHOULDN'T BE ASSOCIATING WITH NIGGERS!"

That last comment came from Mr Joseph Schmidt, aka the town priest, a man as passionate about worshipping Christ as he was defiling underage boys. Fucking hypocrite.

"Antonia, we love you and speak with kindness in our hearts, not wickedness. But you must know that the devil has tainted you. You have become corrupted by his seductive embrace and have fallen into his dark web of chaos.

All who are good and moral and just know this man and his ilk are not those with whom you should consort. Their hearts, their very minds and their very souls are every bit as filthy as their faecal-coloured skins.

Our whiteness is a state of inherent purity and virtue. The white man alone has the burden of shepherding the animals of this planet into the kingdom of God. Still, in order to do that, we must remain pure and unsullied.

Just as a crisp white shirt will quickly become dirty when touched by filth, so will the cleanliness of your white soul become sullied should you continue to fraternise with such creatures.

Do not let his excrement destroy your purity, Antonia."

"Well, that ship has sailed!" Antonia replied, smiling sadistically.

"Why?"

"I'm pregnant."

"Excuse me?"

"Oh, didn't I say it loud enough?" Antonia replied with a contemptible smirk. "I SAID I'M PREGNANT!"

A stunned silence fell across all present.

One which lasted far longer than Antonia was comfortable with. One in which disgust and hatred grew on every one of the faces of all present. One in which Antonia slowly began to just realise how big of a mistake her revelation was.

"MY UNMARRIED DAUGHTER IS PREGNANT BY A NIGGER!?"

"What's the matter, Daddy? Jealous?"

"HOW DARE YOU!?"

The man who called himself Antonia's father slapped her across the face as the men present proceeded to rain blows upon Winston's face and stomach.

"WINSTON!"

"I CAN'T BELIEVE MY DAUGHTER IS A NIGGER LOVER!"

"YOU SHOULDN'T BE ASSOCIATING WITH NIGGER SCUM!"

If Antonia had been thinking clearly, she wouldn't have said what she said next. If she had been thinking clearly, she'd have known that comment would do nothing but make everyone more irate than they already were and potentially put Winston in danger.

But alas, Antonia was not thinking clearly. Not by a long shot. She'd snapped. She'd simply taken more than she could handle. Dealt with too much hypocritical racism.

Seen too much injustice.

The arrogance of those idiots was infuriating, and she'd been pushed well beyond her limits.

"Y'ALL FUCKIN' HYPOCRITES! Y'ALL THE BIGGEST SCUM I EVER MET! MY BLACK FAMILY ARE THE ONLY ONES WHO WAS NICE TO ME! MY WHITE FAMILY ABUSE ME AND TREAT ME LIKE I AIN'T NOTHIN'!"

They acted like the colour of their skin somehow made them better than black folk, but nothing could have been further from the truth. They were idiots, all of them. Dumb, stupid, uneducated idiots who didn't know a damn thing about anything.

"They don't belong in this country!"

"THEY BUILT THIS FUCKIN COUNTRY! I HATE Y'ALL! I HATE ALL Y'ALL! FUCK Y'ALL! FUCK Y'ALL FUCKIN CRACKERS!"

"That's it. We gotta end this fool!"

"NO! NO! WINSTON!!"

"Come on! Grab his legs!"

"You ain't never gonna see your nigger friend again!"

"NO!! NO! PLEASE!!!"

"Time to go, lil nigger."

"NO!! NO! PLEASE!!! DON'T KILL HIM!"

"We ain't gon' kill the lil nigger. We just gon make for damn sure he ain't never gon' put that nigger dick inside another white woman for as long as he lives."

"It's time to kiss your little friend goodbye, nigger."

With that, the townspeople carried Winston out of Antonia's life forever.

This would be the last time she would see him alive as her so-called parents would move her out of Moss Bluff the very next day, and his family would do the same. Antonia would spend years wondering what happened to Winston and whether he was OK.

Years of silence. Years were spent enduring the agony of not knowing if the love of her life was alive or where he was, even if he was.

However, as terrible as what was about to happen to Winston would be, Antonia now had problems of her own with which to contend.

Why?

Because the people of the town of Moss Bluff had not forgotten what she did or how brazen she was about defending it.

It might have been OK if she threw Winston under the bus like they asked, but she didn't, and while that was admirable, it probably wasn't wise.

Both her so-called parents and the town priest believed her to be sexually immoral and wicked, meaning that something needed to be done immediately.

Antonia was now viewed as a whore, a Jezebel, or a succubus. One imbued with a demonic curse from Satan himself. A curse which infected her heart and soul with the rotten impurity of sexual debauchery.

This was a plague which both her parents and the priest believed would leave her very essence as black and stained as the 'faecal coloured men with whom she chose to fornicate'.

According to Mr Joseph Schmidt, aka the God-fearing, ever-loving town priest, the source of Antonia's curse was her clitoris.

Not to mention the half-breed offspring growing in her womb.

13 | BEAUTY, PAID IN BLOOD

KARA | New York Streets: Present Day

A still bloody but now completely youthful and beautiful Kara ran through the streets at full pelt, thanking God that nobody was there to see her. Truth be told, she wasn't running for any good reason other than to keep her mind distracted because she couldn't face the reality of what she'd just done.

Her chest was tighter than an anaconda's grip, and her hands shook like jelly in a monsoon as the growing weight of her actions dawned upon her.

She'd killed someone.

She took a man's life and watched him die.

She saw the life drain from his eyes. What did that make her? Who was she becoming?

What kind of person does that?!

"A person like you."

I'm not! I'm not a killer! This isn't who I am!

"Your actions speak the opposite."

Those were the voices. The collection of dark, echoing feminine voices that spoke to Kara when she died and also in the bathroom.

"Who are you?!" Kara cried, fearful for more reasons than one.

"We are the saviours of your once worthless existence."

"What?!"

"We are Kalizar."

Kara couldn't stop running. She had to keep running. She just had to. She couldn't face the reality of what she did.

She just couldn't.

The look on that man's face as he died was bludgeoned into her memory, and she couldn't get rid of it. At that moment, she felt him. She felt his presence.

She felt like she knew him.

He was a kind and sweet soul who wanted to see if she was OK, but she killed him. He died scared and confused because of her. He didn't know what was happening or even why. He died scared and confused because of Kyra.

She'd killed him.

She kept wondering what his name was, where he went to school, and what shows he watched on Netflix. Was he a follower of hers before that party? Did he keep updated on her posts? Did he regularly like her content, not knowing she was the woman who would eventually take his life? If she knew his name, could she enter it into her follower list and see his profile?

Would she still be able to see the latest story he posted the previous evening, utterly oblivious to the fact that it would be his last ever?

Kara didn't know how she could ever live with herself.

"Death is to life as life is to death, Antonia."

"Stop calling me that!"

"It is time for you to know the rules."

"What rules?!"

"The conditions under which we have bestowed this gift."

"What?!"

"Now you see, our gift is not eternal or free.

If you wish to keep these blessings, you must serve us three."

"What do I have to do?!"

"Life is to death as death is to life."

"What?!"

"If youth and beauty is what you require, it must be paid for with death."

"Mi affi kill people!?"

"If youth and beauty is what you require, it must be paid for with death."

“No. No, I can’t!”

"Then youth and beauty shall not be yours."

"No! Wait!"

"Then youth and beauty shall not be yours."

"Anything else, please! Anything!"

"If youth and beauty is what you require, it must be paid for with death."

"Please!"

"Then youth and beauty shall not be yours."

"What if..."

"Then youth and beauty shall not be yours."

"PLEASE!"

"If youth and beauty are what you require, it must be paid for with death."

Kara had nothing left to say. The reality of her situation was beginning to become apparent.

“A who mi affi kill?!”

"You will be informed in due course. Goodbye, Antonia."

"No! No! Wait! Wait!"

But it was too late. Kalizar had left, and Kara was once again alone, running barefoot through the city streets like a woman possessed. Once again, she heard the faint whisper of a distant cry.

A cry of pain.

A cry of despair.

A cry of anguish which possibly could have been her own. Kara had to kill people to stay young and beautiful.

Could I even do that?!

She thought of all the years she spent longing for this. All the years she spent telling herself she'd do anything to look how she currently did. But could she actually kill people?

Am I willing to go that far? And how many people would I have to kill?

Was she really going to do this?

What would her life become with more killing? She wanted youth and beauty, but not like this.

Never like this!

She couldn't become a serial killer!

I can't!

That feminine cry faded into the background of Kara's psyche as she realised her phone was ringing. It was Blake. She picked it up without a second thought.

"Hey, sup?" he asked.

"What up!?" she replied, panting.

"Where are you?"

"Running!"

"Why?" he asked.

"Cause I felt like it, nigga damn!"

"You need to come back."

There was a painful silence, punctuated only by Kara's laboured breaths and the pounding of her bare feet on the concrete.

"Did you hear me?" Blake continued.

Kara didn't know what to say. She couldn't have mustered words if her life depended on it, which, as it happens, wasn't too far from the truth.

"What?!"

"Some guy got killed."

Unsurprisingly, Kara's mind was gripped by the particular brand of paralysing fear that only comes with the harrowing knowledge that one is about to receive their comeuppance.

"Did you hear me?! I said some guy got killed!"

“I....I....I...”

"You need to come back now!"

"Why?"

"50 called the police; they're gonna need to talk to you!"

"Mi a suspect?!"

"What?!"

"Mi a suspect!?"

"The fuck are you talking about?!"

"Mi a suspect?!"

"Of course not! No! No! Of course not! It's fucking weird, people are saying this disfigured demon ghoul thing killed him! It doesn't make any sense!"

A profound silence followed. One in which Kara's heart rate lowered, and she finally gathered enough wits to realise what had happened. You see, nobody actually saw her that morning.

They saw a hideously deformed ghoul wake up in that bed and burst out of the bathroom covered in blood. Kara Clark, the gorgeous Instagram influencer, wasn't even close to being a suspect.

It would be ludicrous to consider.

This was something. This was good. This was hope. Knowing this made Kara feel a sense of control returning to a previously hopeless situation.

"Look, I know that sounds fucking crazy, but it's what they're saying. Everyone's fucking freaked. You gotta come back."

Exhausted, Kara finally stopped running and hunched over on the street, heaving into her phone.

"Nigga... I ain't... see shit... I was gone... before any... of that happened, and... if there is.... some crazy demon... in that mansion... I don't wanna be... anywhere near it!"

"That's a fair point."

"All of this is scaring the fuck out of me, and I don't wanna be alone. Can you come to my place tonight? I need someone to hold me."

"No problem, Queen. I got you. I just need to go and check up on my gramps, but after that, I'll be there."

"Thanks... bye, King."

Kara hung up and started running once more, realising she now felt terrible for lying to Blake but also realising she had no other choice. What was she supposed to do? Tell him she was the disfigured ghoul? Tell him she killed that man at a demon's behest and had been commanded to do so again?

She couldn't ever tell Blake the truth.

Ever.

And so, painfully, regretfully, Kara began to feel distance forming between her and him. He was still a powerfully comforting presence, second only to Winston. Still, she couldn't tell him who or what she was, which meant their connection could only go so deep.

And Kara hated lying.

This wasn't who or what she was. She had always been honest to a fault, even to her detriment, but now she was being forced to be anything but. Now, she was being forced to question her own humanity.

As she mused on that; Kara realised she needed to get off the streets post haste. Yes, she was young again. Yes, she was beautiful again; both were wonderful; however, she was covered in blood, which was anything but. Her perfection was tainted by the blood of the man whose life she'd taken.

His splattered DNA was a very literal stain on her beauty, which terrified her for more reasons than one. Firstly, the thought of what she had done to earn that beauty chilled Kara to the core. Secondly, the idea of what she must continue to do to stay beautiful made her feel sick. Thirdly, the realisation that she could do so again haunted her psyche.

Was it possible to separate her exquisite beauty from the violence required to maintain it?

Probably not.

In any event, Kara needed to get home, shower, and burn her clothes in her bathtub yesterday. She couldn't risk getting caught on the streets the way she was.

And so she ran, pushing her new and young body to unseen limits as she struggled to get home before said streets once again became awash with human traffic. One or two people were out now, and all looked at her curiously.

Was that because she looked like a slaughterhouse employee or because seeing a woman sprinting for her life while dressed to the nines in the early morning hours was weird?

Kara didn't know, nor did she care to find out.

All she knew was that the longer she spent on those streets, the more they became alive.

Not only could she see the sky brighten as daytime approached, but the background hum of city life was slowly intensifying. Birds sang, factories hummed, and the distant tremor of cars and trucks slowly became a close and deep rumble. The city that never slept was rising from its oxymoronic slumber and Kara needed to be gone before it was fully awake.

However, as she continued to sprint through said city streets, she once again heard the faint echoes of a cry.

A cry of pain.

A cry for help.

The cry of a woman.

She briefly considered pausing to listen intently but rapidly ditched that notion. Deep down, Kara suspected she knew exactly who that woman was and what she wanted.

And that's why she had to keep on running.

She simply couldn't face the truth.

14 |
BY ANY MEANS NECESSARY

ANTONIA | Atlanta: March 1963

Antonia couldn't get Winston out of her mind. It had been years since she last saw him, but he still occupied her thoughts on an hourly basis.

Was he still alive, and if so, where the hell was he?

She had absolutely no idea, and sadly, she had no way of getting in touch with him or his family. Unsurprisingly, they'd moved from Moss Bluff shortly after the incident and could have been anywhere in these United States.

Now, as for where that would likely be, she remembered Winston talking about how the northern states were kinder to black folk and guessed that was where they'd moved. Winston also had a child in New York, so maybe they went there?

In any event, her finding them was like finding a single blade of grass in the Amazon.

As for Antonia, she no longer lived in Moss Bluff and now resided in Atlanta. What's more, her surname was no longer Hoell.

She was now Antonia Parker, wife of Richard Parker, a wealthy banker far more interested in gallivanting worldwide 'on business' with his cohort of mistresses than being with her. But, that said, she didn't mind at all.

Not one bit.

Seriously, Antonia genuinely didn't give a shit. That wasn't a lie she told herself to make herself feel better; it was how she felt.

Why?

Because, after the incident at Moss Bluff, her ever-loving parents, dearest Jonathan and Margaret, eager to improve their social standing, orchestrated opportunities for her to meet men of note.

Through a planned introduction through one of her father's somewhat dubious associates, Antonia was introduced to Richard, who, unlike most white men, was somewhat drawn to her.

Upon witnessing Richard's interest, Dearest Jonathan and Margaret eagerly pushed her to him, convincing her that he was her only chance to escape the pain of her past and build a new life.

They manipulated her guilt over what happened to Winston, saying that a fresh start was what she needed to atone for her past. In fact, Daddy Jonathan even hinted that marrying a wealthy man like Richard would ensure she was never vulnerable or powerless again.

Effectively, Antonia's parents painted this marriage as a way for her to shield herself from the harsh realities of life and being under immense pressure, both from them and her emotional turmoil, and she agreed to it.

Also, if she were to be honest, she was more than a little flattered by his desires because she'd never have expected a man like him to find her attractive.

Of course, Richard didn't take too kindly to Antonia's missing tooth, mind you, but that aside, he seemed to like her.

Not love, but like, and outside of Winston and her black family, that was more than she was used to getting.

This said, however, their marriage was essentially a business transaction.

Richard saw Antonia as a little more than a model wife to complete his stellar image. She was to be a beautiful and refined woman who would look scintillating by his side at social events while having enough sense to keep quiet when the men were speaking.

To him, it wasn't just children who were to be seen and not heard but women too.

Richard had made it abundantly clear that as his wife, it was Antonia's duty to always look her very best. Because of this, she was made to follow a rigorous beauty regimen from dawn till dusk. All to transform her into the perfect wife, or at least one he considered acceptable. First things first, the gap in her teeth had to go, and she was made to get dentures post haste.

Second things second, each of Antonia's days began with the ritual of cleansing her face with cold cream, followed by toning, moisturising, and layering of foundation to create a flawless mask.

After that came the subtle swipe of eyeliner, the delicate application of mascara, and the ever-present ruby red lipstick that Richard so demanded.

Her hair was to be meticulously styled in either bouffant or neat waves, requiring regular expensive salon visits. Then, when at home, she was expected to maintain said hair's perfection with costly products and treatments.

You see, Richard Parker operated a zero-tolerance policy to imperfections of any kind. And so, any chipped nails, stray greys, or gains of weight were met with severe disdain.

Every flaw reflected upon him.

Every blemish tarnished his carefully curated image.

Antonia had to be immaculate, as though her very existence depended on it.

But there was more.

Third things third, she was to adhere to a near impossibly strict diet, one that certainly kept her slim but also left her in a perpetual state of hunger. Also, her wardrobe was not her own. It consisted of perfectly tailored and accessorised outfits with gloves, hats, and handbags that Richard himself had carefully selected with a keenly critical eye.

Each item of clothing was intended to showcase her figure without crossing the line into vulgarity, a delicate balance of allure and restraint that Antonia was made to navigate daily. Even her posture, how she walked, sat, and carried herself, was under constant scrutiny, with her husband perpetually reminding her of the elegance she was expected to exude at every social gathering.

Every flaw reflected upon him.

Every blemish tarnished his carefully curated image.

Antonia had to be immaculate, as though her very existence depended on it.

It wasn't enough for her to be beautiful; Antonia had to be perfect. A living, breathing testament to his enviable success.

Richard knew nothing of Antonia's love for technology, nor did he care. He also knew little of her fondness for black folk, but besides once commanding her to never associate with 'their ilk', nor did he care. Antonia existed purely as an extension of his material status and nothing more.

But nor did she care.

Why?

Because no man, anywhere, and at any time, could ever lace the boots of Winston Poole. Antonia had no idea whether the man she loved was alive, but she did know that her heart died on that fateful day. She was going to be miserable for the rest of her life no matter what, so she could either be miserable and poor or miserable and filthy rich.

The choice was obvious.

If her marriage to Richard taught her anything, it's that while wealth isn't everything, it's preferable to pull up to your problems in a Ferrari than trudge your way to them barefoot.

Sure, their marriage was empty, but who cared? She was already dead inside.

He was exceptionally wealthy, which meant Antonia now lived a life of luxury, which was leagues superior to the alternative.

And in fairness to Richard, outside of the demand he placed on her looks, he didn't mistreat her. He was a saint compared to Daddy Jonathan and they did have mildly positive experiences together. Also, she had to admit that he did have exceptional taste in fashion.

Mildly suffocating as it all was, the outfits he put together for her were nothing less than scintillating, and she was genuinely impressed by his stylistic choices.

But still, the mystery of the whereabouts of her true love and family was permanently wedged into Antonia's brain, and it drove her up the wall.

She had to find him. She had to find them. She had to see if he was OK and apologise for her part in what happened. She had to reconnect with her black family.

Her real family.

She had to.

As Richard spent most of his time away 'on business', Antonia had little to do besides stay pretty, watch science fiction shows, twiddle her thumbs and spend her hefty allowance. This meant it wasn't long before she found herself back in Moss Bluff, trying to find anybody who could tell her what happened to the Pooles.

To that effect, she'd revisited their old neighbourhood and talked to former neighbours, but nobody would tell her anything.

She then went to all the Black churches, hoping to find people who could help her, but again, nobody would say a word.

What was infuriating was that she knew that they knew exactly where Winston's family were. In fact, they knew that she knew that they knew where they were.

But they didn't care.

They didn't give a single fuck.

Why?

Because none of them trusted her.

All looked down on her with suspicious contempt, like she was the police. They all clearly blamed her for what happened, which, in fairness, placed them in great company because she blamed herself, too.

It was her fault Winston's family had to move. Her fault that the love of her life was beaten to a pulp and possibly worse. Antonia was the one who got her and him caught by those men. Antonia was the one who howled like a lunatic and attracted attention.

So yes, people might never forgive her for that, but she understood because she knew she'd never forgive herself.

She'd never forgive herself for what happened to their baby.

Antonia and Winston had created life. The good Lord had blessed her with that man's child, but she somehow found a way to mess it up.

She hated herself for that.

She'd never forgive herself for that.

But she was going to make it better.

However, Antonia had no idea how until she heard about Malcolm X, read his books, and had the biggest revelation of her existence. His writing was earth-shattering. He was so angry. So passionate. So fiercely intelligent that she knew she needed to work for him.

She just knew it.

She'd come across Martin Luther King, too, of course, but just couldn't get behind his 'neutered Uncle Tom bitch ass' message. Antonia knew from first-hand experience that radically transforming the lives of Black people in America meant taking decisive measures. Serious measures.

It meant being 100% committed to achieving the outcome.

By any means necessary.

These evil hypocrite crackers who prayed to an all-loving Jesus yet somehow thought Black people deserved to be treated like second-class citizens deserved force. Nothing less than less than swift, brutal, full-scale, overwhelming force.

The kind of force that only Malcolm X could impart.

The kind of force Antonia had no problems helping him inflict.

Malcolm X was a towering figure in the fight for Black liberation, a man whose presence alone commanded attention and respect. With his sharp intellect, piercing gaze, and unwavering conviction, he became a symbol of defiance against a system built to oppress. His speeches electrified crowds, stirring a powerful blend of fear, admiration, and hope in those who heard them.

To his followers, he was a beacon of strength, a man unafraid to speak the harsh truths that others dared not utter. To his enemies, he was a threat, a relentless voice of resistance that could not be silenced.

And, when Antonia first laid eyes on Malcolm X, she felt an almost palpable force radiating from him. A bold combination of powerful charisma and ever-present danger.

This was the man she had come to find, the man she knew could help her find redemption and create a better world for Winston and his family.

But how on earth could she join his team? How on earth could she convince him to let her help him? Antonia didn't know, but she knew she had to try. And that's what brought her to his speech in Atlanta, Georgia.

She didn't know when she'd get a chance to talk to him or even what she'd say when she did. All she knew was that she supported his message 100% and had to help in any way she could.

She'd read his works; in fact, Antonia had probably read his books more than any of his black followers and agreed with every single chapter, page, paragraph, sentence, word, and punctuation mark.

But Antonia was no fool.

She knew her deficiency of melanin would be a huge detriment to her ability to convince him to let her join his cause, but still, she had to try.

She had to.

She owed it to Winston, his family, and the memory of the child to whom she never got to give birth. Those crackers needed to be humbled by any means necessary.

That much was certain.

So then, standing outside that rain-soaked building amidst throngs of jeering protestors and well-wishing supporters, Antonia finally saw him. She finally saw Malcolm X leave the building, flanked by his personal security. He walked with such power, such confidence, and such poise; he was clearly a man on a mission.

A man who knew he was beset on all sides by enemies but didn't give a single fuck. A man who was led by a purpose greater than the safety of his own physical form. One which gave him the strength to stride head first into the lion's den and yet emerge without receiving as much as an inquisitive sniff.

Antonia fought her way through the throng of jeering crackers and cheering blacks and got close to Malcolm before one of his bodyguards stopped her in her tracks.

"I need to speak to Malcolm!"

"No, you don't."

"Let me speak to him! MALCOLM! MALCOLM!"

"You ain't got nothing to say to him!"

"MALCOLM! MALCOLM!"

Malcolm X carried on walking, so Antonia went out of the crowd, ran in a giant semi-circle, spotted another small opening in said crowd, squeezed her way through and finally ended up right in front of him, this time, managing to get a hand onto his shoulder.

"MALCOLM!" she screamed.

"Get your hand off me," he replied dismissively, pulling his shoulder away.

"I NEED TO TALK TO YOU!"

"Go away."

"I WANT TO HELP YOU!"

That same bodyguard from before shoved her out of the way with mild authority, which made the baying white members of the crowd even angrier. They didn't know Antonia wanted to join his cause, nor did they care.

They just saw a white woman being touched by a black man and were incensed. Within seconds, bottles were thrown as insults were hurled right and left. Antonia, however, taking advantage of the confused chaos, ran to Malcolm's car and leapt right on top of the bonnet, looking him dead in the eyes through the windscreen.

"MALCOLM! MALCOLM!"

"GET THAT CRAZY WHITE WOMAN OFF MY CAR!"

"NO! NO! I AIN'T GOING NOWHERE UNTIL YOU TALK TO..."

Before she could finish her sentence, someone grabbed Antonia from behind and yanked her down. After that, she watched in abject misery as Malcolm X's car sped off down that road and out of her life forever.

Well, not forever. She'd definitely try again.

15 | BOUND TO A WEB OF CHAOS

KARA | Kara's New York Apartment: Present Day

Kara couldn't escape the pain. She just couldn't. No matter how badly she wanted it gone, there it was.

Ever present.

Undeniable.

She'd killed someone.

She'd killed a man, a good and decent soul who didn't deserve any harm to come to him.

She'd killed him.

And she had to do so again.

That's what Kalizar told her.

The price and penance for youth and beauty was life.

Kara needed to take life.

She needed to kill, but she couldn't bear the thought of it. The memory of that man's face was burned into her psyche, and she couldn't get rid of it. She was right there as he died. She saw it happen. She saw the life drain from his eyeballs as he left this world, and she couldn't bear to see that again.

She just couldn't.

But there was something else that Kara couldn't bear. She couldn't bear the unavoidable fact that she would indeed kill again. Deep down, she knew it.

Kalizar knew it, too. Kara couldn't take even another second of life as either the woman she was before or the disfigured ghoul she became at the party.

She just couldn't.

Kara needed that youth.

Kara needed that beauty.

Kara needed those social media followers.

Kara needed that sexual attention.

She craved it. It was her life force.

And so, there she was, deeply submerged within near-unbearable levels of psychological trauma and faced with the unavoidable fact that there was indeed more left to come. But Kara couldn't face that reality. She couldn't face the person she would have to become, and she couldn't face the person she already was.

And so she stood, stark naked as the day those voices known as Kalizar made her, admiring herself in the mirror. Kara had done that a lot lately. It was one of her favourite activities, and understandably so. Her body was beautiful, toned, and curvaceous.

Gazing at her reflection, she almost lost herself in it. The femininity of its contours, the softness of its smooth skin, and the flexibility and strength of its muscles.

It was enchanting.

But once again, she felt blistering pain. The pain of guilt. The pain of remorse for the terrible thing she did and her sheer inability to forget it. Once again, she saw that man's dying eyes, panicked, fearful, terrified, confused.

But once again, Kara saw the way he looked at her. Like the flashback of a vivid nightmare, it all hurtled back in crystal clarity. Even though he knew she was the one who'd killed him, he couldn't bear to die alone. He still needed her by his side as he passed.

Even though she'd killed him.

And the gorgeous body standing before her in that mirror was why she did it.

"ARGHHHH!!!"

Another scream. Faint, distant, but very real. Once again, Kara heard the low whisper of a cry of despair. A cry which was not her own but one she suspected had everything to do with her. A cry which, when mixed with the already crippling guilt she experienced, made her feel like her heart was roasting from the inside out.

Kara needed to escape from such torment and did so via the only method she knew, dissociating through a haze of sexual impulses and social media browsing.

She grabbed her phone and scrolled through her Instagram notifications with her right hand while her left hand made its way to her clitoris. As she read all of those comments of praise and applause, she felt her fingers glide against the fleshy bulb of sensual delight which was now engorging between her thighs.

And her breathing softened.

Benjamin1257

"I'll be honest. I'm lonely as hell, and seeing you on here reminds me there's someone out there I could actually love. You're my dream."

Her muscles relaxed.

Jacobbyboy

"I could worship your body from head to toe. I mean that literally from head to toe."

She melted into herself.

Julienverde332

"I don't think you know how much you mean to me. Seeing your posts every day is what gets me through."

She collapsed into herself.

Carlosescobar887

"You're stunning, obviously, but there's something else. Like a sadness? I feel like I could understand you if we ever met."

That pervasive scream lost potency.

Ramandala

"You are such an inspiration girl! I love your confidence and every day your sexy feminine energy inspires me to embody my inner goddess too!"

The guilt began to fade.

Akirachunnin

"I'll pay you $2000 for a single date. I'm not asking for sex. I promise you. I'd never disrespect you that way. I just need to meet you in person."

And slowly, but surely.

Joellassecretlife

"I keep telling myself I'll hit the gym, but then I see you and wonder if I'll ever look that amazing. You're unreal."

An orgasm began to build.

Mattheuswolfelyfe

"I dream about you, you know. I know it's crazy, but there's something about you I can't get out of my head."

Kara's clitoris melted into an electrical torrent of bliss that melted into lava that flowed hot throughout the arteries of her chocolate body.

Kerciaoliveira

"Honestly, I'd do anything to feel as powerful as you look. I don't know how you do it, but you're magnetic."

Kara was lost. Lost on a voyage of erotic expansion. Stranded in a faraway galaxy of sexual decadence that had her panting breath turn her mirror into a wet, foggy mess before her quivering body.

An orgasm was coming.

Joeelvin

"I don't want to sound pathetic, but I'm one of those people who refresh your profile daily. You give me hope."

An orgasm was coming.

BlackActionMan

"I wonder if you'd even notice someone like me. Just the thought that you might actually see this makes my day."

It was almost here.

HippocraticOath22

"Fuck you, you ugly whore."

And then, just like that, one message brought Kara back to her painful reality of guilt and shame.

HippocraticOath22

"You think you're so fucking special, but you're nothing. Just a sad, pathetic piece of shit who takes half-naked pics to prove to the world she's something she isn't. You have nothing else to offer society except for your body.

That's it.

You have no talents and no skills. If you didn't look the way you do, nobody would give a fuck about you, and you know it too.

You're not funny. You're not interesting. You're not intelligent. All you are is a whore whose body cuts light well. A whore who uses the fact that she's willing to degrade herself in ways most people aren't to make money and get attention.

But just know that the attention you crave is fleeting. You aren't going to look this way forever, and when the day comes that your beloved beauty starts to fade. People will stop giving you the attention heroin you're so addicted to. You know what you're going to do?"

Ordinarily, Kara ignored this pipsqueak. Ordinarily, she didn't take his insults to heart, but today was different. Today, his words cut to her psyche in ways they never had before. Today, her heart skipped a beat as the impact of his words began to register.

KaraClarkHadoken

"What?"

HippocraticOath22

"You're going to end yourself. When the world has moved on, and younger women are getting the attention you need just to breathe, you're going to end your own life."

If that bastard had been in the same room, he'd have seen that Kara was now in floods of tears, so thank God he wasn't. No way in hell she could give him that satisfaction. No way in hell.

HippocraticOath22

"Yeah. That stung, didn't it? Don't like the cold, hard truth of reality, do you, Kara? Just realise that no matter how many 'followers' you have and how many men around the world are dying to put their peepees in you, I know who you really are. You're just pretending. You're fake. You're nothing.

And guess what?"

KaraClarkHadoken

"What?"

HippocraticOath22

"You're going to die alone. You'll waste your prime years fucking everything that moves and wake up one day as a 42-year-old woman who men don't want.

But you'll want them to want you.

You'll think they SHOULD want you, and you won't be able to accept that they've moved on to younger women. So then you'll keep chasing the NBA players and 7-figure businessmen, but while you'll be able to have sex with them, none will actually stick around.

You won't be able to keep them.

You'll be increasingly depressed as the years go by, and your looks continue to rot until one day, you walk past a group of construction workers and realise that not one of them looks up at you.

Not even one. And you know why? Because you'll be old, and they no longer register you as a sexual option."

Kara had experienced this very scenario in her first life as Antonia, and it was nothing short of harrowing. The stark truth was that when she was young, she'd taken men's sexual interest for granted and even found it annoying. Winston was the only man she thought she needed validation from, so she didn't care about anyone else's.

However, that said, the fateful day on which she realised that no man anywhere would ever find her attractive again was one of the most traumatic of her existence. That was when she'd realised how much she'd subconsciously been validated by the attention she consciously thought she hated.

HippocraticOath22

"The builders you wouldn't look twice at today won't look twice at you tomorrow, and when that happens, you'll truly realise it's over. You'll know deep down and to the very core of your being that you're fucking finished.

You won't have a husband because you'll never have developed the requisite social skills to keep a man interested in you beyond your looks, and that will mean you won't have a family.

Maybe you'll have grabbed some NFL player's used condom out of the trash and used it to get yourself pregnant, but that man will never give a DAMN about you, so you'll be raising that kid alone. Then again, that kid would have grown up with a useless, vain, talentless whore for a mother and would no doubt hate your guts too.

But then again? Maybe said NFL player decides he doesn't want an entitled whore like you birthing his child and beats your stomach so bad you miscarry?"

KaraClarkHadoken

"Fucking leave me alone!"

That was a mistake, and Kara knew it. She shouldn't have said that. She shouldn't have done it. Now he knew. Now he knew he was getting to her. Now he knew his words were cutting deep. And now he wasn't going to stop.

HippocraticOath22

"You're more than welcome to block me, but you haven't, and you know why?"

KaraClarkHadoken

"Why?!"

HippocraticOath22

"Firstly, because you know I've got hundreds of dummy accounts to harass you from, so you can't ever get rid of me. Secondly, because you also know what I'm saying is true. I'm telling you what nobody else will. I'm giving you shit you need to hear. I'm saving your life, nigger."

KaraClarkHadoken

"Please go away!"

Kara blocked HippocraticOath22 and sat shivering on the floor of her bedroom, crying her brown eyes out with her toned arms wrapped tightly around her trembling knees. She hated everything he said. She hated all of it.

But she couldn't escape the fact that he was right. She couldn't escape the fact that she deserved to have someone make her feel that way after what she'd done. She deserved to be hated. She deserved to have someone do that to her. She fucking deserved it.

After less than a minute of uncontrollable sobbing, Kara's phone vibrated. This time, it was a text message.

(UNKNOWN SENDER)

"You're going to die a miserable and lonely old woman. You will have nobody who cares about you. Nobody whatsoever. You will spend your final years on this planet stalking young women who still have everything you have lost. You will wish you could be like them again. You will want it more than anything, but you will know it will never be, and it will eat you up inside.

That pain will fester. It will consume you from the inside out, and you will think about suicide every day but won't have the guts to do it because you're a coward. But don't worry; one day, all the cowardice in the world won't matter because your subconscious will do what your conscious mind can't, causing your heart to stop beating.

You'll commit suicide via the scenic route of intense grief and loneliness. That's your fucking future."

This message was terrifying, but not only for the reason you think. Yes, everything he said was ugly, traumatic and painful, all of that was true, but:

KARA CLARK

"How did you get my phone number?!"

(UNKNOWN SENDER)

"Me having your number is the least of your concerns, Kara."

KARA CLARK

"Leff mi di rass alone!"

(UNKNOWN SENDER)

"What kind of dumb nigger language is that?

KARA CLARK

"Leave me alone!"

(UNKNOWN SENDER)

Me leaving you alone is the least of your concerns, Kara."

KARA CLARK

"What the fuck are you talking about?!"

(UNKNOWN SENDER)

"I know what you did at that party."

Kara didn't respond to that. She couldn't. Her fingers had lost their connection to her mind and twitched involuntarily while her eyeballs bulged in their sockets. She was wrapped and trapped in an airtight and suffocating web of chaos, unable to type a single word.

(UNKNOWN SENDER)

"That's right, nigger. I'm onto you."

Kara was shocked. Stunned. Completely at a loss for words and barely able to process what was happening. She stood in silence for at least two minutes, staring into space with her mouth agape as her brain struggled in a futile attempt to understand what was happening.

But, eventually, it did understand. Eventually, that dark fog of confusion cleared from her brain and left her with the stark reality of her current situation.

Kara was being stalked.

But how?! Where the fuck is he? Is he tracking me online, or is he closer than that? Is this real, or am I losing my grip on reality?? How the fuck could he know what happened at the party?!

Was he there in person? Or was someone at the party his accomplice?

The blonde bitch maybe? Was that why she hated me so much? No that doesn't make sense because if she knew it was me, she would have told the police!

Did he hack into the security cameras and use them to spy on her? But then again, were there any security cameras at the mansion?

I don't remember seeing any! And even if there were, how would he have known where they were and how to hack them? And how the fuck does he know what I did when even people who were at the party don't?!

None of it made any sense, but as confusing as it was, it didn't detract from the now very real, ever-present, and unavoidable truth.

Kara was in real, present, and physical danger.

Him follow every move mi a mek? She thought in Jamaican patois.

Possibly. Or was she being paranoid? Were those messages even real or imagined? Her guilty brain's way of punishing her for her misdeed?

Kara didn't have a clue, and as she wracked her brain trying to work out all of the above, she jumped at the sound of her phone vibrating against her wooden table. She quickly picked it up and looked at the screen but saw no notifications.

16 | I GOT HEART & I'M SOLID

ANTONIA | Elmhurst, Queens: May 29, 1964

Antonia had been sitting in near pitch-black darkness for hours, waiting for Malcolm X before he finally arrived, but it felt much longer. By that point, she couldn't even see her own hands and had lost track of time.

But still, once she heard that key turn in the door and Malcolm's signature, unmistakable, powerful voice talking outside, she was hurled back to the present moment with a burst of excitement.

The last time she'd spoken to him hadn't panned out well, but that was then, and this was now

Back then, she didn't get to speak her peace. This time would be different.

This time, she wasn't leaving his house until he agreed to let her join his organisation.

One thing Antonia had learnt from that encounter was that simply attending rallies and meetings wouldn't be enough to get close to Malcolm X. She needed more information on his private whereabouts. She needed to be able to speak to him alone.

And this was when being the wife of a wealthy banker came in handy.

This was when she leveraged the connections she'd gained through her husband, Richard, to track his ass down. Richard Parker moved in circles of extreme influence, rubbing shoulders with politicians, high-powered businessmen, law enforcement, gangsters, and, most importantly, even those in the press. He knew people who could connect Antonia to Malcolm.

But Antonia was no fool.

She knew she had to be careful. The incident at Moss Bluff proved just how incendiary the wrong words could be when uttered inappropriately, and she'd never repeat that mistake. A white woman openly expressing interest in Malcolm X would raise suspicion, especially among Richard's upper-class associates.

So, with that in mind, she framed her curiosity as part of a broader interest in social reform, a cause that could be easily linked to her husband's business dealings.

During a cocktail party at Richard's firm, Antonia subtly mentioned her desire to be involved in charitable housing and education efforts for underprivileged communities. With wealth inequality becoming a pressing issue in society, she proposed reaching out to community leaders nationwide (including those from Harlem) to better understand their challenges.

She was deliberate with her wording and made a point to not state or imply that she was specifically interested in the plight of either black people or Malcolm X himself.

It worked like a charm.

One of Richard's colleagues, a man named John Blackwood, who was eager to demonstrate his knowledge of current affairs and whom Antonia suspected harboured more than a slight crush, called a journalist named Reginald Callam. This was a man who had recently penned a story on influential figures in the black community.

She seized the opportunity to ask for his details, suggesting that understanding their perspectives could help shape more effective charitable programs, and dear old John bought that piece of fiction hook, line, and sinker.

Just like that, Antonia was now connected with renowned journalist Reginald Callam, who was eager to share his insights.

Over a series of lunches, Antonia played the part of a well-meaning philanthropist, subtly steering conversations toward Harlem and its key figures. As a result, dearest Reginald eventually let slip Malcolm X's address, thinking it was just another random detail in the landscape of Harlem's social scene.

But this was exactly what Antonia needed.

Jumping for joy inwardly while outwardly maintaining a deadpan expression, she calmly continued that conversation for another 25 minutes.

All, mind you, while mentally repeating the address thousands of times to make sure she didn't forget it.

With her heart pounding in fear and excitement, Antonia knew she was close to success. Now, all that was left was to find out when Malcolm X would be in New York, head to his home, and make her move.

It would be risky, of course, because this was America, and Antonia was reasonably sure it was legal to shoot someone who trespassed on your property, even white women. But that said, she had to try something and was bereft of other ideas.

Simply put, she was willing to either pull this off or die in the attempt.

So, with that in mind, she had arrived at Malcolm X's house on that fateful night just as dusk began to settle over the streets of Harlem. Of course, she had been there before, however. Quite a few times, in fact. She'd previously explored that neighbourhood many times while wholly covered from head to toe to hide both her identity and race.

As Antonia had conducted her reconnaissance of Malcolm X's neighbourhood, she'd made an effort to seamlessly blend in, her presence utterly unnoticed by passers-by who passed her by as she studied the environment.

Tonight, however, she needed to be extra cautious. She couldn't afford to be seen. Her heart pounded in her chest as she approached the house, trying her best to maintain her composure despite the sheer gravity of what she was about to do.

She'd circled the block twice, making sure the coast was clear before zeroing in on her pre-planned method of entry into Malcolm's house.

It was a side window partially obscured by an overgrown bush, which seemed less secure than the rest. The paint around the frame was chipped, and she'd noticed it didn't sit flush with the sill. After a few tense moments, she approached it, glancing around again to ensure no one was watching.

The latch inside was old, and with the help of a thin, sturdy hairpin concealed within her coat sleeve, she'd managed to slide it open.

Her nerves were ablaze with the thrill and fear of what was happening. Antonia could hardly believe what she was up to. Conceptualising it was one thing but following through on it was another thing entirely.

Even for her, this was crazy.

Once inside, she paused, letting her eyes adjust to the dim light filtering through the curtains while doing her best to stomach the thick tension which permeated the air. She moved carefully, taking in her surroundings while breathing deeply to slow her heartbeat and calm her nerves.

She'd found a way in and now just had to wait. So with that, she slipped quietly into a corner of the living room, her pulse still racing despite her best intentions as she braced herself for the inevitable confrontation.

However, Malcolm X wasn't alone when he finally turned up several hours later. Antonia could hear two, maybe three, other people with him, which wasn't unexpected. He had enemies in white America, the government, and even other black folk in the Nation of Islam, so it was no surprise that he didn't travel alone.

However, this also meant Antonia was about to be outnumbered while caught trespassing on someone else's private property and who knew what might happen next. There was a fair chance she wouldn't leave that house without sustaining at least a few injuries.

But it was a chance she was willing to take.

Also, if there was one thing dearest Daddy Jonathan had taught her, it was how to take a beating, so Antonia was somewhat sure she could handle whatever might happen.

Malcolm X entered his living room with two other men Antonia recognised from her research as his bodyguard, Gene Roberts, and associate Leon Ameer. Decked out in their dapper Sunday best suits, ties, and matching hats, they gasped in shock as she held her hands up and said:

"I ain't your enemy. I just want to talk to you."

"You're that crazy white woman from Atlanta," said Malcolm in disbelief. He, Gene, and Leon studied Antonia closely, their startled eyes a mixture of anger, shock, and even some fear.

"That's me, and I need to talk to you."

"How the hell did you get into my home?!"

"How the hell did you know where his home is?!" cried Gene.

"That ain't important. I just need to work with you!" Antonia replied, doing her best to curtail the fear circulating throughout her bloodstream.

"This bitch..."

"She must be out of her Goddamn mind," Leon sneered.

"Get the hell out of my residence right now."

Malcolm spoke with a cold conviction as authoritative as it was intimidating. At the same time, his steely eyes remained fixed on Antonia's. Her trembling fingers and jaw made her wonder if she'd made a mistake, but there was no backing out now.

The only way out was through.

"No. I want to work with you, and I ain't leaving until you let me."

"Malcolm, she's FBI, you know this is a trick," snorted Gene.

"You think the FBI would be dumb enough to try to infiltrate you with someone who looks like me? It would more likely be someone like him," Antonia replied, nodding to Gene, who clearly didn't take kindly to that comment.

"Get the hell out of my home, now," came Malcolm's command, this time even more powerful than before and literally chilling Antonia right down to her bones.

She could see bitter resentment burning within him; well, within all of them, and understandably so. To them, she was the enemy, a privileged member of the most privileged class of humans to ever live.

One who hated and feared them while simultaneously living a blessed life with zero problems and who, despite all of the above, actually had the gall to invade Malcolm's private residence.

"No," she replied.

"Woman, have you taken leave of your senses?"

"I want to work with you."

"You want to work with me?"

"Yes."

"Why?"

"Cause you the truth. Everythin' you say is a fact, and I want to help you get justice for our people."

Malcolm, Gene, and Leon looked at each other in shock and confusion for exactly 25 silent seconds before eventually looking back at Antonia. When they did, Malcolm saw that she was standing firm and staring right at him.

"You hear this woman?" asked Malcolm, incredulously.

"Our people?" Gene snorted.

"Yes they are," Antonia replied, matter of factly.

"No, they're not," Leon replied with a snarl.

"Yes, they are!"

"Why?!"

"My white family ain't do nothin' but beat on me, touch me when I ain't want to be touched, tell me I was ugly and say I don't mean shit to nobody. My black family loved me unconditionally and made me feel like I matter."

As Antonia spoke, her lips quivered, her voice trembled, and her body tremored, partially from fear but also from overwhelming emotion. Unimpressed, Gene took several steps closer and entered her personal space. Soon, he stood less than a foot away, looking down at her with vengeful eyes.

The air in that tiny living room was smothered with tension so thick it was almost suffocating.

"You know that whatever a man does to an intruder in his home is legal, right? Even if that intruder is a cracker," he snorted, disdain oozing from every syllable.

Not only was Antonia outnumbered, but with every step that man took, he flooded more of her field of vision until she was almost submerged by his considerable physicality.

However, Antonia had been in such situations many times in her young life, meaning that, in a bittersweet manner, those repeated experiences had taught her exactly how to overcome them.

With force.

And so, Antonia didn't flinch. She simply let his words hang in the air as her gaze remained steady and jaw clenched. She slowly squared her shoulders, standing tall despite his size, her expression unwavering. She just looked at him for a long, tense moment, her silence as sharp as any threat.

Without breaking eye contact, she took a small step forward, inching closer into his space, a defiant spark igniting in her eyes. Her hand flexed at her side as if itching to strike but barely restrained by her will.

Then, just loud enough for him to hear, she said in a low yet dangerous voice: "Say it again."

Despite this, however, Antonia was afraid. Afraid because Gene was a grown man and far stronger than her. Afraid because she suspected he was itching for a justified excuse to take out 400 years of righteous frustration on her white woman self. Afraid of what might happen if she was forced to follow through on her threat.

"Cracker."

Antonia punched Gene Roberts with full force, causing a small explosion of blood to burst from his now ruptured nostrils as she adopted a defensive posture to brace for whatever he might do next.

Luckily, Malcolm and Leon Ameer quickly pulled him away before he could retaliate.

"Never fuckin' call me that."

But the main thing Antonia feared was fear itself. Antonia simply hated caving into it. She detested the hold it tried to exact over her and refused to let it control her life.

She refused to let the little bastard win.

"She broke my fucking nose!" Gene cried, holding said nose in pain. He then dove at Antonia but was stopped in his tracks by a simple, silent hand gesture from Malcolm, who probably didn't want to deal with the fallout from his assaulting a white woman.

"Just let me work with you!" Antonia shouted.

"Go work with Martin!" Leon replied.

"Who?! Luther King?!" she replied, disgusted.

"Yes. He loves white women like you more than God, so go bother him. I'm sure he'll find lots of room for you at his many 'fornication gatherings,'" Malcolm retorted.

"I ain't got no time to talk to that fool. Comin' here with all that 'I have a dream' bullshit."

"That right?"

"Yeah, nigga. If we gonna get change for our people, we gotta use any means necessary."

Antonia slipped.

"You calling me the n-word now?"

She really messed up there, but not from malice. The simple truth is that countless hours spent with her black family had acclimatised Antonia to using the n-word ad infinitum. She didn't even think about it; it just popped out randomly at the appropriate conversational junctures.

Well, appropriate for a black person.

But alas, while Antonia was no fool, she was also not black and thus, no matter what the context, her use of the n-word would always ruffle the feathers of negroes who hadn't provided their expressed consent for her to do so.

"I'm sorry. I ain't mean it like that. I meant it the way y'all sometimes say it," she said, feeling genuinely remorseful.

"You have the audacity to break into my home, refuse to leave, and call me the n-word? A word used to demean me and my people for centuries?"

"I told you I ain't mean it like that! I'm sorry!"

"Apologise right now."

"Malcolm, I'm sorry!"

"Your black family teach you to talk like that?" Malcolm asked, studying her closely. His eyes scanned her body from top to bottom for the slightest hint of deception.

Maybe, just maybe, he was starting to believe her. Ironically, something about her inappropriate outburst had swayed him somewhat.

"Yeah, I got it from them," Antonia replied honestly as Gene stood by, glaring while pressing a now bloody handkerchief against his apparently broken nose.

"Malcolm, you can't be buying into this," he added.

"Look at how she talks, stands, and acts. It's just like a black woman. Have you ever seen a white woman act like that before?" Malcolm replied.

"I ain't actin'. This who I am."

"Who are your black family? Tell me everything about them." Malcolm asked forcefully.

"The Pooles from Moss Bluff, Louisiana. They the only people who ever showed me love. They made me feel like I was somebody and not nothin'. I love them more than I love breathin'."

As Antonia spoke, tears began to form in her eyes. Small tears, for sure, not torrents in any way, but tears nonetheless. Tears, which, when added to the genuine quiver of her lips and timbre of her voice, caught both Malcolm X and Leon Ameer off guard.

They were starting to see she was genuine.

"You say you like my books," Malcolm pressed.

"I ain't say that shit, but it's true, I do."

"Which ones have you read?"

"All of them."

"Tell me six things you've read in them that you liked."

"She won't be able to do it," Gene hissed.

Her heart pounding in its rib cage, Antonia made exactly seven seconds of uninterrupted poker-face deadpan eye contact with Gene before speaking.

Standing in that living room across from Malcolm X and his glaring associates, she knew this was her make-or-break time. She had to deliver.

"Only six? Alright."

"The first thing that hit me was how strong you are 'bout education. The way you soaked up knowledge, even in prison, like it was food for your soul. It really spoke to me. You showed me that education ain't somethin' that just falls in your lap; it's somethin' you gotta reach out and take for yourself.

Second, you tore apart that whole stupid idea of the American dream. You showed us how it ain't made for black folks but built on your backs, and that also shook me bad.

Third, the way you push for Black folk lovin' yourselves in a world that's always sayin' you ain't worth nothin'. It's powerful. I seen that myself. My black family are the best people I ever met, but they don't know it because the world tells them they ain't shit. I hate it. I hate it so much, Malcolm. I hate that they feel that way."

The more Antonia spoke, the wider the eyes of all men present became. If they didn't believe she was sincere, at the very least, they knew she'd done her homework.

"Fourth, I respected how you faced your own beliefs and grew, even when it meant breakin' away from the Nation of Islam. That taught me that growin' sometimes means doing the hard thing that scares you and that nobody else understands.

Fifth, how you connected your fight here in America to the struggles of black people worldwide made me see the big picture. This ain't just about black folk Stateside. Them crackers been colonisin' and rapin' all the way from here to Africa and beyond.

And last, you honest. You never tried to pretty up your story or your beliefs. You showed me that truth, no matter how hard it is, is the strongest weapon we got. That's why I want to work for you, Malcolm."

"Wow. The FBI done done their homework." snorted Gene sarcastically. Antonia didn't even justify the comment with a response. She simply shot him a bored expression before turning back to Malcolm, whose eyes had never once left her face.

"And how are you going to help our cause? Explain it to me fully. What possible value could you bring to what we are trying to achieve?"

"Whatever the fuck you want me to. I'll do anything. There's nothin' I won't do to help you."

"Will you fix Gene's nose?" Leon asked.

"Nah, he can do that himself with his bitch ass."

Malcolm and Leon chuckled at that comment, causing Antonia to smirk inwardly with satisfaction. Malcolm stopped first, but Leon continued to laugh until Malcolm silenced him with a hand gesture.

"That's funny, but you didn't answer my question," Malcolm added, serious as a heart attack.

"My husband got connections, powerful connections in banking, press and media. If I'm on your team then they your connections too."

"What else?"

"I know a lot about technology, high-tech gadgets and such. Most don't know about that shit, but I do. Technology 'bout to change the world, Malcolm. Soon we'll be able to have telephone conversations with Chinamen in Beijing and look at them like they on TV."

"Is that right?" Malcolm asked.

"Yeah. Imagine being able to send letters to reporters and TV companies that arrive in seconds instead of days. Imagine having a machine, like a typewriter connected to a powerful computer, that lets you send a message across wires to another machine or even thousands of machines far away.

You wouldn't need to write that letter on paper, put it in an envelope, and wait days or weeks for delivery. It would be instant."

"So?"

"I'm sayin' that technology 'bout to change the world. Everythin' I said, and more is gonna happen, and I can help you use it to benefit our cause."

"Our cause?" Gene sneered.

"You heard what I said," Antonia replied dismissively.

"So let me get this straight," Malcolm continued. "You sneak into my home, refuse to leave, break my associate's damn nose, give me some cock and bull story about future technologies..."

"It's true!"

"And still expect me to want you on my team?" Malcolm asked somewhat incredulously.

"I don't expect you to want me on your team. I expect you to have me on your team."

Antonia replied calmly, noticing a glimmer of respect flash across Malcolm and Leon's eyes.

"Ain't nobody can ever tell me I ain't solid," she continued, staring Malcolm dead in the eyes with a completely straight face.

He looked back just as seriously before pulling out a chair and gesturing for Antonia to sit on it at the dinner table. She did as she commanded, and he sat opposite, casually tapping his fingers against his table's varnished oak surface.

"You got money?" he asked.

Antonia didn't say a word. She simply pulled out her chequebook and a pen and carefully wrote on it. After that, she tore it free and slid it across the table to Malcolm, her expression both calm and resolute. Her eyes met his, screaming her commitment, readiness, and willingness to give everything.

Malcolm's pupils widened when he saw how much money she was offering.

"You're willing to give that much money to help me?"

"You can have everything I own, Malcolm."

"Why? Why do you care so much?"

"I already told you," she replied.

"Do so again and with greater clarity," he pressed.

"I can't stand by no more and watch what happens to Black folks every day. I've seen too many of my people treated like dirt, like they ain't worth a thing, just 'cause of the colour of their skin.

I seen the way they have to step off the sidewalk when a white man walks by, or the way crackers look at them like they ain't nothin' but trouble. It ain't right, and it ain't fair. I remember when I was a little girl, seein' my aunt get beat just for talkin' back to a white man!"

"Your black aunt from your black family?" Malcolm interjected.

"Yeah."

"And why was this so traumatic to you? Why do you, as a white woman, give a damn about the plight of a filthy nigger?"

"Cause she a human being, she my family, and she damn sure ain't fuckin' filthy. Cause it weren't right. Cause nobody did a damn thing about it. Cause it broke somethin' in me, and ever since, I been carryin' this weight in my heart that's only getting heavier with all the things I keep seein'."

There was another silence. Another deeply uncomfortable silence as Malcolm continued to tap his fingers against his oak table without ever taking his eyes off Antonia's quivering pupils. Eventually, when he was ready, he finally spoke.

"She clearly isn't your family, so why do you keep saying she is?"

"Family's more than blood. Family's the people you'd die for and who would die for you."

"And if she were just another Black woman, would you care about what happened to her?"

"Of course."

"Really?"

"It hurts every time I see injustice happen to Black folk. But, yeah, it hurts more when I know them personally. I can't help that."

"Yeah, I'm sure you have a damn good cry about it all in the limousine on the way to the health spa every morning," Gene retorted.

This comment hurt Antonia somewhat, and she hung her head in sadness. Something Malcolm noticed.

"You say it broke something in you. Why? Plenty of white people see Black folk suffer every single day, but it doesn't weigh on them. What makes you different?"

"Because it ain't right!" Antonia cried, her voice cracking as she slammed her fist down onto Malcolm's stiff oak table.

She didn't do any serious damage with that, but it stung badly. She grimaced in pain, rubbing her palm softly as Malcolm repeatedly glanced from her hand to her face.

"You OK?" he asked, with genuine concern.

"Yeah," she replied. They sat in silence for another 15 seconds before she eventually spoke.

"Malcolm, it ain't just the beatings or the hateful words. It's how they try to keep you down in every part of life. They keep you poor, keep you from good schools, keep you from havin' a say in your own lives. They make sure you stay in your place, and I'm sick of it."

"If that's true, what did you do to protect your aunt? You call her family and say families protect and die for each other. So, what did you do when she was beaten? Did you stand by? Did you fight for her? Tell me what you did."

"I ain't do shit, Malcolm! I was a young little girl and scared! I ain't know what to do! But I hated myself for that, and I promised to never let that happen again!"

"Which is just the type of cowardice I can't have in my organisation."

"I was a little girl! But I ain't like that no more!"

"And how do I know that?"

"A few years ago I fought a whole entire town to protect my black boyfriend! I even punched out two white bitches!"

"Really?" asked Leon Ameer.

"Really!"

"What makes you think you can help us, Antonia?" Malcolm asked thoughtfully. "White people have been our problem for centuries. Associating with them brings us nothing but harm, so why do we need you, and how does your guilt change anything for us?"

"I can help because my white skin opens doors to me that are closed to you. You can't even get close to the circles I can and are just tryin' to take this fuckin' system apart from the outside. It's like shootin' a fuckin' tank with a pea shooter."

"She's not wrong there," said Leon thoughtfully.

"But I'm in these circles, Malcolm. I'm on the inside. I'm married to a wealthy banker, and people trust me. I have some influence."

"Is that right?" Malcolm asked dismissively.

"How do you think I even found your address?"

Malcolm's eyebrows raised in response to that comment. She clearly had a point.

"We can use that trust and my influence against them, Malcolm. I can help you destroy this fuckin' system from the inside out on some Soviet Commie spy-type shit.

I can help by using my privilege as a weapon against the system that makes life easy for people who look like me and miserable for people who look like you.

You can keep firin' your pea shooter at that armoured tank and see how that works, or you can drop a grenade under its hatch and blow that mother fucker up from the inside out."

"And you're the grenade?"

"Hell yeah. But don't get it twisted, I ain't guilty, Malcolm, 'cause I ain't the fuckin' problem, and I ain't never been. What I am is angry. Real fuckin' angry."

Yet another silence followed. One in which the weight of Antonia's words and the emotional resonance behind them could be seen firmly imprinting upon Malcolm's mind.

"If the world changed tomorrow if Black people were free and equal, would you still care? Or is your guilt only important because of the injustice you see? Do you really love us, or do you love feeling like a saviour?"

"Look into my eyes, Malcolm. There's your answer."

Malcolm and Leon exchanged glances and nodded thoughtfully.

"You say you're sick of this situation, but what have you sacrificed? What have you lost? What do you stand to lose if you're seen standing with us?"

"I lost the love of my life, I lost the baby I was pregnant with, and I lost my lady flower after them racist crackers mutilated me. I done lost a whole lot, Malcolm, and I got even more to lose by bein' with you."

"Why?"

"I'm a white woman, and people call you the biggest domestic terrorist in these United States. The fuck you think gonna happen if people catch me workin' with you? I could lose everythin', my social standin', my marriage, my money, my freedom. Everythin'."

"And you're willing to lose all of that to work with us?"

"A thousand times over."

"How are your black family doing, and where are they? You didn't finish talking about them," Malcolm asked.

"And I don't want to continue."

From the stark change in Malcolm's expression, Antonia saw that she spoke with poor strategy. The simple fact was that while her situation with the Pooles was understandably traumatic for her to discuss, he didn't know that and, nor did he care.

He simply needed to ascertain whether she was someone he could trust and hence didn't give a damn about her issues.

"If you don't want to talk about that then you and I haven't got anything to talk about at all," he said, matter of factly.

"I don't know where they are, alright?"

"Why?"

"They had a son called Winston. Or have a son called Winston, I don't know if he's still alive."

"Why?"

"We was in love. We are in love. I loved him since I was 10 and we was always together in secret. We did everythin' together, me and Winston. Nobody knew. My parents ain't know. The town ain't know, but we knew. My black family knew."

Malcolm's eyebrows raised. He clearly had some idea of where this was going.

"Anyway, some years back, I was kissin' Winston in the woods, and some white men from the town caught us. They beat on Winston real bad."

"And let me guess, you got scared of looking like a race traitor whore to the crackers and said he raped you."

That was Gene, interjecting dismissively as Malcolm and Leon looked on expectantly, clearly suspecting the same thing.

"No. They wanted me to say that, but I didn't."

"Bullshit. That's exactly what you white bitches do when you get caught with black men," Gene replied.

"I ain't say that! I fought the whole town to protect him! I already told you that!" Antonia cried, standing her ground.

"Really?" Malcolm asked with a raised eyebrow.

"Yeah. I told everybody I loved him and was pregnant with his baby. They pulled me away, but I fought with everythin' I had to get to him. Like I said, I even punched out two white bitches."

"You actually knocked out two white women?" Leon asked, clearly impressed.

"Yeah," Antonia replied nonchalantly.

"Seriously?" he added.

"You know I'm good with these hands," she said with a deadpan expression, glancing in Gene's direction.

"So what happened after that?" Malcolm asked.

"I cussed out the entire town. I called them evil fucking hypocrites and said I hated them. Then they took Winston away. I don't know what happened to him after that."

Tears began to stream down Antonia's cheeks. Malcolm looked right at her, and she looked right back. His eyes were so keen, so rabidly intelligent.

She could feel them taking in every inch of data possible to analyse her behaviour for the slightest tinge of deception. It was as intimidating as it was impressive to behold.

"I never saw Winston again," she continued. "My white family moved me to another state the next day, and I know Winston's family moved him away too, so I don't know what happened to him. I been tryin' to track down my black family for a while, but I can't find them Now I got nobody."

"You got your husband," said Malcolm.

"Fuck him. He don't like me and I don't like him. All he do is chase his floozies, and, and he just as racist as all of them. I'm alone, Malcolm. If I can't help you, I ain't got nothin'."

"How can I trust you, Antonia? History is full of Black men ruined because of white women's lies. How do I know you won't turn on us like so many others?"

"I had an entire town of angry crackers beggin' me to tell them a black man raped me, and I ain't say that shit. I said I loved him, and because of that, I lost my baby and my flower."

"Your flower?" Malcolm asked, confused.

"Yeah," Antonia replied, pointing to her vagina."

Malcolm's eyes widened with shock and sympathy as he gradually understood her meaning.

"They mutilated you there?"

"Yeah, they said I'd been corrupted, so that was the only cure. They ain't use nothin' to numb the pain, either. And they killed my baby.

"I'm sorry."

"I been through all that and more and I'm still here, Malcolm. I ain't goin' nowhere."

"But what if we don't want your help? What if Black people are better off without white folks 'helping' us? What do you say to that?"

"Why make things tougher than they have to be? I'd rather push a truck up a hill with 10 men helpin' me than just nine. If my money and connections can make life even one per cent easier for you and other Black folk, then why are we wasting time debating when we got serious work to do?"

For the first time since he found her in his home, Malcolm X broke eye contact with Antonia and gazed at a painting of the African continent on his wall. He stared at it for at least half a minute in deep thought while stroking his chin.

"Malcolm, is it so surprisin' that I want to help?" Antonia added. "You really think every white person in America hates you? Some of us are good, and I'm one of them."

Malcolm didn't respond; he simply stared at that painting while stroking his chin in deep thought.

"You know, you're not the first white woman to offer her help. A white woman approached me once, asking how she could help my cause, but I dismissed her. I told her that, as a white woman, there was nothing she could do to help me or my people. I often look back and ask myself if I made a mistake by not finding a way for her to contribute."

"I don't know nothin' 'bout that bitch, but if you turn me down, it will be the biggest mistake of your life," Antonia replied without a shred of irony or humour.

“Somethin' gots to change," she continued. "Either they need to stop this shit, or we need to make them stop the shit."

"By any means necessary," said Malcolm, reestablishing eye contact with a smirk. Antonia replied with a brief smirk of her own before steeling her gaze.

"Any fuckin' means necessary. Look, I get it. I'm a white woman, and you don't trust me, and I don't blame you. But I'm here, and I want to help. I need to help."

"You realise you'll be watched, right? Our entire organisation is going to watch and study your every move."

"I ain't expect nothin' less. But I ain't what you need to worry about." Antonia stated confidently.

"What do you mean?" Malcolm asked curiously.

"Look, I ain't sayin' this to make you trust me, OK? Watch my ass as much as you possibly can and make sure I ain't no snake. I want you to do that. Don't tell me any piece of useful information that I could possibly use against your organisation or your cause. I'm fine with that. That's not a problem."

"So what are you saying?"

"What I'm sayin’ is that even outside of me, you need to be careful, Malcolm. You got enemies."

"You think I don't know that?"

"I ain't talkin' about the crackers, the government, or the cracker fuckin' government. I'm talkin' about the Nation of Islam, Elijah Mohammed and them. They ain't happy with you, Malcolm."

"You think they're going to try to kill me?"

"I do. You got enemies on all sides, Malcolm. We need to be careful."

"We?"

"Yeah, nigga. We."

There it was, yet another unsolicited and wholly unintended use of the n-word. However, this time, Malcolm didn't react. Instead, the two simply shared another silence. One in which she and he continued to gaze into each other's eyes without blinking. One in which they both took the measure of each other.

One in which they saw past their superficial differences of gender and skin colour and connected with the energy of the soul opposite. One which finally ended with Malcolm cracking what could only be described as a genuine smile.

"I don't got nothin' better to live for, Malcolm. I want to help you make this country a better place." Antonia continued.

"I appreciate that."

"But we need to fix your security. It was far too easy for me to break into this place."

"Tell me exactly how you did that."

17 | THE WHORE YOU CRAVE & CONDEMN

KARA | Sons of God Recording Studio: Present Day

There were times in both of Kara's lives when she wondered what the fuck she was doing and why the freak she was doing it, and this was one of them. There she was, sitting in a pitch-black studio opposite the Christian fanatic forward slash influencer known as Adrian Phillips while brutally aware of what was to come next.

Phillips was a stuck-up, prim and proper, grey-haired white man dressed like a 1940s college professor. He was, in Kara's eyes, a clear nutjob, one who ran an organisation called The Sons of God. They were a group dedicated to bringing planet Earth back to a state of purity and beauty apparently not seen since Eve convinced Adam to eat the apple.

Phillips believed modern society was cancerous at the core and also believed that said cancer needed to be cut out sans anaesthesia.

Sex was wrong.

Music was wrong.

TV shows, movies, and novels were wrong.

Fashionable clothes were wrong, in fact, so was wanting to look good in any way.

Social media was nothing less than abhorrent (a somewhat hypocritical stance, considering he ran an active IG with no less than 127,529 followers).

And, of course, homosexuality was a personal affront to the honour of his Lord and Saviour, Jesus Tap-Dancing Christ.

Essentially, anything that diverged from strict conservative beliefs was as wicked and sinful as defiling a puppy.

Now, considering the above, it should come as no surprise to hear that Adrian Phillips detested Kara Clark and everything she apparently stood for. And so, with that in mind, she once had to ask herself why the hell she was there.

The studio was black. Almost pitch black with very little light except for the two spotlights that shone on Kara and Adrian's faces. It was moody, creepy, and surreal all at the same time, almost like they weren't people but souls.

Two disembodied yet diametrically opposed consciousnesses communicating through a timeless ether of nothingness to resolve their differences.

Which, on second thought, was clearly what Adrian had intended.

His face was so punchable, so smug, so self-righteous. So unbefuckinglievably arrogant that Kara wanted to slap him. Every fibre of his being oozed with the supposedly undeniable truth that he was better than her. He knew he knew better than her. He knew he was right, and he knew she was wrong.

All that mattered was for him to educate her black ass and school the masses at exactly the same time.

"I am better than you, Kara," Phillips said, in near telepathic fashion.

"What a nice thing to say to your honoured guest. You happy to have your viewers hear you talking to me like that?" Kara replied.

This interview took place on Adrian's popular Children of Eden YouTube channel. It was also simultaneously live-streamed to his Facebook page. Between her followers and his, over 85,000 people were watching live.

"I don't deal in pleasant falsehoods, Kara. I tell the cold, hard, unflinching truth of reality, which my audience admires and respects. When I say I'm better than you, I don't do so with a shred of ego, but for two reasons. One, because I see the insecurity in your eyes, and two because it's simply a faithful representation of reality."

"And why? Why are you better than me?"

"Never has the answer to a question been so patently obvious."

"Humour me."

"Have you even seen that abominable video you made on that balcony?"

"You mean the video in which a private and tender moment between me and my lover was both filmed and broadcast online without our consent?"

"Kara, don't be coy. We both know what that video was."

"What was it?"

"Your obvious attempt at going viral."

"No, Adrian, it was not."

"You knowingly and deliberately shot and leaked that sex tape, didn't you?"

"No, Adrian, I did not."

"You want to be another Kim Kardashian, don't you?"

"No, Adrian, I do not."

"You want to be just like that whore, Rihanna? Don't you?"

"Now that I wouldn't mind."

"So why did you do it?"

"Why did I do what?"

"Why did you film that video? Come on. Everything about it was just too 'perfect'. The moaning, the screaming, the panting, the way you were moving."

"So you're saying you were turned on by it."

"I didn't say that."

"Not consciously."

"Not in any way."

"So why is it perfect?"

"I know theatrics when I see them."

"But you said it's perfect, which implies you think it's a textbook expression of erotic sensuality, and that implies you were turned on by it."

"I can assure you that I was not."

"Is that so? Or did you find yourself rock hard at the sight of watching me getting fucked?"

"Watch your language."

"And when that happened, you had to have a little conversation with yourself, didn't you?"

"About what?"

"You had to face the ongoing fact that your cock gets hard for women like me no matter how much you wish it wasn't so. What is it, Adrian? Do I look like the kind of woman you know you could never get? Is that it?"

"You're a filthy whore, and it's pathetic."

"Who's more pathetic? Me, the filthy whore, or you, the man whose cock gets hard for said filthy whore?"

"Watch it, Kara. You're dealing with a real man here. Not one of your online simps."

"Adrian, I've only known three real men in my life. Two are dead, and only one's still alive. Trust me, you can't hold a candle to any of them."

"Is that so?"

"Let me ask you a question. Why do I get all the blame for that video in your eyes?"

"Because you deserve it."

"But what about Blake?"

"Who?"

"Exactly."

"Who's Blake?"

"The man who fucked me. Why doesn't he receive any scrutiny? Why is it all on me?"

"Because he isn't parading himself on social media like a whore and selling videos of himself to the highest bidder."

"Firstly, he's got a very sexy IG with lots of hot pictures of himself. Secondly, that's cap, and you know it. You didn't say a damn thing about my social media. It's all been about that video."

"I have a whole litany of grievances with you, Kara. Don't worry."

"Hit me."

"Well, speaking of the gentleman in question. Is he your husband? Your boyfriend?"

"Not in the traditional sense."

"Meaning?"

"He's someone I deeply care about, and we share an intense emotional and sexual connection, but we haven't put a label on what it is exactly."

"So you allow any Tom, Dick, or Harry to enter you?"

"Did you even listen to what I just said? He isn't just anyone."

"But you're free to cavort with whomever you choose?"

"Yes, and so is he."

"And you think this is acceptable behaviour?"

"As long as nobody's being hurt."

"Why don't you get yourself a real job, Kara?"

"Excuse me?"

"You're so young and so beautiful; why don't you get a proper job?"

"Do you not see how wild what you just said is?"

"Why?"

"My youth and beauty are precisely what make me able to make money the way I do. The fact that people like you want to fuck me is exactly why I'm able to live this life. If you didn't want me, if I wasn't beautiful, I would have to get a 'real job.' So telling me that being in possession of something that saves me from the drudgery of a 9-5 as being the reason why I should have that 9-5 is crazy."

"But why degrade yourself?"

"Am I degrading myself?"

"Of course you are. Look at your social media and your Onlyfans. Only a woman whose self-worth is in the toilet would do such things."

"So you think women like me are the lowest of the low."

"I know you are."

"So, do you think you could get me?"

"What?"

"If we were both at a bar or club and you saw me, do you think you would possess the balls to approach me and the requisite charisma to keep my interest and take me home?"

"I would never engage in such immoral behaviour."

"I didn't ask if you agree with the concept from a moral perspective; I asked if you could do it."

"Well, erm, I, erm..."

"After all, I'm the lowest of the low, right?"

"Yes, and that is true, but erm..."

"So taking me home should be easy, right?"

"Well, yes, erm..."

"Adrian, stop it. We both know you couldn't."

"How dare you?"

"That's gotta be really fucking infuriating, knowing that the real reason you despise a certain type of woman is that you know you can't have her."

"You don't know what you're talking about."

"If that's true, then show me your phone."

"What?"

"Your phone. Let's go through it right now and look at your search history."

"We're not doing that, Kara."

"Yeah, that's what I thought."

"Why don't you get a real job instead of being a whore?"

"Give me your phone right now, and let's look through your search history. Let's see the sorts of websites you browse when you're all alone, Adrian."

"That's not going to happen."

"Hypocrite."

"You had sex on camera for millions to see."

"Like I said, that was filmed and shared without my consent. Are you really stupid enough to think the dozens of people who stood by filming on their camera phones dozens of feet below were plants?"

"You share obscene and degrading content on your Onlyfans."

"Which is a shame because I'm so beautiful, which apparently means that beauty should be hidden from the world, right?"

"Which is a shame because you're lowering yourself. No doubt you think it's empowering, though."

"Isn't it?"

"I couldn't think of anything more degrading."

"You think I'm giving up my power?"

"I know you are."

"Some 32-year-old man in Minnesota works 9-11 every day at a job he fucking despises for $500 a week. He then joins my Onlyfans for $30 a month and buys 2 private videos in his first hour for $150 a pop. In less than an hour he's given me almost half his wages, and for what? Two 60-second videos of my legs.

He's never going to meet me, let alone touch or fuck me. Those videos are as close as he's ever going to get. What's more, he's never going to see more of me than that, no matter how much he pays. He'll never see my intimate areas, only pay to see parts of me that anyone who saw me on a beach in a bikini would see for free. Tell me, Adrian, which of us is being degraded in that scenario?"

"So what you're saying is you love the attention."

"Most women do."

"Not true."

"Oh, I'm afraid it is. The only difference is that not all of us have the ability or confidence to capitalise on it."

"So you're saying all women want to be objectified."

"Firstly, I didn't say all; I said most. Secondly, I wouldn't say objectified; I'd say appreciated. How many women do you know who are attractive enough to be models, dancers, singers, or any other kind of 'hot girl' profession but have opted instead to work in Starbucks?"

"So, again, you love the attention."

"I do. I love knowing that people..."

"Men."

"People all over the world get off on looking at me."

"Why are you so insecure?"

"Am I?"

"You clearly are. What's more, you're using the supposed insecurities of other women as an excuse for your own need to chase external validation."

"You're chasing validation right now, Adrian."

"Is that right?"

"It's not enough for you to just privately disagree with my lifestyle and keep it pushing, you have to virtue signal to your followers so they know what an amazing person you are. Your whole self-image lies in comparison to me. You're using me to affirm to your followers and yourself that you're moral and worthy, and it's because you don't believe in yourself the way you want everyone to think."

"You don't know what you're talking about."

"Don't I? What are we even doing here? You haven't brought me here to help or change me; you just want to prove that you're better than me. It was literally the first thing you said.

"I've brought you here to learn the truth and the way."

"And the best way to do that is to start the interview by telling me I'm beneath you? You thought that would make me want to listen to whatever you had to say?"

"Sometimes hard truths need to be expressed, Kara."

"Well, I'm sorry, Adrian, but I don't want your' truth', your way, or your unrealistic desires."

"Unrealistic? There is nothing unrealistic about..."

"You're hypocritical. You want me to have a gorgeous body that people want to have sex with, but you hate for me to actually have sex with this gorgeous body. You like that I'm beautiful because that beauty is attractive, but to act or capitalise on that? That makes me Hitler."

"You're wrong on so many levels..."

Adrian's phone lit up upon the table between them, shining a multicoloured hue into the near pitch-black expanse. Kara immediately grabbed it and started going through it.

"Got your phone!"

She then saw Pornhub in his browsing history as well as various sexy pics of Rihanna in his image library.

"Why have you got half-naked pictures of Rihanna saved in your phone?"

"Erm... well... erm..."

"And why the fuck do you have Pornhub in your browsing history?!"

"Erm... erm..."

"Adrian you're a fucking hypocrite. You look at content like this, jerk to it..."

"Why I would never..."

"You jerk to it and then hate on the women who make the content you've been jerking to!"

"Kara, I'm going to ask you to watch your language!"

"And I'm going to ask you to drop the crap! Why engage with something you apparently hate?!"

Kara waited in silence for Adrian to reply.

"Don't worry. I'll wait!"

Kara sat with her arms folded for another 15 seconds, waiting for a reply that never came. Clearly, Adrian Phillips had nothing to say.

"You called me a whore before, and you know what? Here once was a time when I was a whore, but not in the way you think! Back when I used to get up every morning at 6:30 am and head to a fucking job as a fucking secretary for a fucking company, I didn't give a fucking shit a-fucking-bout!

I had to wear an outfit I didn't want to wear, talk to people I didn't want to talk to and have conversations about things I'd rather dip my head in battery acid than discuss. When I had to go to that fucking office and consign myself to 11 hours of imprisonment every fucking day just to get enough cash to pay my rent! That's when I was a whore, Adrian!

"Den! Not now! Wah mi do right now gi mi freedom! Freedom weh mi neva feel since mi did a work wid Bredda Malcolm!"

"What?!"

"I said, I haven't had freedom like this since I worked with brother Malcolm!"

"Malcolm X?!"

"Yeah, nigga!"

"Have you lost your damn mind?!"

"No, Adrian, I've finally found it. And I don't care what you or anyone else thinks."

With that, Kara sat back in her chair, feeling powerful and victorious. She'd won that battle of wits. She'd beaten Adrian Phillips and was now free to bask in the warm glow and sweet scent of success.

But then, once again, she heard something.

Something louder than before.

Something more haunting than before.

Something more passionately frightful than before.

It was a cry. A scream. A wail imbued deep with traumatised feminine energy.

One that gave Kara a chill right down her spine.

As a frustrated Adrian Phillips stammered and stuttered his way through an attempt to regain control and wrap up the podcast before he could suffer more humiliation, Kara began to feel a deep fear emanating from her core.

18 | THE UNKNOWN WATCHER

KARA | New York Uber Journey: Present Day

Exactly five minutes after the end of her podcast appearance with Adrian Dickhead Phillips and while heading to Blake's apartment in her Uber, Kara received a text message. It was from an unknown sender, but even an elderly gentleman with late-stage dementia could have deduced from whom it had been sent. Said message read:

UNKNOWN SENDER:

"Great job on Adrian Phillips' podcast, you nigger slut. You did such an excellent job of painting yourself to be a sympathetic human being that I almost forgot you're a delusional and talentless whore with no worth to society. Almost. Almost. That is until I remembered the things you do when nobody's looking, the things that eat you up from the inside out. You know, THOSE things.

The things nobody else knows but me.

I wonder how the rest of the world will feel when they know your dirty secret?

Will they still cherish and idolise you? Or will they rightfully dispose of you like the filthy jungle bunny you are?

Maybe one day you'll find out."

Kara blocked the number, of course, but truthfully did so, knowing no good would come of it. Whoever this person was, he was obsessed with her and wasn't going to stop harassing her. What's more, he said he had multiple devices to harass her from, and she had every reason to think that was true.

But how on earth does he have my private number?

It was one thing for him to message her on Instagram, but on her private phone number? That was mortifying. That said, however, it was nowhere near as chilling as the fact that he seemed to know what she'd done.

But how? How is that possible?!

How could he have known? Hippocratic Oath wasn't at the party; she knew that for sure.

Or did she?

Do I?

It didn't make sense. None of it made a lick of sense. How the hell could he have known?

What did he know, and how did he know it?

What the hell is he going to do?

She just didn't know.

19 | SAY YES TO US TODAY

KARA | Blake's Apartment: Present Day

Kara was wrapped within Blake's arms lying on his couch as they binged Breaking Bad on Netflix. Experiencing a turbulent rollercoaster of emotions running the gamut from fear to dread and all the way back, his presence was a source of mild comfort. However, that slight tinge of support wasn't close to being enough meaning Kara wasn't able to think straight.

She could focus on the show for all of five consecutive seconds before her mind began racing in 36 different directions, and she was now panicking. Her new heart slammed against its ribcage like the galloping hooves of an antler fleeing a lion as a cold sweat leaked from her chocolate skin like condensation on a car's rear window.

"What's wrong?" Blake asked with a concerned expression.

Something she was growing to love about him was just how attentive and observant he was. Despite how bad she felt, she had been doing everything in her power to mask it and was sure most people wouldn't have noticed.

Blake, however, wasn't most people.

"Don't look so surprised, Queen," he added. "It's obvious when you're upset. Wanna talk about it?"

"I wouldn't know where to start," Kara replied, partially out of honesty and partially from a desire to run away from the problem."

"You sure?"

"I'm sure."

"Would it help if I wrapped you up in my strong arms super tight?"

"That would actually help a lot."

"Would it help if I planted some soft and tender kisses on that delicious forehead of yours?"

"That would also be wonderful."

"And would the wonder further increase if I told you how proud I am for how you handled yourself on that podcast?"

"It would, but you've told me that already!" Kara replied, laughing.

"Well, it needs to be repeated," Blake said, matter of factly.

"Why?"

"He rocked up to that interview expecting you to be this dumb, ditzy, airheaded IG model who didn't even have two brain cells to rub together to start a fire.

However, you, my dear, you, Miss Kara Clark, utterly destroyed him. He kept trying to trap you but you wouldn't let him, and I saw him getting more and more flustered as you consistently called him out on his bullshit."

"Like what?" Kara replied with a coy smile.

"Fishing for compliments?"

"You better believe it," she replied.

They both laughed tenderly for half a minute before Blake continued.

"But firstly, what the hell was that Malcolm X comment about?" Blake asked, confused.

"Nigga, I just felt like fucking with his ass," Kara replied, lying through her teeth.

"Well, you definitely did that. But to answer your question, it's like you said with the sex tape thing; nobody gave a damn about me when that dropped. All the attention was on you, and it's unfair."

"Jealous I got all the followers?" Kara smiled.

"Hell yeah! There I am, breaking my back, sweating like our ancestors, putting in alllll that good work and don't nobody give me no credit for nothing!"

"Life's not fair!" Kara laughed.

"Where the fuck are my followers!? Where are my residuals?!" Blake shouted with a massive smile before they both burst into passionate laughter. After half a minute or so, he continued.

"It is unfair, though, and to you, Queen. It's totally wrong that people have been calling you all sorts of names online but ain't nobody said shit to me. It's wrong that people like that dickhead Adrian Phillips think they have the right to tell you to your face that they're better than you just because they don't approve of how you live your life."

"I guess that's just how the world works. People hate on women for doing things men are praised for."

"Well that don't make it right. It's a stupid double standard, and I hate it," Blake replied, stroking her forehead softly as she gazed into his oceanic blue eyes.

"You know something?" Kara added. "You're like the second most mature man on earth."

"Only the second?" Blake replied, pretending to be offended. "What? So I got competition?!"

"Stiff competition," Kara replied with a smirk.

"Well, there's like, what? Four billion of us dudes on the planet, so I guess I'll take that," he replied with a smile.

"You should because I meant every word."

"I got it from my gramps," Blake smiled. "He's the most mature man I know."

"Yeah?"

"Yeah. He taught me everything about..."

Before Blake could even finish his sentence, Kara's heart was stabbed by intense grief as she once again heard that feminine scream echoing all around.

It was everywhere.

Literally everywhere.

Imbued deep into the molecules of the air in Blake's living room and rapidly ricocheting off the walls with spectral freneticism.

It clattered against her eyes.

Screeched within her eardrums.

Penetrated the frontal lobe of her brain.

It was the desperate wail of a woman lost between worlds.

A woman in true, unrelenting torment.

Unforgiving torment.

A wail which filled Kara's heart with dread and sent adrenaline pumping down her spinal cord.

Once again, she began to panic, looking to and fro like an infant impala cornered by a Bengal tiger, desperate for a way out while also knowing resistance was futile.

Blake was concerned.

Genuinely concerned.

"Queen, what's wrong?"

"Yuh nuh hear dat?!"

"Huh??

"Can't you hear that?!"

"Hear what?"

Kara didn't reply. She just kept looking left, right, up, and down in a desperate search for something she deep down knew she'd never see.

"Kara, I'm getting worried. What's wrong?"

She couldn't see anything. No matter how hard she looked, she couldn't see a damn thing. But she could feel it. She felt it with every fibre of her soul.

That presence, that terrified, angry, and panicked feminine presence. It was everywhere but nowhere in particular and in total awareness of her. It was watching her.

"What do you want?!"

"Kara, what the fuck's wrong?!"

Blake grabbed her by her shoulders, spun her to face him, and began shaking sense into her with mild to moderate force. Surprisingly, it worked, and after about 15 seconds, the shrieking faded into nothing, leaving them all alone.

Who the hell was that?! Was it Kalizar?!

It was the only idea she had, but that didn't make sense because why the fuck would they mess with her like that?

"Kara, what the hell is going on?" Blake said softly yet firmly, staring straight into her soul with those endless blue eyes. His masculine, grounded, and protective energy perfectly matched the contours of his beautiful milk chocolate face and was as soothing as it was nurturing.

"Blake, I can't tell you. I wish I could, but I just can't."

"You can tell me anything."

"But not this. I, I don't even know what to tell you, King."

At that moment, Kara's phone vibrated and she picked it up, eager for a distraction, any distraction. Sadly, however, it was yet another text message from:

UNKNOWN SENDER:

"I wonder what your black buck would think if he knew the things I know about you, Kara? Think he'd still want to cuddle and call you his 'Queen' if he knew the piece of shit you really are? Still think he'd want to slide his coon dick inside you then?"

Oh my God, him a watch mi! How di rass him a watch mi?! She thought in Jamaican patois.

As floods of tears streamed from her quivering eyeballs, Kara thumbed out a panicked reply, her fingers slipping over her wet screen, making her words barely legible.

"Leav em the fcuk alon!"

"Never going to happen."

"What d yuo want form me?!"

"I want you to take a knife and end it."

"Go awya!"

"In your fucking throat, Kara."

That last comment gave Kara a traumatic flashback to a time she wished she could forget. She was still reeling from its aftershock when a very concerned Blake spoke.

"Kara, what the fuck is going on?!"

He forcefully grabbed her phone and read the chat.

"Who the fuck is this?!"

"I don't know! I've got a stalker!"

"A what?!"

"A stalker! This man, I, I don't know who he is or where he's from! He started harassing me on Instagram, so I deleted him, and now he's messaging me here!"

"How the fuck has he got your number?!"

"I don't know!"

"How the fuck does he know you're here?!"

"I don't know!"

"And what the fuck is he talking about?! What don't I know about you?!"

"Blake, mi nuh know! Mi nuh know!" she cried in patois.

“I can’t understand you!”

“I don’t know!” Kara repeated in regular English, lying through her teeth.

"I'm scared, Blake!" she said, being honest again.

"You don't know what it's like! It's like there's this person dedicated to destroying me.

It's like he has nothing better to do than hurt me, and it's like he knows everything about me! He knows exactly where I am and how to contact me; I don't know what to do!"

"If he knows everything about you, then what does he know that I don't?!"

"Blake, I don't know!"

"Kara, we need to go to the police!”

"I, I don't know!"

"Are you out of your fucking mind?! You've got a stalker! We need to do something!"

Both were silent for almost 5 minutes as Kara paced Blake's living room like a psych ward mental patient, and he nervously studied her every move.

Eventually, her phone vibrated again, and she grabbed it from him immediately. It was another message.

UNKNOWN SENDER:

"Good idea. Go talk to the police and see what happens when I'm forced to tell them what I know about you."

"Steady the tempest in his veins.

His anger howls, a beast unchained.

Lean on we, in faith remain,

To pass through silence, free of pain."

"Kalizar, is that you??"

Indeed, that was Kalizar. Yet again, speaking in riddles.

"Kara, who the fuck's Kalizar?!"

Oh fuck!

UNKNOEN SENDER:

"You're so dead, and you don't even know it."

Calm down, calm down. I can do this. I've got to stay calm.

"Give credence to your words.

Resist to go berserk."

"OK, Kara, sit down with me. Right here, sit."

Blake placed Kara on his couch and sat beside her with his strong arms wrapped around her shaking shoulders.

"Stay calm, Queen; stay calm. It's going to be OK. I'm here."

"The price for life is death.

The heart within your chest."

I don't know if I can do this. I don't know if I can.

"The beauty of your breasts.

The ecstasy of sex."

"I don't know what's going on, and I don't need to know. Kara, but I got you. You're not alone."

"The fee is more than less.

The price for life is death."

Unknown Sender:

"Someday and someday soon, we're gonna meet in person, you filthy cunt, and when we do, you're fucking dead."

"A price you have to pay.

A life you have to slay."

"You hear me, Kara? You're not alone. You hear me?"

"If this is all OK.

Say yes to us today."

"Yes."

"You hear me, Kara?"

"Yes."

"If this is all OK.

Say yes to us today."

"Yes."

"Do you hear me, Kara?"

"Yes."

Unknown Sender:

"I'm coming for you."

20 | I'M NOT GOING ANYWHERE

ANTONIA | Atlanta: September, 1964

To say things were wild for Antonia was an understatement because Malcolm's life (and, by extension, hers) had become a frenetic whirlwind of pandemonium. On the one hand, his profile, and therefore the civil rights movement as a whole, was growing.

He gave talks worldwide and was even asked to debate at the Oxford Union in September. Again, that was amazing. Incredible. Beautiful. Antonia felt blessed to see this. It felt great to see the fruits of their labour begin to manifest.

Malcolm's profile was growing for sure, and she was so proud to have played a small role in helping that happen. That said, however, he still didn't completely trust her, nor did any of the other folks in his organisation.

No matter how sincere or helpful she was, or how much of her racist husband's money she secretly syphoned their way, there was always a black and white coloured barrier wedged firmly between her and the other members of Malcolm's movement.

But once, Antonia was no fool.

She understood exactly why that was.

But that said, it didn't make it hurt any less. Yes, they were wise to keep eyes on her, and yes, she would have done the same thing in their situation, but it still left her feeling desperately lonely.

If Richard or white America in general knew what she was doing, she'd have been divorced, cut off from her allowance, and socially ostracised, or worse. So, with that in mind, some recognition would have been nice.

Hell, her now mutilated flower still bore the permanent wounds of what could happen if she was caught fraternising with black folk. Antonia hadn't felt the slightest tinge of sexual arousal since what the good father Joseph Schmidt did with her own parents' blessing those years ago, and it left her feeling barren inside.

And this was not to mention Winnie, the baby she lost. Winston's baby. Their baby. Antonia had been robbed of the chance to be a loving mother and, truthfully, didn't think she was still fertile.

In her dreams she saw the child she and Winston never got to meet. In her dreams, she played with little Winnie, nibbled her cheeks and stroked her curly hair before Winston wrapped them both up in his strong arms and kissed their foreheads.

But alas, Antonia never got to meet little Winnie, and she might never meet Winston again, and, what's more, it was all their fault.

America's fault.

The racist crackers who made his and their family's lives a living hell and took Winnie away needed to pay.

She'd never forgive them for that. Never. Never in a million fucking years. Something needed to happen. Something was going to change.

But that said, there were real stakes involved in the game Antonia was playing. High stakes. Heavy stakes. In fact, this wasn't even a game; this was literal life or death. On the one hand, she had the chance to make a better future for millions nationwide, but on the other, she might spell her own downfall in the attempt.

It was a choice she was willing to take, but that didn't make it any less terrifying, and that's why it hurt to have the very people she was helping keep her at arm's length.

Yes, she understood where they were coming from, and yes, she would have done it herself, but that was just rationality speaking. All of the rationality in the world couldn't change the fact that she was desperately lonely and needed a family.

She was taking a massive risk to her own livelihood by helping Malcolm X's cause, and she simply craved more appreciation than she was getting.

That said, Malcolm had graciously agreed to help her track down Winston's family in exchange for the help she provided to his cause. He hadn't found them yet, but he said he was on the case, and as a man of his word, that was all Antonia needed to hear.

Born Malcolm Little, Malcolm X was a prominent African-American Muslim minister and a human rights activist during the 1950s and 1960s. A key figure in the Civil Rights Movement, he advocated for the advancement and empowerment of African Americans through self-defence and self-determination.

A prodigiously bright child, he had harboured dreams of becoming a lawyer but had said dreams crushed when he was told by his eighth-grade teacher that:

"Being a lawyer is no realistic goal for a nigger."

But that sadly wasn't the worst of it. As a child, he witnessed his family's struggles with racism and violence on a daily basis, including the Ku Klux Klan's burning down of his family's home and the murder of his father by white supremacists.

Disillusioned with life, he became a violent street hoodlum who was involved in various criminal activities such as theft, gambling, and drugs during his teenage years and early adulthood. In fact, Little (as he was known at the time) and his gang had a reputation for violence, and such behaviour actually had him sent to prison in 1946 for burglary.

However, while inside, he educated himself, converted to Islam, joined the Nation of Islam, and eventually left in 1952 to begin his ascension to becoming a prominent spokesperson for Civil Rights.

While the passionate fire which made him such a feared hoodlum never left his soul, even in his calling as a leader, Malcolm X's stance on violence evolved throughout his lifetime. In the early stages of his activism, he advocated for self-defence and the use of violence if necessary. However, his views changed after leaving the Nation of Islam and making his pilgrimage to Mecca.

He then began to embrace a more inclusive approach to civil rights and rejected violence as a means of achieving it. Malcolm X now understood that violence only perpetuated the cycle of hate and therefore believed that nonviolence and peaceful protest were more effective in bringing about change.

Also, his views towards white people evolved throughout his life. In the early years of his activism, he believed that as whites were responsible for the oppression of his people, both races should be separated. He even advocated for the establishment of a separate Black nation within America.

However, after his 1964 pilgrimage to Mecca, he began to see that not all white people were racist and that some were working towards racial justice.

However, since Malcolm had split from the Nation of Islam, things were becoming progressively dark. Tensions between him and The Honourable Elijah Muhammad were boiling, and Antonia was seriously starting to fear for his safety.

In fact, she'd actually begun to hear whispers of profound discontent aimed in his direction from within certain factions of the black Muslim community.

Not everybody liked Malcolm X. Not everybody was on his side, even in the black community. Some were turning against him, and the sentiment among various elements started to get ugly. In fact, he and Elijah Muhammad had exchanged increasingly harsh words about each other in the press, making Antonia feel queasy to her stomach.

Malcolm accused Muhammad of having multiple affairs and various financial improprieties while Muhammad questioned Malcolm's loyalty, criticised his focus on civil rights over the Nation of Islam's religious teachings, and laughed at his rumoured appointment of a white woman (Antonia) as a fundraiser and outreach advocate.

Honestly, the whole thing baffled her. Both men were on the same side. Both were fighting the good fight for Black Americans against a sick white society that both hated and feared them. Surely that was more important than any personal squabbles they might have had?

Apparently, they disagreed with that notion, proving to Antonia that the male ego was just as potent and potentially self-destructive no matter what race in which it was found.

She was also beginning to feel the need for serious worry, however. In the course of her fundraising activities, she'd heard rumblings of not only significant resentment towards Malcolm emanating from a mosque in Newark, New Jersey but was becoming increasingly sure that the FBI was spying on him.

She also heavily suspected his inner circle had been compromised but had no way of knowing for sure or proving it.

All she knew was that there were:

- More and more police officers at Malcolm X's speeches and public appearances
- Wiretaps and surveillance cameras were placed at the locations where he and his associates met

- Various leaks of sensitive information to the press clearly indicating that someone close to him was working with law enforcement
- Multiple attempts to sow discord and distrust within his inner circle by planting false information and rumours

And so on, none of which made Antonia even slightly comfortable. Also, there was a growing cultural sentiment that he'd betrayed the Nation of Islam and was becoming a problem that needed to be fixed.

You see, many people were mortally offended by his accusing Elijah Muhammad of being senile and sleeping with young girls. Such folk demanded he receive his comeuppance.

A climate of fear and suspicion was growing, one which would have no less than dire ramifications for the movement unless the problem was quashed.

Malcolm X was flanked on all sides by enemies, both in the Nation of Islam, the US government, and even his own personal circle.

To be honest, if Antonia were smart, she would have cut her losses and run. She would have focused on being married to her cheating husband, doing her daily beauty treatments and forgetting Malcolm X ever existed.

But, alas, while Antonia certainly was no fool, nobody anywhere and at any time had ever accused her of being either a genius or a quitter. She wasn't going anywhere; she was going to help Malcolm X as much as she could right until the bitter end.

By any means necessary.

Antonia owed it to him, she owed it to her people, and most importantly, she owed it to Winston and his family. She simply owed it to the one love of her life. The man she had a sinking feeling she'd never see again until after her soul had forever left its body.

Antonia couldn't allow what happened to him to go unanswered. Justice had to be served. Good had to prevail against evil, and if that meant risking her own life, then so be it. Antonia and Malcolm were becoming deeply embedded in an all-encompassing web of chaos, but that was OK.

That was fine.

She welcomed it.

Antonia was going to help him bring about his dream of securing equal rights for black people in America. Even if he didn't trust her. Even if he didn't appreciate her help.

And she'd do so by any means necessary.

21 | THE BALLAD OF THE TIGER & THE TURTLE

ANTONIA & KARA | New York Residential Home: Present Day

Kara had arrived at the location of her next kill feeling both morally uncomfortable and downright terrified. She didn't know who she was supposed to kill or if they even deserved it, and the thought of doing the deed sent her senses into a tailspin.

And so, for exactly 45 uninterrupted seconds, she stood silently with her eyes firmly closed in a futile attempt to block out the avalanche of terror that cascaded across her brain.

She'd asked Kalizar to tell her who she had to kill. She'd pleaded for that information but received nothing in return, her desperate pleas being met with nought but empty silence.

Kalizar was not on her side.

Kalizar was malevolent.

Kalizar enjoyed seeing Kara in confusion and pain. They were toying with her, and deep down, she knew she had to break free from their grip. However, she also knew she needed what they had to offer.

As Kalizar's presence lingered in her mind, a creeping numbness spread through her fingertips, winding up her arms like the slow tightening of an invisible vice. Her chest constricted as though an unseen force pressed down on her lungs, making each breath shallow and heavy.

Kara needed the youth. Kara needed that fit, firm and strong body. Kara needed the body that wasn't wracked with pain when it moved. Kara needed the body that could sprint without tiring, leap like an athlete, and manoeuvre with sublime grace.

She craved the breathtaking beauty it possessed and its intoxicating effect on every single person who laid eyes on it, men and women alike.

Kara coveted that power.

It was her life force.

It nourished her soul, and she couldn't go back to the way things were before. She couldn't be that old decrepit fart sitting alone, obsessing over the lives of Instagram models a quarter of her age.

She just couldn't.

But then Kara had an unsettling thought. One which iced the bones of her young frame so cold she felt them chill the blood that flowed around them.

Antonia Hoell died that day.

She literally died.

That meant that if she refused Kalizar's demands, she wouldn't just go back to her old body; she'd cease to be. If she wasn't Kara, there would be no other life, only death.

But Kara didn't want to die; she really didn't. The thought scared her so much her lungs almost stopped.

But she couldn't kill either.

This isn't who I am.

She wasn't perfect, but she wasn't a killer.

Am I?

She didn't have it in her to take another life.

Do I?

Did she desire youth and beauty so much that she was willing to commit the most cardinal of sins to attain them?

Am I really prepared to go so far?

Was she?

I can't do that.

She didn't have that inside her.

I just don't.

But maybe she did.

Do I?

She couldn't be that type of person.

I can't.

She couldn't live with herself.

I have to tell Kalizar no. I have to just tell them no and let whatever happens happen.

At least I'll be able to look myself in the mirror.

But that wasn't true. She wouldn't be able to look herself in anything because Antonia died on that day.

Antonia Hoell died in that hospital.

I don't want to die.

Kara didn't want to die.

I don't want to die.

And she couldn't live as that ghoul.

And then, once again, she heard that harrowing shriek and felt that familiar energy.

Young, feminine, and distressed.

In pain.

Lost.

Abandoned.

All alone and desperate for help.

Kara asked herself who it was while knowing that doing so was nothing more than an act of self-denial. The more she tried to convince herself that she didn't know who that scream came from, the more she knew she was full of shit.

A soft, unsettling hum filled her ears like the faraway murmur of staccato voices. The whispers twisted and dissolved before she could grasp their meaning, leaving her with only a sense of foreboding that tightened her grip on reality.

"Remove such thoughts right from thy mind.

Open thine eyes; it's time to shine."

That was Kalizar, once again, communicating with Kara through the synapses of her new body's nervous system from a location she both couldn't begin to guess and instinctively knew she'd never want to see.

I can't do it. I can't.

She couldn't do it. She couldn't.

Kara was in a nursing home, of all places, and didn't know whether that was great or awful.

Who am I supposed to kill? A member of staff? Some old man? A child?

Would she be able to go through with it again? Could she take another person's life to preserve her own?

Could she accept the alternative?

She didn't know if she could.

I don't think I can.

She knew she couldn't.

I'm not a killer.

But she couldn't die.

"Enter the room."

Time itself seemed to shudder and slow as she reached for the doorknob, each second stretching out until the world around her dissolved into a dreamlike blur. The distance from the door to the bed felt like miles; each step weighed down with the gravity that only nightmares possessed.

Kara then saw a sight she wasn't prepared to see in a thousand centuries of leap years. She was in a patient's room with all the usual trappings one would expect.

Bland green painted walls adorned with cards from various well-wishers, assorted medical instruments nobody knows the name or function of, that trademark disgustingly sterile hospital smell, and a black man lying fast asleep on the bed.

An old black man.

A very old black man.

One Kara knew intimately but hadn't seen for over half a century.

Winston?

One she never thought she'd see again.

Winston!?

She collapsed to the floor in shock and joy, her young legs unable to function as her mind processed the gravity of what its eyes had borne witness to. It was Winston!

"WINSTON?!"

His face was ravaged by time. Etched with deep wrinkles, his once prominent hairline was now a clear figment of the past, but it was him! It was Winston! He was alive!

It didn't take two seconds for a river of tears to flow from her young eyeballs as she sobbed with joy, literally using her arms to drag her body along the floor to his bed.

Winston's alive!

But it didn't take a further three seconds for the harrowing reality of why she was there to come crashing down upon her soul.

"NO! NO, NO! YOU CAN'T BE SERIOUS! I CAN'T! NO! NO NO!"

And it didn't take more than another second for Kara's heart to become just as paralysed as her malfunctioning legs.

"You know, of course, what you must do.

All the rest is up to you."

"NO! NO! NOOOOOOO! I CAN'T DO IT! I CAN'T DO IT!"

"The price for life is death."

"NO! NO! NO! FUCK FUCK FUCK FUCK FUUUCK! OH GOD OH GOD OH GOD OH FUCK GOD NO NO NO NO WINSTON NO FUCK WINSTON NO!"

"Tiger?"

"PLEASE ANYBODY ELSE, ANYBODY ELSE BUT HIM, PLEASE ANYBODY ELSE!"

"Tiger.... is.... that.... you?"

"WINSTON?!"

“Is.... really.... you?”

"HOW DO YOU RECOGNISE ME?!"

“What’s.... happening.... how.... are.... you.... here?”

"HOW THE FUCK DO YOU RECOGNISE ME?!"

Antonia pulled herself to the bed, dragged herself to her very unsteady feet, threw her arms around Winston's bedbound frame, planted a long kiss on his lips, and gazed into his eyes with tears in her own.

"WINSTON, I LOVE YOU; I LOVE YOU SO MUCH; I ALWAYS HAVE! I NEVER FORGOT YOU! NEVER WINSTON! I NEVER FORGOT YOU!"

"Tiger, calm.... down, please.... calm..."

"I'M TRYIN', I'M TRYIN'!"

"What's.. going....on? Why....are you young...."

"AND BLACK?!"

"Yes... What.... is going.... on?"

"HOW DO YOU RECOGNISE ME?!"

"It's.... you."

"Turtle! My Turtle! My Turtle! My Turtle! My Turtle!"

There currently exist no words in the English language that can accurately depict the dizzying range of emotions that assaulted Antonia at that moment. Shock, disbelief, joy, elation, bliss, ecstasy, wonder, amazement, sadness, remorse. All these and more were felt to a degree impossible to quantify or convey with mere words.

Her system was overloaded with emotion. It overflowed with an energy which had her synapses spasming uncontrollably.

"Tiger..." said Winston, tears forming on his now ancient face.

He was old now, worn and weathered by time, but it was still him. Winston was still there. The quiet strength and love that burned behind those blue eyes of his had never gone away. It was still there. No matter what happened to his body, his spirit was still intact. His soul was still strong. Winston was there. It was Winston. He was alive.

Winston was alive.

"Mi glad fi see yuh! Mi miss yuh so much!" Antonia sobbed.

"I've.... missed.... you.... too..." Winston replied, his voice breaking with raw sincerity.

"I've missed you so much."

"I've been.... praying for.... this day..." Winston added.

"Fi real?! Why yuh neva link mi?!"

"I..... I ain't know.... how. My mind.... ain't.... so good since what.... they done. I find it.... tough to think.... now. I can't.... remember your.... name, Tiger."

"It's Antonia! My name is Antonia!" she replied tearfully.

"My family.... would not tell.... me..."

Antonia felt a lump in her throat as the weight of Winston's words dawned. He'd been cognitively impaired since the incident and couldn't think clearly or remember her name.

What's more, his family refused to tell him. That's how committed they were to keeping her out of his life. As heartbreaking as that was, she got it. She understood.

"Why.... are you.... here.... like this?"

"I don't know."

But she did know. Antonia knew precisely why she was there, and that single question sent her mind into another tailspin.

"What's.... wrong?" Winston asked, reading her emotions perfectly.

Antonia didn't say anything. Antonia couldn't say anything. She didn't even know where to begin.

"What... is it?" he pressed.

"Someone, or somethin'..." Antonia said, struggling to find the words to express herself."

"What....?"

"Someone...."

"What....?"

"Someone wants me to...."

"Antonia... say it..."

"Some things want me to do somethin' to you."

"What....?"

"Kill you."

As the impact of those words registered on Winston's tired eyes, he didn't look angry, upset, or even scared. Just confused. Also, this was when Antonia noticed that his left eye was now grey instead of blue and lazy, too. It didn't focus on her like the right one did.

"Why....?"

"I don't know."

"Who....?"

"I don't know. Some sort of ghosts. They speak to me in my mind."

"Tiger... you... OK...?"

"No, Turtle, I ain't."

"What... is going... on?..."

"I died."

“You... what...?”

"I died. I was all alone at home and so miserable. I never met another man like you, Winston, and my life was terrible after we was separated. I was disabled, in cripplin' pain day after day, and I just felt so old and ugly."

“I.. always.... told you.... you.... beautiful....”

"But I never believed it. Not really. And the older I got, the more I hated my body. The more I hated life. So I started lookin' at young women on social media, young black women who had lives I didn't. And I'd touch myself when I looked at them."

“You like.... girls....?”

"No, no, it wasn't that. It wasn't about them, it was that I needed to look at them to forget how shitty my life was, but the more I looked, the more I realised I'd never be them. And it hurt. It hurt so much to know that I'd never be the one thing I wanted more than anythin' in the world. So I touched myself to feel better."

There was an incredibly long silence as the two did nothing but share emotionally charged eye contact. As bewildered as Antonia was, Winston was even more so. This was perhaps too much for him to process, and he looked like he thought he might still be dreaming.

"You always.... said.... only that.... and me.... made you.... happy..." he finally added.

"And it was true, but after what happened to you and what they did to me, I ain't never feel anythin' down there ever again."

“What did.... they do.... to.... you....?” Winston asked, tears forming in his eyes.

"Somethin' bad. I don't wanna say."

However, it was with this statement that Antonia remembered what the racist mob implied they were going to do to Winston all those years before. It was a realisation that gave her an icy yet sinking feeling deep in her gut.

"Oh my God," she gasped, terrified to hear the answer to her upcoming question.

“What.... did they.... do to.... you? What did they do to it?"

“They.... removed.... it....”

A dam of heartbreak burst in Antonia's soul, bringing with it torrents of more tears, wails, and sobs as she hugged Winston tightly.

"Oh my God. Oh my God!"

"It's.... OK..."

"NO! NO IT NUH ALRIGHT! IT NUH RASS ALRIGHT! IT NUH RASS ALRIGHT!"

"Don't cry.... Tiger..."

"No! No! It's not right!" Antonia sobbed, laying her head on his chest.

“Was a long.... time.... ago...”

"But that don't make it OK! Look what those fuckin' bastards took from you!"

"Made....my peace..."

"I HAVEN'T!"

"It's OK..."

"I haven't."

Antonia collapsed into a crumpled heap on top of the body of the love of her life, emptying her tear ducts all over his hospital gown while he stroked her head lovingly.

“You.... know what.... you.... need....?”

"What?"

"Circular.... back.... rub...."

It had been over half a century since she'd heard those words, and their shock made Antonia laugh in genuine happiness. Giggling softly like the teenager she was when they were separated, she collapsed further into Winston's aura.

With her head resting snugly against his now frail chest, she listened intently as the familiar heart not heard in decades slowly beat within his rib cage. It was slower and weaker than before, but she'd still recognise its signature anywhere.

That was Winston's heart.

She'd finally found him.

She'd found Winston.

"I'd have stayed by you, Winston. What they did to you wouldn't have meant nothin' to me. I'd have stayed by you even if you had no arms or legs. You my human," she said tearfully.

Winston said nothing, and neither did Antonia; he just continued to stroke her back in the soothing way that never failed to melt her troubles. After about a minute of silence, he finally spoke.

"You lose.... the baby....?"

Antonia's audible wails gave Winston his answer. Together, they lay without speaking for another three minutes before she continued.

"I ain't never been able to feel much down there since what they done did to me that day. Maybe a tiny bit, but nothin' much. That day, I lost the only three things that gave me joy. But one day, I felt something.

One day, when I was old, I felt somethin' like I used to. It was so beautiful, strong, overwhelmin', I needed more, so I kept goin', I kept touchin' myself. But it went away. The feelin' vanished quick. I spent decades chasing that feelin', and I had it back for maybe a minute."

"What did.... you do....?"

"I kept goin', harder and faster. I had to get the feelin' back; I just had to. But it never came. All I had was pain. A black pit of agony I couldn't escape no matter how much I tried."

"But.... you.... kept trying....?"

"Yeah, and I felt my body diein'. The strain was too much. I felt my life end. I died, Winston. Well, I was in a black space, and I heard the doctors working on me. Then I died. Fuckin' bastards let me die because I was lookin' at pictures of black women."

"Really....?"

"Yeah. But I heard a voice. It asked if I wanted to have everythin' I ever wanted and I said yes. Then I had an orgasm and opened my eyes in this body."

"My.... God..."

"But that ain't it, Turtle, there's more."

"What....?"

Antonia didn't say anything. She was clearly trying to muster the courage to speak.

"What....?"

"The voice that gave me this body sent me to kill whoever was in this room."

"Me....?"

"They ain't say you was here, but yeah."

"What.... if you.... don't kill.... me....?"

"That don't matter."

"Answer.... the....question....."

"Mi nah go do it"

"What.... happens....?"

"I ain't gonna do it, Turtle!"

"Answer.... me."

Antonia raised her head off Winston's chest and gazed into his now grey and blue eyes. She wanted to speak and tried to do just that, but she couldn't. Her lips and lungs were paralysed.

"What?..."

"I... think... I'll... die..." she finally replied.

"Really...?"

"I died in that hospital. My body is dead. Antonia don't live no more. If I don't do what they want, I don't get this body, and I think that means I'm dead."

"Kill.... me..."

"What?"

"Kill.... me..."

"I can't."

"You.... can..."

"I just found you again."

"Tiger.... do it..."

"I can't bear to lose you. I can't."

"Look.... at me. I'm.... an old.... man.... and I'm.... tired. My life's.... over. I'm ready.... to meet.... my end. The only reason.... I kept going.... was to see you again.... and now.... I have. Now I know.... death ain't.... the end. I've got no reason.... to stay. Do.... what you need.... to do.... Tiger... I'll.... find you.... on the other side."

"Turtle, I can't."

“You can.... you.... will.... We’re gonna.... be together.... forever.....”

"Winston, I can't."

"It's OK. I’ll.... go to.... the.... other side.... and wait.... for you. I'll.... find you.... when you die..."

"Turtle, I can't!"

"You... can...."

"I can't!"

Horrifically, the skin on Antonia's body began to char, wither, and rot as she morphed into the walking dead right in front of Winston. She moaned in fear and anguish, but surprisingly, he wasn't scared.

Shocked, yes, but not scared. He definitely wasn't. In fact, he continued smiling at her in utter defiance of her physical circumstances, seemingly determined to show his apparent comprehension of the utterly incomprehensible.

"Do it", he spoke softly. “I don’t.... have.... long.... left. I want to go.... on.... my... own terms."

Antonia didn't want to do that. She couldn't bear the thought of it. She wanted nothing more than to spend her remaining days with the love of her life.

"I love you, Winston Poole."

She wanted to rest her head on his chest for hours, days, weeks, months, and if his health allowed it, years.

“I love you.... too.... Antonia Hoell.”

But the more she looked into his eyes, the more she saw the truth. He wasn't just ready to die.

"I love you."

He wasn't just willing to let her kill him.

"It's OK.... My time has.... gone."

He wanted to die.

"Mi love yuh so much."

She saw it in his eyes.

“Make me.... a.... promise.”

She saw over half a century's worth of physical pain and mental confusion.

"What?"

She saw the endless humiliation he suffered from his mutilation and frustration at his inability to be the man he once was.

"I don't know.... what you've.... gotten into.... but you.... need to.... get out.... of it..."

He couldn't even remember her name.

"I don't know what to do."

He couldn't even remember her name.

"I love you so much."

Young Antonia kissed old Winston passionately, with tears streaming down her cheeks. It was long, soft, sensual, and loving.

"Cover.... my nose.... and mouth. You.... can.... do it.”

Antonia did as she was told and put her left hand over Winston's nose, planting a long kiss on his forehead.

"It's OK.... Tiger.... It's OK. You.... can.... do it...”

With fresh tears streaming down both of their cheeks Antonia covered his mouth with her right hand and squeezed tightly, forming an airtight seal.

After that, she leaned down next to the ear of her one true love and kissed it softly. After about 30 seconds, he began to shudder slightly.

"Turtle, mi waan thank yuh fi everyting yuh do fi mi. Di memories mi have wid yuh a di happiest inna mi life, an' mi blessed fi even meet yuh," she said in patois.

Winston took his trembling hand and placed it on top of her own as his body started to spasm. She kissed his ear softly before continuing.

"I never met a man who could hold a candle to you, and I never will."

After a minute, Winston's spasming became even more powerful. He gripped Antonia's hand tightly and turned his head to look at her. As his body convulsed with the throes of death, her eyes convulsed with fear and love.

Together, the two soulmates gazed lovingly at each other as the light of consciousness slowly faded from Winston's eyes.

Eventually, he was completely gone. Antonia didn't know how much time had passed before that happened, nor did she care.

All she knew was that the eyes that were previously so vibrant were now dull and devoid of life, leaving her soul just as vacant.

There she stayed, her own eyes now beetroot red and her cheeks awash with salty tears as she cried a river of pain onto the lifeless chest of the love of her life.

"You did well, Antonia. We approve..." came the staccato feminine voices once again echoing directly into her mind.

Antonia realised just how much she hated them. How much she hated Kalizar. She was trapped in a dangerous situation from which she might not be able to escape.

"WHY DID YOU MAKE ME DO THAT?!"

No reply. Silence abounded all around. Kalizar was gone.

"WHY DID YOU MAKE ME KILL HIM?!"

Silence there, and nothing more.

"WHY YUH MEK MI KILL HIM?! WHY YUH MEK MI KILL HIM?! WEH YUH DEH?! WEH YUH DEH?! ANSWER MI?!"

Silence there, and nothing more.

She laid on Winston's still warm but completely lifeless chest without a hope in the world. The best day of her life was simultaneously the worst.

In the dim light, the shadows around her seemed to writhe, drawing closer, darkening as they crept along the floor, almost as if reaching out to pull her deeper into the darkness Kalizar had woven.

She couldn't shake the feeling that she was no longer alone, that the shadows bore witness to her terrible choice.

"Why did you make me kill him?!" she sobbed.

"WHAT THE FUCK!?"

And this was the moment Antonia heard a voice, one familiar as day but completely unexpected.

This was the moment she remembered that the door to Winston's bedroom was unlocked and wished to God that this wasn't the case.

This was the moment when Antonia looked up to see Blake, of all people, standing in the doorway in utter disbelief.

The moment she saw that his eyes were starting to tear.

"WHAT THE FUCK!?"

The moment she saw his trembling hands quickly forming into a tight fist.

"WHAT THE FUCK!?"

22 | TO TRUST A WHITE WOMAN

ANTONIA | Queens: February 14, 1965

Things were getting serious. Life threatening. Deadly. Antonia was at The Plaza Hotel in New York discussing campaign strategies over the phone with Malcolm when it happened. Sadly, however, he was home with his wife, Betty and their children.

Antonia liked Betty; she liked her very much, and the two had a respectful and amicable relationship, which she appreciated. Of all the mistrust and mild hostility she faced from Malcolm's organisation, the least seemed to come from her. For whatever reason, Betty appeared to trust Antonia and maybe even somewhat admire her too, which wasn't unappreciated.

The fact that she trusted Antonia enough to work alone with her husband wasn't lost on her and meant everything. Of course, whether that was down to some great insight into Antonia's character or the fact that she knew Malcolm would never again touch a white woman was anyone's guess, but ultimately, it didn't matter.

They had a friendly, cordial, and respectful relationship. It seemed they both understood they were on the same team.

In fact, Betty had been instrumental in the search for Winston's family, putting out feelers in community groups and churches all across the northern states. They hadn't been found yet, but with her and Malcolm's hard work adding to the sheer size of their network, Antonia guessed it wouldn't be long.

Provided they were alive.

Antonia had noticed that most of Malcolm's team had come to hold a somewhat grudging respect for her devotion to their cause.

Did they like her?

Not particularly.

Did they trust her?

Not particularly.

Why?

Because her presence was a constant reminder of her privilege and the oppression they had suffered for their entire lives.

Antonia represented institutional racism just by her mere existence, and they clearly didn't like that.

However, the value she brought to their cause over time couldn't be denied.

Her unassuming appearance as a wealthy white woman allowed her to move through circles otherwise closed off to the movement. She navigated high-society events and leveraged her connections to discreetly gather information, raise funds, and secure resources crucial to Malcolm's operations.

One of her most significant contributions came when she helped organise a fundraiser with several influential and wealthy donors sympathetic to civil rights but hesitant to engage directly with Black activists. Antonia acted as a go-between, using her charm to gather substantial donations that kept the organisation afloat during critical periods.

Additionally, she quietly passed along valuable intel about government surveillance and police activities, information she obtained through her husband's connections in the press.

Antonia even arranged for discrete safe houses and transportation for those who needed to move undetected across state lines, all at considerable risk to her own safety. The simple fact was that while many in the organisation still struggled with the concept of trusting a white woman, they couldn't deny that her efforts were effective.

Antonia used her privilege as a weapon against the system, slipping through the cracks of segregation and racism to work behind the scenes, all while deflecting attention away from the more visible members of the movement. And such, as said before, her commitment, while initially doubted, was now respected, albeit grudgingly.

She had become a bridge between worlds, a tool that Malcolm X himself saw the value in, even if he never admitted it or fully let his guard down around her. Antonia was an outsider who had forced her way in, her relentless dedication making it difficult for anyone to argue against her being there.

She had lost count of how many times she'd been told she was like no white girl ever and honestly didn't know how to take it. On the one hand, it was clearly a compliment. But, on the other hand, being compared to the bastards who hurt Winston made her want to put her fist through a wall.

Still, she, Malcolm, and his family had much more pressing matters to attend to because if it wasn't clear before, it was now painfully apparent that somebody wanted him dead. Someone or some group had actually set his house ablaze to kill him, his wife, and their sleeping children.

Everyone was stunned.

Antonia didn't even know how to process it.

One moment, they were discussing sources of funding and planning the logistics of a proposed trip to India, and the next, she heard the mother of all commotion down the line as his wife Betty screamed blue murder about there being a fire. The situation went from zero to 100 in the blink of an eye.

Antonia didn't even know how to process it.

From what she'd heard, Malcolm dropped the phone and sprang into action like a man possessed, navigating the rapid inferno to get his wife and children to safety. Antonia then tried to hang up to call the police.

Still, as Malcolm had left his phone off the hook, she couldn't do a damn thing but sit and listen for sixty frustrating seconds before she threw on her jacket and shoes and headed to Harlem at top speed.

On the way there, she asked herself who could have done this, but the truth was that it could have been anyone.

The police.

The FBI.

Someone from the Nation of Islam.

A spy from within Malcolm's camp.

The possibilities were endless, and honestly, Antonia was scared because she knew she'd likely be seen as a suspect. Not in the eyes of the law but in those of Malcolm's inner circle, i.e. the only eyes that mattered.

She was genuinely terrified.

Not only for his safety, not just for his family's safety, but for hers. In fact, as her taxi brought her closer to his neighbourhood, she asked herself what the hell she was doing at least five separate times. There was no chance she wouldn't have fingers pointed at her. No chance in hell. Her safety could be in real danger.

The intelligent thing to do would have been to turn the taxi around, head back to her hotel at high speed, quit the organisation and forget Malcolm X ever existed. That would have been the smart thing to do.

But, alas, while Antonia certainly was no fool, nobody anywhere had ever accused her of being either intelligent or a quitter.

She wasn't going anywhere, she was going to help Malcolm X as much as she could right until the bitter end.

By any means necessary.

But now Antonia had to focus on the big picture because the real perpetrators were still at large. Also, this wasn't just an explicit attempt on Malcolm's life, it was also a warning. There were those who hated his powerful message, despised his outspoken personality, and yearned to see him fall or be psychologically broken.

Seemingly by any means necessary.

Malcolm would need increased security at every last one of his events and at his home, too, from this point forward. Round-the-clock protection to ensure his safety was of paramount importance, but to be frank, Antonia knew that wouldn't happen. The danger surrounding him had grown increasingly dire for months. Still, the police had ignored all of her requests for extra protection.

And she knew exactly why.

To them, Malcolm X wasn't a freedom fighter or a hero. He was an amalgamation of a dumb nigger who needed to know his place and a domestic terrorist they needed to neutralise. Irrespective of whether or not they had anything to do with what was happening, they sure as hell weren't going to lift a finger to stop it.

The only people Antonia knew Malcolm could trust were her, his wife, Clarence 37X Butler, and John Ali. Everyone else was up for suspicion, especially his slimy bodyguard Gene Roberts with his bitch ass.

There was something about that man that rubbed her the wrong way ever since she first laid eyes on him, and the feeling was clearly mutual. She could tell he didn't really believe the things he was pretending to believe. She didn't know how she knew it, but she knew. She just did.

She didn't trust him.

His aura wasn't pure.

But as just stated, Gene Roberts also didn't like Antonia. They had a contentious relationship which went much deeper than the fact she once broke his bitch ass nose. Everyone else seemed to buy into him, but she didn't, and he could sense it. Something about that made him very uncomfortable.

Antonia could tell. She knew.

She didn't trust him.

His aura wasn't pure.

With his bitch ass.

When she arrived at Malcolm's house, a crowd of onlookers had gathered as firefighters fought to subdue the blaze. Malcolm's wife, Betty, sat with the children a few feet away as he stood next to Antonia and looked her suspiciously in the eye.

"Malcolm. They're coming for you," Antonia said honestly.

"They?" he asked, studying her eyes closely for the tiniest hint of deception.

"They," she replied, factually and with emphasis. No deception to be found.

"How do I know this wasn't you?" he asked seriously.

"You don't, and that's my fuckin' point. We need to step up your security," Antonia replied, looking him right in the eye without flinching.

"You come here making all of these claims about wanting to help make things better for black folks..."

"And I mean every fucking word."

"But yet, here you are, just after my home has been firebombed."

"You think I'm stupid?! You think I ain't know you'd suspect me!? I knew, but I came anyway because I care about you and want to tell you face to face that this wasn't me!"

A long but tense silence followed in which Malcolm and Antonia did nothing but stare at each other's eyes.

"I ain't do this, Malcolm."

"So you say."

"Don't be a fuckin' idiot."

"What the hell did you just call me?"

"I ain't call you anythin'; I told you not to be a fuckin' idiot, and you know why?"

"Why?"

"Because I already done said we to step up your security, Malcolm. We got enemies. I been sayin' this."

"We?" he asked, still scanning her eyes for deception but finally starting to see that there was none to be found.

"We," Antonia replied seriously. "I don't care what you think of me. I know you don't fully trust me and never will. I get it and I know why but that don't matter because what matters is the mission. You too important to our cause, Malcolm. We can't have nothin' bad happen to you."

"I'll accept whatever plan Allah lays out for me."

"Or you will keep yourself and your family alive so you can bring in a new world for our people."

"I've got bigger problems to deal with than that, Antonia."

"Like what?!"

"My home's just been firebombed. I'm standing outside the remains barefoot with few clothes on my back and no money in my pocket. Hell, I don't even have pockets to put the money I don't have in."

"I can give you money."

"Not necessary. I'm saying I need to figure something out."

"I can give you money."

"That won't be necessary."

"Malcolm, stop being proud and accept the help."

"I don't need it."

"Yes, you do."

"Still trying to prove yourself to me."

"This has nothing to do with that."

"Then what is it?"

"When we started workin' together, I said I was gonna help you any way I could. I said my man got money. He rich, Malcolm. He got plenty of money, and he a whorein' racist who don't give a damn 'bout me. Just use that white man's money. Call it reparations for slavery."

"Are you sure?"

"This ain't the time for pride, Malcolm. You homeless, right?"

"I am," Malcolm replied before looking over at his wife and children. "We are."

"Then let me help. Tell me how much money you need, and it's yours."

"Thank you."

"You got snakes in this organisation, Malcolm. But I promise I ain't one of them."

"Who thought the day would come when I would begin to trust a white woman?"

"Don't y'all always say the Lord works in mysterious ways?"

"That's Christians. We say Allah's ways are beyond our understanding," Malcolm replied with a smile.

At that moment, Gene Robert's' bitch ass appeared on the scene, causing Antonia's slight smile to turn into a snarl. In fairness, he clearly wasn't pleased to see her either, as evidenced when he walked straight up to her, looked her dead in the eye and said:

"Strange timing, you showing up right when all this goes down."

Antonia didn't dignify his comment with a response. She simply bit her lip in anger while defiantly meeting his gaze.

"Brother Malcolm, haven't we questioned before what it means to let an outsider walk our path? She's not one of us, and she never will be."

"Excuse me?" Antonia asked.

"Faith, blood, and history. You don't share any of it. And it shows."

"Want me to break your nose again?"

"Prepared to face the consequences of making that attempt?"

"You two, this isn't helping. We're on the same side," Malcolm said.

"Having her in the mix, Malcolm... it's like leaving the door open and wondering why the wolves wander in."

"You think I did this? If I did, I'd be a million miles away from here by now."

"Malcolm, I'm telling you, she's not one of us. Feels more likely she's here carrying someone else's agenda. Maybe the NYPD's, maybe worse," said Gene suspiciously.

"If the NYPD were going to put a spy in our camp, you really think they'd be dumb enough to send a white woman?" Antonia retorted.

"This isn't helping," Malcolm said.

"If it were me, I'd use one of his bodyguards," Antonia continued.

"Stop this," Malcolm commanded.

"Who better to plot Malcolm's downfall than a member of his inner circle who knows his whereabouts and is trusted to keep him safe, too?" Antonia pressed. "Seems perfect to me."

"You're lucky I'm a good man because if not, your family would be filing a missing persons report tomorrow," Gene snarled.

"Do your worst, nigga. I ain't runnin'."

"Then again, you have no one who truly loves you, do you? A husband who's never there, a 'family' who abandoned you... and the ones who didn't? They did things to you that no one deserves. Well, most at least."

"Gene," Malcolm said firmly.

"Nobody's watching out for you, least of all here. You're just... nothing," Gene continued, looking Antonia dead in the eyes as she looked back without flinching.

"Alright, that's it, stop. Stop this right now," Malcolm said, raising his voice to a commanding pitch.

With that, Antonia and Gene both softened and relaxed their postures. They didn't like each other, that much was sure, but not nearly enough to disrespect Malcolm.

We can't afford to argue amongst ourselves. We need to think and focus on the real enemy," Malcolm continued.

"My first thought is Newark," Antonia said thoughtfully.

"Is that right?"

"Yeah. Lot of them niggas be loyal to Elijah Muhammad and they angry 'bout the shit you been sayin' 'bout him. People say he talkin' 'bout you like you a problem that needs fixin'."

How the hell do you know that, white girl?" Gene asked incredulously.

"Cause I pay attention."

"Malcolm, this white woman's just trying to pit you against your own people. We don't have reason to think this was the Nation of Islam or anybody in no stupid mosque in New Jersey; it's probably just some crazed lunatic. We just need to wait for the police to get their shit together..."

"The police don't want to help us, you fuckin' idiot. They probably in on it. Look how long we been out here waiting on them and they still ain't show up!"

"You have a point there," Malcolm nodded thoughtfully.

"Malcolm, what are we gonna do?!" Antonia asked.

"I need to sit down with Elijah Muhammed. Antonia, contact his people immediately. We definitely need more security, too, but only men who have been thoroughly vetted and we can fully trust. Gene, look into that yesterday. As for the police, I want both of you to study their reactions for signs of deception or glee when they arrive. If they had something to do with this, we'll be able to tell."

"OK," said Antonia,

"Got it," said Gene.

As firefighters continued to battle the blaze, the otherwise black night sky was now alight in hues of red and orange as the resulting heat sent beads of sweat dripping down the necks of all present.

The scent of burning wood, oil, plastic, and rubber permeated the air as Malcolm gave Antonia a brief nod before walking away to check on his wife and children.

After that, Antonia stood deep in thought, pondering how to implement Malcolm's orders but without an honest clue how. What would happen if Elijah Muhammad declined the offer of a sit-down?

Then what? Also, could and should they reach out to the Mosques in Newark to broker a truce? Could Gene be relied on to provide extra security, and if not, what should Malcolm do instead?

She just didn't know, but she did see the situation was grim. The climate around Malcolm X was more foreboding than the flaming sky around his blazing home. Something needed to happen; that much was obvious, but what? What could they do?

What should they do?

But alas, while Antonia definitely was no fool, she certainly was no genius, and this dilemma taxed her mental faculties to the limit. With that said, while she wasn't sure what the next course of action should be, one thing she knew for sure was that she was going nowhere.

Despite their distrust of her, Malcolm and his wife Betty were the closest thing to family Antonia had and his movement was the only thing that gave her life meaning. Without it, she might as well be dead anyway because nothing else mattered.

But then, an uncomfortable feeling in the back of her neck told her she was being watched. Hence, she turned around to see Gene Roberts using his eyes to burn a hole through her flesh.

She calmly folded her arms and looked back as the two made painfully aggressive eye contact. Both stared daggers at the other, and both refused to be the first to back down or look away. It was a battle of wills, a contest for dominance that Antonia was going to make damn sure she didn't lose.

It would be another two and a half minutes before a winner would be crowned.

23 | FIGHTING TO LIVE, READY TO DIE

ANTONIA & KARA | New York Residential Home: Present Day

Blake's balled fist hit Antonia's jaw like a sledgehammer from hell, ricocheting her brain against her skull. Within seconds, she'd lost all track of where she was, having forgotten down from up and right from left.

Dancing, twirling, churning stars proliferated in her field of vision, making it almost impossible to see, let alone remember what the hell was happening. And seconds later, his fist cracked her again, this time flush on the nose. Searing pain erupted in her skull from temple to skeleton, but what was worse was that Blake wasn't stopping.

Blake wouldn't stop.

He was right on top of her, driving repeated punches into her face. He was trying to end her.

"WHAT THE FUCK DID YOU DO?! WHAT THE FUCK DID YOU DO?!" he screamed.

His voice trembled with utter heartbreak, a deep and genuine pain which ironically brought Antonia back to the present moment.

"YOU KILLED HIM! YOU FUCKING KILLED HIM! YOU KILLED MY GRAMPS!"

She couldn't believe what was happening. She couldn't process it. Blake was Winston's grandson? It didn't make sense.

DIDN'T THEY MUTILATE WINSTON?! DIDN'T THEY KILL HIS ABILITY TO HAVE CHILDREN?!

"BLAKE! STOP! STOOOOPPPP!"

But Blake wouldn't stop. He just wouldn't stop. He was all over her, pinning her down to the cold, tiled floor with those overwhelmingly powerful arms and core. The same body which had brought her to exquisite realms of pleasure on so many occasions was now solely focused on terminating her existence.

"YOU KILLED HIM!" he screamed, saliva leaking from his own mouth all over Antonia's face.

She tried to get her hands up to stop his fists but might as well have been trying to hold back a tidal wave with a piece of string.

Said fists drove right through her hands like they weren't even there, slamming them back into her face with devastating force. She was bleeding. She didn't know which blow had caused it, but her face was bloody, and that blood leaked into her eyes, stinging them and coating her vision in a thick crimson hue.

"WHY WHY WHY DID YOU DO IT WHY?!"

Antonia was tired. Exhausted. Spent. Not only from trying in vain to protect herself from Blake's overwhelming onslaught but from everything.

She was tired of life.

Tired of being.

Tired of living.

A near century's worth of struggle and pain was too much to bear, and this was the coup de grace. This was the straw that finally snapped the camel's spine.

She couldn't go on like this. She just couldn't. She wouldn't. Not now. Not after she'd been forced to kill the only man she'd ever loved.

Not now.

Not now that Blake wanted her dead. What was she going to do? Fight him back? Kill him too?

And then, an eerie whisper echoed in her mind, darker than the night itself. Each word laced with an ancient, twisted promise.

"Sever soul from bone.

Claim this fate, make it your own".

She felt a chill coil around her spine as if an unseen force had slithered through the darkness to crawl beside her, urging her hand.

"Blood must be shed.

End him now, leave words unsaid."

"NO! NO! MI NAH GO DO IT! MI NAH GO HURT BLAKE TOO!"

"WHO THE FUCK ARE YOU TALKING TO?!"

"NUH MEK MI DO IT! MI A BEG YUH, NUH MEK MI DO IT! "

"YOU'RE FUCKING CRAZY!"

In an instant, a wildly sobbing Blake leapt off Antonia, darted to the body of Winston, aka his deceased grandfather and threw his arms around his lifeless form. Rocked with pain, she slowly picked herself up off the floor and staggered towards him.

"His essence you must take.

His body you must break.

Antonia stood next to Blake with a persistent torrent of tears streaming down her cheeks to match his own. He looked so distraught, so helpless; she just didn't know what to do.

All she felt was an overwhelming sense of guilt, shame, and a desire to set things right. A desire which had her fling her arms around Blake's chest just as he had his flung around Winston. It was a desire that ultimately proved foolish, leading to her taking yet another hard fist to the jaw.

Now, he was back on top of her. Now, he was using his unstoppable strength to smother her while fighting with the deadly intent of a tortured soul who'd just witnessed the murder of a loved one.

The punches were so fast, so intense, so brutal that Antonia couldn't do anything to stop them. She was powerless. Helpless. Even in her new, fit, strong, youthful body, she still couldn't do a thing to stop him.

And the more they fought, the more she saw that enraged glare in his eyes. Eyes that once were so full of affection and love were now anything but, and now Antonia realised the truth.

Blake was going to kill her.

And she deserved it.

Blow after blow rained down upon her jaw, but Antonia didn't mind; she welcomed it. It was all for the best. She deserved everything that was happening, and what's more, she was just tired.

Tired of the pain.

Tired of the torment.

Tired of the struggle.

And tired of life itself.

Winston was her only reason for living.

Her reason for being.

And now that reason was gone.

Winston was gone.

The kindest, sweetest, most loving human she'd ever met was no more, and it was all her fault.

She'd killed him. She'd killed the only person she'd ever truly loved, and whatever price she had to pay for that was more than sufficient.

Each successive blow brought pain, yes, but also a sense of peace.

A sense of calm.

While her young body was being blitzed with agony, her soul began to feel as light as a feather.

Lighter than it had felt in years, decades even.

With each bludgeoning blow her soul became awash within a tranquil ocean of joy. One of contentment. This was exactly where Antonia needed to be. This was precisely what she needed to do. She had to let Blake do this. She had to.

She wanted to.

Not that she could stop him if she tried.

Still, she was too tired, and besides, she deserved it.

Snowflakes gradually began to enter her field of vision. Tens of thousands upon millions of dancing crystalline white stars slowly formed in front of all she could see, including the man doing his best to end her existence.

Soon, she could see nothing but a dancing and pulsating field of static. Soon, for all the pain she knew she was experiencing, she just couldn't identify with it. She couldn't even locate it.

And nor did she care.

Antonia slowly faded from this world into the next. Embracing the very oblivion which should have found her many decades before.

She was dying. Antonia was becoming one with death. She was finally dying.

And all was well.

She deserved this.

All was well.

Maybe she'd see Winston soon.

"You cannot perish, not just yet.

For Winston's soul, they crave to get."

"TIGER! TIGER HELP ME! TIGER HELP MEEEEEE!"

That was Winston. Hurting. Screaming. In pain.

Winston?!

And just like that, Antonia was snapped back to reality. The ocean of stars in her vision parted like the Red Sea as she locked eyes with the man attempting to smash her into oblivion.

"TIGER! YOU GOTTA HELP ME, PLEASE TIGER!"

"WINSTON?!"

"DON'T SAY HIS FUCKING NAME! DON'T YOU DARE SAY HIS FUCKING NAME!"

That was Blake, screaming at the top of his lungs.

"Winston's soul they'll feast upon.

If you defy what must be done."

"NO! NO! PLEASE DON'T HURT HIM! WINSTON?! TURTLE?! TURTLE ARE YOU THERE?!"

"YOU'RE INSANE! YOU'RE FUCKING INSANE!"

As Antonia and Blake fought, Kalizar's eerie words echoed throughout her mind. As Blake's rage erupted, his words lashing like barbed wire across her mind, a coiled chill seeped into Antonia's bones.

The air thickened, time dilated, and an ancient whisper slithered into her thoughts in the dim stillness between breaths. It was cold. It was venomous. It was undeniable.

"Tasks await, a quest to heed,

Defy our words; his soul shall bleed.

In flames eternal, he will yearn.

Endless torment, no peace to earn.

For in your soul, his screams will tear.

Echoes of pain, cries of despair.

Guilt and blame, forever nigh.

Haunted by this until you die."

"NO! NO! NO! NO! PLEASE PLEASE! WINSTON!!"

"YOU FUCKING PSYCHOPATH!"

"BLAKE! STOP! STOP! STOOOOOPPP!"

But nothing could make him stop. Nothing would make him stop. Blake was a man possessed. Those eyes, those blue eyes, were filled with vehement rage.

He would stop at nothing until she was dead. But that couldn't happen.

"I CAN'T DIE!"

Winston's soul would be lost if she did, and she couldn't let that happen.

"I CAN'T DIE!"

"Antonia Hoell, you know the game.

Erase Blake's life and end his name.

Resolve to do what must be done.

Then, claim his heart and be the one.

A soul for life, your choice is clear.

Winston or Blake, whose end is near?"

"I'M NOT DOING IT! I'M NOT KILLING BLAKE!"

And she wouldn't. She couldn't. But the pain was intense. Otherworldly. Unbearable, her skull felt like it was being repeatedly struck with flaming meteors. But why couldn't she just pass out? Why couldn't she just die like Blake wanted?

"WHY CAN'T I JUST DIE?!"

"Not until your work is complete."

"I DON'T WANT TO DO THIS ANYMORE!"

Kill Blake to save Winston. Could she even do it? Did she have it in her?

This was when Antonia felt another blow rock her jaw. A blow that did real damage. A blow that fractured said jaw and left her unable to talk. A blow which sent a white-hot streak of pain searing from her brain to her neck.

Antonia staggered as the blow fractured her jaw, pain flooding her senses, the shock of it like a lightning bolt searing through her. Yet, as she should have crumpled, something dark and insidious took hold.

Antonia's body surged forward, moving with a ruthless precision that was not her own, hands clamping down on his arms with a strength that defied her form.

She slid behind him, her chest pressing against his back, trapping him in an embrace as cold and relentless as death itself. His struggles grew frantic, but she somehow held him fast, her body an unyielding cage around him, her strength terrifying, final, unstoppable.

She could feel him struggling, but he couldn't get free somehow. She could feel him fighting with everything he had, but he couldn't free himself.

WHY?!

Blake was so strong; why couldn't he get free. Why? Why couldn't he free himself?

Antonia then watched on in horror as her arms locked themselves around his throat and began to squeeze with a strength she didn't think was humanly possible. Within seconds, he began to choke, splutter, and convulse.

"NO! NO! NO!"

It was Kalizar. It had to be.

"WHAT ARE YOU DOING?! NOOOOOO! DON'T KILL HIM!"

Blake thrashed wildly like a fish on dry land, trying to get Antonia off his back. He repeatedly slammed into walls and tables but to no avail. Her body was now just too strong. It was Kalizar. This was Kalizar's doing.

"STOP! STOOOOPPP! LEAVE HIM ALONE! PLEEEEEASEEEEE!"

Blake's struggles were becoming weaker by the second. His body was being denied the necessary oxygen to fuel his muscles and, hence, save his own life.

His brain was being denied the requisite oxygen to stay conscious and operate his body. Blake was weakening rapidly. He soon slumped to the floor, slowly twitching and spasming on the spot with Antonia still on top.

"STOOOOPPPP! STOOOPPPPP! LET HIM GOOOOO!"

But Kalizar wouldn't let go. Antonia's arms were wrapped tighter and tighter around Blake's neck with no sign of relenting. Soon, he was unconscious, but still, her hands wouldn't relent.

Still, they kept choking him. Still, they kept on trying to kill him.

Still, they wouldn't relent.

Antonia fought. She fought like a caged lion to pull them away. She couldn't lose Winston and Blake in one day. She couldn't kill Winston and Blake in one day. No way. No way in hell. Antonia was locked in a one-on-one battle with Kalizar not just for control of her body but for Blake's life.

But Kalizar was so strong, so unbearably potent.

It was like battling against a tank. But she had to keep fighting; she had to, Blake wasn't even moving now. He wasn't moving.

"HE'S NOT MOVING!"

He was unconscious. She had to do something.

"DON'T KILL HIM, DON'T!"

Antonia screamed, grunted, and strained, veins bulging out of her sweat-ridden forehead and merging with the fresh tears pouring from her blood-red eyeballs.

It was working.

It was working.

Somehow, some way, she managed to pull her arms about five inches away from his neck before her strength gave way, and they clamped down on it yet again.

She couldn't do it. She wasn't strong enough.

Blake's body was twitching in shock.

Blake was going to die.

This was when she heard the door to Winston's bedroom open.

"OH MY GOD!"

This was when she saw a young Asian female nurse standing quivering in the doorway, looking positively mortified.

"WHAT ARE YOU DOING?!"

What happened next was too fast even for Antonia's mind to process. All she knew was that she found herself leaping to her feet, darting to the nurse, and blasting her jaw with an explosive punch that had her unconscious well before her head hit the ground.

After that, she escaped.

Antonia ran at full speed through that corridor, out of the nursing home, and away into the night.

She genuinely didn't know if it was her controlling her limbs or Kalizar.

But then, somehow, amid the frenetic anxiety of sprinting for her life, not knowing if Blake was dead, and trying to deal with the fact she'd definitely killed Winston, she heard her phone ring.

There it was, vibrating incessantly against her leg with ever-increasing intensity. While she tried to pretend she didn't know who it was, deep down, there was no doubt. Deep down, she knew precisely who was contacting her. Deep down, she knew why she was going to answer them. Antonia needed to be punished. She needed to be humbled.

And with that, she grabbed her phone, looked at the screen, saw it was an unknown number, picked it up and cautiously said:

"Hello?

Only to hear an ominous yet electronically distorted male voice say:

"You evil fucking bitch, I knew you were vapid and shallow, but I didn't know you were capable of this. What the fuck's going to happen when the whole world discovers exactly who you are."

"Who is this?!" she cried.

"It doesn't matter who this is. What matters is that you're fucked. What matters is that now the whole world will know exactly what you're all about."

It was him. Somehow, he knew exactly what she was doing and when.

But she had no idea how.

All she had was a deep feeling of panic, fear, loneliness, and dread.

She was in real trouble. And she didn't know what to do.

She didn't have a clue.

She just knew she was going to be caught, and all because of him.

Something about that made Antonia angry, a white-hot, surging anger that didn't belong to her. She felt it growing like a storm inside her chest, swirling and dark, edging out her fear and confusion with a new, dangerous clarity.

This wasn't Antonia's anger. This was Kara's rage.

Her breath quickened, her fingers tightening around the phone, a chill running down her spine as strength spread through her veins. Kara wanted to scream, to tell the voice on the other end to run, to hide, because if she ever found that prick, she was going to do unspeakable things to him.

The thought flickered through her mind like a lit match, sparking something deeper.

Antonia could feel herself slipping, her fear dissolving under the weight of Kara's dark determination.

She could almost hear Kara's voice. It was steady. It was focused. It was calm, urging her forward to hunt and destroy.

She'd already killed Winston and might have killed Blake, too. What harm was one more?

The idea settled over her, cold and sure, as if Kara herself had reached through the void and placed it in her mind.

And why not?

Why shouldn't Kara murder her stalker?

Why the fuck not?

24 |

LOVE, LUST, & DAMNATION

KARA | Nondescript Hotel: Present Day

Hours later, Kara had paid cash to check herself into a cheap, run-down, and nondescript hotel and was now frantically pacing her room without a clue of what to do. She couldn't go home; Blake would have sent the police there. No. No, She couldn't do that. But then again, was Blake even alive? She had no idea. Not even one.

Didn't have a clue.

But still, she couldn't possibly have killed the nurse, and between her and him, surely that's what would have happened. But then again, how could the nurse have possibly known who she was? And what about her stalker, Hippocratic Oath? What would or could he have told the authorities? What did he know?

And how the fuck does he know it?!

Did he know where she was at that exact moment? He clearly had some way of tracking her, so maybe he knew where she was hiding?

He probably does!

She was completely in the dark, a terrifying state of affairs. Her only idea was that he'd found some way to hack her phone and track her via GPS or the microphone. She couldn't begin to think of how he could have done that, but it was her best idea, so she'd ditched her phone and bought a new burner with pre-paid credits and data en route to the hotel.

That has to be enough!

He was just one man, so there was no way he'd have been able to discover the details of her new device.

Is there?!

But still, there she was, alone. Waiting for the inevitable as her stomach became a churning chasm of dark emotions. Ice-cold blades of pain slowly serrated her gut alongside psychic flames of horror, which steadily burned her soul.

However, the more Kara stopped moving, the more she realised the true reason for this pain. It wasn't the thought of police capture; it wasn't her stalker, Hippocratic Oath, and it wasn't even Blake.

It was Winston.

Her beloved Winston. She'd waited over half a century to see him again and finally had. It had finally happened. She'd held his hand, kissed his lips, heard his voice and felt the warmth of his breath on her neck.

It was Winston.

Kara saw Winston. She saw her Turtle. He was old, yes. Tired, yes. Broken, yes. But it was him.

It was Winston.

The warm, grounded light of his being still shined through, even when trapped within the confines of an aged frame. He still made her feel safe like no other ever had. Those minutes she spent with him still felt like a lifetime of bliss.

And yet Kara still killed him.

I killed Winston.

It didn't matter that he told her to do it. It didn't matter that he'd said he was happy to go. She still did it.

I still did it.

She smothered him to death and felt his body tremble as he went. She looked into those beautiful, sweet blue eyes as the energy that made them so captivating was slowly drained away.

I saw it happen.

In fact, she continued to look into those same eyes after he died. She then saw them devoid of that energy, devoid of that spark. She saw Winston's eyes devoid of life and didn't know how to cope. Kara couldn't handle the guilt of what she'd done to the love of her life. She couldn't deal with the guilt of what she'd done to Blake.

And how the fuck are they related?! Blake's Winston's grandson?! Winston was the grandfather he talked about?!

What the fuck was going on?! How did this happen? Did she kill the only two men she'd ever truly cared about in one day?!

She couldn't handle it. She wanted to cry, scream, shout, curse, anything. She couldn't take the pain; she couldn't.

So with that, Kara stood in front of her mirror, stripped down to her red lacy underwear and admired her seductive body.

God damn, it was incredible.

God damn, she looked sexy.

Her curves were sensual, and her breasts were full, thick, and ample. Her butt was bulbous, her thighs were muscular and feminine, and her skin was a deliciously edible shade of caramel.

Gazing at her body helped, it helped a lot. Gazing at the divine vision of perfection that was as orgasm-inducing from head to toe as from heel to crown helped.

It helped a lot.

As did sliding her fingers underneath her panties. As did feeling them probe, caress, and stimulate her sensitive clitoris. All of the above sent a flood of dopamine washing throughout her system as her underwear slowly began to moisten.

Her breath deepening, she stared intently at her reflection, vividly remembering the likes and comments it had earned her on social media. She didn't need to look at her phone to imagine the multitudes of men who fantasised about her to the point of obsession.

She saw them in their hundreds of thousands, sitting hunched over their devices and stroking themselves to oblivion through the openings of their boxer shorts.

She saw the women who were intimidated by her body's perfection but couldn't bear to tear themselves away from looking at it. She saw the proud heterosexual women who, when confronted by her beauty, became awash with conflicting emotions their egos fought hard to suppress.

She saw all of the above and felt a soft satisfaction enter her spirit. It was a satisfaction that compelled her right hand to tap against her clitoris, slowly, sensually, but consistently, as her left hand trailed along her waist up to her breast and squeezed.

That pressure was everything; that pressure made her gasp. And, as Kara felt a stream of blood slowly course into her nipples, causing them to thicken with her fingers' deliberate touch, she shuddered at the throbbing waves of ecstasy that crashed against the shores of her consciousness.

Charged pulses stimulated her nervous system as a warm electrical vibration penetrated her ears and made her eyes glaze over.

She was forgetting.

Forgetting the pain.

Forgetting herself.

She was just being.

And the feeling was electric.

Electrifying.

Captivating.

It took her mind away to never-before-seen realms of pleasure as soft moans forced their way past her wet tongue and lips.

But then, somehow, and some way, Kara was no longer alone.

Suddenly, she was with Winston. Suddenly, Winston stood right behind her, but not as he had been before he died or when she knew him. Winston was now in the prime of life, in his early 30s, the same age as his grandson Blake, and every bit as handsome.

And just like his grandson, Winston's body was powerful and grounded with energy that was unapologetically masculine yet nurturing at the same time.

Energy he used to grab and spin Kara around on the spot before she looked deep into his piercing blue eyes as they looked right through hers.

Tilting her chin back with his chocolate fingers, Winston kissed her neck softly while her own hands continued to probe and explore her breast and clitoris.

She moaned, of course. She moaned in sweet, breathless pleasure as he pulled back and once again looked her close in the eye.

Deep in the eye.

Winston looked at her with a furious intensity reserved only for his nickname for her.

Tiger.

He stared into her very essence with the passion of a wild animal that had contained its fury for far too long. Winston stared through her eyes and past her heart to penetrate the quivering soul of the girl who resided within.

However, as he stood with his rock-hard cock pressed against Kara's thigh and his breath on her lips, she saw another figure enter from behind.

It was her.

It was who she used to be.

It was Antonia.

The young and white version of Kara.

They locked eyes for a second and smiled knowingly before Antonia looked at Winston and smiled again, stroking his face tenderly. Winston smiled back, and Antonia slid her tongue deep into his mouth while her hand stroked Kara's left breast and his hand stroked her right.

Kara took Winston's hard, thick, and veiny cock into her hand and slid her fingers down into Antonia's increasingly wet pussy. Antonia gasped, and Winston moaned as Kara slowly but rhythmically penetrated her pussy and stimulated his engorged tool.

Slowly, reality began to merge and distort. Slowly, time began to displace. Colours faded in intensity before tripling in brightness and coalescing into the surrounding air to create colours never-before-seen.

Nothing else existed. It was just Kara, Winston, and Antonia alone in a carnal realm of desire as Winston lifted Kara, wrapped her legs around his waist and unapologetically entered her with his cock.

She shuddered at its thickness, taking delight in every last inch of the penis she hadn't felt in over half a century as it began to drill her with increasing speed.

It was too good.

Too exquisitely painful, too delightful agonising, too blisteringly erotic.

God, it hurts. Fuck it hurts.

Winston's fucking cock fucking hurt. It was pain. Pain she'd forgotten. Pain she'd forgotten she needed and craved like no other. Pain she didn't know if she could take.

Kara's moans turned into gasps, cries and shrieks as Winston fucked her to the bleeding edge of insanity. Her legs and toes twitched like the death throes of a gunshot victim as Antonia took her pale white hand and firmly placed it over her mouth, stifling her moans.

"Shhhh," said Kara's younger self, putting her finger to her own lips as Kara's muffled noises caused a cushion of air against her palm.

However, none of this stopped Winston from continuing to drill Kara like she were his enemy. Each thrust was deliberate. Each thrust came with purpose. Each thrust came hard and deep into her cervix with a strength as intimidating as it was commanding.

And Kara felt the urge to surrender. She felt the overwhelming desire to yield to the unrelenting abuse that lovingly assaulted her vagina.

"Shut up," Antonia said firmly, her hand cupping Kara's lips.

But it wasn't enough; Kara couldn't keep quiet. Her muffled moans fought through the gaps in Antonia's hand to emerge into the atmosphere as powerless whispers of delirious submission.

She was weak.

Broken.

Defeated.

Powerless to overcome this sexual onslaught and wouldn't have had it any other way.

With every long, constant, aching, penetrative thrust, the love of her life turned her mind to mush, soul to mist, and pussy to jelly.

She saw stars, galaxies, and universes. She felt their presence all around. She felt them merge with her life force. Millions and billions of trillions and quadrillions of conscious life forms were everywhere the mind could fathom and anywhere it could not.

They were embedded into the air she breathed and immersed within the cells of her now chocolate skin. They floated into her ears with every sound she heard and she tasted their vibrant energies on her wet tongue.

But there was more.

The conscious entities that Kara now realised had permeated all of existence were not just conscious of themselves. They were also conscious of her.

Each and every one knew her by name. Each and every one found her situation highly amusing. But each and every one bore her no ill will and wished her nothing but the best. She felt their undying acceptance ooze into her vulva with every sustained thrust of Winston's long, thick, pulsating black cock.

And she never wanted that feeling to cease.

Antonia leaned in and kissed Kara passionately, sliding her tongue against hers in rhythmic unison with Winston's thrusts, stroking her cheeks tenderly while Kara's vagina was lovingly destroyed with force.

By now, Kara's limbs had lost all ability to reason with her brain, flailing and writhing into the ether as her lungs both hyperinflated and hyperventilated.

Kara couldn't breathe. She didn't know what was happening but knew she couldn't breathe. No matter what she did or how hard she tried, she couldn't take air into her lungs. She just couldn't. They were bereft of oxygen, heaving like never before in sexual futility.

She began to thrash wildly against Winston's hard body, but the more she did so, the less she had to breathe.

Or to live.

Her vision became an endless sea of colours. First ruby red, then emerald green, then golden yellow, and then a brilliant white. All while her young and sexy body struggled to function amidst intense vaginal assault and sadistic oxygen deprivation.

Somehow, her wild screams of delight flowed through Winston, through Antonia, fused with the giggling entities all around, and melted them into an ether of sexual bliss.

Kara was cumming, and it was going to be big.

Huge.

Unstoppable.

Awe-inspiring.

Jaw breaking.

And true to form, that orgasm hit her like a tidal wave of erotic violence. It ploughed through her vulva, clit, thighs, calves, twitching toes, and up to her back, aching breasts, engorged nipples, sweat-ridden neck, quivering lips, bulging dilated pupils, and disoriented brain.

She roared like a gazelle being devoured by an anaconda. She screamed like an abuse victim finally pushed acres past her breaking point. She cried like a goddess of universal life force revelling in the sadistic act of beautiful, murderous creation, which was her eternal birthright.

She didn't know how long that orgasm lasted. Nor did she care. Kara was lost to a sacred plane in which the laws of physics and relativity held no meaning. A place she'd never before seen but had somehow always known. One in which the concept of pain became a distant, fleeting memory as every fibre of her physical and spiritual beings was imbued with enduring, everlasting love.

By the time her cries, wails, moans, and orgasmic throes had faded into the ether from whence they came, her vision had begun to return to normal. Kara then realised she was lying on the warm carpeted hotel room floor with Antonia sitting square on her face.

Antonia's fat ass was pressed tightly against Kara's face as her wet pussy clung to her lips like honey-laced salt, smothering her moans and systematically robbing her of oxygen.

And still, Winston fucked Kara powerfully, rhythmically, intensely, perpetually.

He wouldn't stop, and she wanted him to.

She wanted him to stop.

She needed him to.

But she also needed him to keep going.

She needed him to fuck her like it was her last moment on earth.

She needed him to rail her with his cock until the laws of physics lost all meaning.

Until time and space collapsed inward and folded into a singular point.

But she still couldn't breathe.

No matter how hard she tried.

Breathing was futile.

She was fucking choking.

Resistance was futile.

She was fucking choking!

She had Antonia's bare ass smothering her face and Winston's cock ramming further into the unseen regions of her pussy, destroying parts she didn't think it was possible to reach.

Kara moaned into Antonia's dripping pussy, her now slick with salt-and-honey-tasting lips reverberating against the squelching vulva that suffocated her. Her arms spasmed and quivered. Her legs shook.

Her toes trembled. Her body vibrated like a pneumatic drill as the absence of the sweet oxygen of which she was being deliberately denied sent the cells of her beautiful body into shock.

She lifted her quivering arms and felt Antonia's breasts with her hands. Squeezing them, probing them, accepting their weight as their owner moaned in response.

"You gonna cum, Kara! You gonna fuckin cum!"

Who was that? Antonia? Or Winston? She didn't know. She wasn't sure. She recognised the vocal imprint, but her brain lost the ability to connect vocal imprints to human identities.

All she knew was that she was being fucked into madness as the buildup of CO2 in her bloodstream, mixed with the relentless pounding of Windston's engorged tool, sent her into a realm of shock reserved only for the most clinically insane.

“MMMMHUHFFFFGGGGHHHHH!”

It was building. The pressure was building. Increasing. Swelling. Throbbing. Ballooning. Bulging against the frontal lobes of her brain and slowly squeezing her consciousness out of her body. She was passing out. There was nothing she could do to stop it. She was passing out. Losing consciousness.

Dying.

Dying?

Dying.

Maybe she was dying.

Until Antonia randomly sat up from her face. Suddenly, a sudden gust of oxygen forced its way into her lungs with the reverse force of the vacuum of space.

Until the cells of her body sparkled with life-giving oxygen and until Antonia sat her fat white ass right back down on Kara's face and sent her spiralling over the edge of sexual insanity, hurtling headfirst into the abyss of primal psychosis.

"NGHGHGJGHGGHHHHHH!"

She babbled and gasped in a frenzy of hysteria as Winston's cock rammed her like a jackhammer. Antonia placed every last ounce of weight on top of her now sweat-ridden face and pussy tasting lips.

Kara's mind, lost in the throes of her fantasy, suddenly fractured with the cutting chill of a painful memory.

"But I'm serious, Peter. Like if I ever stoop so low, just put a knife in my throat. My fucking throat. You'd think a woman from her generation would know better than to be a fucking nigger lover."

The words echoed, sharp and unrelenting, slicing through her mind like shards of glass. A sickening knot twisted in her stomach, the rage rising fast, uncontrollable. Her teeth clenched, nails digging into her palms as the fantasy dissolved into the harsh reality of the past.

The fire within her burned hotter, surging through her veins, threatening to consume her. For a moment, she could hear the cruel laughter that followed those words. The fury was blinding, suffocating, a force that demanded to be unleashed.

But then, as suddenly as it had come, it receded. The present snapped back into focus. She was no longer in the memory. No longer standing powerless.

And just like that, she was back in the present, shook free from the shadow of a past as her body bucked and moaned in delight for a moment of eternity, thrashing wildly in the throes of passion as her second orgasm took her to a domain of delight she didn't know existed.

"AHHHHHHHHHHHHHHH!"

Kara was lost. Lost to herself, lost to the universe, and even lost to time and space. It was indescribable! Out of this world! Bullets of murderous pleasure tore every facet of her being, laying waste to everything in their path while somehow healing them at the same time.

She was a ship stranded in a thunderous night's sea with no captain to guide her. A lost plane spiralling from the heavens above to the ground below with no pilot to save her. A candle in a storm, her flame trembling in the fierce gusts, barely holding on as the darkness pressed ever closer.

But she wouldn't have had it any other way.

This orgasm was her destruction. Her beautiful, sweet, sensual, loving, caressing, dominant obliteration. It belonged to nobody else but Kara.

It was hers.

Hers to own.

Hers to cherish.

Hers to exalt.

With every passing second, that violent explosion of love cascaded throughout her being; she felt more and more at peace. There was a stillness in the chaos. Serenity in the agony. True joy was buried deep within the exquisite physical agony of sexual destruction to which she was being subjected.

It was everything to her. She was reborn from the flames. Reborn from the ashes. A true phoenix. The alpha and the omega. Death and rebirth. And as she died, so was she reborn.

However, as long as her orgasm lasted, it certainly did not last forever. It eventually abated. It eventually subsided. And then, much to Kara's dismay, she saw Winston and Antonia beginning to fade from existence right before her eyes. She tried to cling to them, of course; she did everything she could to hold on to them.

Kara grasped at those fading phantoms like a survivor of the Titanic clinging to a thin plank of wood in the ice-cold North Atlantic sea.

But it was all for nought.

She wasn't strong enough.

Try as she might, she couldn't hold onto them. Try as she might, she could do nothing to prevent them from evaporating into mist.

Disturbingly, the more they evaporated, the more reality restructured, and soon Kara realised that she wasn't actually lying on her back on the floor of her hotel room. She was still standing in front of her mirror with one hand cupping her mouth, the other deep inside her dripping pussy, and a puddle of her own making collecting on the floor between her painted toenails.

None of it was real.

She must have been standing there the whole time.

And then she heard a collection of whispers emanating from the air just behind her long neck. Whispers which spoke in unison but just ever so slightly out of sync. Whispers which created an eerie and unsettling echo that made the fine hairs of her long neck twist and turn.

"A sensual gift, we have bestowed.

Passion, lust, pain, and throes.

In pleasure's grip, you were astray.

But now, a life, you have to slay.

Before too long, the task shall fall.

A dark command, embrace the call.

A chilling dance, blood will be shed.

And by your hand, they will be dead."

And then, for the first time, Kara saw the entities she'd been communicating with.

"We are Kalizar."

Kalizar was a feminine being with three cackling heads that slowly rotated on the spot.

She slid into view behind Kara, smiling sadistically in the mirror as she squirmed in place, hunched over to one side, her body continuing to writhe and squirm like a stalking cobra.

Kara had already come to realise the real trouble she was in. Still, now that fact was crystallised beyond all rational ability to deny.

She had made a deal with the devil. And the price she would have to pay would far outweigh the exceptional gift she'd been given.

"If I do this, will you let Winston go?" Kara asked.

"Yes."

"Do you promise?"

"Yes."

"Will his soul be ok?!"

"Kill for us as we require.

And Winston's soul shall not expire."

"How do I know I can trust you?"

"Such is the beauty of duality."

Kara was in trouble.

She'd made a literal deal with the devil and had no idea how to get out. But something else was true. She didn't know how, and she didn't know where, but she'd seen this demon before. She didn't know how, and she didn't know where, but she definitely had.

She'd seen this demon before.

Or have I?

25 | ALL HELL BROKE LOOSE

ANTONIA | Audubon Ballroom: February 21, 1965

Antonia hardly knew where she was. The level of sexual excitement she'd experienced made it nearly impossible to think. Somehow, she'd had an extremely vivid experience of having sex with Winston and a beautiful black woman, and she didn't know what to make of it.

It didn't feel like a dream.

It felt just as real to her as standing in the Audubon Ballroom on that Sunday morning in New York. Her mind was hazy, confused, aroused, and she was moist in places she was embarrassed to be in public.

But she saw Winston. She felt Winston. She felt his energy. His beautiful face. His incredible body.

She felt him. He was there. He didn't speak, and he didn't have sex with her. But he was there. But why? Why didn't he have sex with her? Why only the black woman?

Why do I feel like I know that woman?

And why could Antonia feel every last inch of his deep thrusts into that woman's vagina?

And why did Antonia now feel like her own vagina was sore?

And where did all of that come from? She hadn't felt any sexual satisfaction in years, not even the tiniest drop, but suddenly, all of this? It didn't make sense.

She forcefully tried to snap back to reality just after three men walked by her booth. She'd seen one or two of them before; she was sure she had.

Are they from Newark? And are they carrying something? Did I charge them for their entries and forget I'd done it?

She didn't have a clue, but before she could call them back, a large group of smartly dressed men and women arrived at the booth to pay their entrance fees.

Just as with everyone else who'd happened by on either that or any other day she'd worked for Malcolm, they clearly wondered what the hell she was doing there. Seeing a white woman working with the biggest Civil Rights leader in America was jarring, and they clearly had questions.

Some weren't sure if they were even in the right place.

In fairness, she didn't want to be there herself. She was happy to be at the event to support it, but she'd rather have been in the shadows for this specific reason. She didn't want her presence to take the shine away from either Malcolm X or the movement itself.

All Antonia cared about was helping to usher in a new world of equitable treatment for black folk and nothing else.

However, several staff at the Audubon Ballroom hadn't turned up that day. Also, Elijah Muhammad had rejected her offers for a sit-down, and Gene Roberts had come up short in his search for additional security. Both had Antonia not wanting to leave Malcolm high and dry by not helping out.

She had to step up to the plate.

In any event, Antonia reassured that confused group that they were indeed in the right place, took their payments, and turned to the next group, who were waiting patiently behind them.

Malcolm X was to give a speech at the Organization of Afro-American Unity that day, and something wasn't sitting right with Antonia. Despite their best efforts, they weren't able to get a police presence, and given the threats that had been made on Malcolm's life, that was more than worrying.

Besides her, Gene Roberts (with his bitch ass), Rasul Abdullah Suliman, Abdul Kareem, and a few other members of Malcolm's circle, there was nobody present to ensure his safety.

Antonia was left with a sinking feeling of dread as that ballroom slowly began to fill. The haunting sense that something awful might occur.

She prayed it was all in her head, but there was an energy in the air that day. A presence she couldn't quite put her finger on. Something dark and malevolent. Between the lingering afterglow of her sexual fantasy of Winston and the beautiful black woman and this ethereal existential mist of darkness, she knew something wasn't right.

Antonia put those thoughts to the back of her mind when Malcolm's talk began and took her position, watching silently from the side of the room. Benjamin Goodman, Malcolm's close associate and personal assistant, opened before he eventually came on stage to deliver a speech called "The Importance of Organization."

In it, he addressed the need for African Americans to unite and coordinate their efforts to gain political power to overcome racial injustice and achieve equality in the United States.

It was a good speech, brilliant in fact. Delivered with Malcolm's trademark ferocity and articulate nature.

Truly a wonder to behold. The black audience was transfixed as he spoke, soaking up every word with rapt expressions.

Malcolm X gave them hope.

Malcolm X gave them a reason to believe.

People who had been beaten, raped, enslaved, demeaned, and trained to hate themselves were overjoyed to finally hear that there was another way to live and see themselves.

Malcolm X reminded them that they had worth.

He showed them they had an intrinsic value that was every bit as meaningful as the white man's. Thanks to him, they were beginning to envision a future where they could live lives of dignity, happiness, and prosperity. Thanks to him, they were starting to believe they, too, could become doctors, lawyers, and architects.

Thanks to Brother Malcolm, the black folk in that room were finally beginning to realise that they could finally be proud of their beautiful brown skin.

And Antonia loved that for them.

So many black people wanted to trade places with Antonia. So many of them wished they had the privileges of being white, but she thought they were insane. She'd happily have traded places with them in a heartbeat.

Being black was beautiful both inside and out, and Malcolm X helped them truly feel that in their hearts.

This man was a prophet and a true visionary. Antonia felt so blessed to be working with him in any capacity. She was so honoured to be helping spread his message in any way she could.

Also, he and his wife Betty had finally delivered on their promise to locate Winston's family! It turned out that they were now based in New York, as she'd suspected! Winston said he had a child in New York, so was that why they'd moved there? So he could be close to them? Antonia prayed that was the case because if so, he was OK.

She still had no idea if he was alive, so this tiny nugget was everything to her.

Everything.

Antonia didn't know what had happened to Winston, but she now had his family's address, and that was all that mattered. Now, the question was whether she would go to see them in person or if she would write. She honestly didn't know, but one thing she did know was that whatever she did, she would do it soon.

Antonia was going to be reunited with her real family.

But then, at that moment, Antonia once again felt a wave of conflicting emotions penetrate her psyche.

Suddenly, she saw images of Winston, herself, and the black woman having passionate sex. Tens of thousands of images littered her vision, and she felt them, too. She felt their hot and sweaty bodies writhing and thrusting against one another. She felt the lust coursing through their bloodstreams.

She felt the carnal energies permeating the air. She felt her vagina once getting wet and her breathing beginning to quicken.

But why? Why is this happening? I've been barren for so long. Why now?

Antonia tried to suppress it, but it wouldn't work. Nothing would work. She was enraptured within the throngs of a dark sexual energy, and something was wrong. Tentacles were slowly wrapping around her, organic vines that constricted her neck as a trio of echoing feminine voices began to speak words she couldn't understand in tones that deeply unsettled the soul.

She felt darkness there but nothing more.

Pure darkness.

Evil incarnate.

But nothing more.

A deep sense of foreboding invaded her consciousness as those voices spoke, cackled and laughed.

And then, at that moment, the Audubon Ballroom went black as pitch.

And then, at that moment, Antonia looked at Malcolm on stage and saw a bright light emanating from his heart, illuminating the overwhelming darkness like a beacon of true hope.

And then, at that moment, she once again heard the cackling of those feminine voices.

And then, seconds later, she looked to her right and saw three men rise from their seats. Three men who literally had a three-headed female demon hovering above them casting a red beam of energy from its eyes straight into their hearts.

And then, at that moment, Antonia's vision returned to normal.

And then, in an explosion of violence, all hell broke loose.

Those men ran to Malcolm, brandished firearms, and fired round after round after round directly at him as the entire ballroom erupted and fled in terror. Antonia didn't know how long the attack took from start to finish. It felt epically long, like an hour, but realistically, it couldn't have been. It must have only been seconds.

In any event, during those hour-long seconds, Antonia found herself running towards the man at the front. The one wielding a shotgun and pumping constant rounds at Brother Malcolm. What on earth was she going to do when she got to him?

She had no idea and would never know because once she had her hand on his back, an unseen bullet perforated her gut and sent her spiralling to the wooden floor, writhing in agony.

Immediately after that, that shotgun-wielding man blasted Malcolm X straight in the chest.

He fell to the ground, twitching next to Antonia with blood pouring from his nose, mouth, and sternum while his bodyguard, Gene Roberts, tried in vain to keep him alive.

As Antonia lost consciousness, the last thing she saw was Malcolm X's face.

His eyes were completely open but devoid of life.

His mouth was completely open but devoid of life.

He was devoid of life.

Malcolm X was lifeless.

Malcolm X was dead.

And Antonia was dying, too.

26 | BBC WORLD SERVICE

In a chilling act that sent shockwaves across cyberspace, infamous social media influencer and OnlyFans model Kara Clark was captured on camera, committing murder and assault in a bizarre, unhinged manner.

Jamaican-born, 23-year-old Clark, currently based in New York, was seen entering the room of Jackson Bennett, an elderly resident at Xavier's Institute care home.

Bennett immediately recognised and feared Clark despite the two having no known affiliation. Reports state that he was seen begging for his life as a bloodthirsty Clark, performed a bizarre sex act and then smothered him to death.

After Bennett's death, a wild-eyed Clark was confronted by his traumatised grandson, Blake Poole, known to some as Clarke's collaborator in her viral sex tape.

Stunningly, Clark then assaulted Poole, nearly killing him before Sara Dartmouth, a nurse who heard the commotion, intervened. Clark brutally assaulted Dartmouth, leaving her unconscious before fleeing into the night.

Poole remains in a coma from severe injuries inflicted by the influencer. Dartmouth is also comatose, having suffered significant head trauma.

Clark is now wanted for murder and assault, with the potential to incur extra charges depending on Poole's and Dartmouth's respective conditions. Local authorities urge anyone with information on her whereabouts to come forward immediately.

Stay tuned to the BBC World Service for updates on this breaking news story.

27 | VODKA, GUILT, & A GLIMMER OF HOPE

KARA | Nondescript Hotel: Present Day

Kara was sitting in the lobby of her hotel, trying to keep her head down while nursing her glass of vodka. Well, that wasn't strictly honest. It was actually her fifth, and so much drinking had her head spinning in circles like she was on a perpetual Ferris wheel.

It was good, though. It helped a lot. She could feel the liquor's warm glow as it slowly intoxicated and poisoned her body, and she welcomed that feeling. It damped her pain, if only slightly. Sure, she still wanted to die. Sure, she felt like her heart was melting slowly from the inside out, but the liquor made it better.

The liquor made it tolerable.

The warmth the liquor generated behind her eyes was everything.

The fire it ignited within her gut was the world.

Her gut, her disgusting, fucking, beautiful, fucking, traitorous gut.

The gut of a piece of shit who didn't deserve to live.

The gut of a heartless whore who'd killed the love of her life just so she could continue being young and beautiful.

She didn't deserve to live. She didn't.

In what universe was it right that Winston died while she drew breath? It was fucking absurd. A travesty against humanity, and Blake, too? The news said he was in a coma. The news said Blake might die. And Kara so badly wanted to speak to him. She wanted it more than anything.

The owner of the same acidic heart that was steadily dissolving in its rib cage wanted nothing more than to talk to Blake. She wanted to hold him again and beg for his forgiveness. She wanted to kneel before him and plead for him to either absolve her of this guilt or just be done with it and decapitate her at the neck.

Kara wanted the pain to go, but she also needed it to stay because she had to be punished for what she did. She had to pay a penance for who she was.

She had to.

Maybe that was why she was sitting in a busy hotel lobby while there was a nationwide manhunt out for her..

Maybe.

Maybe she subconsciously needed someone to spot her and put her out of her fucking misery.

Maybe.

But even if that were true, she still wasn't committing to what needed to be done. She couldn't woman up and end it.

At the very least, she could turn herself into the authorities, but she didn't have that in her either.

All she could do was sit in that bar, decked out in baggy jeans and an even baggier hoodie while doing her best to make sure nobody noticed her.

Truth be told, it was working.

She'd heard several people having conversations about the psycho OnlyFans model, Kara Clark. Still, none realised she was the one they were talking about.

Maybe.

But why would they?

Whoever expects to see the murderous psychopath who's just been reported on the news right before their own eyes?

Nobody, that's who. But still, what was she going to do? Where was she going to go? She didn't have a clue.

Maybe she'd just sit in that drunken stupor, slowly poisoning her gorgeous body with vodka until she had a cardiac event.

Perhaps.

Perhaps if she was too chicken shit to kill herself quickly, she could take the scenic route to suicide?

Perhaps.

Death by a thousand shots.

Death by intense alcohol poisoning.

Death by staggering degrees of ethanol.

A death most deserved.

A death most welcomed.

This was the moment when a middle-aged white man sat down directly opposite Kara in her booth.

She looked at him, startled and scared, before he opened his mouth.

"I know who you are," the man said matter of factly.

Mi nuh know weh yuh a talk 'bout," she replied in Jamaican patois, drool seeping from her thick, juicy lips.

"Sorry?" the man asked.

"I don't know what you're talking about," Kara replied.

"Yes, you do," he said bluntly, prompting her to immediately get up to leave.

"I wouldn't do that if I were you."

She turned to look at him properly. Somewhere in his forties, entering middle age with a receding and greying head of brown hair, dark brown eyes, and decked out in an expensive grey business suit. He somehow seemed very sure of himself.

"Think about it; if I wanted to run you in, I already would have. I'd have called the cops from a distance and just let them catch you."

That was a good point. He now had Kara's attention.

"Who are you?" Kara asked.

"My name's Peter, but that's not important right now. What's important is that you know I'm on your side."

"Are you?"

"I am. I've seen the actual video of what happened in that hospital room, and it didn't go down like the news is saying."

"It didn't! It didn't!"

"I know. Any fool with a functioning pair of eyeballs can see that. It's obvious."

"Him tell mi fi kill him! Him tell mi!" Kara cried in patois, slightly forgetting where she was.

"Keep your voice down. There's people around."

"He told me..." Kara continued, speaking quietly.

"That's exactly what it looked like. I saw what happened with the other man, too. You were just trying to protect yourself. In fact, the savage almost killed you before you got the upper hand.

"I honestly was. I, I, I didn't want to hurt him."

"I know, Kara. I know."

"So what do I do?!"

"We need to clear your name."

"How?!"

There was an intense silence between the two as the man pursed his lips and stared into the distance.

"Look, I'm a doctor, not a lawyer, so this isn't my area of expertise, but essentially our first step."

"Our?!"

"Our first step, yes."

"Why are you helping me?!"

"Keep your voice down, Kara, please."

"Why are you helping me?"

"I hate injustice, I abhor lies, and I'm also an admirer of yours, too, so that helps."

So, Peter was a fan. That made sense. There had to be people who were still on her side, and it was logical that most would have been her long-time admirers.

"So what are we going to do?" she asked, hopeful she might have someone to help her.

"Look, this isn't the best place for us to talk. Come to my room, and I'll fill you in on my plan. I know how to get you out of this situation."

"I, I'm not going anywhere with you," Kara replied, feeling threatened.

"At this point, haven't I proved you can trust me?"

"No."

"If I wanted to harm you, I'd have called the cops the moment I saw you."

"Maybe you did?"

"OK, I understand. No hard feelings. All the best."

Peter stood up, adjusted his tie, and started to walk away before a burst of trepidation and panic had Kara grab onto his arm.

"Don't go," she whispered, her thick lips quivering in fear.

"You said you don't trust me, so there's no point in continuing this conversation."

"I'm sorry. I'm just terrified, and I don't know what to do."

"So you do trust me?"

"I do, I do, Peter."

"Good because for this to work. I need you to believe in me. Without your faith, this entire operation will be ruined."

"OK."

"Come, take me by the arm and keep your hood up. We don't want people to see you."

"OK."

And with that, Kara held Peter's arm and led her out of the hotel bar as oblivious customers ate, drank, and chatted. She wasn't sure where he was taking her but she thanked the Lord above that she wasn't alone.

Now she had help.

And that was something.

That was everything.

But she didn't have a clue of where he was taking her.

28 | NOT YOUR LIFE, NOT YOUR BODY

KARA | Nondescript Hotel Room: Present Day

Kara's head was spinning.

Spinning like she'd been strapped to a rocket and blasted into orbit at unfashionable speed.

Kara's head was spinning.

Spinning like a comet flung into the vast reaches of outer space.

Kara's head was spinning.

Spinning like a whirlwind, twisting and turning like cosmic debris trapped in the almighty pull of a black hole.

And Kara barely knew what was happening.

She was in Peter's meagre hotel room while he droned on about everything she apparently needed to do to clear her name.

He spoke about getting legal advice, gathering evidence, maintaining a consistent stance in the media, cooperating with the police investigation, documenting public support, and using both traditional and social media to her advantage, amongst other things.

Kara heard everything he was saying, but it was too much for her brain to process. Too overwhelming. Too overpowering. What the fuck was happening? This wasn't what she signed up for. She just wanted to be young and beautiful.

That was it.

She didn't want to be a killer. She didn't want to be a fugitive from the law. And in any event, whether Winston told her to or not, she clearly did kill him, so she was legally fucked no matter what.

But still, she felt uneasy. She felt on edge as if Peter had anterior motives. Then again, everyone she met in her new body did, so that wasn't new. He wanted her; that much was obvious. Were it not for his undeniable attraction to her, he wouldn't give a damn about helping.

Kara wasn't stupid.

She saw the way he looked at her. He was clearly thinking more things than one as he spoke.

Kara wasn't dumb.

She caught him glimpsing at her ass several times when he thought she wasn't looking.

Kara was no fool.

But then, once again, Kara heard and felt that oh-so-familiar feminine wail of pain. That dark yet resonant scream of despair bleeding into torment. The feminine howl of misery that overwhelmed her soul with torrents of guilt and caused her skin to crawl with discomfort.

"NOT YOUR LIFE!"

Who was that?! she asked herself, knowing damn well what the answer was.

Kara felt the woman's agony. She couldn't ignore her pain. She resonated with it like it were her own. It tugged on her eyeballs and raked tramlines along the skin of her back.

It smothered her.

Suffocated her.

That woman's pain was everywhere, ever-present; she couldn't escape it. And she also couldn't escape the guilt. The guilt was too much. The guilt was too intense. She couldn't outrun it. She didn't deserve to be alive. She shouldn't have done what she did. She took a life so that she could live, and she deserved to burn in hell.

No, that wasn't right. Kara took three lives.

"Are you OK?" Peter asked, looking at her curiously while presenting a glass of brandy and coke. She grabbed and downed it in one, nearly retching at its sickly strong and acidic taste before immediately asking for another to help numb her pain.

As Peter stood up to fulfil her request, she held her head in her hands and tapped her feet to ignore said pain, but to no avail.

It was still ever-present. Still growing in intensity. Still pulsating against the cellular walls of her gorgeous body like the rhythmic pounding of a heart under siege, each pulse a reminder of the choices that haunted her.

"Kara, are you alright?" he asked, inappropriately placing his hand on her waist as he looked her in the eye. A relentless wave of pain battered her nerves, tightening its hold just as the presence emerged again, its scream shattering the silence.

"NOT YOUR BODY!"

It clanged loudly against her eardrums and echoed throughout her mind, smashing it harder and harder still.

The guilt. The horrible, awful, fucking, agonising guilt. Kara just couldn't get away.

Peter offered her another drink, and she accepted gladly, taking it straight into her throat and belly and almost bypassing her taste buds altogether.

But not completely.

While 85% of that drink went straight to her neck, 15% did indeed splash against her tongue. When that happened, Kara once again encountered a taste sickly, strong and acidic in nature. But this time she realised something.

This time, she realised that the drink didn't taste like brandy.

Brandy was in it, for sure, but something else was present.

Something artificial.

Something chemical.

And this was when she knew.

This was when Kara realised she had been drugged.

"What did you say this was, again?" she asked, doing her best to look nonchalant.

"Brandy and coke," Peter replied, matter of factly. She looked into his eyes and, not for the first time, felt uneasy.

Tense.

However, now it was for other reasons. Now, she didn't just see him as an opportunistic follower willing to move The Great Lakes and MT. Everest for the chance to experience the sensuous delights of her naked flesh.

Now she realised he harboured ill intentions. The bad vibes he consciously tried to downplay now radiated from his being like steam evaporating from a boiling pot of coffee.

Kara was in trouble.

She needed to do something.

"I'm just going to the bathroom," she said, trying to buy herself time.

"OK," he replied suspiciously.

Kara's head was spinning.

She needed to do something fast.

What the fuck did he put in that drink?!

She had no idea but knew she needed to get it out of her body yesterday. It might have been a matter of life and death. With that, she made a beeline for the bathroom, went inside, locked the door, turned on the faucet, and shoved her two longest fingers as far down her tight throat as she possibly could.

To call it uncomfortable was an understatement. She felt like she was choking, but nothing would come up.

"Kara. Kara, are you OK in there?"

Shit, he thinks something's wrong!

"Mi good, just mek mi go pee, man, cho!" Kara anxiously replied in Jamaican patois.

She shoved her fingers even deeper still, feeling them rub against her sensitive tonsils as her gag reflex finally kicked in and hurled half a litre of lumpy chemicals into the green porcelain sink.

That's not alcohol!

She kept those fingers deep inside her neck, operating in violation of her body's natural instincts, desperate to get as much of whatever the fuck he'd poisoned her with out of her body as possible.

However, nothing else would come out. Again and again, she tried, but her stomach simply heaved and wretched to no avail. Her abdominal muscles were tight like iron knots, but nothing happened.

Kara couldn't throw up any more.

Did I get rid of it!? Is it all gone?!

The fear was palpable. Thick. Ever-present and staring right into her face.

Kara just didn't know what was going to happen.

But then, in the midst of that overwhelming web of chaos and confusion, she heard that wailing scream yet again. The echoing cry of feminine despair that reverberated from her eardrums to her panicked eyeballs.

She slapped her own face no less than five hard times to shut that voice up before realising Peter would be wondering why she was taking so long.

Fuck, I need to go back outside.

She took a moment to compose herself, her head now reeling from the effects of untold amounts of alcohol, and left the bathroom to see Peter standing right by the door, looking more than concerned.

"Is everything OK?" he asked.

"Never better," she replied.

"Are you sure?"

"Yeah, I see clearly now."

"What does that mean?" he asked with a worried expression.

"It means I want another drink."

"You want another one?" he asked, clearly pleasantly surprised.

"Did I stutter?"

"Well, no, but, erm, I..."

"Let's party tonight. You want to party with me, right, Dr Peter?"

"Well, yes, I'd love to..."

"Great, so pour us both a couple more drinks and let's have some fun."

Blushing with shy excitement, Peter did exactly as he was told and poured two more drinks. Kara turned her back and pretended to use her phone while secretly spying on him through her screen's reflection.

Her eyes widened at what she saw.

Peter was discretely pouring a strange powder into one of the drinks and quite a lot of it too. He then stirred both, starting with the regular brandy and coke and ending with the powdered concoction of poison.

"Here you go," he said, looking Kara closely in the eye as he placed his drink on the table and handed her the poisoned one.

Kara's head was spinning.

And she needed to do something immediately.

Without thinking, she stood right in front of Peter, inches away from his face, and looked square at his rapidly dilating pupils.

He was scared.

Intimidated.

Aroused.

He wanted this, for sure.

He craved the chance to be this close to the body he'd spent so much time lusting over from afar. But he didn't expect this union to occur willingly. He didn't consider himself worthy of the honour.

Deserving of the privilege.

And you aren't. You fucking aren't. Kara thought.

And thus, when confronted with his cock's innermost desire, Peter teetered on the precipice of restraint, poised to be swept away by the rising tide of sexual arousal.

Kara could use this. Kara would use this. She'd turn Peter's undeniable attraction to her against him.

She'd turn the tables, and she'd win.

So with that, she kissed him passionately on his thin, dry, chapped, and middle-aged lips, doing her best to ignore the two-inch nub that strained to penetrate her from within his crotch. Still able to taste her own chemically laced throw-up on her own tongue.

Maybe he can too, but probably not.

You see, poor Peter was now in seventh heaven and babbling like self-control was fast becoming an abstract concept. There he stood with the stiffest of stiff pricks, exploring the same curves he'd spent so long yearning for with the same hands he'd often used to beat his microdick over them until it bled.

Poor Peter couldn't believe his luck.

Poor Peter was now in seventh heaven.

However, as poor Peter fell prey to his own body's autonomic arousal response, Kara used this element of surprise to secretly switch both drinks before pulling away and forcing herself to form a smile. All while her brain secretly resisted the urge to descend into insanity.

What the fuck did he put in my drink?! And how much of it did I throw up?! What's going to happen to me if and when whatever he drugged me with starts to kick in??

Kara didn't know. But she did know her best shot at safety came from getting him to drink whatever the fuck that was. So, she quickly downed her brandy and coke and gestured for him to do the same.

Poor Peter necked the entire thing in one go. He clearly didn't suspect a thing.

Let's do this you piece of shit.

It must be said that Kara took more than a moderate amount of satisfaction from seeing Peter tremble nervously before her, that erect nub of his still pitching a microtent in his slacks.

Ray Charles could see the effect she was having on him. Stevie Wonder could see how badly he wanted her. Helen Keller could see how having her merely kiss his dry, chapped, thin lips had already stiffened his tiny prick to near bursting point.

Peter was horny. Powerfully so. But Kara couldn't get overconfident. She couldn't afford to get complacent. His current state needed to be handled with care because the situation was both good and bad.

Bad because she was still clearly in physical danger. You see, while Peter couldn't hold a candle to Blake in terms of physicality, he was still a fully grown man who could probably overpower her with a moderate degree of effort.

However, what was good was that as he was now thinking with the ant brain above his balls and not the one behind his eyes, he would be easy to manipulate. And guess what? Kara could and would use every last one of his surging hormones against him.

I just need to be careful.

However, at that moment, her phone vibrated, so she took it out of her pocket and looked at the notification. It was a Google alert which read:

Kara Clark Murder Enquiry: Victim Blake Poole's Condition Worsens

Shocked for more reasons than one, she quickly clicked on the article.

"Blake Poole, victim of attempted murder at the hands of the infamous Internet personality, Kara Clark, is now in critical condition."

I can't believe Blake's surname is Poole! Kara thought. *How the fuck did I not know that?!*

"Poole, who is also the grandson of Clark's murder victim, Jackson Bennett, is currently in a coma, and his situation is said to be deteriorating. Health officials report a decrease in responsiveness to external stimuli, severe respiratory complications, and potential brain damage.

Regarding the bizarre sexual murder of her father and ritualistic assault of her son, Blake's mother, Leticia Poole, made a statement an hour ago, which you can hear on the video below."

Leticia Poole!? She must be the child Winston had taken from him! Kara thought.

She quickly tapped on the video and watched while Peter looked on curiously. She saw a teary-eyed and middle-aged black woman standing outside a hospital while flanked by dozens of reporters, and knowing that this was the child Winston had spoken about all those years before was bittersweet.

"My father, Jackson, was the kindest man I have ever known and a ray of sunshine in an otherwise dark world. In my entire life, he never hurt anyone. He treated everyone he met with the same kindness and respect. He always made me feel safe. He always let me know that I was loved.

And even though I met my father a little late in life, he gave me enough love in that relatively short period to last multiple lifetimes. He may not have been strong of body, but his spirit was the mightiest I have ever seen.

He had a light inside him that refused to be dimmed, making my father the strongest man I have ever known. For him to live to such advanced years with such injuries to die not from old age but from murder is a testament to the power of his spirit. Our family already misses him more than words can ever say.

My son, my Blakey, is my entire world and a constant source of love and support to our family. He is my single greatest achievement, and seeing him in this state breaks our hearts. We hope and pray for his full recovery.

We want nothing more than to see him smiling, laughing, and joking with us all. We want him back in our lives. We miss him so much, but we're scared. We're afraid that this is the end, and we don't know what to do.

Blake, please come back to us. Come back to our family, please. Please don't let that evil demon steal your light from us like she stole Daddy's.

And Daddy, if Blake is to meet you in the great ever after, please look after him. Please shelter and guide him in death as you always did in life. We all love you both so much. We love you more than words can say. We love you more than life itself. And we miss you. We miss you both so much.

To anyone who has information about this evil bitch, please go to the police. We beg of you. Please help bring her to justice. Please help the police catch this woman before she kills again. Please, please help."

The news report ended with sobs of despair from Leticia that cut through Kara's soul. It was just too much. Even more guilt than before, if that were possible. She'd always wondered what Winston's child was like, but to find out like this was crippling. To see a grown woman who was his near exact likeness call her evil incarnate without a hint of irony smothered her soul.

To realise that she agreed with almost everything that woman said crushed her spirit and left her hardly able to breathe. To deduce that Winston's family had changed his name to make sure she couldn't track him down made her want to cry. Kara exited that video with teary eyes of her own and noticed another notification just underneath that read:

Unknown Sender:

"Fucking hell, slut, you've been a bad girl, haven't you? Are you physically incapable of being a productive member of society? Are you only able to be an evil fucking degenerate piece of shit? But you know what? Maybe I should be proud of you because you've killed one nigger and almost two in one day. I guess, in your own strange way, you're making the world a better place."

Hippocratic Oath yet again.

How the fuck did he get this number?

It didn't make sense. She'd dumped her old phone and replaced it with this, so how on earth did he know how to reach her? It just didn't make sense.

The level of terror Kara experienced at that moment had risen to nuclear proportions, possibly on a par with those felt by the people of Hiroshima on August 6th 1945.

And she still had Peter to contend with.

"Kara, are you alright?" Peter asked, displaying a look of concern that she wasn't sure was real or fake.

Kara didn't even respond. She ignored him for the moment and thumbed out a reply to Hippocratic Oath, writing:

"How the fuck did you get this number???!"

However, once she hit send, something happened, making her young and beating heart nearly lodge in her throat.

At that moment, at the precise moment she hit send, Kara heard a deep vibration emanate from Peter's trouser pocket.

She looked down at his leg and up at him, clearly concerned.

He looked down at his leg and then up at her, clearly concerned.

There they stood, staring right into each other's souls, each refusing to be the first to look away.

“Kara, what’s wrong?” Peter asked, feigning ignorance.

Kara didn't say a single word. She simply took her phone, sent another message to that same number, and locked eyes with Peter as they both heard another vibration coming from his pants.

Kara's head was spinning.

Spinning because she realised she was trapped alone in a room with her stalker, Hippocratic Oath.

Kara's head was spinning.

Spinning because she knew exactly what was going to happen next.

Proving her intuition correct, Peter punched her square in the jaw and sent her straight to the ground, her head slamming against the cold, hard hotel room floor. With stars proliferating in her vision, she saw and felt him on top of her in microseconds, fighting to tear her clothes off.

"OK, I'll kill her. I'll fucking kill her!" Peter screamed.

"You're not gonna kill me!" Kara howled.

"I'll fucking kill the bitch!"

Peter had Kara pinned to the floor, but she fought to get free. She did everything in her power to get him off her, but alas, nothing worked. She struggled and kicked and bit, feeling bile rise to her throat every time her leg brushed against the swollen nublet in his groin.

Feeling nauseous every time, he groaned in sick pleasure at that intimate piece of contact. Kara clawed and scratched at his face, drawing blood, but to no real avail.

Where the fuck is Kalizar?!

Where the fuck were the voices?

"Help me!" she screamed.

Why wouldn't they give her the demon strength they used on Blake?!

"HELP!" she screamed, hoping to hear something, but sadly hearing nothing.

"Nobody's going to help you, you fucking whore!"

Peter drove his forehead into Kara's no less than three times and unsurprisingly had her seeing triple. While she was dazed, he removed her hoodie, tore off her bra, sucked her right breast forcefully, and undid the fly buttons of her jeans.

She somehow summoned the strength to punch him in the face twice, but nothing happened. She couldn't stop him.

"Help me! Heeeeeelp meeee!" Kara screamed, begging Kalizar for help but receiving absolutely none.

She drove her knee into his balls as hard as she could, feeling her thigh slam yet again against the pebble which poked out through the now undone fly of his suit trousers.

All it did was make Peter angry.

And suddenly, he had a blade. A lengthy, monstrous, and razor-sharp blade. A blade Kara had never seen before. A blade which was now pressed against her sweating, bulging neck. All while grinding his leaking 2-inch dicklet against her bone-dry crotch.

Kara screamed in both pain and rage, feeling its cold, hard, and sharp steel press into her throat and begin to pierce the skin. Again, she begged Kalizar for help, and again, nothing happened. And now the knife began to slice said skin, causing blood to seep out of its freshly created wound.

Kara looked at her would-be rapist, her eyes a stark amalgamation of fear and rage as he looked right back, clearly intent on harming her for reasons known only to him. He seemed utterly demented. Clinically insane. The huge pupils of his now bloodshot eyes gave him the aura of a rabid bull. He seemed crazed, rabid, angry, vengeful, and drowsy.

Drowsy?

Yes. Drowsy.

All of a sudden, Peter was drowsy. Disoriented. Tired. Confused. His pupils bulged, squirmed, and ballooned until they completely overtook the brown parts of his irises. His strength began to fade. His spirit began to desert him. Suddenly, he lay on top of Kara with trembling fingers that were now failing miserably in their quest to hold onto his blade.

His thin lips were twice their usual size and flushed with blood, as were his dry cheeks. In fact, Peter's whole face was turning red, and dangerously so.

Beads of sweat poured from his forehead down to his lips and mixed with the saliva that flowed from his tongue into Kara's open and screaming mouth.

She heaved so much that her abdominals ached. If she hadn't already emptied the contents of her stomach in the bathroom, she would have done so right then and there.

But still, none of that mattered. What mattered was that Peter was weakening.

Kara bit his hand hard enough to draw blood, and he dropped the blade to the floor next to her face.

Then, she used every ounce of strength to punch him repeatedly in the temple.

Peter winced in pain.

Peter was hurt.

Peter staggered, but not in the way she expected.

What's wrong with him?!

But then she remembered.

The drugs!

The drugs were kicking in, and hence, Peter was losing consciousness.

Kara's head was spinning.

I've got him.

Kara had him.

She had the little piece of shit.

I'm gonna fuck his whole world up! Rip him from pillar to post!! I'm going to inflict so much harm on this cunt that his life will never be the same again!

"Yuh hear mi, yuh likkle piece a shit?! Bad tings a go happen to yuh!" Kara screamed in Jamaican patois.

But Kara wondered what was going on. That was her voice, for sure, but not her personality.

Why am I being so violent?

That just wasn't like her.

Why do I feel so strange? So hot? So aggressive?

This was when she realised she was high, too. Not just drunk but chemically high.

Her vision was more vivid than ever before but slightly wavy. She felt a deep and enduring heat emanating from her brain and flowing through her neck, shoulders, arms, hands, chest, stomach, legs, and feet.

Everything in her body felt hot.

Baking hot, like she was coated in close to boiling molasses, she felt her inhibitions evaporate into mist. At that moment, the concept of performing unspeakable acts on another human seemed amusing, and the idea of wreaking utter humiliation upon them was downright compelling.

She had to giggle. She gave in to the uncontrollable urge to laugh in the face of the man who'd stalked and tried to rape her. She surrendered to the overwhelming desire to cut him deeper than he'd ever cut her and make him beg for forgiveness.

I'm going to hurt you. I'm going to tear your soul out of your bones, and you'll thank me for the experience!

Peter passed out at that moment, right on top of Kara. Whether that was from his drug-induced stupor or the fear of her promised retribution wasn't certain. All she knew was that she now had his entire weight pressing down upon her frame as his two-inch nub was still harder than Captain America's shield and still violating her crotch sans consent.

She pushed him off, smiling as his head slammed off the floor. After that she reached into his pocket, grabbed his phone, pulled his eyes open, used his face to unlock said phone, and had herself a look.

Unsurprisingly, it was a treasure trove of information that confirmed one thing without a shadow of a doubt. Peter was, indeed, Hippocratic Oath.

There was a massive log of messages he'd sent Kara on and off Instagram, but there was also more. He had downloaded hundreds of gigabytes worth of pictures and videos of her. Countless files were saved on that phone, not just of her but of other black models.

The man was obsessed.

There were definitely far more of her than anyone else. However, still, scores of scantily clad black models adorned the phone of a racist prick who claimed to hate them on account of their colour.

You couldn't make it up.

He had a messaging app called WhatsApp installed. Kara opened it and then saw a private group with 27 members called the Aryan Brotherhood, in which they were all talking about her. Peter, aka Hippocratic Oath, was gleefully telling everyone exactly what he was going to do to her, and they eagerly listened.

HippocraticOath22:

"She's at the Saint Jameson Hotel. I've just got myself a room."

White Power 4 Eva:

"Shall we call the cops?"

HippocraticOath22:

"Are you mad? Of course not. I'm gonna find her, degrade her, and remind her why the white man is superior."

NiggerKiller:

“Do that, but don't get yourself into trouble.”

HippocraticOath22:

“With who?”

Aryan Unity:

“With the police. Ain't nothing they love more than showing sympathy for filthy niggers these days. Be careful.”

HippocraticOath22:

“Yeah, but this ain't no regular nigger. This is a nigger who half the world hated even before she killed another nigger and put a second in hospital. Trust me, no matter what happens to her, nobody's gonna give a fuck. Who's she even going to tell, anyway? She's on the run and would have to face the music for murder to put me down for rape and assault.

She'll just have to shut her fucking nigger mouth.”

White Power 4 Eva:

“But aren't you scared?”

HippocraticOath22:

“Of what?”

White Power 4 Eva:

“She killed a man.”

HippocraticOath22:

“No, she killed a nigger, not a man. I can and will outsmart her. Anyone of us could. I'll charm her, make her dumb ass think I'm on her side, take her to my room, spike her drink, wait till she passes out, and get to work. I just need to make sure I don't kill her, but even if I do, no one's gonna care. Easy money.”

Kara's head was spinning.

She looked at Peter as he lay slumped on the floor, still drooling, still snoring, cock still harder than Thor's hammer. Words can't describe the level of rage she felt. The hatred was palpable. The loathing was through the roof.

She wanted revenge.

As she slowly removed his clothes, stripping him until he was stark naked with his thick pot belly perpetually expanding and contracting, she had a damn good think about everything she was going to do.

As he took laboured unconscious breaths on his hotel room floor, Kara smiled with the dark satisfaction of knowing his day was only going to get worse while hers could only get better.

She would do unspeakable things to this man. She would wreak unforgettable harm upon him. She would wreck him in every possible way.

Kara was going to destroy Peter in mind, body, and soul.

An' yuh a go thank mi fi di privilege too, yuh racist piece a shit.

Kara's head was spinning.

29 | WET TEARS ON A NUMB NECK

Antonia | Columbia-Presbyterian Medical Center: March 3, 1965

Antonia awoke in a hospital patient room with a body wracked with physical pain alongside a mind drowning in guilt. She didn't need anyone to tell her Malcolm X died in that ballroom because she already knew.

She saw it.

She saw what those bastards did to him. They gunned him down right in front of her, so she didn't need to be told.

Sne knew.

She already knew.

Antonia knew Malcolm X was dead. And Antonia knew who did it, too. It was them. Those fucking assholes. The suspicious cats she saw walking into the hall but didn't stop. The men she maybe could have prevented from entering if she wasn't lost in the middle of a stupid fucking sex fantasy.

And who was that black woman, anyway?

God, she was so beautiful.

She looked just the way Antonia wished she could but knew she never would.

No! That's not fucking important! This isn't important!

What mattered was that Malcolm X was dead, and it was her fault.

It was all my fault!

What mattered was that the world had lost an influential leader, a talisman who would usher in a new era of fair and equitable treatment for black folk.

What mattered was that black America's hero had been slain.

What mattered was that all hope for creating a world in which racist fucks would see justice for what they did to Winston was lost.

What mattered was that she'd failed.

I failed!

This was when Antonia noticed something horrific. She hadn't done so before, but she did now, and now it could never be unnoticed. Now, she was painfully aware.

How had she not realised before?

Antonia couldn't move.

What the fuck?!

Antonia was trapped inside her skull and looking up at the wall. She couldn't move.

Not an inch.

She couldn't even feel her body. It was like it wasn't even there.

This was when fear exploded from her heart and erupted from her mouth in the form of a blood-curdling wail.

When panic exploded from her soul and erupted from her eyeballs in the form of fresh salty tears.

When her hospital room became awash with the harrowing cry of a soul who knew she was in a situation she couldn't begin to handle.

One who knew life would never be the same again.

One who knew she was fucked.

"I CAN'T MOVE!! I CAN'T MOVE! AAAHHHHHH AHAHHHH AHAHHAH I CAN'T MOOOOOOVE!"

Antonia screamed until she went hoarse, repeatedly banging her head, the only part of her body that still moved against her hard pillow. Eventually, someone came into her room, standing over her flaccid body, both plain-faced and emotionless, as she both cried and screamed.

"I CAN'T MOVE!!"

"I know, Mrs Parker, I know."

"I CAN'T MOVE MY BODY!!"

"Mrs Parker, I'm going to need you to calm down."

"HELP!!"

"I'm trying to help you, but I can't do so if you won't shut the fuck up."

"WHAT?!! WHY ARE YOU..."

"Antonia, considering what you've been up to, you're lucky I'm helping you at all. If you're going to be a traitor to our people and do everything in your power to take us down, then none of us owe you the tiniest shred of support. You were out there evangelising that filthy animal and his wretched cabal of apes and finally got your comeuppance.

The good lord saw fit to punish you for your many misdeeds, and such is life. Hopefully, this will be a learning experience. Still, honestly, based on what I've heard about you, I'm not holding my breath."

Antonia looked meekly at the person speaking; it was a doctor, male, white, and maybe 50 to 60 years old. Armed with a stern face smothered in wrinkles and a relatively heavy-set frame, he glared from unsympathetic eyes that didn't give the tiniest fuck about her situation.

He certainly wasn't taking pleasure in it. He clearly wasn't a sadist. But he didn't care either. As far as he was concerned, Antonia was getting exactly what she deserved, her comeuppance, if you will.

"What have you..."

"Shut up."

A prolonged silence followed, punctuated only by the echoes of Antonia's sobs and moans. Her trademark strength and ferocity had now abandoned her, along with the use of her limbs. Now, she simply felt defeated in every possible capacity.

Emotionally.

Spiritually.

Mentally.

Not to mention physically.

"Now, Mrs Parker, do you want to know what's happened to you?"

Antonia didn't even register his words. Her ears detected reverberations of sound but were unable to transport them to the brain for processing. She simply didn't understand a damn word the doctor said.

As she felt wet and sticky tears uncomfortably tickling her cheeks and realised she couldn't wipe them off, she wanted to die.

"Now, are you going to be quiet and let me explain what's happened to you or not?"

"I want to die," Antonia whispered meekly.

"Mrs Parker, do you want to know what happened to you?"

She nodded softly before trying to rub her face against the pillow to remove her tears. She couldn't do it, though. Her neck wouldn't turn far enough.

And so, more tears flowed.

"Firstly, you have significant spinal cord trauma as a bullet has damaged it, resulting in paralysis from the neck down, paralysis of which you seem to be acutely aware.

Secondly, said bullet may have ruptured the nerves surrounding the aforementioned spinal cord, leading to further damage. Thirdly, you also have a vascular injury. The aforementioned bullet's trajectory seems to have ruptured various blood vessels that supply said spinal cord, leading to decreased blood flow and oxygenation.

All of the above will have long-lasting to permanent implications for both your sensation and motor function."

"Am I going to be like this forever?"

"How smelly is a wet turd in a ditch? You may indeed recover some sensation and motor function. It is possible. Through intensive rehabilitation over an extensive, and I do mean extensive, amount of time, you may regain some movement and sensation in certain parts of your body.

However, it is essential to note that this improbable recovery would be slow, painful, and challenging. Mrs Parker, I must also inform you that you'll never be the same again. One way or another, your life as you know it is over."

A torrential downpour of tears burst forth from Antonia's eyes as she cried and begged for help that nobody cared to give. Finally, her doctor's face cracked with the slightest twinge of empathy. But that was all it was, mind you.

The slightest twinge.

The tiniest microscopic flicker of the dying ember of the last vestiges of the human potential to give a fuck about the pain of another.

Antonia was alone.

Bereft. Distraught. Crushed. Overwhelmed. Smothered. Defeated.

And once again, she wanted to die.

"I want to die."

That was all she wanted, all she needed.

"I can't live like this."

She couldn't live like that.

"Please kill me."

"Mrs Parker, please pull yourself together. We both know that's not an option; besides, you have a visitor."

"I can't live like this." she sobbed.

“Mrs Parker, there is someone here to see you."

"Who?"

"Your husband, Richard."

On cue, Antonia's husband, Richard Parker, walked into view from behind the doctor, who smiled and tapped him on the shoulder before exiting the room.

"Wow," Richard gasped, studying Antonia from head to toe with a baffled expression emblazoned on his lips.

"He said I might not walk again," Antonia replied, weeping.

"Antonia, honey; that's not even the worst of it," he replied, matter of factly.

"What?"

"He, along with the press and half of these United States, says you've been fraternising with niggers," Richard stated bluntly.

If the above exchange hasn't made this clear, let it be known that Richard Parker was nothing like his wife, Antonia. Standing at over six foot two and having just completed his 37th lap of the sun, he had a full head of brown hair beginning to grey at the sides alongside a sturdy and robust frame. Gross racism aside, he honestly was the symbolic visage of distinguished white masculinity of the time.

A wildly successful and affluent banker, Richard Parker took many overseas trips, so many in fact that he was more acquainted with the interior of his suitcase than his marital bed. Honestly, it was clear to both that their relationship was an arrangement rather than a union.

A dutiful obligation, if you will.

A social masquerade, as it were.

A carefully choreographed yet utterly fallacious dance the two performed solely to uphold societal expectations and nothing more.

Richard was an attractive man and exceedingly so. His tall and significantly built frame was perpetually housed in embroidered three-piece Italian suits, nylon socks, and wingtip brogues from dawn until dusk. All of which blended with his natural boyish charisma to make him a devil with the ladies.

Women were drawn to Richard Parker everywhere they went, and he loved the attention. He took it deep into his lungs with the ferocity of a man trapped several leagues underwater, sucking oxygen through a single straw. In honesty, Antonia had lost count of the number of times he'd flirted with barely legal ditzy blonde air hostesses right in front of her face, but neither did she care.

She didn't need powers of clairvoyance to know what happened on his many 'business trips' because it wasn't like he was subtle about it. Richard Parker was about as discreet as a marching band at midnight, and neither did she care. Richard did what Richard did and didn't give a damn if Antonia knew or not.

And neither did she care.

His hefty bank balance gave her a tidy monthly allowance, which wasn't just a consolation; it was more than worth it. She had no desires for either his heart or those belonging to any men whose names weren't Winston Poole, so who the fuck cared who he had sex with? As long as he didn't bring the floozies home, Antonia couldn't possibly have been less interested.

Also, let it be reiterated that Richard Parker did indeed bestow upon Antonia a princely sum of coin for the honour of being his lawfully wedded wife. In fact, she'd have been overjoyed with half the amount. Maybe his generosity was due to some tiny vestige of guilt trapped deep within his soul, or perhaps he just had more money than God.

Probably a bit of both.

But in any event, said allowance had been critical to Antonia's support for Malcolm X's campaign. For that, she was secretly grateful.

However, at that moment, the sham status of their marriage didn't matter to Antonia because she was just overjoyed to see him. She was delighted to see someone, anyone, who could help navigate the torture she was enduring.

Someone who at least had some positive inclination towards her. Sure, their marriage wasn't loving and was fraught with expectations and pressure. Still, Richard didn't mistreat her in any way. Their interactions were somewhat positive overall.

"Malcolm X, Antonia? You were in league with Malcolm fucking X and his sick cabal of animalistic porch monkeys? Jesus H Tap Dancing Christ, I heard you once had a thing for niggers, but I never thought you'd stoop so low as to be a traitor to your own kind. What the fuck were you thinking?"

Antonia's tears now streamed down past her cheeks and onto a paralysed neck, which simply couldn't feel them. She opened her mouth to speak, but Richard waved her off before continuing.

"Malcolm X, Antonia? Malcolm fucking X? The terrorist coon who's trying to destroy our country? Our way of life? That's who you've been helping?"

There was a long and painful silence as Richard looked into his wife's sobbing eyes in disbelief.

"I saw you've been making huge withdrawals from the account I set up for you. Money so big you couldn't possibly have been spending it on yourself. It was for him, wasn't it?"

Antonia didn't say anything; Antonia didn't do anything. She simply looked at her husband with fear and tears flowing from her eyes as disgust and rage burned within his.

"IT WAS FOR HIM, WASN'T IT?!" Richard shouted, losing his composure. Realising that, he took a moment to stiffen his posture, readjust his blue tie, and pull himself together before continuing.

"You've been spending my money, my hard-earned money, to help that filthy nigger. That terrorist. I can't even look at you."

"Richard..."

"You know how hard I work! You know how much I hate what I do! The long, laborious, tedious fucking hours I put into this fucking job! You know all of this! You fucking know this, you whore!"

“Richard...”

"You fucking know this! I've given you everything a white woman could want, but do you appreciate it? Do you care? Do the sacrifices a good, clean, working white man makes to provide for his fucking woman mean a damn thing to you? They don't, do they? They don't mean anything. I've given you everything. Everything!

Everything a woman could ever want, and instead of appreciating it, instead of appreciating me, instead of giving me sons like an honourable white woman, you're whoring around with monkeys and using my money to destabilise our fucking nation! How am I supposed to show my face in public after this?! What the fuck will our friends think?! I'm the husband of a fucking race traitor!"

As Antonia lay on her back, continuing to sob, Richard walked away out of her comfortable eyeshot. This was when she realised that while she couldn't move her neck from left to right, she could do so from up to down, albeit with extreme difficulty.

She struggled and strained to look at her irate husband, but the pain was unbearable. 15 seconds later, her exhausted head collapsed back onto the pillow.

Shortly after, she heard the sharp staccato click-clacking of high heels as Richard walked back into eyeshot with his arm wrapped around the shoulders of a blonde 21-year-old who was too beautiful to not be a model.

She smiled sheepishly, her lips adorned with bright red lipstick and her body wrapped within a blood-red form-fitting bodycon dress which did little to hide her ample cleavage.

"I'm divorcing you, Antonia; we're done. You no longer have access to me or my resources. Also, this is Nancy, the true love of my life and the woman with whom I'm going to start a family."

"Hi," said Nancy in a friendly but shy manner.

"But, but, but," Antonia stammered.

"But what?”

"But I'll need money for my treatments. I can't afford them on my own," she continued.

"That's something you should have thought about before you started literally sleeping with the enemy."

"I, I didn't..."

"Don't insult my intelligence. You sure as hell weren't following that banana-eating monkey around the country for his intellect, and we both know it. If you need money for your treatment, you can speak to him.

Oh, wait, that's right, he's dead, and good fucking riddance. Also, I've taken my money out of your allowance account, so that's that. So long, Antonia. My lawyer will be in touch to finalise the divorce when you're back on your feet, figuratively speaking, of course."

Richard turned to walk away once again, taking Nancy with him.

"No! Wait! Please!" Antonia cried in despair, painfully craning her neck to look at him.

He casually turned around with a bored expression.

"I might never walk again! I can't even move my arms, Richard! You need to help me!"

"You're always raving about all the high-tech gadgets that will be available in the future, right? Apparently, we'll all be living in an episode of The Outer Limits or The Twilight Zone in a few decades, right? So sit tight and wait.

Soon they'll come up with a way to fix your broken body and have you able to walk, feed yourself, and wipe your own ass, but that's going to be a journey you face alone. Goodbye, Antonia. Let's go, Nancy."

With that, Richard and Nancy left Antonia all alone in the hospital room continuing to cry a river of tears past the cheeks and chin that still could feel them down to the neck which could not.

She would lay like that for another three and a half hours before a nurse came to check on her.

30 | YOUR LITTLE JOHNSON'S STANDING UP

KARA | Peter's Hotel Room: Present Day

Still near blind drunk, still higher than Neptune from whatever the fuck Peter put in her drink, and still seething with rage from the realisation that he was her stalker, Kara was exacting revenge. To her, he was no longer a man, no longer even a human being.

He's a thing. He's not a he, he's an it.

And it was scum.

Worthless.

Infested.

Infected with bacteria like warm shit, she'd scraped from the bottom of her Jimmy Choo.

Kara was going to treat it like the diseased lump of excrement it was. Kara was going to humiliate it.

She was going to revel in it.

Take pleasure in it.

Truly savour every last drop of its sweet, delicious taste.

She'd stripped Peter's podgy, pasty white body butt naked, tied its wrists and ankles to all four corners of his hotel room's bed, and gagged his mouth with used tissue from his bathroom bin.

All she could hear were cries and moans coming from his stuffed mouth, the same cries and moans he'd previously had no qualms about doing his best to induce within her.

Annoyingly, however, Peter's weren't the only cries Kara heard. She also heard those of another, one she knew but refused to admit the existence of. One with whom she was linked inextricably, bonded not only at the cellular level but the spiritual too.

And Kara really wished that bitch would just shut the fuck up.

"I DON'T WANT TO BE HERE!! LET ME GO, PLEASE! LET ME GO!"

Her pain was potent, palpable, vivid, visceral, undeniable, and agonising to the core and Antonia...

No! No! My name's not Antonia! I'm not that ugly, worthless piece of shit! I'm someone special! I'm important! I'm beautiful! I'm Kara!

That's right. Antonia wasn't Antonia.

I'm not Antonia!

Antonia was weak, ugly, old, disabled and worthless. But Kara was different. Kara was beautiful, powerful, and feminine, and Kara could take the pain. She could handle it. Kara could rise above it. Kara could endure. That's who Antonia was. She was Kara.

Not Antonia. Antonia wasn't Antonia. Antonia was Kara.

She continued to remind herself of that fact as she looked at the pathetic worm lying spread eagle on the bed before her. She continued to remind herself of that fact as her mind simultaneously reaffirmed just how much she hated the pile of human waste lying helpless on that bed.

She hated it like she'd never hated another being in both of her lives and wouldn't rest until she'd wreaked unforgettable harm upon it.

"I HATE YOU! I FUCKING HATE YOU!" she screamed right into Peter's face as lumps of congealed yellow phlegm flew into its quivering eyeballs.

Peter was an *it*. And it was so scared.

It was terrified, and even more intoxicated than she. It barely knew its own name, let alone where the fuck it was; that much was clear.

Good.

Kara climbed off the bed, grabbed more of the white powder it had drugged her with, walked back, pulled the tissue from its mouth, poured the drugs down its neck, and forcefully held its jaw shut while it all went down its throat. It nearly choked on its own tongue.

GOOD!

"SWALLOW IT! FUCKING SWALLOW IT! SWAAAAALLLLOOOWWWW IIIITTTTT!" she screamed straight into his spasming pupils.

Kara took a moment to truly appreciate the terror that permeated its being and realised how much she loved witnessing it. She revelled in appreciating seeing how petrified it was.

Its dilated pupils were quivering like a rickety bridge caught in a monsoon. Its body was somehow freezing cold yet coated from bald head to stubby toe in slimy sweat that gave it the look of a freshly salted slug in the throes of death.

But it wasn't enough. Not even close.

"LET ME GO PLEASE!"

That wasn't Peter. Kara had already gagged its stinking mouth, so it couldn't possibly have been him. No, it was her, the woman Kara had no choice but to push away.

Far away.

Kara had to push that woman deep down into the depths of her consciousness, and she was trying. She was trying with everything she had, but it was hard. So fucking hard. So difficult to ignore. So ever-present. So undeniable. Screaming right in her eardrums and seemingly impossible to escape. And it was its fault.

"IT'S YOUR FUCKING FAULT!"

It was all Peter's fault.

"IT'S ALL YOUR FUCKING FAULT!"

"MMMGHHHGHH MGHFHHFHFH MMMMMMMGGGHHH!"

It was all his fucking fault.

Kara grabbed a bottle of liquor, she wasn't sure what kind, and poured it straight into Peter's mouth, dissolving the tissue paper on its tongue while it nearly choked on it all. As she peered deep into its bloodshot eyes, she felt no sympathy. No remorse or compassion.

Nothing but venomous hatred burning from every last blood cell.

"You wanted to kill me. You piece of human shit. No! No, no, no, you wanted me to kill myself, didn't you? Didn't you? You wanted me to take a knife and lacerate my own throat, didn't you? You'd have loved that, wouldn't you?

To see me slowly go insane, you wanted that, didn't you? You wanted to cause me pain, but why? Why? What did I ever do to you? What did Kara do to you? Nothing. I did nothing. Kara did nothing. We did nothing! But still, still, you had to hurt me! Still, you had to harass me! Didn't you?! But why?! What the fuck did I ever do to you?! What the fuck did we ever do to you?!"

"TIGER! TIGER, I NEED HELP! PLEASE! YOU'VE GOT TO HELP ME!"

That wasn't the woman, and it certainly wasn't Kalizar. That was a voice not heard since she'd recently murdered its owner and in over half a decade prior to that. This was someone else. Someone Kara loved dearly.

"WINSTON?!"

"HELP ME, PLEASE, TIGER!"

"WINSTON, IS THAT YOU?!"

Peter's phone beeped and vibrated from its pants pocket on the floor. She hopped down and picked it up. There was a notification from:

Wifey Claire

Kara waved its phone in front of its twitching face to unlock it and opened the message. It was a voice note from a relatively young-sounding woman who said:

"Baby, I'm going to be in serious need of some TLC when you get home tonight, I swear to God, 'cause you won't believe the evening I've had. I was out with Jess and Estelle at that Italian restaurant. Do you know Mario's? That place on 38th and Broadway? Anyway, I had a super spicy pizza with extra strong chilli peppers and my God, the thing was so hot!

Baby, it was like eating lava, and guess what? One of the peppers got stuck in the back of my throat. My fucking throat!"

What the fuck? Kara thought, feeling a strange sensation wash over her.

"I honestly thought I was gonna die! Seriously! I was coughing and sputtering so much I'm surprised I didn't heave my lungs up! Anyway, you'd think Jess and Estelle might help a bitch out or at least offer some sympathy, but nah! They just sat there and laughed! They fucking laughed! Fun times!

Anyway, a bitch drank about two litres of water, so she's OK now, though. But like I said, I'm gonna need one of your massages tonight and some real TLC because Jesus fucking Christ, baby, my fucking throat is killing me. Kisses!"

Something about that voice note gripped Kara right by the balls she didn't possess, but she didn't know why. She found herself replaying the last five seconds.

"Jesus fucking Christ, baby; my fucking throat is killing me. Ciao!"

Who's voice is that?

And again.

"Jesus fucking Christ, baby; my fucking throat is killing me."

Who is that?

And again.

"My fucking throat is killing me."

Where do I know her from?

So she went back again.

"My fucking throat!"

And again.

"My fucking throat!"

Until it hit her.

Like a blade that stabbed into her conscious brain through the form of a traumatic memory, Kara was hit with the stark realisation of what triggered her. She had a vivid flashback. One in which she was all alone and trapped in an endless void of darkness. One which went like this:

"But I'm serious, Peter. Like if I ever stoop so low, just put a knife in my throat. My fucking throat. You'd think a woman from her generation would know better than to be a fucking nigger lover."

Kara's head was spinning.

Adrenaline raced through her bloodstream at such a rate she thought her heart might exit her mouth.

The woman in that voice note was the female nurse who mocked her when she was dying. It sounded insane to even comprehend, but it was true.

But there was more.

"But I'm serious, Peter."

Much more.

"I'm serious, Peter."

"So much more.

"Peter."

No. It can't be. It fucking can't be. It's not possible!

Kara didn't know what to do. She didn't have a clue. This was just too much. After she took another huge swig of that unknown liquor, she cradled her head in a desperate attempt to self-soothe. Little did she know, but she now looked just as she did when cowering in fear of her father as a small child.

"Was it you," her words asked a question, but her tone was anything but inquisitive. She was telling Peter who he was. She wasn't asking anything.

"Was it you." she repeated, frustrated when he didn't say a word.

Kara grabbed the bottle, prized its mouth open, poured copious amounts down its neck while it gagged, and punched it five times in the jaw with every ounce of her strength she could muster.

But it wasn't enough. It still wouldn't talk.

She punched it again, tensing every muscle in her right arm and back upon impact to will her body to generate even more force.

"UREEKKKHHH!"

This was a good one. She hurt it with that. She hurt it for sure.

But it wasn't enough.

"IT WAS FUCKING YOU! IT WAS FUCKING YOU!"

Peter wasn't just Hippocratic Oath. Wasn't just the man who'd been stalking her and making her life a living hell. It was also the cunt doctor who'd killed her. It was the one who let her die. It was literally Peter's fault, and you know what?

Because of that, it wasn't enough to hurt Peter. Causing physical harm wasn't going to be sufficient. She needed to break Peter. She needed to wreck Peter.

Kara needed to harm it irrevocably.

But she wasn't strong enough.

"EERRRKKKKGGG!"

Kara wasn't strong enough.

"NNNGGGGGGGNNN!"

Powerful as her body was, it couldn't do the kind of damage she needed to inflict.

"GUUGGGHHZ!"

But Kara had the spark of an idea. One that had her stand above him on the bed and stomp on its face like a woman possessed.

Its moans and cries both soothed and irritated her concurrently. She hated the sound of its fucking voice, but she loved the agony she heard radiating from it. She delighted in the fear she knew it was feeling, and knowing that she alone was the cause of that fear was everything.

Peter deserved all that and much more. Cunts like Peter took Winston away from her.

She punched it again.

"GARRKKKZZ!"

"CUNTS LIKE YOU ARE THE REASON I SPENT HALF A FUCKING CENTURY WITHOUT THE LOVE OF MY LIFE!"

Cunts like him mutilated Winston for life and robbed him of his dignity.

She punched him again.

"URQQQV!"

"CUNTS LIKE YOU ARE WHY I'VE ALWAYS FELT SO ALONE!"

Kara hopped to the bedside table, grabbed a large black remote control, saw one of Peter's worn socks on the floor and grabbed that, went back to the bed, stuffed the sock right in his mouth, prised his legs apart, and drove the remote right into his asshole.

She didn't know from where in her psyche the urge to do that arose, but upon seeing his features contort in shock and agony, she was glad it had.

Once it was halfway in, she quickly rotated it left and right in 180-degree circles while repeatedly violating his orifice.

Muffled roars of pain escaped the fabric of the wretched piece of shit's sock-gagged mouth, and Kara laughed at the sight.

One must remember, however, that Kara was not sober at this point. Not even close. In fact, words such as high, buzzed, wasted, blasted, twisted, wrecked, or destroyed would have been far more accurate depictions of her mental state.

However, one must also remember that this was all Peter's doing. With her vision tinted blood red and her heart racing faster than a NASCAR engine, she could barely remember her own name.

Peter awoke this demon within Kara when he tried to drug and rape her, so whatever happened next was on him.

However, as intoxicated as she was, she had enough sense to know her mental state was compromised.

Peter was in no better state, mind you. He was near delirious, in fact, both from pain and the deleterious effects of whatever the fuck he'd tried to drug her with. His pupils had now ballooned to five times their standard size, wiping out his irises to make his eyes utterly black as he bucked in confused agony. He seemed possessed, like the sad victim of demonic affliction.

But that wasn't just it.

There was more to the story than that.

Peter was in pain, yes, indeed. His pain was real. His pain was true. His pain was all-encompassing.

But that wasn't just it. That wasn't everything. Peter, it wasn't just pain.

Peter was also aroused.

"You're enjoying this, aren't you?" Kara asked, smirking sadistically.

Yes. Yes, he was. Peter, aka the stalker formerly known as Hippocratic Oath, aka the doctor who allowed her to die and laughed about it, was visibly stimulated.

Stiff.

Erect.

Bricked up.

Harder than Iron Man's armour.

While his confused and drugged body lay twitching on that hotel bed, all 2.5 inches of his pathetic manhood stood to attention. All while he rapidly became drenched in a sweaty puddle of his own making.

"Your little johnson's standing up, Peter."

No lies were spoken. Peter's penis stood to attention like a soldier giving the final salute to the coffin of his fallen comrade.

"You enjoy this."

He did. He enjoyed it. The sick, racist rapist fuck who'd abused her for no other crime than being black enjoyed this.

"You like being humiliated," Kara smiled with a twisted glare.

He did. He definitely did.

"Don't you?" she prodded sadistically, once again twisting that hard, thick, lumpy, rectangular remote inside his stinking asshole.

He didn't say anything, not one word, but then again, none needed to be spoken because his groans betrayed him. They gave the game away. Poor

Peter was in sweet, delicious, delirious sexual agony, all while his stiff nub quivered like a hairless Daffy Duck nervously covering his privates.

He looked so pathetic.

"You're so pathetic."

"PLEASE, I DON'T WANT TO BE HERE!"

Was that Winston?!

"WINSTON?!"

"IT HURTS! IT HUUUUURTS SO MUCH!"

Was that Winston?!

"TURTLE?! TURTLE ARE YOU THERE?!"

Nothing. She couldn't hear anything.

"WINSTON, ARE YOU OK?!"

Kara repeatedly called her dead lover's name in vain, desperate to hear his voice but unable to hear a damn thing. Now, she was panicked. Panicked, angry, frustrated, and filled with hatred.

"TURTLE?!"

Her Turtle wasn't there. She couldn't hear his voice. She couldn't feel his presence. She was once again alone. She had heard his voice; she was sure of it, but it was a fleeting tease, a whispering fantasy that dissipated in the winds and was now lost to the annals of time. She was still alone.

I'm still alone.

She was always alone.

I'm always alone.

Once more, Kara felt a dark urge emanating from the unknown depths of her psyche. And once more did Kara surrender to that urge rather than resist.

"Look at me," she said menacingly.

Kara spoke powerfully and with an unconcealed air of malice as she waited calmly for her captive's eyes to meet hers.

He eventually did as he was told. His eyes, now a mixture of terror, confusion and unbridled lust, fixed a terrified gaze right into the two cold voids pinned to Kara's face.

They then followed her seductive chocolate-skinned form as it walked to the other end of the room, propped her phone against the wall, checked it had enough storage, switched on its camera, set it to video, made sure it was angled towards him, zoomed in to capture the perfect frame, switched to 4K to maintain the bitrate quality, and hit record.

Then, those same eyes trailed Kara as she slowly walked towards their owner, seductively peeling away her clothes until she stood right in front of his spread-eagled body, wearing nothing but a blood-red and lacy Victoria's Secret lingerie set. His jet-black eyes widened at the sight, and that made her smile.

It made her feel powerful.

It felt good.

The shit felt right.

"PLEEEASSSEEE! PLEEEEAAAASSEEEEE! HELP MEEEEE!"

An explosion of guilt burst into her consciousness and gripped her heart, causing her to lose balance and stagger to her knees in shock.

It was her.

She was haunting Kara. Glued to her soul like hot napalm that Kara knew she couldn't escape. But she had to. She had to try. She couldn't go back to being who she was, and she didn't want to die.

I don't want to die.

Kara's fists clenched as she picked herself up and gritted her teeth for her prisoner to see.

"You spent all that time trying to make my life a living hell. Following me, stalking me, threatening me, contacting me on my private phone, and for what? Why? Why would you do that?"

"NGGGGHHHH!" came Peter's response.

"I know. I know exactly why, Peter. But I want to know if you do too. Do you know why you stalked me? Do you know why you hate me so much?"

Peter tried to speak, but his nervous system was fried beyond all comprehension, meaning all he could do was babble incoherently through the fabric of his worn, wet sock.

"Come again? I can't hear you."

Peter babbled again, his gurgling drug-induced splutters grating like screws against the chalkboard of Kara's psyche before she went over to him and slapped him hard in the cheek, her long nails lacerating his skin and causing him to bleed in multiple places at once. He cried yet again, with his solidified pecker still twitching from left to right like a caterpillar squirming in its chrysalis.

"SHUT UP!" Kara screamed, punching and scratching him again, causing even more blood to spill as the sock fell out of his mouth.

"HEEELLLLLLLPPPPP!!" Peter cried, his mouth finally unfettered.

"SHUT UP!"

"STOOOOPPP!"

She leapt on top of him, her bulbous, thong-clad ass cheeks pressing right against the micro penis that shuddered in response while its owner moaned in agonised delight.

"SHUT UP!" Kara cried, punching him right in the jaw with everything she had.

“STOOOP, PLEEEEEAAAASEEEE STOOOOOOPPPP!”

"SHUT THE FUCK UP!" she demanded, punching him two more times while the gargling groans from his shuddering mouth betrayed his rampant sexual desire.

"STOP CRYING OR I'LL GIVE YOU SOMETHING TO CRY ABOUT!

"I CAN'T! I CAAANNNNN'TTT!"

“UUUUKKKKKKRRRRGGGGHHJ!” she punched him again.

"STOP CRYING OR I'LL GIVE YOU SOMETHING TO CRY ABOUT!”

"NRRRRGGGGGHHH!"

And again.

"NRRRRGGGGGHHH!"

And again.

"GRKKKRHHHH!"

"STOP CRYING OR I'LL GIVE YOU SOMETHING TO CRY ABOUT!"

She continued to rain punches upon his skull like a woman possessed.

"WHY THE FUCK WON'T YOU SHUT UP!? WHY THE FUCK WON'T YOU SHUT UP?! I SAID SHUT UP! I SAID SHUT UP! SHUT UP WHEN I'M TALKING TO YOU! YOU HEAR ME?! ANSWER ME!"

She bucked back and forth on his rock-hard nub, continuously slamming both fists onto his face as he groaned and grunted like a wounded bull. This had her looking at her captive in both satisfaction and disgust.

"HOW THE FUCK IS THIS TURNING YOU ON?! HOW THE FUCK IS THIS TURNING YOU ON?! STOP CRYING, OR I'LL GIVE

YOU SOMETHING TO CRY ABOUT! STOP CRYING, OR I'LL GIVE YOU SOMETHING TO CRY ABOUT!"

She continued to grind the crack of her thick ass seductively against his bloated tool to further torment him, laughing in his face before whispering into his ear.

"Why's your johnson hard, Peter? Why is it fucking hard?"

"Mmmrrggghhh!"

"Lawd Jesus, yuh like dis, nuh true? Yuh like dis, nuh true, yuh likkle bitch? Yuh really like dis." Kara sneered in patois.

As Peter continued to groan beneath her, his handcuffed wrists pressing into the cold, hard steel of their restraints, Kara continued.

"So the 2-inch cock of the Neo Nazi who hates black women actually gets hard for the very same black women its owner claims to hate. Quite the conundrum you have there."

Kara smiled in his face, savouring the moment.

Now, in objective terms, that room stank. Peter's mildly unkempt musk permeated the atmosphere, along with the stench of alcohol and sweat. Still, right now, Kara didn't mind such smells at all. She rather enjoyed them, in fact. Now, they were the sweet scents of victory.

"And you know," she continued, "it's such a shame for a moment like this to be private, don't you think? Something like this should be shared with others. I mean, you're so discreet about your hatred for us, posting in private groups, trolling, stalking, and doing everything you can to make our lives a living hell, but why?

Why be so secretive? Why not let people know who you really are? Why not reveal yourself to the world? Why not unburden yourself? Don't you want that, Peter? Don't you want to finally be free?"

As Peter blabbered an inaudible stream of gibberish, Kara grabbed his phone, pointed it at his face to unlock it, and began filming herself.

"To the arrogant, ignorant, racist fuck who's watching, this is Kara Clark, and as you can see, I'm black as fuck. Coated from head to toe in chocolate and I know just how much that offends you.

The colour of my skin makes you want to put your fist through a wall, doesn't it? In fact, I can feel your anger burning through my phone. Oh, sorry, I'm being dumb; this isn't actually my phone at all; it belongs to Peter. Say hello, Peter."

She then stood up and flipped the camera around to point at Peter. She slowly panned all over his body as he lay sweating profusely, groaning, writhing, and still embarrassingly erect.

"Peter has been stalking me and making my life a living hell. He's harassed me on Instagram, X, and even through messages on my private number. How the fuck did you get my number, by the way, Peter?"

Peter didn't say anything. Peter couldn't say anything. Peter was in no fit state to talk. Kara continued.

"Oh, that's right, Peter can't talk right now, but why? Because I gave him a solid mouthful of the white powder he tried to drug me with. See how he's sweating? He doesn't look too good, does he? But I promise he's fine, I promise you he's great. In fact, he's having the time of his life. Look."

She once again angled the camera to his stiff cocklet and kicked as hard as she could with her pantyhosed right foot, smirking at his delirious groans of traumatic pleasure.

"Yuh see how him hard like rockstone? Look pon dat. Yuh coulda use dat ting as a weapon if it neva smalla than a baby toenail. An look yah, look pon dis."

She pointed the camera at the remote, which was still poking from his anus, bulging in and out with every breath he took. It was pushed out by about five inches, so she bent down and filmed herself thrusting it all the way back in, and guess what?

Peter groaned like a baby pig with a knife in its neck.

His body shuddered like he'd been struck by lightning, and he bucked wildly against his restraints as a massive globule of yellow, smelly, sticky semen erupted from his cocklet and landed on his soft, round belly.

Kara had caught the whole thing on camera.

"OHHH MY GOOOODDDD! OHHHH MMYYYYY GGGGOOOOOODDDDD! PLEASE! PLEASE SOMEBODY HELP ME!"

That was Winston. Not Peter.

"WINSTON?! WINSTON, BABY, MI DEH YAH!"

But then, just like that, Winston disappeared as quickly as he arrived. But poor Kara didn't know. Poor Kara spun her head in erratic circles in search of her lost lover but sadly found nothing.

"WINSTON?!!"

Until he returned.

"TIGER! TIGER, YOU HAVE TO KI...! YOU HAVE TO ...LL HI.... SO I CAN BE.."

"WINSTON?!!"

Winston was gone yet again, but she did feel him, if only for a brief moment. Kara felt his presence. She did, she really did, if only for a brief moment. And that brief moment was excruciatingly conflicting. Beautiful to hear his voice but horrific to listen to his pain.

"WINSTON?!!"

She bent down on the bed, sobbing violently.

"I don't know what to do."

She just didn't know.

"I'm lost."

That was until she once again made eye contact with the petrified eyes of her stalker and would-be rapist.

"You."

Until the sight of his sweaty, disgusting face filled her with more rage than she could handle.

"You."

Until every muscle in her body tensed tight, and saliva began to seep through the gaps in her clenched teeth.

"You killed me. You killed me. You killed me, and you took Winston from me. YOU FUCKING TOOK WINSTON FROM ME!"

She held the camera, pointed it at her face, and began to speak.

"Peter killed me."

However, before she could finish, Kara doubled over in psychic agony, clutching her gut and grunting in pain like she'd been shot. She didn't know what that was or where it came from, but she knew it wouldn't stop her.

"One way or di odda, mi ago finish dis video."

She composed herself and squared the camera on her sweaty and half-crazed face.

"Peter fucking killed me. He could have saved me, but he killed me. Him and you, his racist fuck of a wife. You said I was pathetic. You said I didn't deserve life. You decided to let me die. You fucking killed me, and you laughed about it. Well, now it's time for you to pay. Now you're gonna get what you deserve."

She turned the camera back to Peter's semen-laden belly.

"Look at all that man milk. It's all over his stomach, God damn. Wifey, are you watching? I did this to your husband without even touching his little pecker. Are you jealous?"

She turned the camera back to her face.

"When's the last time you made him spunk like that?"

She stopped the recording, opened Peter's chat app and forwarded the video to his wife. After that, she spent exactly three minutes and 59 seconds sitting silently. A conflicting yet anticipatory silence. One in which the absence of external stimuli was enough to remind her of the perplexing array of chemicals and emotions that blitzed her consciousness.

One which brought fear, self-loathing, and guilt to the forefront of her soul as she gritted her teeth in distress at the distant feminine wails she felt reverberating through her psyche. The long, drawn out, and agonising cries of trauma that sliced like a razor-sharp Stanley knife on soft flesh.

Before she even knew what she was doing, she'd opened Safari on Peter's phone and saw he had Google alerts set up to track all news coverage concerning her. The top alert was called:

The Kara Clark Scandal Continues, Blake Poole Wakes Up.

She clicked on it and read the following article.

31 | WHY DID SHE DO IT?

KARA | Peter's Hotel Room: Present Day

Blake Poole, the victim of attempted murder at the hands of the estranged fugitive and Instagram model Kara Clark, awoke from his coma this afternoon. Poole, having suffered numerous long-term injuries due to respiratory issues caused by extreme oxygen deprivation inflicted by the hands of the aforementioned Clark, is unable to speak or breathe unassisted. As such, he is currently being tended to by family and medical professionals.

Interestingly, while the media had opted to approach doctors and family for comment, Poole insisted on providing a written statement to the world. A statement which is reproduced below in its entirety:

"Honestly? I don't even know what to say. I'm angry, sad, heartbroken, confused, and even scared. I just don't know what to even think, let alone speak, because that woman is pure evil. People told me how bad she was, but I didn't listen. I should have, but I didn't. I thought I knew better, and my poor Gramps paid the price for my (expletive deleted) arrogance. I don't understand why she did what she did. I can't make sense of it.

I saw her. I actually saw her murder my grandfather, and for what? Why? It just doesn't make sense. She's a (expletive deleted) psycho. An absolute (expletive deleted) psychopath and even that doesn't do her justice. She killed my grandfather, and for what? Why? He was such a kind and sweet man; why on earth would anyone want to do that?

She's evil. (expletive deleted) evil, and I pray to God that she's brought to justice. Finally, I suspect she had something to do with the murder at 50 Cent's mansion party and have informed the police of th..."

The shock of having Blake out Kara as being the mansion party killer was cut short by Peter's ringing phone and interrupting her reading of the article. It was Claire, his wife. She was video-calling him.

And when Kara saw who it was, her thick lips and vengeful eyes formed a smile.

A menacing smile.

32 |

SECRETS LAID BARE

KARA | Peter's Hotel Room: Present Day

The frantic face of Peter's wife, Claire, filled his phone's screen as Kara looked back from behind, cold and dead eyes. Claire was a 30-something and decidedly average-looking blonde with shock and confusion plastered over every last millimetre of her pasty, freckled skin. She looked at Kara in terror, clearly unaware of what was happening or why.

But Kara loved that terror. It fueled and motivated her.

She wanted to cultivate that terror.

Nurture that terror.

Kara wanted to destroy this woman, and that's exactly what she would do.

"Where's Peter?!" Claire begged frantically.

"Who?" Kara replied, playing dumb.

"Peter! Where is he!?"

"You saw the video. He's laying strapped at the wrists and ankles with a TV remote sticking out of his asshole and a fresh batch of sticky baby gravy on his belly."

"PETER! HOW THE FUCK COULD YOU DO THIS TO ME!?"

"Bitch, calm down."

"PETER, YOU PIECE OF SHIT! YOU CHEATED ON ME WITH A FUCKING NIGGER!"

“Gyal, mi a go need yuh fi calm down.”

"I HATE YOU!"

Kara hung up the phone and sat for a while, twiddling her thumbs. Twenty-five seconds later, Claire called again. Kara, of course, answered nonchalantly.

"Are you going to calm down?"

"WHERE'S PETER?!"

She hung up yet again, sat down yet again, and played with her nails yet again. 10 seconds later, the phone rang once again, and she answered.

Yet again.

"Ready fi behave?" Kara replied in Patois.

"Where's Peter?" Claire begged with tears streaming down her freckled, pasty white cheeks.

"Bitch, how many times do I have to tell you? He's tied to the bed I'm sitting on and drugged out of his mind with a pile of his own nut butter on his stomach."

"Why are you doing this?" Claire sobbed.

"Why did you kill me?" Kara asked, matter of factly.

"Huh?"

"Bitch, did I stutter? Why the fuck did you kill me?"

"I don't know what you're talking about."

"Let me jog your memory. Antonia Hoell, an old white woman in hospital being operated on by you and your cunt husband, Peter. You said: 'Oh my God, Peter, that's so pathetic.' 'No, but that's top tier of pathetic. That's honestly what she was doing?' Jesus H Christ. How fucking embarrassing.' 'If I found myself in even half as worthless a state as that at her age, I'd just fucking end it.'

'She's so fucking worthless.' 'But I'm serious, Peter. Like if I ever stoop so low, just put a knife in my throat. My fucking throat. You'd think a woman from her generation would know better than to be a fucking nigger lover.' 'Let's do it. Let's switch off the life support.'"

With that, Claire's pasty white face became even paler than usual. She looked as though she'd indeed seen a ghost, which, upon reflection, wasn't far from the truth.

"How do you know that?"

"Why yuh kill mi?"

"What are you talking about?"

"Antonia Hoell, white woman, old. You killed her. Why?"

"She's you??"

"You know what? Forget it. It's not important."

"What's going on?"

"You and your husband don't like black people, right?"

A long silence transpired in which Claire didn't say a word but looked at Kara with the most delightfully worried expression.

"You and your husband hate black people, right?"

“No...I...I...”

"Bitch, you were just screaming about him cheating on you with a nigger."

“That....that's not true...”

Kara pulled the camera back to reveal her sexy lingerie-clad body. Her thick breasts bulged within the tight confines of her lacy bra as her right hand slid seductively over their soft contours. Her wet tongue licked her thick lips in a slow and sensual circle as she smirked malevolently at the woman gawking back.

To say the pupils of Claire's eyes widened with shock would be an understatement of biblical proportions.

"Yuh see dis?" Kara asked in Patois, smiling.

"What the fuck is wrong with you?!"

"Yuh see dis, Claire?"

"PETER!? PETER?!"

"Do you see my body? Do you see how smooth my skin is? How toned it is? You don't look like this, do you, Claire?"

Claire said nothing. She just stared at Kara in disbelief.

"Do you?"

Again, Claire said nothing.

"Did you know your husband's a secret nigger lover, Claire?"

"THAT'S A LIE!"

Kara pointed the camera onto Peter's cum laden stomach. After that, she grabbed a tissue off the floor and carefully used it to soak up most of the semen while making sure none of it touched her.

Then she shoved the tissue in his mouth as his wife Claire watched aghast.

"Claire, I want you to ask yourself a serious question. Have you ever made him cum as hard as that? Ever?"

She flipped the camera back onto herself and smiled.

"Have you ever seen your husband spunk like that before?"

"HEEEEELLLLLPPPP!"

It was her again. The feminine presence that Kara knew she couldn't outrun but also knew she couldn't bear the consequences of encountering.

With that, the abdominal walls of her fit frame clenched in pain as her knees buckled, causing her to fall to the ground and drop Peter's phone. It landed directly underneath her, with Claire's intimidated face perfectly positioned on its screen.

For a moment, they looked at each other, both in near intolerable amounts of pain and both searching desperately for an end to their suffering. For Kara, that moment felt like an hour, a long and laborious hour in which she suffered the indignity of having her hated foe bear witness to her weakness.

She couldn't let that happen. She wouldn't let that happen.

Never again.

She'd never give that bitch the satisfaction.

So she stood up, turned around, arched her butt to the camera, twerked, then bent down and smiled at Claire, who said:

"You fucking nigger."

"Wow, you're really sticking the hard 'r' on that, aren't you?? But Claire, did you know your husband subscribes to this nigger whore's Onlyfans? Did you know he regularly beats his meat to pics and videos of this fucking nigger whore? Did you know his phone, this phone, this phone I'm talking to you on right now, is a shrine to my nigger whore beauty?

Did you know that, Claire? It's full of my content. Did you know that, Claire? Or has your racist fuck of a husband been keeping secrets from his equally racist fuck of a wife? Tell me, did you know that, Claire?"

"You're lying."

"See for yourself, bitch."

Kara then forwarded about 15 minutes of videos and 100 megabytes of pictures. Unsurprisingly, fresh tears emerged from Claire's eyes as moans erupted from her lips.

"Your husband's living a double life, Claire."

As Claire continued to wail and sob, Kara got up, climbed onto the bed next to poor Peter, and lay beside him with her head next to his. He was sweaty, confused, and delirious, and now poor Claire could see them both together on her screen.

Kara grabbed another tissue, wiped Peter's face dry, and then planted long, soft kisses on his cheeks, forehead, and chin. She took no pleasure in this, of course. It was only marginally preferable to sticking her hand in a used toilet. But that said, she had to send a message and was willing to take one for the team to do so.

However, what happened next shocked her to her core.

Firstly, Peter moaned in pleasure. Nothing surprising about that, of course. It was to be expected at this point. However, what wasn't to be expected was that so did Claire.

That's right. It wasn't just poor Peter who loved being humiliated, but poor Claire too.

His fucking wife.

You couldn't make it up.

Kara looked at Claire's face; so many emotions were present. Pain, misery, sadness, anger, frustration, but also lust.

But also lust.

Claire was aroused.

"Yuh like dis too, nuh true, gyal?" Kara sneered in patios.

Of course she liked it. That fact was engraved onto the faint wrinkles of her pasty white face. But she didn't say anything. Not a single word.

"HEEEELLLLPPPPP!"

It was her again. The feminine presence.

"FUCK OFF!"

Kara felt a searing sensation in her heart from her cry, but she suppressed it. She had to.

“Dis turn yuh on, nuh true?” Kara snarled, focusing back on Claire, filming everything as she slowly ran her manicured fingers across Peter's trembling neck, shoulders, and chest.

She then pointed the camera at his dick, which was, of course, still harder than advanced calculus. Still standing to attention like the world's tiniest flickering candle in the wind. Still having not gotten even the tiniest bit softer.

"Look at that," Kara said, smiling at Claire. You'd think that after such an epic nut, his johnson would be spent, but I guess not. I guess it still wants more."

She trailed her hand down slowly across Peter's chest, stomach, and crotch but never directly touched his dick. Instead, her fingers snaked around it, twisting and turning in undulating circles while he moaned in delirium and Claire's breathing deepened.

"Claire, tell me you're not getting aroused by this. Tell me you're not."

Claire didn't say a word. She just continued to breathe deeper and deeper while staring intently at what Kara was doing to her husband.

"My God, you are. The white Neo Nazi's pussy gets wet for seeing her husband get humiliated by a dirt-skinned nigger. Who knew?"

Kara turned the camera back onto herself.

"But then again, I can't blame you. You've never had that effect on him, have you, Claire? We both know it's true.”

Kara slowly pointed the camera at her entire body, starting with her head and moving down to her shoulders, thick breasts, firm stomach, muscular thighs, smooth calves, and painted toenails, before slowly coming all the way back up to her face.

"Claire, tell me. Did you really see how much cum was on your husband's belly?"

Claire didn't say anything.

"Did you?"

Claire stayed as silent as a Pharaoh's tomb. She just sat in place with her mouth agape in fear and lust as her breathing became loud enough to be audible down the line.

"Claire, I'm asking you a question."

"I saw it," Claire finally replied, breathlessly.

"Yeah, that's right. Now tell me. Have you ever made your nub dick husband cum that hard?"

"No."

"No, you haven't. How many years have you been together?"

"Ten years."

"Ten years, an it only tek dis gyal ten minutes fi mess up him belly wid more nut dan yuh ever could."

"I'm wet."

"Of course you are."

Kara turned the camera back onto poor Peter. He was also moaning softly and writhing against his restraints as she slowly trailed her hand in circles around but never against his purple and bloated two-inch cock. The little thing was bulging like a freshly salted slug ready to burst.

"What's crazy is I still haven't really touched his johnson, but look at him. He's on another planet like Coruscant, Caprica, or Vulcan. He's literally in another world. Do you think he even knows you're here, Claire?"

Peter moaned loudly in response to his wife's name.

"Peter, ah wah dat? Yuh know seh yuh wife deh yah?" Kara sneered in Patois.

Peter responded with a near-orgasmic but wholly unintelligible stream of gibberish.

"Oh, he does, Claire, he does. He does know you're here. I imagine he's embarrassed; I mean, he has to be because he still has that remote sticking right out of his starfish. Actually, I think it's fallen out a bit, lemme just readjust that real quick."

Kara slowly, methodically, but forcefully thrust the remote deeper into Peter's rectum while twisting it sadistically. He arched his back like a steel beam bending under unfathomable pressure while grunting like a dying boar. All while Claire's breathing perpetually deepened, and soft gasps escaped her thin lips.

"Claire, did you know your husband's cock gets hard for being humiliated? Did you know he secretly wants to be fucked like a little bitch? Did you know that's what he really wants?"

"....No...No...Oh fuck, I'm wet..."

Kara kept the camera trained on her hand as she slowly violated poor Peter's rectum with that remote. He was wild with frenzied lust, and his wife wasn't far behind, both of which gave Kara the spark of an idea. She then crawled on top of him and saw he'd swallowed the cum-filled tissue she'd put in his mouth.

"Lard, Peter? Yuh really swallow up all dat cum? Claire, mi did know seh yuh husband was a freak, but mi seh, Lard Jesus."

Kara sat her ass back down on his crotch, his stiff cock going exactly one inch up the crack of her butt cheeks, barely reaching her thong. She sat down with all her weight rocking and gyrating back and forth against it, grinding her cheeks into his swollen testicles, and delighting in seeing his eyes roll back into their sockets."

"OHH...GOD....." Peter groaned.

"You hear that, Claire? This nigger's ass is like God to your man. Do you want more, Peter?"

"GOOOODDD.."

"You know, you're lucky I'm giving you as much as I am with a cocklet that small. Seriously, you wouldn't be able to even fuck me. I'm sitting square on top of your dicklet johnson right now and it's barely touching my thong. Claire, how the fuck does he satisfy you with this?"

Kara continued to grind her butt rhythmically against Peter's hard penis, twerking back and forth and in sensual circular motions along its pathetic length while keeping the camera trained on his face. His eyes were closed, his jaw was clenched, and he bit his lip in frustration as his body convulsed underneath her.

"You're enjoying this a little bit too much. Claire, I think your husband's going to cum for my thick black ass. He can't handle it. He's gonna explode."

"Yeah... he is..." Claire panted as Peter's shaking and convulsing intensified underneath Kara's ass.

“Touch yuhself. Touch yuhself like a dutty likkle slut.”

"I'm touching myself," she gasped.

"Do it.”

"Fuck, I'm so wet."

Kara continued to sadistically assault Peter's bloated crotch as his body trembled beneath her, his vibrations causing her hand to shake as she held the phone.

"Take your fingers, and play with your swollen clit, bitch."

"I'm touching myself."

"Finger yourself until you squirt."

Claire did exactly as she was told while Kara continued to grind her ass all over Peter's crotch. He shuddered and jerked violently. He was clearly going to cum, his orgasm was imminent.

"You're going to cum, aren't you, Peter? You're going to cum with something thick shoved up your starfish and my butt on your nublet."

Indeed, he was.

"NGGHGHGHGH!"

Peter couldn't hold it in. He couldn't. He was trying, though; God bless him. Lord knows why, but he was doing his gosh darndest, even though it was clear to all concerned that said darndest wasn't close to being darndest enough.

"Oh... oh fuck... Oh fuck oh fuck oh fuck..." Claire moaned. Her pale skin now a very pink hue and coated in sweat."

"No, no, no. Mi jus get a idea."

Kara climbed off Peter's swollen nub and giggled as he repeatedly thrust his hips upwards into thin air in a vain attempt to reestablish contact with her butt. Then she freed his left hand from its restraint, placed it on his cock, and laid down on the bed next to him on his right side with her face almost pressed against his.

With her lips grazing his sweaty earlobe and her eyes still locked onto the conflicted face of his wife, Kara smiled as her own words dripped from her lips and tongue like moist, wet honey.

"Peter, why don't you touch yourself. Oh, hold on... are you even left-handed? No, I guess not, but you can make it work. Go on, touch your little nub. Well, I'd say stroke it, but I don't see how that's possible with something so small. Flick it. Flick your little nublet until it sprays like a fountain. You can do it. You can make it work."

Peter did as he was told and used his index finger and thumb to rub his cock furiously while Kara had the camera locked on selfie mode so Claire could see them both at the same time.

That said, it didn't look like Claire could see much, as her eyes had rolled back so far she must have been staring at her own brain. Soon, Peter was bucking and moaning so violently that the entire bed was shaking.

"He's touching it, Claire. He can't stroke it like a real man, but he's rubbing it as best he can. But how does that make you feel? Your husband, the man who's supposed to have eyes for no other bitch is lying naked on a bed next to a woman who's done nothing but humiliate him but is still hornier than you've ever made him in your life.

Can you see how fast the bed's shaking? He's doing that. That's how wild I'm driving him. Look at his face, Claire."

Kara turned the camera onto Peter's frenzied face as he rubbed himself into oblivion before laughing at how clearly aroused Claire also was.

"Claire."

Claire didn't respond, but then again, she didn't need to. Her heavy breathing could be clearly heard down the phone.

"Claire, it's OK, you don't have to be shy. I know you're fucking horny. I know you can't take this. It's OK. Touch yourself."

"HEEELLPPPP! I CAN'T TAKE IT HERE! YOU GOTTA LET ME BE FREE!"

"Fuck off!" Kara screamed into the ether before looking back at a startled Claire with burning venom.

"Touch yourself like your husband is right now. Take your fingers, slide them under your panties, and explore your clit."

Claire didn't say a word but was clearly doing as told.

"NNNGHGHGHGHGHGXZZXCCC!"

That was Peter, relieved of his senses by copious amounts of alcohol and drugs and submerged within an overwhelming cascade of sexual frenzy.

"Your husband's gonna nut, Claire. He's gonna nut for a filthy nigger bitch. He's gonna nut harder for me than he ever would for you."

Kara turned the camera onto Peter's crotch. He'd gripped his penis between the tip of his thumb and index finger and was masturbating so furiously that his hand was now a pink blur. Kara was impressed he was able to go so rapidly on a cock so small it didn't allow for much vertical exploration, and on his weak hand nonetheless. He'd clearly had a lifetime of practice.

"GUUUUHHHHHHHH!"

"HEEELLLPPP MEEE!"

"LEAVE ME THE FUCK ALONE!"

"TIGER, HELP ME!"

"I'M COMING! I'M COMING! OH FUCK I'M COMING!"

"SHUT THE FUCK UP! SHUT THE FUCK UP!"

"OHH GOOODDDD... PLEASE... PLEEEEEEASSSEEE!"

"TIGER, PLEASE, YOU HAVE TO KILL HIM!"

"WINSTON?!"

"OH GOD.... I'M CUMMING!"

"GIVE ME MY BODY BACK!"

"FUCK YOU! FUCK YOU LEAVE ME ALONE! LEAVE ME ALOOONNNE!"

"UUUUUUUUUUUUUUUUUFFFFFFFFFFFF!"

"OH MY GOD.....OH....OH FUCK...."

Kara screamed, howled, and thrashed as Peter did the same, his wrist and ankles digging into their restraints as his wife could be heard and seen hyperventilating on his phone's screen. Kara didn't know how long it lasted. She was a slave to the moment and simply wasn't sure.

Seconds?

Minutes?

That was anybody's guess, but she did know that when she came around, Peter had another huge globule of unborn sons on his soft, round stomach, and his wife was a sweaty, heaving, dishevelled mess.

She'd made them both cum, and at the very same time.

How truly humiliating.

With that, Kara replaced Peter's restraint and left him alone while she went to the bathroom to take a long and luxurious shower. She made a specific point of taking the phone in with her and positioning it so Claire could see every inch of her gorgeous body as she bathed.

She tried to tell herself this was all to torture Claire, but it really wasn't. It was to save her own sanity. She needed Claire's cries to serve as a distraction from the haunting voice that refused to leave her in peace.

33 | TICK, TOCK, CRACKERS

KARA | Peter's Room: Present Day

At least half an hour later but possibly more, Kara was finally out of the shower and sitting on the bed next to a still chained up and still somewhat confused Peter. Claire was also on the phone, and neither looked close to being OK. Kara was no expert, but she was beginning to feel a deep sense of shame emanating from both.

And rightfully so.

"OK, so here's the deal. Claire, you don't know this, but I recorded that entire affair. Everything I did to Peter was captured on camera, look."

She got up, walked to the phone, which was still recording on the other side of the room, picked it up, and showed it to a positively mortified Claire. Afterwards, she returned to the bed and sat beside Peter's waist.

"Let me go!" he shouted.

"Oh, look. Your husband's back from Neverland. How are you, Peter? Or should I say, Hippocratic Oath?"

"LET ME GO!" he screamed even louder, clearly somewhat recovered from his drug-induced stupor.

"In good time, I got some stuff to say first."

"FUCKING LET ME GOOO!!! HELP!!! WHY AREN'T YOU HELPING ME?! SHOW ME HOW TO BEAT HER!!" Peter screamed, looking erratically in all directions while thrashing against his restraints.

"Shut up, Peter."

But alas, Peter would not listen. Instead, he insisted on shouting and thrashing against his restraints like a man possessed.

And so, in response, Kara stood on the bed and kicked him in the face as hard as possible with her right stockinged foot. All while making sure to film it so Claire could see.

"Are you ready to shut up now?"

The artist formerly known as Hippocratic Oath finally did as he was fucking told but kept on looking around the room in search of something Kara simply couldn't see.

His beady eyes darted in every possible direction like a compass situated slap-bang in the middle of the North Pole. In response, Kara administered a few deft foot slaps to the face, which had him finally make eye contact.

"Peter, I don't know if you're aware, but this is your wife Claire on the phone. Say hi, Claire. No? Feeling shy? OK then, well anyway, she saw everything that just transpired. She saw what I did to you, and she saw how hard you came all over yourself without me even needing to touch your little pecker."

A now mortified Peter made eye contact with his equally mortified wife. Both were as silent as a morgue at night.

"Like I just said," Kara continued. "I recorded all of that on this phone, and here's what's going to happen. You two will take all the money in your bank account and forward it to the Malcolm X Foundation; don't worry, I've sent the payment details to Claire's phone. If you do as you're told, I'll delete this video, and you racist pieces of shit can go on with your lives.

However, if you don't, this video gets forwarded to Peter's Facebook, Twitter, sorry, X, Instagram, and LinkedIn pages. When that happens, everyone you know will see what just transpired. Everyone you know and respect and who knows and respects you, friends, family members, cousins, nieces, and colleagues, will see the two of you humiliated by a chocolatey-skinned black nigger, bitch. How's that sound?"

"You're evil," said Claire in shock.

"Apparently so, but that's not an answer," Kara responded.

"You wouldn't," Peter gasped.

"You sure about that?" Kara said, smiling.

"All of our money?!" Claire pleaded.

"All of it."

"Please."

"Where was please when I begged you not to let me die?"

"What are you talking about?"

"Withdraw all of your fucking money and forward it to the Malcolm X foundation, or I'm going to destroy both of your fucking lives. Do you understand me, yes or no?"

"Go fuck yourself," Peter replied resolutely.

"OK, you asked for it."

Kara hopped onto the floor and took a full body shot of Peter's utterly naked body chained to all four corners of that hotel room bed.

"What are you doing?"

"Just updating your Facebook status."

She then posted that picture onto his Facebook page along with the caption:

“There's nowhere else I'd rather be.”

Within a minute, his phone lit up with Facebook notifications. Comments and DMs came in faster than Kara could count. She showed Peter and Claire what was happening, and, unsurprisingly, both were mortified.

"YOU FUCKING BITCH!" Peter screamed, thrashing against his restraints and desperately trying to grab Kara with his chained left hand.

She casually stood out of his reach with a smirk.

"Claire, you need to speak to your husband because if he even tries to lay another hand on me, this day will end badly for both of you."

"You want us to send you all of our money??" Claire asked frantically.

"Talk to your husband, Claire."

Kara turned the phone to face Peter. Now that he and his wife could see each other, he became teary-eyed.

"Baby, I'm sorry," he blubbered, his eyes quivering like a wilting daffodil in a violent hailstorm.

"Oh, my God, Peter. Oh my God!" Claire replied, sobbing.

"What?? What is it??" Peter asked.

"Baby, I'm getting calls and messages. Oh fuck... but oh fuck it won't stop... oh my God.... Oh my God, Mom's just messaged me! And Sheila from work! Oh my God!"

“Fuck! Fuuuuuuccccckkk!”

"And that's just from one picture," Kara added with a smirk. "Now, you have exactly sixty seconds to do as I commanded, or I'm posting the full video on every social media account Peter owns."

"FUUUUCCKKKK! FUUUUUUCCCCKKKK!" That was Peter, of course, but you already knew that. The poor guy was sobbing and bawling like a freshly butt-slapped newborn.

Seconds later, his phone began to ring. It was his mother, apparently. A woman who answered to the name of Jackie.

Kara briefly wondered why on earth he had his mother's name saved in her contact but ultimately decided she had more pressing matters with which to contend.

"Oh, look, Peter. It seems Jackie's trying to call you. Do you think it's about that post? Want me to answer and let her know you're preoccupied? Or maybe we can have a four-way husband, wife, mother, and stalkee video call?"

"NO! NO! FUCK, DON'T ANSWER IT!"

"Peter, we have to send the money!"

"IT'LL BANKRUPT US!"

"This will be worse. Tick, tock, crackers."

"We're gonna do it! We're gonna do it!"

"Sorry, what's that?"

"WE'RE GOING TO SEND IT!"

"I didn't hear you. Can you repeat that?"

"I'M SENDING THE MONEY!"

"HOW, WE CAN'T SEND EVERYTHING WE OWN! IT'S NOT POSSIBLE!"

"Explain."

"WE HAVE SAVINGS AND INVESTMENT ACCOUNTS THAT WE CAN'T WITHDRAW FROM IMMEDIATELY. IT'LL TAKE DAYS TO GET THE FUNDS FROM THEM!"

"So, how much do you have in your regular account?"

"ABOUT 50,000!"

"Lovely. So you're going to prove that to me and then send it all to the Malcolm X foundation. Like I said, I've already forwarded the payment details."

34 | WE DON'T WANT YOU

ANTONIA | The Hoell Residence: April 5, 1965

As Antonia awoke in her wheelchair, she was greeted with the intense yet familiar physical throbbing she'd begun to suspect would be present until her dying day. Her body pulsed with pain from the tip of her neck down to the base of her spine, making the mere act of existing something she now questioned the importance of.

Moving wasn't just effort; it was agony. Turning her neck to look to her right sent blades of trauma slicing through said neck, meaning she had to turn her whole body instead. However, she couldn't move her legs and had to swivel in her fucking wheelchair as a result, but still hadn't fucking figured out how to fucking do that fucking yet.

And, to make matters fucking worse, her fingers kept getting caught in the fucking spokes of the chair and getting semi-crushed between them and the wheels every time she had the temerity to try to move from point fucking a to fucking b.

It was all so fucking miserable.

All so devastatingly traumatic; however, not quite as excruciating as the sad truth of where she now was. Having been cut from Richard's wealth and being so disabled she couldn't currently work, Antonia had nowhere to go but back to her parents' home, a fact as humiliating as it was soul-crushing.

She hated everything about that place. Everything.

She loathed the smell, detested the decor, and despised the endless array of painful memories it invoked.

The constant unprovoked attacks on her beauty, intelligence, and character. The unprovoked punches to her jaw. The unprovoked knees to her ribs. The many unconsented nighttime jaunts Daddy Jonathan made to her bedroom.

Jaunts, she was powerless to stop.

Jaunts she suspected her mother was well aware of but somehow didn't mind.

And now she was back. Antonia was back in Moss fucking Bluff. Back in that same old fucking house.

Fucking penniless.

Fucking powerless.

Robbed of the use of her fucking lower extremities and still entirely in the dark about what had happened to Winston.

Her mother was dead now. She'd died the year before while Antonia was working with Malcolm X, and she honestly wasn't sure how she felt about it.

Overjoyed? On the verge of tears? As numb as the two useless lumps of flesh jutting out from the base of her torso?

Antonia didn't know, but she did know that she hated dealing with Daddy Jonathan. She hated dealing with her father. She couldn't stand seeing his fucking face. That conflicting mixture of shame, guilt, judgement and maddening happiness to see Antonia made her want to scream with rage.

Even more, she hated the mixed fucking feelings she felt about watching him fucking age. He was losing his strength, bit by bit and month by month. He was becoming weak, doddery, passive, confused, and old.

And a part of Antonia revelled in it.

A significant part of her soul rejoiced in the knowledge that even despite her own extensive injuries, he still didn't possess the requisite strength to ever again do to her what he once did with impunity.

He was broken, beaten, unsure of himself, and guess what? The vengeful side of her soul relished every last scent of the sweet taste of victory. It drew great comfort from seeing him reduced to a mere shadow of what he once was and relished the resulting power it felt. With a broken and disabled body that looked just as ugly and worthless as it felt, seeing his now derelict form gave Antonia meaning.

It gave her soul purpose.

However, that wasn't the only side of Antonia's psyche, for there was also another. There was also a loving, caring and compassionate side of her that she wished didn't exist but sadly couldn't escape. This part of her being felt agonised by her father's ongoing demise and wanted nothing more than to see him return to full strength.

Oddly enough, this side of Antonia's soul would rather have him back to the way he was and able to abuse her at his discretion if it meant she didn't have to bear witness to his ongoing decomposition.

And Antonia detested that aspect of her being.

Anyway, she was, somewhat unsurprisingly, rolling by in her wheelchair when a random hand dropped a letter through the mailbox to the floor, and her heart lit up with hopeful anticipation. It's not an exaggeration to say that her soul immediately began to shine.

But why?

Because, if you recall, the late and great Brother Malcolm X had managed to track Winston's family before his untimely demise, meaning that Antonia had since reached out to them.

She had been waiting with bated breath for their reply and hyperventilating whenever a letter manifested, and today was no different. More excited than a four-year-old on Christmas morning, she rolled over as quickly as possible, a phrase which meant little considering how poor she still was at operating her chair. But still, she eventually made her way over to see that the letter had her name on it, which excited her even more.

Now she just needed to pick the damn thing up.

Her first instinct was to grab it with her toes, but her feet weren't up to the task. It was like they were submerged in a deep field of static and received only 6% of the commands her brain decreed, so that wasn't an option.

Fuck.

The fucking letter was so near. It was right at her feet, but still so far that she felt nothing short of helpless sitting there and looking at it. It was both a painful reminder of how far she'd fallen as well as a grim totem of her future reality as a cripple.

Antonia tried to grab the letter with her hands. However, her arms weren't long enough to do so without falling from her chair, so she used her right hand to grab the corner of the wall and steady herself while she reached for it. However, said arm lacked the requisite strength for the task and hence had her face planted onto the cold floor in seconds.

Still, as painful as that was, and it certainly was no tiptoe through the tulips, it did mean that Antonia was now right next to the letter.

Success.

Exasperated, she finally picked up the letter and opened it.

It was from Francine, Winston's mother. This fact had Antonia brimming with more excitement than a child at their first taste of Christmas pudding.

This was the moment she'd been waiting for, one over seven years in the making. She had finally heard from Winston's family. From her real family.

Finally, the lines of communication had re-opened. Finally, she could re-enter their lives in some capacity. Finally, she could find out what had happened to Winston and whether he missed her as much as she missed him.

Finally she might be reunited with the love of her life, the only thing that gave her existence meaning.

Antonia read the letter.

"Antonia. I know you have been trying to contact my family. I also hear that you are now back in Moss Bluff, and I am writing this letter to tell you to stop looking for us, especially Winston. We no longer want you in our lives and never will.

Winston suffered life-changing injuries from that attack and is now permanently disabled. He forgets who he is, your name, how to tie his shoelaces, and wakes up every night screaming, sometimes in his own filth. You did that to him, Antonia.

Knowing you has ruined my son's life. Your presence put him in danger, but you didn't care. You shouted, screamed and drew attention to my sweet boy, knowing what those people would do if they found him, but you didn't care.

You didn't care.

You didn't care about Winston. You only cared about Antonia. You never cared about Winston. You have only ever cared about Antonia.

You were my son's world, but he was your plaything. Your pet. Your black monkey to enjoy when you got bored of your perfect life of white privilege and needed a short vacation. He meant nothing to you. He was nothing to you. And, Antonia, now you're nothing to us. We don't want you.

He is blind in one eye, Antonia. And confused, and in constant pain, and permanently mutilated, The things those animals did to my boy are too painful to write, and we all wish we never laid eyes on you.

We can't even do anything about it. We can't go to the police because they don't care. We can't go to the government because they don't care. Nobody cares. Nobody cares about us the way they care about you. You're so lucky to be white, and you either think everybody is or don't care how your actions can affect people who aren't.

There were so many beautiful black girls who wanted to be with my lovely son. He could have been happy with any of them. He could have started a family with any of them. But instead, he had to fall in love with you, an ugly white bitch who isn't even 5% of the human being he is.

We hope never to see you again. Please stop searching for us. Go live your ugly white bitch life and leave us alone, Antonia. Your father was right to do those things to you.

I'm glad Winston has forgotten your name; it's far more than you deserve.

We don't want you.

Goodbye."

Tears swelled in Antonia's eyes as she read that letter. However, by the time she finished, her eyeballs were home to a torrential downpour of grief. Her arms and head collapsed lifelessly against the hard floor of her father's hallway as her torso and toes flopped weakly like a fish three minutes out of water and thus nearing the end of existence.

Antonia was alone. She didn't have Malcolm. She didn't have Winston, she didn't have a family, and after her husband left, she didn't have money. She was just alone. Alone, disabled, ugly, and poor.

As Antonia's mind, soul, and lungs wailed in mutual agony, the stark realisation of her situation sliced through her being.

She had nothing.

Antonia had nothing.

35 | WHEN LOVE DEMANDS BLOOD

KARA | Peter's Hotel Room: Present Day

"Another life you have to claim.

His soul awash with pain and shame.

For his existence ends this day.

His destiny, the price you pay.

For Winston's soul, doth hang askew.

So Peter's life, you must undo.

By moonlight's touch, their paths will cross.

A sacrifice, a soul is lost."

Kara heard that all too familiar collection of feminine whispers emanating from the air behind her chocolate-coated neck. Speaking almost at the same time but just ever so slightly out of sync, they created an eerie and unsettling echo which made the molecules of her skin twist and turn as they secreted sweat.

"We are Kalizar," they smiled sadistically.

Kara wasn't even looking in their direction, but their sinister delight bled through every syllable.

"Help! Help! You gotta help me!" Peter screamed, looking past Kara. Could he see them?

How is that possible?!

"He can see you?!" Kara shouted at the unperturbed demons who stood rooted to the spot, hunched to the left and smiling malevolently. Their heads slowly twisted and nodded in multitudinous directions like the serpent locks of Medusa.

"Peter's life must end this eve," Kalizar replied nonchalantly.

"You can see them?!" Kara screamed at Peter.

"Baby, what's going on?!" Claire cried from Peter's phone.

As Kalizar's body writhed and squirmed, their three giggling heads looked at Kara. They slowly rotated on the spot, never once taking their eyes off her.

"Kill him. Kill the man who caused this pain."

"WHAT THE FUCK?!"

That was Peter, unsurprisingly.

"End his days, erase his ways. When he has died, Winston will thrive."

Once again, Kara heard cries, screams, wails and moans. She wasn't sure if she was hearing or feeling them from deep within her soul, but either way, there they were.

Harrowing moans.

Agonising moans.

Tens of thousands of haunting moans.

Moans, which all sounded like Winston in various states of torture.

Moans are interspersed with flashes.

Glimmers.

Impressions of Winston in despair.

Winston was hurt.

Badly.

"Obey this call, or Winston falls."

"Wah yuh plan fi do to him?!" Kara screamed.

"Obey this call, or Winston falls."

"YOU'RE SUPPOSED TO BE ON MY SIDE! YOU'RE SUPPOSED TO BE ON MY SIDE!"

That was Peter, once again.

"Baby, what's happening?!"

"HELP! HELLLLLP!!"

"Please, don't do anything to Winston!"

"YOU'RE SUPPOSED TO BE ON MY SIDE!"

"Obey this call, or Winston falls."

"YOU CAN'T DO THIS! I DID EVERYTHING YOU AS..."

Kalizar slithered across to Peter and pressed a single bony finger into the flesh of his brain through the space between his eyes. Seconds later, his body fell limp against the bed as his wide-open eyeballs darted left and right in fear, and frantic breaths escaped his lips.

"Baby?! Baby! What's happening?!"

That was Claire, utterly oblivious to what had transpired.

"Mi nuh waan fi kill nuhbody," Kara cried, fresh tears forming.

"This we understand."

"Mi cyaan keep do dis," Kara continued in patois; tears now streaming down her cheeks."

"You will do what we must."

"I don't want to kill anyone."

"What are you doing?! We paid you the money, just leave! What do you want from us?!"

That was Claire. Peter, if you recall, had been relieved of the ability to move and speak.

"We yearn for the delicious nectar of Peter's soul... Antonia."

Antonia. Fucking Antonia. That name seared Kara's beating heart like a red-hot blade.

"Nuh call mi dat."

"Wish to see Winston once more?"

"Yes. Yuh know seh mi do. Yes."

"End Peter's life, and this shall be yours."

"Fuck."

Kara looked directly at Claire down the phone. She was quivering with terror and confusion.

"Claire, let me ask you something."

Claire didn't say anything; she just looked intently at Kara with a panicked expression, which let her know she was hanging on her every word.

"Do you remember an old white woman called Antonia Hoell, who you and your husband operated on? She'd been found masturbating to 'ebony porn', as you called it?"

"How do you know about that?"

"Do you remember what you said?"

"How could you possibly..."

"Do you remember what you said?"

"What on..."

"Oh my God, Peter, that's so pathetic. No, but that's a next level of pathetic. That's honestly what she was doing? Jesus H Christ. How fucking embarrassing. If I found myself in even half as worthless a state as that at her age, I'd just fucking end it.

She's so fucking worthless. I'm serious, Peter. Like if I ever stoop so low, just put a knife in my throat. My fucking throat. You'd think a woman from her generation would know better than to be a fucking nigger lover."

"How on earth do you know..."

"I was that old white woman, Claire. I was the old bitch dying in front of you. The one you and your racist fuck of a husband decided to not help. You fucking killed me and never thought twice about it. Did you?

Well, now I'm here. Now I'm back, and I'm in this body. This beautiful, sexy body that your husband's been slapping his Johnson to behind your back. Did you know Peter subscribes to black women on Onlyfans? Did you know he sleeps with you but secretly wishes he could be with them? Did you know that, Claire?"

"No."

“Well, now yuh know, white gyal. Mi beg yuh not fi kill mi, but yuh neva care. Yuh laugh afta mi. Yuh laugh an seh mi worthless. Yuh seh mi was nuttin, an mi did believe yuh. Mi did hate bein like yuh. Mi did hate bein’ white,” said Kara in Jamaican patois.

“My white family punched me, kicked me, told me I was ugly in one breath and used my body to satisfy their sick pleasures in the next. They were just like you. Just like you. But one thing they didn't do was kill me. You did that, Claire. You did it.

You killed me.

But now mi back. Mi back inna dis body, an it feel good, it a everyting mi ever want. It is everyting mi ever want. But it come... it come wid a price. Dis body nuh really mine. No matta how much mi love it, no matta how much it a everyting mi ever want, it nuh really mine, an mi get remind of dat more an more every rassclaat hour.

I hear voices, Claire; I hear voices in my head; they don't counsel me or understand, but they talk to me. They talk to me. They tell me things that I must do. They tell me things I'll do to you, and I just don't know what to do. I don't fucking know what to do, Claire.

But mi know dis. Mi know seh everyting mi a go through a yuh fault. Mi know seh people like yuh a di reason Winston get tek weh from mi. Mi know seh racist eediat like yuh a why mi black family disown mi.

I know ignorant shit stains like you are the reason why they, brother Malcolm, and the rest of my people had to suffer so much injustice. You're why I was shot and lived most of my life disabled in agonising pain, Claire. You are."

"What? I don't know what you're talking about,"

"Mi know."

"Oh my God..."

"What? Oh."

Kara looked down at her arm and saw that it, along with the rest of her body, was withering away on the spot. She was becoming a corpse again. Genuine dread bled throughout her entire being.

"Please, please let me go..."

Claire's eyes widened in near-paralysing horror as she saw the ghoul Kara was becoming. It was a genuine fear which haunted Kara's soul in ways she couldn't consciously articulate, but knew she'd never forget.

"Yuh husband stalk mi an mek mi life a livin hell, an mi nuh even know how him do it. Mi nuh know how or why, but fi some reason him decide fi mek mashin mi up him life mission." Kara said in patois.

"As if killing me once wasn't good enough, he had to do it twice, but I'm better than him, Claire. I'm better than your husband. I actually don't want to kill him. Despite everything he did to me, I don't wanna kill him, but I got to."

Kara grabbed what was left of Peter's powder and began pouring it all into his mouth while looking at his frantically quivering eyes. His pupils were so big they entirely covered his irises. He still couldn't move, but she clearly saw that he was straining to do so.

Peter was completely paralysed from head to toe, but so help him God, his eyes still functioned. He was still conscious, and he'd heard everything Kara said. He knew what was coming. He knew he was about to die, but he couldn't even scream. All he could do was let out the most sad and pathetic whimper.

Once she'd finished pouring the powder down his neck, she held his mouth open and began emptying bottle after bottle of hard liquor down his throat. She did all of this while Claire cried and screamed down the phone line like it was going to make a damn bit of difference.

By the time Kara was finished, Peter's eyes had rolled into the back of his head, and his body convulsed like a wounded gazelle twitching in the jaws of a lion, fighting futilely against its inevitable demise.

Kara didn't like what she'd done; she hated it, in fact. But Winston came first. Winston always came first. Winston was everything. If there was even the tiniest chance she could save his soul by erasing another, she'd take it. It wasn't even up for debate.

Kara would kill anyone for Winston if she had to. Anyone.

"Peter a dead," she said to Claire; her skin slowly regaining its youthful beauty as his body shuddered like a dying ember flickering in the cold, desperate for a last gasp of life.

"What the fuck are you?!"

"Claire, remember what you said you'd do if you were ever in such a pathetic position? You said something about taking a knife to your neck."

"Peter! Peter! Peter!!"

"Claire, stop."

"HELP!! HELP!! HEEELLLLLLPPP!!!"

"Claire, stop."

"SOMEONE HELLLP!!"

"Nobody's here to help you, Claire. Anyway, remember the video I made of you and your husband? I'm about to post it to his Instagram, Twitter, LinkedIn, and Facebook pages.

Not only will the entire world see your husband having the biggest orgasm of his pathetic life by being fucked in the ass with a foreign object, but you frigging yourself to orgasm at the sight of it too."

"NO! NO!!!! PLEASE!"

"You said you'd take a knife to your neck if you ever stooped so low, Claire, and I think you just have. Let's see if you're true to your word."

"NO! NO! PLEA-."

Kara ended the call and turned away from Peter's trembling body as she began sharing the video on his social media accounts. However, as she did this, Kalizar once again began to speak.

"There is but one more life to end.

When deed is done, you'll see your friend.

Winston shall be returned to thee.

Eternal love, most true and free.

Unbound by anguish, strains or woes.

A love long lost, now yours to hold.

A chance, once more, to be his wife.

So kill for us, and kill tonight."

"A chance to be Winston's wife?? Are you going to bring him back to life??"

"Kill for us, and kill tonight?"

"Answer me!"

"A love long lost, now yours to hold.

A chance, once more, to be his wife.

So kill for us, and kill tonight."

"A who yuh want mi fi kill?!"

"All will be revealed in time."

"When?!"

"Exit this room, Antonia. You are not safe."

"What!?"

"Get out, escape, and make haste before grievous harm is inflicted upon you."

"What?!"

"Now."

With Kalizar's words, Kara heard the faint yet growing sounds of sirens in the distance. It sounded like the police.

36 |
IN THE EYES OF AN INNOCENT

KARA & ANTONIA | Central Park: Present Day

Kalizar was right. Kara definitely did need to escape because as soon as she left the hotel building, the police stormed in after her.

They then saw Peter's dead body, meaning that not only was she now definitively labelled a serial killer, but her manhunt had exploded like nobody anticipated.

Kara Clark was now public enemy number one.

Everyone was looking for her.

Literally everyone.

In fact, Kara hadn't just gone viral this time; she'd made international news. They talked about her from London to Sydney, Tokyo, and even Canggu.

Between the scandalous reports of the circumstances surrounding Peter's untimely demise alongside the now mega-viral video of what transpired in that hotel room, the situation looked beyond grim.

Kara was seen by all of society as a baying and deranged psychopath who needed to be imprisoned for the good of mankind.

And she didn't exactly disagree, truth be told.

She had to turn herself in.

She had to.

She just had to.

But not before she brought Winston back.

Not until then.

She'd use her own life to bring back the only love she'd ever known.

And then she'd turn herself in.

And then she'd let whatever happened happen.

But she couldn't live like this.

She simply couldn't go on like this.

Living on the streets,

Living on the run.

Haunted by those voices.

She wouldn't go on like this.

It had been over 24 hours since Kalizar made her kill Peter. Now, Kara was sitting on a park bench next to a little Indian girl and facing the dark reality of the next gruesome act she was set to commit.

In stark contrast to the blitzkrieg of emotions from which she suffered, the little Indian girl happily minded her own business. In fact, as she sat with her legs casually crossed at the ankles, a relaxed air of contentment emanated from her being.

She seemed soft, warm, nurturing, composed, and entirely at peace with her surroundings. This little Indian girl radiated an air of quiet contentment that touched Kara in ways she couldn't understand or articulate, even if she could. Ways which made her stomach tie into thick knots.

Knots of pure, unadulterated, unavoidable guilt.

As birds and children sang and played all around, as the sun shone brightly 93 million miles high with its warm rays caressing everything in sight as well as everything beyond, and as the faint echo of sirens could be heard in the distance, the little Indian girl's energy was as light as spring's fresh rebirth.

Kara's, however, was darker than an ancient Egyptian tomb.

She knew what she had to do. But she didn't want to do it.

She knew what she had to do. No matter what she tried to tell herself, she knew. But she also didn't know what terrified her more. Was it the horror of what knowing was required or that she knew she would go through with it?

Kara just didn't know.

Why? Why her? Why this little girl?

Those thoughts clattered left and right in her brain as she felt bile rising to her mouth from her throat.

How old is she? Seven? Nine?

It was wrong. Evil. Too evil. Too extreme. She wouldn't do it. She couldn't. She wouldn't. Not a child. Not like this. She wanted Winston back, of course. Of course, she did. She wanted that more than anything, but at what cost?

At what cost?

As Kara sat clad in that hoodie, doing her best to obscure her face from the smattering of human traffic all around, the irony of that fact was not lost. There she was, finally inhabiting the beautiful and attention-grabbing body she'd always craved, but now being forced to hide said body from the world at large.

She could no longer revel in the delights of her beauty and would never be able to do so again.

With that thought, the little Indian girl shot Kara the sweetest smile she'd seen in years and said:

"Hi."

"Hi," Kara replied sheepishly.

"Wow, you're so pretty," the little Indian girl continued. She had a British accent.

She's British??

Of course, that wasn't a major shock as New York was an international city that attracted a lot of tourism, but it was still unexpected. Kara assumed she was American.

"Thank you," Kara replied.

"I hope I look that beautiful when I'm an old lady."

What the hell did she just say?

"Old, lady? I'm not old," Kara replied, confused.

"Yes, you are, silly," the little Indian girl said, smiling sweetly. "You're older than my grandma."

That comment knocked Kara for six.

How the fuck does she know that??

Kara didn't know what to do or say. She didn't even know what to think. She ran tripping circles in her mind while twitching erratically on the spot for fifteen seconds before she found the strength to speak. The little Indian girl, however, never once took her eyes off her.

"What do I look like to you?" Kara asked timidly.

"Huh?" the little Indian girl replied, confused.

"What do I look like? Can you describe me?"

"You're a really pretty old white lady."

As if to add intentional emphasis to this shock, Kara felt Kalizar's presence once again squelching against her mind.

She felt tentacles coiling tight around her neck and growing tighter with every last futile attempt to take a breath.

No words were required.

Kara knew precisely why Kalizar had arrived. Kara needed to do as commanded.

"Thank you so much," came her forced reply. It felt so hard to utter those words. Almost suffocating. Amongst other things, Kara was now fighting the urge to cry.

"But why are you seeing me like that? That's not who I am."

"Yes, it is. You've never been anyone else."

Kara looked down at her hands and saw they were still caramel brown. Still youthful. Still beautiful. She gasped an inward sigh of relief but was now even more confused.

"Where are your parents?" she asked, limbs a-quiver with emotion.

"Back in England," said the little Indian girl.

"Then what are you doing here all alone?"

"I came here for a holiday with my cousin and her family, and we went swimming for her birthday party. There was a big group of us, though, and we took two minibuses to get here from the house. When we came out from swimming, I asked my uncle if I could go to the shop to get a Double Decker chocolate bar, and he said yes, so I went, but they didn't have it!

They didn't have any Double Deckers. They didn't even know what it was! So I had to get this thing called a Hersheys which is nowhere near as good. But when I came back, everyone was gone. None of the minibuses were here."

"How long have you been alone?" Kara asked.

"I don't know, maybe 20 minutes, I think."

"So you're lost in a foreign country all on your own?"

"Yeah, I guess."

"How old are you?"

"I'm eight and a quarter," The little Indian girl said proudly.

"But you're not scared. I would have been terrified if that happened to me at your age."

"I don't know. I guess I've been through worse," The little Indian girl replied with a shrug.

"Like what?"

At this moment, and for exactly two whole seconds, Kalizar's embrace strangled her neck like a boa constrictor. The little Indian girl watched on in confusion as Kara's face bulged and contorted in agony.

It was a warning.

Kara needed to do what she needed to do.

"Please don't make me do this," she sobbed quietly.

"GIVE ME MY BODY BACK!"

Both Kara and the little Indian girl gasped in shock.

"Who was that?" asked the little Indian girl, stunned.

"Did you hear her?" Kara asked, with a tear running down her cheek.

"LET ME GOOOO, PLEASE!!!"

"Yes," the little Indian girl replied, looking frantically in all directions before noticing Kara's tears.

"Are you OK?"

"No. Mi nuh alright. Mi deh far, far from alright."

"Huh, my friend talks like that too..."

Before the little girl could finish her sentence, the scream came yet again, making her jolt on the spot like she'd been bitten by a cobra.

"GIVE ME MY BODY BACK! GIVE ME MY LIFE BACK!"

"Who is that?" asked the little girl.

Unbeknownst to Kara, a middle-aged black woman had walked past both her and the little Indian girl, studying them both with a concerned expression.

"Mi nuh want fi do dis," Kara cried, tears streaming down her cheeks. The little girl rested a hand on her knee and looked up at her with a sympathetic smile.

"What don't you want to do?"

"This."

"What?"

"GIVE ME MY LIFE BACK!"

"LEAVE ME ALONE!" Kara screamed, slamming her fists hard into the park bench. The little girl rubbed her knee and smiled into her eyes in soothing support.

"She's speaking to you, isn't she?" the little Indian girl asked. Kara said nothing and simply continued to cry for a few moments.

"Yes," she finally replied.

"And you're in her body? Is that why you were surprised I could see you're an old lady?"

Who the hell was this girl? How could she be so observant and intuitive?

"How do you know all this?"

"I'm smarter than the average bear," the Indian girl replied with a shrug.

"Can I ask you a question?"

"Yeah?"

"Would you do anything to save those you love the most?"

"I always do," the little girl replied matter-of-factly, once again leaving Kara stunned.

She always does?? What kind of small child has ever had to save anyone once, let alone more than that??

Kara and the child made soft yet uninterrupted eye contact for an undisclosed moment in time. Neither speaking. Neither saying a single word. For that moment, two souls shared a genuine connection as the sun shone in the skies above and the birds and children sang and played all around.

However, as Kara continued to gaze into that small child's eyes, she sensed her energy. She felt her soul. And somehow, some way, she felt her age. Her true age. The little Indian child was much older than she looked.

Which didn't make a lick of sense.

But there was more. Kara knew this little Indian girl, too. She didn't know from where, but they'd met before.

"It's terrific to see you again," the little Indian girl said, as though reading Kara's mind.

Kara needed to explore this. She needed to know where she could have possibly known this little girl from, but her guilt was too intense. It overpowered her curiosity, and she needed to confess.

"Someone wants me to hurt you," she said sadly.

"Who?"

"I'm trapped. I'm trapped and, and I don't know what to do."

"But it's not the screaming woman, is it?"

"No. No, it's not."

"Who is it?"

"Something else."

"Someone else, or something else?" the little girl asked in a comforting tone.

"Something else," Kara replied, the pupils of her brown eyes quivering like brittle leaves in a snowstorm.

"It's OK," said the little girl softly.

"I'm supposed to be dead. I'm not supposed to be here. I'm not supposed to be in this body! This is her body, but if I give it back to her, I'll die! I don't want to die again! I don't want to! But I have to hurt you..."

"Do you mean kill me?" the little girl asked, still looking into Kara's eyes with nothing but pure understanding.

"Who wants you to kill me? Is it Kalizar?"

"How do you know..."

"It's Kalizar, isn't it?"

"How do you know?"

"They gave you this body and are using you to try to kill me, aren't they?" asked the little Indian girl.

"Yes," they have my soulmate and, and she said terrible things will happen to him if I don't do this."

"Oh."

"If mi a go do it, him will be alright, but mi haffi live wid dis torment. But if mi nuh do it, if mi gi dis gyal back her body, mi a go dead an him soul a go get tortured!"

"It's OK," said the little girl, somehow understanding Jamaican patois perfectly.

"No, no, it's not! And why aren't you scared of me?! Didn't you hear what I said?! I have to kill you!"

"But you won't do it."

"MI HAFFI KILL YUH!"

"But you won't. We both know you won't."

"BUT I HAVE TO!"

"No, you don't. You're not a bad person, Antonia."

Antonia. Antonia. For some reason, hearing that name spoken by that child touched Kara's heart. Kara spent so much time hating everything Antonia represented and wanting nothing more than to be anything but her that she'd convinced herself she was someone else.

But she wasn't.

Kara was Antonia.

She always was Antonia and always would be Antonia. Why was she ashamed of who she truly was?

My name is Antonia.

Kara's name was Antonia.

My name is Antonia.

Her name was Antonia.

"Yes, your name is Antonia, and you're beautiful."

As an ocean's worth of salt water streamed from Antonia's eyes, she heard the real Kara's screams growing louder. She desperately clamped her ears shut to escape them. However, such attempts were sadly futile because said screams originated from her own psyche.

There was no escape.

Also, little did she realise but police sirens wailed in the distance. Sirens, which were becoming louder. Sirens she probably would have been able to hear had she not covered her ears.

"I'M NOT! I'M UGLY!"

"You're not. Of course, you're not. You're so pretty."

"BUT THIS ISN'T MY BODY!"

"I'm not talking about her body. I'm talking about you. You're pretty, Antonia."

"GIVE ME BACK MY LIFE!"

"Kill the girl. Kill the girl, or Winston will howl in pain for all eternity."

Kalizar's words permeated the air, thicker than molasses mixed with clay and more haunting than the ruins of a Nazi death camp. And then, as if to accentuate Kalizar's point, Antonia heard Winston's anguished voice begging for mercy somewhere in the ether.

"WINSTON!" she screamed!

"Kill the girl, or you both shall know nought but unforgettable harm."

"Kalizar!" the little girl shouted. "Stop it! Let her go! This has always between me and you! I'm the one you really want!"

"Kill the girl."

Tragically, horrifically, and sadistically, the skin on Antonia's body once again began to wither and rot. Once again, she felt the moisture slowly being sucked out of its pores and evaporating into the sunny air.

Once again, she felt her lips, cheeks, arms, and legs shrivel and decay on the spot until her body had gone from thick and luscious to thin and decrepit.

Her hair greyed and fell off her scalp in matted clumps, and everything in her vision went a pale shade of orange as her vocal cords lost most of their ability to function.

Gripped by terror, she grabbed a knife from the gut pocket of her hoodie. She held it to the Indian girl's throat seconds before a young black female police officer arrived on the scene. She gasped at Antonia, her face contorted by disgust and horror.

"PUT THE KNIFE DOWN AND BACK AWAY FROM THE GIRL!" screamed the terrified officer, pointing her Glock 22 pistol squarely at Antonia's skull.

"Officer, it's OK!" shouted the little girl. "I'm OK, she isn't going to hurt me!"

"I HAVE TO DO THIS!"

That's what Antonia was trying to say. However, what came out was an unintelligible stream of gibberish. As the terrified children and their equally terrified parents took notice of what was happening, they scattered in fear, leaving Antonia, the little girl, and the police officer alone in that park.

"Kill the girl."

"Kalizar, leave her alone! I'm the one you really want!"

"DROP THE KNIFE!"

"She isn't going to hurt me, don't shoot her!"

“MI NUH WANT FI DO DIS!!”

"DROP THE FUCKING KNIFE!"

"Do it. Kill her now."

"LET ME GO! PLEASE LET ME GO!"

"Wait, wait! Is your boyfriend called Winston?!"

"I SWEAR TO GOD I WILL SHOOT YOU IN THE FACE IF YOU DON'T PUT THAT FUCKING KNIFE DOWN NOW!"

"HUH?!"

"Winston's here! He said Kalizar's lying! He said he's fine! He says it's OK! You don't need to do this!"

"WINSTON'S OK?!"

"He's fine! He's fine! He said he's waiting for you like he promised!"

The little girl could somehow understand her, even through her now withered vocal cords. However, before Antonia could ask how the hell that was possible she felt Kara's body acting against her will. Its right hand pulled the little girl in close while its left tried to stab her with the knife.

But Antonia tried to stop that from happening. She tried so hard. She struggled to pull that hand away, but she couldn't. She just couldn't.

Antonia was locked in a one-on-one battle with three demons, one that she wasn't nearly strong enough to win, try as she might. Kara's now haggard and gaunt frame was locked in vicious conflict with her as she pushed herself to the limit to regain control.

But then, as she struggled, she heard the little girl's voice.

"Antonia, it's OK. It's OK. You can do this."

"MI A TRY SO HARD, BUT MI CYAH STOP DEM! DEM TOO STRONG!"

That was what Kara's withered vocal cords tried to say as what little was left of her veins bulged from her now decayed and wrinkled skin.

"The only power Kalizar have is the power you allow them to have. It's the power you give them. You don't have to fight them. You just need to know they can't control you."

"DEM TOO STRONG! KILL ME! KILL ME NUH?!"

Antonia had the quivering blade pressed excruciatingly close to the little girl's throat, but still, she showed no fear. She simply looked at her with nothing less than kindness, compassion, and understanding.

"It's OK. Stop trying so hard, and just let go. Let go, relax and know there's nothing they can do to control you."

"MI CAN'T!!!"

"Your name is Antonia Hoell, and you'll be OK. I love you, Antonia. You can do this. I love you."

"LET THE GIRL GO!"

"Kill the little girl!"

“NO! MI NAH DO WAH YUH WANT!”

"Don't listen to her, Antonia. It's OK. It's alright, you can do this," the little girl said without ever taking her eyes off her.

Antonia then felt Kalizar's grip begin to soften. Slowly but surely, Kara's body became hers again. Slowly but surely, she regained control of its limbs.

"You're loved, Antonia. You're safe, and you're beautiful."

A feeling of calm contentment flowed throughout the body Antonia's soul had been using as its own. A tranquil sensation of peace not known since she was a small child some 80 years before. A sense of relaxation that lifted her spirits and somehow caused her to regain control of Kara's limbs.

"See? I told you you could do it," said the little girl with a smile.

"Thank you," Antonia smiled.

"You don't have anything to thank me for," replied the little girl, smiling sweetly.

Now in complete control of Kara's body, Antonia began to pull the knife away from the little girl's throat. Sadly, however, before she could finish, two bullets tore through the gut of the body she had stolen for her own and sent her spiralling to the floor.

As she lay in a twisted sprawl, rapidly losing her grip on both consciousness and life, she saw the little girl kneeling above her with Kara's hand in her own. She was looking through Kara's eyes right at Antonia's soul.

The more Antonia lost her grip on reality, the more the little girl kept her focus, and as Kara's body bled out, the whole world faded from view. All that remained was her and the little girl.

She never took her eyes off her.

"You're going to be OK, Antonia. I've got you," the little girl said softly.

Those were to be the last words Antonia ever heard on earth. Thoughts of the little girl were to be the last she would ever have. As her borrowed mind began to shut down and her soul slowly detached from it, she faded from consciousness.

She didn't know who, what, or where she was. Reality diluted. Existence morphed, desaturated, and liquefied into nothingness. Antonia knew nought except for one thing, that the little Indian girl never once took her eyes off her. There, she knelt, steady, resolute, loyal, and unwavering, right by Antonia's side.

She never took her eyes off her.

Not once.

37 | THE APOLOGY ACROSS LIFETIMES

ANTONIA | The Timeless Place

"Antonia, I'm sorry. I'm so sorry for what I did to you, and I hope you can believe and forgive me."

Once again, Antonia was lost in that forgotten place. That dark and endless void of nothingness from which she'd heard Peter and Claire callously allow her to die. Once again, Antonia was separated from her body. Once again, she was detached from the experience of living in the three-dimensional physical universe.

Once again, she existed as nothing but a disembodied consciousness floating through an endless ether of thought, heading to an unknown destination from an unremembered origin.

Antonia's senses had abandoned her, once again.

She saw, smelled, felt, heard, and tasted nothing but was somehow and some way more aware than ever before. And because of this, she knew something.

Antonia was not alone.

She felt a masculine presence all around, one she'd known for many years but hadn't felt for decades.

One she'd hated for all of that life yet still missed more than the deserts miss the rain.

The same masculine presence which now felt surprisingly warm, loving and remorseful.

"I'm sorry," he repeated.

However, the masculine presence didn't communicate with words but with energy.

Vibration.

Resonance.

One which permeated Antonia's being and imbued within her the proper depth of his meaning.

"I harmed you in ways no soul should ever do to another, and I want you to know that it wasn't your fault. I take full responsibility."

Antonia had never felt such affection from him before. His thoughts warmed her spirit and shone a healing light on her soul. One which illuminated that dark chasm of nothingness all around and transformed it into a bright expanse of love.

"I wasn't good enough for you," she thought in response, tearful energy flowing from her being in all directions.

"You hated me," she added. "That's why you did those things against my will. That's why you degraded me."

"No," he replied.

"You couldn't be any further from the truth. It wasn't you I hated but myself. I detested the man I was. I hated who I had become, and seeing your youthful innocence was an agonising reminder of everything I had lost. Every day I saw your beautiful little smile or felt that loving energy beaming from your pure heart, mine shattered just a little bit more.

You were brought into my life as a mirror, Antonia. Through you, I saw myself for what I truly was, and through you, I received my soul's most significant challenge in that lifetime.

The complete and enduring support you showed those people, despite what I or others thought, inspired my soul and challenged my ego.

Please know that the more I attempted to kill the light of your spirit, the more I actually killed myself.

Please know that it broke me to do those things to you. It broke me mentally, physically, and emotionally, Antonia."

At first, Antonia resisted, her thoughts tangled in a chaotic web of old wounds and unanswered questions. She wanted to recoil, to cling to the pain she had carried for so long. A pain that had defined and held her in a way he never had.

"Every time I harmed you, I poisoned myself, so much so that my time in that incarnation was shortened as a result. It's why I fell prey to that condition, Antonia, and it's why we spent so much time together at the end. My soul was crying out for a way to apologise, but my mind and body simply weren't brave enough to verbalise it."

But as his words sank deeper, she felt a strange, unfurling warmth like sunlight breaking through a dense mist. Her anger, which had once felt like a shield, now felt oddly heavy, weighing down something she was no longer sure she needed to protect.

"The guilt I felt over what I did to you brought an early end to my life and caused my soul to pay a penance in the great thereafter. However, that penance led me to the level of spiritual understanding I currently have. I have you to thank for that.

I owe everything to you."

His energy resonated within her, filling spaces she hadn't realised were empty. For the first time, she felt the possibility that maybe, just maybe, she could let go. If only a little.

"The steadfast strength of your character in the face of such darkness was my mirror, and Antonia, I thank you. Your love for Winston was the most beautiful thing I ever saw in that lifetime, and I'm privileged to have had you guide me as much as I was supposed to guide you.

You are loved. And you always have been."

With those words, a dam broke within Antonia's psyche. She was shocked, amazed, overcome, elated, and basically emotionally overcome.

If she were still within a body, she would have hugged this male tighter than she'd ever hugged anyone before. If she were still within a body, she would have cried a river of tears onto his chest and bawled hard and loud enough to be heard for a mile in all directions.

But alas, Antonia was not in a body, so she could not hug him nor cry onto his chest. All she could do was think of the words.

"I love you too."

And with that, reality began to morph

38 | THE LAST CORRIDOR

ANTONIA | The Timeless Place

Antonia opened her eyes and looked down at her hands to see she was in a body again.

Old again.

White again.

Decrepit again.

Distraught again.

She was in a long, pulsating, and flickering blood-red corridor that stretched endlessly. One in which the laws of physics seemed more of a suggestion than a strict rule.

Everything was inverted. Up was down, right was left, and each movement felt laboured, like she was trawling through a thick molten soup.

However, a white light glowed radiantly in the distance and its soft, soothing rays called to Antonia. Those rays were warm, inviting, somewhat intoxicating and emanated alongside a beautiful song with an ethereal voice.

Yes, Antonia also heard a voice.

Without any words being spoken, she knew the light was calling her. It wanted her. She knew that. No words needed to be spoken.

But Antonia also heard growls, chuckles, and whispers all around her now ancient and gaunt white body. Ominous and foreboding utterances of malevolent consciousness that bled from the molecules of the ether and the moist surface beneath her wrinkled feet.

She saw Kalizar, not in one place but many, their three heads having grown bodies of their own and flickering menacingly across the undulating tunnel and even slithering over the pores of her skin.

Kalizar was nowhere in particular but everywhere at once.

But there was more. Kalizar had a young black woman locked in a cage composed of dark energy. The woman was ensnared in a chaotic web with tight black vines coiled around her shapely form and piercing her flesh to extract her life force.

That woman was Kara, and Kara howled in distress as her essence was stolen from her, slowly, perpetually, and painfully.

"All your souls are belong to us."

Kalizar's three selves split into two and were all over Antonia's tired and frail body in a flash. They pulled and tugged at her, not at her physicality but her soul. They were tearing Antonia's soul apart. The pain was subtle at first, but what first started as a tug quickly ballooned into an excruciating wave of misery.

"A heavy penance to pay for your misdeeds, Antonia."

Antonia tried to scream for help, but her voice sounded like she was deep underwater, and her body moved in slow motion.

"Welcome to your doom."

She continued to struggle but to no avail. Reality perpetually warped. Colour slowly drained from her vision as it simultaneously grew darker and darker. She felt a swelling within her. Immense pressure.

Overwhelming pressure interspersed with thousands of Itches.

Millions of itches.

Itches that she didn't have nearly enough limbs to scratch. Itches which evolved into streaks of pain that stretched and scraped across her entire being.

The pressure continued to grow. Never stopping. Never halting. That is until one of Kalizar's clones reached straight into Antonia's chest and grabbed her heart. She tried to howl, but all that escaped her withered lips was the smothered gurgles of a drowning gazelle.

Antonia was being ripped apart.

Antonia was prey.

Half a dozen clones of Kalizar tore at her from all sides of that fluctuating blood-red corridor as she prayed for help, release, or just something, someone to save her.

But it was all for nought.

"You will not escape."

There was nothing she could do.

"Resistance is futile."

Lost in a frenzy of panic, Antonia struggled like a wild animal, trapped several leagues beneath the seas but sadly with none of said animal's power. She bucked wildly like a condemned criminal on the electric chair, but with none of the force those words would imply.

It was all for nought.

"Embrace the inevitable."

There was nothing she could do.

"Accept your fate. Embrace death's inevitable caress."

Antonia howled yet again from the pit of her decrepit lungs. Louder this time. Somehow, with more strength. Somehow, with more vigour. Yet, it was still all for nought. It just wasn't enough. Not even close. She was being smothered.

Enveloped. Consumed. Devoured. Eaten.

And as the nerve endings of her haggard body and black soul continued to incinerate at that demon's touch, Antonia once again found an emerging sense of peace. It was time for her to finally stop fighting.

This is too much for me.

Time to stop trying.

I can't fight them.

Time to accept reality.

As Antonia's ever-dimming vision slowly succumbed to total darkness, she looked into Kalizar's eyes.

"Darkness there, but nothing more."

Their faces were emotionless masks that harboured dead eyes while contorted into the shapes of sinister smiles. Faces which hadn't experienced the sweet joy or immense sorrow of emotion for aeons.

This brought a sense of fear which Antonia also felt as one of destiny. This was her ultimate destination. It was inevitable. Her entire life had taken her to this very point.

There was nothing she could do.

I have to give up.

She just needed to face reality.

The last thing she would ever experience was the visage of this demon smiling from behind emotionless caverns for eyes as it claimed what little was left of her soul.

It was time to stop fighting.

Time to accept reality.

Time to accept her fate.

However, before Antonia could succumb to said fate, that Kalizar clone exploded into a swirling column of black dust as a blue, glowing arrow burst through her mouth from behind her neck.

Immediately afterwards, a gold shield crashed into three of the remaining clones, sending them spiralling into the distance.

And then, a blue bolt of electricity slammed onto one of the remaining two. Before Antonia could blink, a tall Indian woman teleported next to the last one and punched it into an exploding column of black dust.

"Don't worry, I've got you," said the Indian woman with sincere emotion as she stood with the majestic aura of an ancient queen.

She wore a tribal outfit with a bow and arrow in her hand, a giant gold shield on her back, and glowing blue energy coming from the spot between her eyes.

"No harm will come to you."

The voice was different, older, but Antonia knew who this was.

"It's you."

While in an adult body, she still radiated that same childlike innocence and beauty.

"But, but how?"

"Yes, it's me," she continued. "Come on, Antonia, let's take you home."

With those words, Antonia's reality slowly became crystalline white as everything in that tunnelway flowed into each other, even with the words of the Indian woman. Somehow, her utterances flowed from her heart as waves of energy that melted into the surrounding landscape.

Antonia also saw that the Indian woman wasn't alone. She actually had a tiger and two tribespeople standing by her side. One was a man, the other was a woman, and both were beautiful but looked like twins. They stood smiling while holding hands as their toned bodies shone in the crystalline white labyrinth.

As for the tiger, it was huge, massive, enormous, menacing, and fearsome, but with eyes that conveyed an oceanic level of intelligence and wisdom that no beast should have. All had their eyes firmly locked on Antonia, but she felt nothing but empathy and compassion coming from them.

Empathy and compassion, which lifted from their forms like morning dew evaporating from a lush Amazonian rainforest to become one with the all-encompassing white soup.

And then, Antonia heard another voice. Another masculine voice. One which was strong, firm, resolute, and prideful. One she'd not heard in over half a century.

"Hello, white girl," he said.

It was a voice she'd missed dearly for decades. One which moved her heart with love and made her feel overjoyed to once again hear. One belonging to a man for whom she had the utmost respect. A man sadly taken from the world too soon.

"Hi," Antonia replied, smiling inwardly.

As Antonia's world continued to become white as snow itself, her energy remained focused on the strength and support which emanated from that masculine presence. She now saw and felt that man's true love and admiration for her. She'd never allowed herself to notice it before, but it was always there.

However, as she continued to journey into another plane of existence with that man by her side, Antonia could also feel the love of the majestic Indian woman and her followers. They were watching over her, guiding her, ensuring she was OK.

And Antonia was better than OK. She was beginning to feel free.

But she also felt guilty. Guilty because she let that man down when he needed her the most.

39 | THANK YOU FOR SHOWING ME HUMANITY

ANTONIA | The Timeless Place

"I'm so sorry," Antonia whispered, her voice trembling.

"Sorry for what?" the man replied gently.

"I killed you."

"No, you didn't."

"I let you die."

"No, Antonia. You didn't."

"I should have kept watch better. It's my fault they got to you."

"It wasn't your fault."

"Yes, it was!"

"Look within yourself."

"What?"

"Do you truly believe you could have stopped them? Someone as small as you?"

"I could have tried."

"You did try. You gave everything you had, even took a bullet with me."

"It wasn't enough."

"You nearly died with me."

"I don't care."

"Your life was never the same afterwards."

"I could have helped you. I could have saved you."

"No, Antonia. Those men were coming for me, no matter what. I'd made enemies too powerful to escape. If it hadn't happened in that ballroom, it would've been outside, the next day, or the day after. My time had come; nothing you could have done would have changed that."

Tears flowed freely from Antonia's soul. Were they tears of happiness? Sadness? Relief? Regret? She couldn't say. All she knew was that a deep love for this man welled up within her, and she finally understood that he felt the same for her. But this love wasn't romantic.

No, it was something warmer, supportive. It was a bond between lifelong friends and comrades at arms who had weathered numerous storms side by side. Antonia felt overjoyed to know she had proven herself worthy of that bond.

"You were always worthy, Antonia. You never needed my approval for that to be true. You are worthy now, just as you always were."

"But you never said that back then."

"I had my own battles to face. The mistrust I held toward you came from my own heart. It was my burden to carry, Antonia. It was never yours."

"Thank you."

"It was my time. Nothing you could have done would have prevented it. But know this: your work helped bring forth the world as it is today. You were instrumental in that. You helped reveal our suffering to those blind to it."

"How?"

"You brought new ideas and tools that allowed us to spread our message far and wide. You provided resources when we were destitute, introduced us to those in power, and helped them see us not as beasts but human beings."

"Was I that helpful?"

"Even more so."

"Thank you so much."

"You played a pivotal role in changing the world, Antonia. Never forget that."

"Thank you."

And then, without limbs to hold or bodies to embrace, they merged in a way that transcended physicality. Love, affection, admiration, respect; all these emotions flowed between them like beams of light.

It was a bond that dissolved the lines between their souls, an embrace where they could no longer tell where one spirit ended and the other began.

All Antonia felt was love. A love that knew no boundaries, crossed all barriers, and rendered the colour of her skin as irrelevant as that of grass.

And then, in the heart of that love, within that soft, endless well of understanding and mutual goodwill, she felt the presence say:

"Thank you. Thank you for showing me that a person's worth is not measured by the colour of their skin but by the content of their character."

And Antonia replied, thinking but not speaking:

"Thank you for giving my life purpose."

"It's time for you to go."

"Why? I want to stay here with you."

"Our journey here is over, and it's time for you to finish your story. You're going to beat those demons, Antonia."

At that moment, she felt a blinding flash of light, an overwhelming surge that carried her from this plane of existence, sending her back through the swirling tunnel. But as she drifted away, she felt and heard that masculine presence presence whisper:

"By any means necessary."

40 |
BOUND BY SHADOWS, FREED BY LIGHT

ANTONIA | The Timeless Place

"Go... our shadows... go..."

As her eyes fluttered open, Antonia's ears were assaulted by Kalizar's dark, hissing command. The voices echoed from every direction, impossible to trace.

Still, she felt their sinister intent wrap around her, thick and malevolent. Shadowy and wet, Spectres began to creep toward her as the hallway twisted into a chaotic maze.

The labyrinth around her was now a churning sea of crimson and jet black, spiralling and flickering out of sight without pattern or order. She had no idea where to go.

"Go to the light!" yelled the majestic Indian woman from somewhere unseen.

"I don't know where it is!" Antonia cried back.

"Yes, you do! None of this is real! They're trying to deceive you! Trust yourself!"

"I don't!"

"Yes, you do! Believe in yourself!"

"How?!"

"Just do it!"

Antonia's heart raced. Her limbs were alien to her. When she tried to raise her right arm, her left twisted, and when she tried to straighten her left, her head bobbed.

All the while, the shadowy spectres glided closer, whispering tens of thousands of distorted voices that filled her mind, coaxing her toward madness.

Panic washed over her as she clung desperately to the woman's words, like a sailor to a lifeboat in a storm.

"Help!" she screamed.

Nothing else came to mind.

"Help!"

It was all she could think to do.

"Help!"

But her pleas vanished into the void as the spectres neared, their icy chill burrowing into her skin, smothering her as if to drown her very spirit. Paralysed, she spun helplessly, frantically.

Just as the shadows reached her, a cry echoed through her mind:

"We've got you!"

Suddenly, an army of tribal warriors materialised in the corridor, defying all reason as they battled the spectres without hesitation.

The majestic Indian woman bounded into the fray, riding that massive tiger as it devoured a spectre with a single bite. Then the tiger's eyes turned a deep black, vibrating with energy as it exhaled a powerful bolt of dark energy that obliterated three more shadows in its path. Kalizar, however, dodged gracefully, twisting like smoke.

More warriors filled the corridor, each moving with a fluid grace far beyond anything Antonia could muster. But as they defended her, the shadows closed in again, tearing at her, consuming her essence.

Just then, a volley of energy arrows pinned the shadows against the walls, dissolving them into a thick mist. In that instant, Antonia felt her body beginning to obey her commands. One shaky step after another, she moved forward, unsteady but gaining control.

"I have to help her," Antonia whispered, hearing Kara's pleas. They were no longer faint, no longer distant, but as close as her own heartbeat. She didn't know how she knew, but she knew precisely where Kara was.

Her focus narrowed as she walked, her mind growing quiet, her senses fixed solely on Kara's presence. Her limbs grew steadier with each step, carrying her forward.

"Where are you going?" called the majestic woman.

"I have to help her! I can't leave her like this!"

"Save yourself!"

"No, I owe her this."

"Then focus! Calm yourself!"

"I'm trying!"

"Kalizar distorts your senses, but you can resist!"

"How?"

"Think of something beautiful!"

Even as the words left the woman's lips, Antonia's mind filled with memories of her loved one. She felt his presence; warm, powerful, protective. She felt his strong, gentle arms around her, his scent of sandalwood musk enveloping her. The memory grounded her, lifting her, allowing her to float toward Kara.

The shadows swarmed around her, but Antonia pressed on, buoyed by the warmth of her love. Energy arrows pierced the darkness, and warriors leapt beside her, their blades slicing through shadows that reached for her soul.

The crimson and black faded into blinding white light as she floated forward. And in that light, she saw a lone figure; a beautiful young black woman, caged and shackled by venomous serpents, her life force fading.

It was Kara.

As Antonia approached, she felt the energy between them merge, Kara's presence enveloping her. Their hearts began beating in unison, and in that crystalline light, their souls became one.

For a single, timeless moment, Antonia and Kara ceased to be separate entities. They were no longer white or black, old or young. They were simply one.

And it was blissful.

41 | YOUR MEMORIES ARE MINE

ANTONIA & KARA | The Timeless Place

"I'm sorry."

"For what?"

"For stealing your life... I'm so sorry."

There was a pause, a tremor passing through both voices like a current in shared waters.

"I'm sorry, too."

"Why?"

"Mi nuh know. It's like... yuh feelings dem a mine too... wow... oh wow... lawd gard..."

"Wah? Wah happen?"

"Your memories. So much pain..., so much misery. I feel it all."

"I want you to know I'm sorry."

"Don't be."

"But I am."

A silence settled, heavy and fragile; neither was sure where one began and the other ended.

"I see it all. I see everything that happened to you and feel like it happened to me. It's crazy. It's like your memories are mine."

"I feel yours, too."

The words seemed to come from nowhere and everywhere, drifting between them like an endless healing mist. Each felt the other's regret, echoing and intertwining between them.

"I know what life was like for you. I know now why you wanted to be me. I see it all...and I understand. I get it."

"I'm ashamed that you can see me for who I am."

"Don't be. There's nothing to be ashamed of."

"But mi mash up yuh life."

"No... Yuh save mi life. Gi it meaning."

"How?"

They paused, breathing together, not knowing if they were answering or being answered. And then, as one:

"I made a living from flaunting something most could never have. I monetised people's deepest insecurities and offered little value to the world besides my body. Feeling how you felt from looking at my pictures has opened my eyes."

"Oh my God... that was crazy."

"I know."

Then again, they spoke in perfect unison, sharing the same mind and soul.

"In your situation, I would have done the same thing. I now understand my effect on people and don't like what I see."

They continued, their voices blending, fading, merging, and coalescing.

"But yuh life done," a voice whispered.

"Mi life jus a start," another answered.

"You're wanted by the police. There's a manhunt after you," a whisper floated between them. The resulting response came as if from both and neither, an answer without a question.

"I'll be fine."

Antonia had ceased to be, and so had Kara. They were nameless now, a singular being with no need for labels.

"How?"

"I just know. None of this has happened by accident. I feel it. I have a higher calling, a true purpose, and you have put me on the path towards it."

"But yuh a go prison."

"No, mi nah go."

"A how yuh can know dat?"

"I wish I knew how, but I just do... You do too."

"Oh my, you're right, I do. I see it, too."

The entity formerly known as Antonia and Kara continued to speak with unified and synchronised voices.

"I'm going to appreciate living now more than ever. I'm going to forget materialism and my image. Pay attention to what matters. Focus on my passions. Do more charity work. Give something back. And, of course, reach master rank on Street Fighter."

"Wow."

"You showed me that my life can have more meaning than I ever thought possible. I'm so inspired by the work you did in the civil rights movement. You were one of the few white people who dared to stand up for black people at a time when the rest of the country saw us as second-class citizens."

But suddenly, a dark presence swelled in the ether. A cold and sharp shadow bore down on both.

"We nuh deh yah alone."

"Lawd God, somebody else here."

A malevolent energy broke into their unified consciousness. Each could feel it, thick, viscous, and poisonous. A voice, neither one nor the other, whispered to both.

"You killed me."

It was the voice of one who intended to do them harm.

"Who?"

"It's him."

"Him?"

"Him."

"Yuh feel him too?"

"Mi feel him."

A masculine entity spoke. One who knew both women and who both women bow knew. One who hated both women and who both women now had reason to hate.

"You killed me."

They felt his anger reverberating through the ether. They felt his hatred oozing into their beings like arsenic.

"You tried to kill us first!" they continued, still speaking, thinking, and acting as one.

"Fuck you!"

"You stalked us! You made our life hell!"

"FUCK YOU! I'LL KILL YOU, I'LL FUCKING KILL YOU, YOU FUCKING WHORE!"

"Let go."

"SHUT THE FUCK UP YOU DISGUSTING JUNGLE BUNNY!"

"Di jungle bunny weh yuh did a fantasise bout."

"We sorry fi how yuh feel, but we neva cause yuh pain."

"WHAT?!"

"We didn't cause you any pain."

"YOU KILLED ME! BOTH OF YOU! YOU FUCKING KILLED ME!"

"We didn't do shit! Nobody told you to obsess over our social media!"

The hatred emanating from that male was so palpable it became tangible on that energetic plane. It was thick like tar made treacle and every bit as disgusting to the senses.

Kara and Antonia continued to speak as one.

"Tek responsibility. Yuh did have di choice fi nuh look pon we page dem, but yuh choose fi do it. Yuh did have di choice fi seek help fi yuh mix-up thoughts bout black woman, but yuh choose not fi do dat. Yuh hatred an attraction fi black woman nuh have nutten fi do wid we."

The male entity said nothing. He radiated dark, vengeful, and malevolent energy into the surrounding ether. The energy deeply unsettled the souls of both women.

"And what were you going to do after you drugged us?" They continued. "Of course we defended ourself. And we thought we had to save Winston! You think we were going to let you live so Winston's soul would die?"

Strangely, fortunately, surprisingly, that masculine energy began to shift. Something about that last statement caused the vitriol to seemingly drain from his being, leaving his energy spent and simply sad.

Had they bodies to inhabit, he would have been hunched over in abject defeat.

Had they forms to occupy, he would have appeared broken, limp, and thoroughly beaten.

But alas, they inhabited no bodies and occupied no forms, meaning his defeated state expressed itself through pure emotion and nothing more.

"I'm so fucking sick of being rejected."

"Is that why you hate black women so much? Because they rejected you?"

"I'm just tired of being discarded and overlooked for who I am. It's always been like that. It always was like that."

"But dat neva we fault."

"What?"

"It wasn't our fault."

"I know."

"It wasn't our fault."

"Oh my God."

"What?"

"Oh my God, I've been so wrong. I'm so sorry."

That was the male entity. For some reason, the anger and hatred that had previously radiated from his being were now dissipating into the ether, leaving a sense of sadness and humility in its wake.

"Really?"

"Yes. I've been so silly, so stupid. I was blind. Blinded by my hatred, I see it now. I see it all, and I'm so sorry."

With that, for the first time in an unknown period, the entity formerly known as Antonia and Kara began to separate into two. Their union, blissful as it had been, was coming to an end.

"It's time for me to say goodbye."

"What's happening? Where are you going?"

"I, I think I'm going back to my body."

"Really?"

"Yeah."

"But you were shot."

"It's OK, I'm going to survive. I know I will. I'm going to be OK, and so will you."

"I can't believe I forgot. How on earth did I forget?"

"Forget what?"

"You guys need to talk."

"I don't want to be alone with him, but I like being connected to you, Kara."

"You always will be. You'll be a part of me forever now. I can tell."

The male entity was Peter, the stalker formerly known as Hippocratic Oath. It was strange; he came with so much venom and hatred, but now it was all gone. Where had it all gone? Where had his hatred disappeared to?

"You're safe with me, I promise."

"Goodbye, Antonia. I have to return to my body."

"Thank yuh fi everyting."

"No, thank yuh."

With that, Antonia found herself back in her body, not Kara's sublime, young, and chocolate form, nor her young pre-disability body, but the ancient frame with which she met the end of her existence.

However, unlike before, there was no disappointment within Antonia's soul. She felt no self-disgust. No self-hatred. In fact, she felt nought but a growing sense of peace.

A sense of contentment.

Of self-acceptance.

"I've been so silly."

That was Peter. He too, was back in his body and now stood before Antonia with a supportive and calm energy.

"Why?"

"Because I forgot who you are. I forgot who we are."

"What are we?"

"You really don't remember?"

"No. What don't I remember?"

Peter smiled softly, sweetly. His eyes flashed with a kindness and understanding they simply didn't have when she met him in person.

"We made an agreement to do this."

"What?"

"Before this lifetime. Our souls made a contract to cause each other immense harm and, in doing so, allow ourselves to grow."

"Are you saying that we're soulmates?"

"That's exactly what I'm saying."

It seemed so strange, so crazy, frankly unbelievable. In what universe could one who caused her so much pain be her soulmate? It seemed impossible to comprehend.

"I thought soulmates were people you loved and who loved you."

Peter smiled softly, the light of love somehow emanating from his being.

"Not necessarily. Soulmates are those who massively impact your journey. They can be people you really love but those you hate too. It's not about how much you love them. It's about how they impacted your journey."

This comment stunned Antonia, both for its simplicity and also for its potential truth. Upon reflection, it made so much sense. The people she intensely disliked were often those who had affected her life's journey the most.

"Yes, you're getting it," Peter smiled as though he could read her thoughts.

"If this is true, then it's clear we're soulmates," Antonia added.

"Exactly."

"But why didn't you say this when you first arrived?"

"I didn't remember. I was still locked into my earthly way of being. However, the more time I spend in your presence, Antonia, the more I remember who we really are."

"And who are we?"

"We've lived many lifetimes together."

This comment floored Antonia. It paralysed her right from the neck down and rendered her vocal cords inoperable. All she could physically do was gaze into Peter's eyes with pupils as large as tennis balls and a mouth wide enough to fit a fist.

"Really," Peter continued. "Our minds may have hated each other in this lifetime, but our souls couldn't possibly love each other any more."

"Oh wow."

"I love you, and I always have."

Antonia felt it, too. She felt love emanating from him. Flowing from him. Glowing from him. She was immersed in it. Enveloped within it. Ensconced within it. And it felt good. It felt wholesome. It felt right.

"You know something?" Antonia said, a warm smile beginning to spread across her lips.

"What?"

"I actually have to thank you."

"Why?"

"Because I lived my life with intense rage..."

"Me too."

"Yes. Rage I kept restrained within me. Rage that grew, swelled, and burned against the inner walls of my mind and soul. It was a rage that devoured me internally, and I spent my entire life waiting for an excuse to explode it all out. You gave me that excuse, Peter."

"I understand. That was the deal we made."

This was too much to comprehend. Too much to fathom. Antonia's greatest enemy, the one she'd hated more than any other, was her soul's closest companion?

That everything Peter did was not an expression of his inner wickedness but simply an act of love? Merely him faithfully carrying out an agreement they both had made before their lives?

"I needed it. It was cathartic, and I thank you for it," Antonia continued, nearly breathless from overwhelm. "Thank you for creating the space for me to express that side of myself."

"You're very welcome, but now that time is over."

"Why? What happens next?"

"Now we leave this phase of our existence. Now we go to the world between worlds to tally our lessons from this lifetime and decide what we plan to do next."

Antonia knew what that meant. On a deep and core level, she knew exactly what that statement meant. In fact, it was clear once she left Kara's body that this was to come next.

She knew this was the next stage of her soul's journey, but that didn't make her any less scared. That didn't make it any less terrifying. She couldn't do that journey alone. She just couldn't.

"Will Winston be there?"

"Winston?"

"The love of my life."

"Erm... oh yes, of course. He's waiting for you to join him. I know he's dying to see you."

"So what do we do?"

"Take my hand."

Was Antonia really prepared to say goodbye forever? Was she prepared to say goodbye to her existence?

"I don't know," she replied. Fear pulsing through every quivered syllable.

"Antonia, I promise, I mean you no ill will, and I humbly apologise for the harm I caused you in this lifetime. Please, let us take this next step together."

Despite Peter's words, Antonia's fear was less about him and more about what his proposal meant. She didn't know if she was ready to say goodbye. But then again, what else was she going to do? Maybe this was indeed the next step? The only step.

With that, Antonia took Peter's hand and felt a slow and soft white flash of light engulf their bodies as he smiled into her eyes. And then, somehow, the two began ascending high, higher, and higher still. Floating weightlessly above things her eyes and mind could not comprehend.

Antonia perceived things for which no earthly words existed to describe. Stars, suns, planets, solar systems, galaxies, universes, dimensions, cells, atoms, molecules, and even more.

These were the best words her mind could uncover in its futile attempt to explain the utterly inexplicable. It was as though she were staring at the source code of reality, the digital sequence of zeros and ones that were the building blocks of the three dimensional plan of existence.

Also, as they soared ever upward to a destination Antonia could not begin to name, she looked into the eyes of the man she once despised and finally saw him as he truly was.

He was just another soul like herself.

Peter was simply another soul making his way through life and doing his best with what he had. Antonia also realised that the negative emotions she felt for the soul formerly known as Peter were locked to her earthly frame.

They were a consequence of having manifested in that three-dimensional realm and hence having experiencin the illusion of duality. However, as said, that duality was not real, for she and Peter were not separate entities but one and the same.

They, along with all of creation, had emerged from the same eternal river of essence, and to that river of essence, they would return.

Her old resentments didn't belong. Not to her. Not anymore. Antonia had banished those sides of herself to the annals of history like a newly emerged butterfly discards its old chrysalis.

Antonia felt lighter than a hydrogen atom as her earth-bound hatred for the soul formerly known as Peter faded away. She felt expansive and blissfully compassionate as he looked into her very being with the exact same emotion.

And then, Antonia felt a particular pull she couldn't articulate. It was a knowing which compelled her to gaze upwards and have her breath wholly stolen by the sight of a gargantuan ball of pulsing energy. One which looked just like the sun but in a brilliant shade of luminescent white.

"Is that what I think it is?" Antonia asked with a heart filling as much with fear as excitement.

"Yes," Peter replied with a smile.

“I’m scared.”

“So am I. But I’m here. We’re in this together, Antonia. Please don’t worry. There’s nothing you need to do. There’s nobody that you need to be anymore. No need to try so hard and no need to keep fighting. Just let go. Let it all go, and allow me to guide us to our next destination.”

Antonia was going to do this. Antonia could do this. She could let go. She could surrender. She could release all the pain, the torment, and the pressure. She could do it. She would do it.

The closer they were to that sun orb, the more brilliant its light became. Antonia felt its incandescent energy beaming through herself and Peter and filling her with,,. unease.

Antonia felt uneasy.

A gnawing sense of discontent increased the closer she got to that light.

This isn’t how it’s supposed to feel. Is it? She thought.

“It’s to be expected,” said Peter, as though reading her mind. “Heading through that light means the end of everything we were in this lifetime, and our egos don’t want that.

Our egos are tied to our current identities and desperately clinging to them like rats on a thin plank of wood adrift in the Arctic. We’re both scared, Antonia. Neither of us wants to do this, which is precisely why it must be done.”

Buoyed by the guidance of her soulmate, Antonia edged closer to the sun orb, embracing the gravitational pull that sucked her into its depths like a whirlpool of finality.

Like the irresistible pull of a black hole, she was drawn ever closer to the end.

To finality.

To her ultimate terminus.

All while doing her utmost to override the palpable trepidation which began to consume her from the inside out. Her chest tightened like an iron knot, and the pores of her wrinkled skin broke out into an icy cold sweat.

The feeling was becoming unbearable.

"It's OK, Antonia. Stay strong. I'm here."

Antonia grasped tightly onto Peter's hand and focused on his eyes. She needed an anchor to help ignore the stinging and burning sensations beneath her skin. She needed a trusted guide, a loved companion, a sworn protector, anything. Just anything to help her navigate that transition.

However, this was when whispers once again slithered into her wrinkled eardrums.

There were tens of whispers. Thousands of whispers. Tens of thousands of whispering whispers. Whispers which unsettled the heart. Whispers which unnerved the soul. Whispers that writhed against the cellular walls of said eardrums to utterly unsettle their owner.

Whispers, which ironically seemed loud like a bullhorn yet quiet like a dying church mouse.

But there was more.

Antonia didn't just hear whispers; she felt fear. She felt terror. Antonia was terrified. Genuinely terrified.

And then the shouts started.

And the screams.

"You're safe, Antonia. Just come with me," Peter added. Trying to reassure her.

"What's happening!? This hurts! This hurts. I'm burning all over! Is it meant to be like this?!"

"It's your ego at play. It doesn't want you to change, so it's fighting to stay the same."

"This doesn't feel right!"

"It's your ego, Antonia! Mine is doing the same thing! Don't worry, just trust me!"

Antonia felt such a strong revulsion. Such an overwhelming sense of dread, along with that painful sensation under her skin. She was burning like a low-level flame had been lit underneath her pores and was slowly increasing in temperature. But she had to keep going.

"NO DON'T DO IT!"

Didn't she?

"Who is that!?"

"IT'S ME, ANTONIA! DON'T TRUST HIM!"

It was the Indian woman.

"DON'T LISTEN TO HER!"

Somehow, the majestic Indian woman's words cut through the ether and revealed the state of Antonia's reality. Suddenly, everything morphed, and she saw where she really was.

She wasn't moving toward rebirth but a dark, writhing pit of doom, a mass of death with countless yellow, slit-pupiled eyes fixed on her.

Vines snaked around her neck, drawing her toward a churning mouth lined with serrated fangs.

She looked down, horrified to see biting insects swarming her skin. She clawed at them, but they wouldn't budge.

"HELP!" she screamed, her voice cracking as she met Peter's gaze.

He'd tricked her.

His face twisted in vengeful hatred, and his grip turned iron-tight as he forced her toward the abyss. She struggled, but it was useless.

Powerless. As always.

The vines squeezed tighter around Antonia's neck, and she spasmed, her body crawling with the relentless, biting swarm.

It was all too much.

And she was all too weak.

"YOU'RE GOING TO BURN IN HELL YOU UGLY LITTLE FUCKING CUNT!"

She was too weak and too tired.

"YOU KILLED ME! YOU FUCKING KILLED ME!!"

She was in too much pain. It was simply time for her to die.

"FUCKING DIE!!!"

Time for her to rest.

"FUCKING DIE!!"

Antonia felt her eyes beginning to close. Antonia forced her eyes shut.

"FUCKING DIIIIIEEEEE!"

But then, in a blue explosion of electricity, the majestic Indian woman appeared in front of Antonia, wrapping her strong arms around her waist. The blue spot on her forehead glowed with a fierce light that matched her gaze, and her voice cut through the darkness in a powerful yet gentle manner.

"Don't worry, I've got you."

Suddenly; Antonia felt a flood of relief flood throughout her being. It was warm, grounding, and real. The burning sensation from the biting insects faded away as they dissolved into nothingness.

Her body then uncoiled from its state of terror. She began to unwind, and her hands, previously so tense, began to soften, releasing the fear that had gripped her bones.

She looked up at the woman holding her and felt a sensation of true safety. One of trust.

And then, as the woman's light intensified, Antonia's world turned blue.

42 | THE CLOUD GAUNTLET UNLEASHED

ANTONIA | The Timeless Place

Antonia was back in the tunnel flanked by the majestic Indian woman, that giant tiger, and the rest of the tribespeople, all of whom had formed a phalanx around her.

As she took ever-increasingly confident steps, the Indian woman marched by her side like a sentinel, pushing and pulling her out of the way of attacks from Kalizar's spectres while dodging those headed for her.

"Nomi! To me!" The Indian woman shouted.

Within seconds, the tiger broke from the formation, ran to the middle, grabbed Antonia by the neck with its teeth, and hoisted her onto its massively muscular back. Within less than a second, the rest of the tribespeople had already readjusted themselves to plug the resulting hole.

After that, the tiger bolted rapidly, and Antonia clung to its back for dear life.

Again, a blue bolt of energy hit Antonia in the chest, startling her but causing no pain. Immediately after, a blue explosion had the majestic Indian woman appear in front of her on the back of the tiger.

"We've got you."

Antonia looked forward and saw another light in the distance. The original light. The real light. She made eye contact with the Indian woman, and the two shared a silent nod. This was where she needed to be. This was to be Antonia's final destination.

She knew that. She understood it.

The Indian woman then fired another bolt of blue energy from her hand into the distance towards that light and teleported both her and Antonia to it.

They were now on the top of the undulating tunnel yet somehow still standing upright as though its ceiling had its own gravitational pull.

A black gargoyle swooped down and clawed at Antonia. Still, the Indian woman pushed her out of the way and shot it between the eyes, exploding it into a swirling cloud of black dust.

"Come on!"

The Indian woman fired a blue bolt further towards the light and again beamed her and Antonia to it. Moments later, another gargoyle swooped down, grabbed her, and carried her away, kicking and screaming.

The Indian woman rapidly became smothered by scores of Gargoyles and shadows but continued to bark orders nonetheless.

"Head to the light, Antonia! You have to reach it!"

Antonia did as she was told, realising she was stronger with every passing second. Her body obeyed her now, and as she took those initially tentative steps towards that light, she began to feel energy and purpose returning to her form.

She could do this.

That walk turned into a jog, and soon, that jog eventually turned into a run. Strangely, the closer she got to the light, the younger and stronger she became.

"Keep going, Antonia! You can do it!"

"Are you OK?!" Antonia cried.

"Don't worry about me! Keep going! He's waiting for you!"

"There is nowhere left for you to be.

Your very soul is ours to bleed."

Antonia was now physically in her 60s and feeling ever-energised while simultaneously panicked. Why? Because seemingly from nowhere, dozens of Kalizar's clones appeared on the morphing tunnel's floor, walls, and ceiling.

They stood hunched over to the left and casually swaying to the right as their many haggard and gaunt faces dripped with malevolence. But she had to continue. She couldn't quit.

"Antonia, you have to keep moving!"

"YOU'RE NOT GOING ANYWHERE!"

That was Peter, aka the man Antonia once knew as her stalker, Hippocratic Oath. He appeared right upon her from behind, but where did he come from? That was anybody's guess.

All she knew was that his hands had gripped her neck tightly with the sadistic intent to choke out the life they both no longer had.

"IF I DESTROY YOU I GET ANOTHER BODY! I GET TO LIVE AGAIN!" Peter screamed.

Her body, now in its 50s, Antonia backwards headbutted Peter and drove her elbow into his nose, shockingly exploding him into a dissipating column of black dust. She then continued her run to the light.

"Don't give up, Antonia, I'm with you," said the majestic Indian woman.

"Kalizar's everywhere!" Antonia cried.

And she was right because Antonia was engulfed in an all-encompassing web of chaos. War blitzed at either side as the Indian woman's warriors did fierce battle with Kalizar's spectres and clones.

"Keep going! You're almost there!"

Snake tendrils burst from the mouths of the clones and buried themselves deep into Antonia's chest. However, before she could howl in pain, the beautiful man and woman pair of warriors leapt in and hacked the tendrils in half and yanked them out of her chest.

In a fluid motion, they spun around and shot four clones with arrows as the giant tiger eradicated two more with a ruby-red beam of force from its mouth.

Antonia was now in her 40s and stronger still. She had to keep going.

"Don't stop! You're almost there!"

And she was. She was almost there. The bright light at the end of the tunnel was closer now than ever, and as the strength returned to her body, she found herself hurtling through the air at speed.

"You're almost there, Antonia."

The light was all around. All-encompassing. Potent. Brilliant. Eternally luminous. However, as Antonia gazed at its beauty, Kalizar and Peter coiled around her from behind.

"Not today, you little whore," said Peter, maliciously.

"Welcome to your doom," Kalizar cackled.

A blue bolt of energy hit Antonia in the shoulder before the majestic Indian woman appeared by her side with a tremendous amount of wind forming around her right forearm. It was as though her arm had become a turbine, creating a near-deafening cacophony of noise.

"Cloud Gauntlet!" she cried.

The turbine intensified until it became a thick and blueish-grey fog of violence that ricocheted around her arm.

"Duck your head."

Antonia did as she was told, and the Indian woman aimed her arm at Kalizar and Peter, who tried to escape. As they attempted to retreat, an unseen force weighed heavily upon them, binding them to the spot.

Like liquid concrete, the air around them had thickened, trapping them in place. The sheer pressure made it impossible for them to even twitch. It was as if the tunnel had turned against them, bending the laws of reality to hold them captive.

Their movements slowed to a crawl, their limbs frozen by the immense gravitational force exerted by the energy swirling around the Indian woman.

They couldn't move.

"Leave Antonia alone!"

A burst of concussive wind rocketed out of the Indian woman's arm, violently obliterating Peter and the remaining Kalizar clone while narrowly missing Antonia.

Immediately, all of Kalizar's minions faded into nothingness.

With Kalizar and Peter seemingly defeated, the majestic Indian woman and her tribespeople gathered around Antonia at the edge of the light.

43 |
HI, MY NAME IS...

ANTONIA | The Timeless Place

Now inhabiting her 25-year-old body, Antonia gazed up at the brilliant ball of light that somehow hovered both above and below her in that undulating tunnel. It was so radiant, so breathtakingly beautiful, that she was beyond enchanted.

But it wasn't just a light; that much was clear. It was alive. It was sentient. And very much aware of Antonia.

Also, that brilliant ball of light was calling her. Whispering to her. Coaxing her. It wanted Antonia to merge with it, but she didn't know.

She just didn't know.

"It's OK," said the majestic Indian woman, taking Antonia's hand in her own, clearly aware of her need for support. "You're safe, and this is OK. You don't have to fear what comes next."

"But what will come next?" Antonia asked, a palpable tremor in her voice.

A tremor which unbeknownst to her, reverberated like a wave against the hearts of the majestic Indian woman and her tribespeople, causing them to smile in sympathy.

"You know. Antonia. You know exactly what comes next."

"I don't. I don't have a clue."

"Yes, you do. And it's OK, you're going to be safe."

Antonia was too overcome with emotion to be physically capable of speech. All she could do was cry. Antonia cried a lake of tears into that undulating tunnel, their many psychic tremors pulsing against the sympathetic hearts of the Indian woman and her people.

Eventually, she spoke, her right hand lovingly cupping Antonia's cheek.

"Antonia, I'm sorry."

"Why?"

"You've been used as a pawn."

"Why?"

"Kalizar used you to get to me. They know they can't do it here, so they used you to kill me in the day world."

"You're the child they wanted me to kill," Antonia said with wonder.

"Yes, I am."

"So all those horrible things I had to do were to prepare me for killing you? To get me used to taking lives so it would be easier to kill a child?"

"Yes, that's right. But they also wanted to torture you specifically."

"Why?"

"They wanted to get revenge on you"

“Why?”

“Do not worry; all will be revealed soon, my love."

"But I've never met them before."

"Not in this lifetime."

"What?"

"Antonia, you and I are old friends."

"We are?"

"Yes, in another lifetime, we knew each other very well."

This comment gave Antonia a flash of remembrance. Tremors, whispers, sparks of old and long-forgotten memories. Those of her as a diligent student and this woman as her...

"Wait, were you my mentor?"

"Yes, I was, and we did something to Kalizar that they have never forgotten or forgiven."

"What did we do?"

"We created Kalizar."

"Oh my. But how?"

"Antonia, that does not matter right now because I promise you that everything will be revealed soon. What matters is that you know that they have a grievance with both of us but mainly myself and were using you to exact vengeance."

"Oh wow."

"But it's over, and now you're free."

"Free to do what?"

"Now you're free to be."

"But what about Kara? She was shot because of me, and, and she's a wanted criminal."

"Kara is going to be fine."

"How do you know that?"

"Antonia, she is going to thrive, so please don't worry. And please don't worry about anything you were forced to do while in her body because Kalizar are to blame for all of it."

"Thank you."

Antonia and the majestic Indian woman slowly rose from the ground and floated towards the light.

"How is any of this possible?"

"The day world in which you've spent your most recent life accounts for less than 0.0001% of everything in creation, Antonia. There is so much more for you to experience."

"Really?"

"Yes. Also, I must tell you something."

"What?"

"Your lifelong preoccupation with acts of the flesh was not what you think it was. You weren't bad, evil, or wicked, but quite the opposite. In the days of old, some women in the day world, women just like you, used vital life force energy to communicate with higher powers.

Their natural abilities provided essential healing and guidance for their communities, and such women were critical to the survival of their tribes."

"I'm one of these women?"

"Yes, and you have performed this role many times. That is who your soul is, and it is that part of you that was focused on those carnal acts. It wasn't about vanity; it was about completion. You felt separated from the divine and needed to become whole.

However, you did not have an outlet for connection in this lifetime as you did in others. You didn't have the necessary guidance to cultivate your natural abilities.

Because of that, you knew only how to revel in divine life force energy but not how to channel and direct it. Between this and the treatment of your father lies the cause of this fixation for you in this lifetime.

But please know this: You are complete, Antonia. You always were."

"Wow. Oh wow," Antonia replied, tears streaming down her cheeks. The Indian woman was crying, too, albeit with a soft smile and supportive gaze.

"Antonia, it's time to enter the light."

"I can't."

"Yes, you can."

"I'm too scared."

"You need not be."

"But I think the light is death."

"Oh, Antonia, you sweet and lovely soul. Of course, it's death."

The majestic Indian woman hugged Antonia tightly yet with a profoundly supportive energy as both continued to cry onto each other's shoulders.

"But it's OK. It's time for you to rest."

"I can't."

"It's OK."

"I don't want to die."

"Yes, my love, you do. This is the end of your journey; deep down, you know this to be true."

The majestic Indian woman pulled back, kissed Antonia on the forehead, and smiled at her, still crying."

"It is your time," she continued sweetly. At this moment, Antonia felt an overwhelming release of emotion erupt from her chest. Her face grimaced with shock as she fell to her knees, shivering. The Indian woman knelt beside her supportively.

"What's happening to me?" Antonia asked fearfully and tearfully.

"That was your heart chakra releasing years of trauma in preparation for your transition," the Indian woman replied. "Don't you feel so much better now?" she asked with a smile.

Antonia did feel better. She felt incredible, in fact. It was like she'd dropped a giant backpack full of boulders that she didn't even know were there. Boulders she now realised she'd been carrying her whole life.

But still, as elated as Antonia felt physically, it did nothing to assuage her fear.

“I need to apologise to Blake.”

“I'll find him and do that for you. I promise. I'll let Blake know who you really are, Antonia. But it's time. It's time to enter the light.”

"But I can't do it. I don't want to be alone again," she replied, her voice quivering.

"Who said anything about being alone?"

Now back in her 18-year-old body, Antonia saw a figure arrive from the ball of light. It was completely white at first and rounded in form like a single droplet of water breaking free from an entire ocean. However, as it reached Antonia, it took the form of a man she knew all too well.

"Winston!"

"Hello, Tiger," Winston smiled. Before he could even dream of continuing, Antonia threw her arms around him and squeezed tighter than a hydraulic press, laughing just as much as she was crying.

"What are you doing here?!"

"I said I would wait for you until you die, and here I...”

Antonia kissed Winston with the molten passion of an exploding star before he could even think about finishing his sentence. It was a kiss decades in the making. The resulting explosion of well Severn decades' worth of painful loss and sorrowful longing. A kiss of true undying love.

As they kissed, Antonia heard the Indian woman and her tribespeople erupt in an almighty cheer. It was thunderous in power yet soft in sentiment. Their collective, unbridled joy penetrated her heart.

Even the tiger roared.

When she and Winston eventually parted, she once again studied the face of the man she'd loved for her entire life. A man who looked exactly like the 18-year-old who was ripped away from her all those years ago.

"Come on, Tiger. Let's go. It's time for you to see what's next."

And with that, Antonia took Winston's hand, and they soared together into the light. As they entered it, she slowly felt her physical form melting not only into him but into the orb of light itself. Slowly but surely, everything that made her 'Antonia' begin to dissipate.

She was losing her identity, losing the labels she had placed on herself and that others had placed on her. She was no longer her skin colour; she was no longer Antonia Christine Hoell.

Now, she just was.

However, as her soul continued to shed the identity of its past life, its essence was fixed on the majestic Indian woman who had never stopped looking in her direction while still crying tears of sympathetic joy.

With what little was left of its ego, the being once known as Antonia looked deep into the eyes and soul of the majestic Indian woman and said:

"Who are you? I don't even know who you are."

As its essence finally became one with Winston and the gigantic oceanic orb of light that enveloped them both.

As a lifetime of mourning turned to joy.

As decades of agony became sweet, unfathomable bliss.

As deeply held insecurities and shame faded away into rays of contentment and self-worth, what little remained of the being formerly known as Antonia felt the still-crying majestic Indian woman say:

"Preeta. My name is Preeta."

Before Antonia was finally no more.

THE END

1ST EPILOGUE | I GOT MY SISTER WITH ME

ANTONIA | The Hoell Residence: Moss Bluff, October 1, 1965

Another letter had arrived in the post that day, another letter from New York, in fact. And so, as Antonia sat in her wheelchair at her small kitchen table, trying her gosh darndest to open it, her fingers trembled both in anticipation and dread.

The envelope itself was simple, small, and unadorned, literally the textbook definition of nondescript, yet despite this, it seemed to carry the weight of the world.

Antonia's imagination started running rampant because she knew it wouldn't be good.

Has something terrible happened to Winston? Has his health taken a turn for the worse?

Was she to blame not only for his poor health on disability but his ultimate demise?

Her heart thudded in her chest as she unfolded the letter, her brown eyes scanning its impeccably neat handwriting and dreading the inevitable.

Dear Antonia

First off, I hope this letter finds you well. I've wanted to reach out for some time now, but you can understand how much has been going on since Malcolm passed. This world has changed for us all in ways we never expected, and I've had to be strong in ways I didn't think I could. But God is good, and He gives us the strength we need when we need it most.

Antonia, I want you to know something important. Malcolm spoke highly of you. He always said you had a fierce heart and an open mind, and I agreed. I still do. Please don't think he didn't notice how you stood up for our people, despite everything you could have lost, everything you did lose, because he did. We both did.

We all did.

And trust me, I know that wasn't easy.

I've always admired you, Antonia. I know our lives seemed worlds apart, but I saw a kindred spirit in you. I saw a fighter. I never said it before because I was shy and had stupid pride, but now, with all that's happened, I need to say it.

You need to hear it.

You are a great person.

I know you've lost a lot, especially with your husband divorcing you and pulling back his support. And I can only imagine that you feel alone right now. But you are not alone, Antonia.

You never have been.

I have received more donations than I could have ever dreamed of since Malcolm's passing. It's overwhelming at times, but I see it as a blessing. I'm using it to help the families that Malcolm cared about, the people he was fighting for. And when I thought about who needed help, you came to mind immediately.

I am sure you have been struggling with your rehabilitation fees, and it doesn't sit right with me to let you carry that burden alone. So, I'm stepping in to cover the costs. It's the least I can do after all you've done for our people, even when it cost you so dearly.

Also, I want to say that you were right about a few things. Firstly, it's come to my attention that the people who killed Malcolm likely did come from a mosque in Newark, New Jersey.

It looks like the police are investigating other men but that's nothing more than a red herring, a smokescreen. It was the men from the mosque in Newark. Were they guided by Elijah Muhammad or NYPD?

We're not sure, but it certainly was them. Secondly, and speaking of the NYPD, Leon Ameer discovered that Malcolm's bodyguard, Gene Roberts, was an NYPD informant, so it seems your mistrust of him was well placed.

Was he involved in Malcolm's death? Or was he merely a spy who reported on our activities? I can't say for sure, and I fear this may never change because Gene disappeared after Malcolm's death. However, even if he hadn't, I'm powerless to fight against the might of the NYPD, so I don't know what I, or any of us, could do.

As for Newark, retaliating to them would only bring more bloodshed.

I'm tired, Antonia. The fight for justice continues, but the violence stops here. The battle was for equity for our people and nothing else. I refuse to see more of my people die.

If we retaliate and kill those men, are we any better than the white men who killed that poor innocent boy, Emmett Till? I don't believe so, but Antonia, I want you to know you were right.

You are family, Antonia. Malcolm saw that in you, and so did I; we always used to joke that you were his big little sister. And he once said you were an angel sent by God to show him that all people can be good regardless of colour.

Antonia, I don't know much about your family situation and what you've got going on with the Pooles. Still, if you are ever on the lookout for a sister, well, you've got one right here. My door is always open for you.

Anytime you need someone to talk to or a place to just be, you come on over. My girls would love to see you, and so would I.

If you need me to come to Moss Bluff and help with your rehabilitation, I'm already there. Just say the word, and I'll come running. I mean that.

Take care of yourself, Antonia. The world ain't always kind to those who stand on the right side of history, but you keep standing anyway.

With all my love, your new sister,

Betty

As Antonia put the letter down, her vision quickly became blurred by tears while a paralysing mixture of emotions assaulted her chest. She had never expected this kindness, this acceptance, from anyone, let alone Betty. Let alone someone who had lost so much herself.

Antonia hadn't considered herself worthy of that kindness, and the weight of those words touched her soul in places she didn't know could be touched.

Her fingers hadn't stopped shaking since she'd picked up the letter and showed no signs of stopping. Her eyes hadn't stopped crying since she'd read the letter and showed no signs of stopping.

Antonia had been speechless since she read the letter and showed no signs of speaking.

However, Antonia wasn't just speechless; she was mind-blown. She didn't even know what to think.

After a few minutes of tearful reflection where shockwaves of emotion made her body tremble like an earthquake's aftershock, Antonia finally regained composure.

She still had difficulty processing her thoughts; in fact, she hardly knew what day it was, but she was elated.

Antonia was elated.

Sad to know who killed Malcolm X and heartbroken to see that bitch ass Gene Roberts was with the NYPD, but elated nonetheless.

She wiped her eyes and folded the letter, placing it carefully in the drawer next to her, safe in the knowledge that her efforts hadn't been in vain. She had made a difference. People had noticed. Malcolm noticed. Even though he didn't show it much, he actually appreciated and cared for her.

Knowing that was everything to Antonia.

It was everything.

As was the knowledge that she wasn't alone. That she had help. Antonia had a sister now. Antonia had a family again. She wasn't alone anymore. And at that moment, for the first time in a long time, she smiled.

Antonia smiled a big fat smile.

2ND EPILOGUE | LE MONDE NE SUFFIT PAS

ADRIAN | Sons of God Recording Studio: Present Day

Adrian Phillips knelt in dark solitude, his entire body trembling with violent rage and shame. The whore Kara Clark's mocking words echoed endlessly in his mind, each syllable an agonising wound that drove his humiliation even deeper.

The evil bitch. The morally defective slut. How dare she speak to him that way?! How dare she humiliate him like that?!

The world had become twisted, glorifying the profane and ridiculing the righteous, and Adrian felt powerless to stop it.

So impotent, so worthless.

And Adrian hated that feeling.

It was an indignity that made him take a blade to his own forearms as penance for his weakness, as he had done so many times before.

Through gritted teeth and bloody arms, he perpetually whispered his prayer, pleading for justice and strength. Adrian had spent hours begging The Lord for a way to cleanse the world of its rot, but sadly, his prayers had not been answered.

But he wouldn't give up.

Pressing his hands to his heart, he beseeched his Lord and Savior to please show him the way.

Suddenly, a blinding light filled the room, and Adrian gasped in shock. Before him stood St. Jude, his face calm but eyes shining with an unsettling intensity.

The faintest scent of sulphur hung in the air, metallic and sharp, permeating Adrian's nostrils. The edges of St. Jude's figure shimmered and pulsated as though he were an image painted on water, always on the verge of dissolving forever.

"Adrian," the saint whispered, each word layered with three echoes.

Three somewhat feminine voices snaked through the studio with the cadence of an ancient hymn, reverberating through its air just slightly out of sync. The sound slid over Adrian like silk, at once comforting but somehow chilling too, drawing him closer with each deliberate utterance.

"The world is lost; the pure pay the cost.

But dark precedes light; in fury, we fight."

Adrian's heart pounded, his fervour mounting with every syllable. Despite the saint's cryptic tone, his message rang clear.

A Holy mandate had been decreed. God himself had finally answered his prayers, and Adrian breathed a silent prayer of gratitude.

"I understand," he whispered, clutching his hands tightly to his heart. "I understand so clearly, and I am ready. I am ready to follow God's will. The world must be cleansed, St. Jude. Please, tell me what I must do."

St. Jude's face twisted into a subtle smile as he leaned forward, his triple-toned voice curling like smoke around Adrian's ears, filling the room with an eerie, rhythmic hum.

"The chosen are few, and the corrupt shall fall.

The earth will tremble, pain consumes all.

From ashes and ruin, purity shall rise.

For in fire and fury, the faithful will baptise.

A storm of reckoning, to cleanse and reclaim.

This world, oh so broken, shall perish in flame."

Each word snaked throughout the room, layered and chilling while filling Adrian's heart with fervour. Lost in the euphoria of his calling, he felt a holy fire swell within his heart, a devotion so fierce he could barely contain it.

However, somewhere beneath, in a dark, silent corner of his soul, another fire flickered, one he could not name, a sensation he dared not explore.

"I accept," Adrian murmured, his eyes wide with devotion and wet with tears. "I accept my purpose a thousand times over. Thank you, St. Jude. Thank you so much for this opportunity."

As St. Jude's figure began to dissolve, the faintest smirk tugged at his lips. Adrian did not notice the subtle shift, nor did he see the dark shadow slinking into the corners, twisting like ink spilt amongst olive oil.

"A soul fed by fire, a fate of desire.

For pure hands to lift, the tainted one's gift."

The saint's voice lingered in a sinister chant, the threefold somewhat feminine echoes weaving in an unsettling cadence.

The words reverberated, layered like an ancient hymn, each tone warped and eerie. Adrian felt a tremor ripple down his spine, one his mind was too consumed with purpose to recognise. The room chilled, the air thickened with an otherworldly presence that seemed almost... amused.

And then, St. Jude faded into the ether from when he came, but not before a whisper, almost inaudible, brushed against Adrian's ear. It was a soft, almost mocking laugh that hung in the air long after the room had once again gone dark.

However, none of this mattered to Adrian because he now had purpose. He now had his mission, and it had been given to him by God himself. The heathens of the world were going to pay.

The fornicators, pornographers, politicians, liars and all else who purveyed sick and immoral filth to God's children were going to bleed. They were going to suffer, and if necessary, they were going to die agonising deaths.

With Jesus Christ by his side, Adrian Phillips realised he had but one option:

To burn the entire global civilisation to the ground and reshape society in His image. To usher in a new Age of Enlightenment on planet earth not seen since before Eve made Adam eat the apple. To make the sinners and evil doers of the world burn in the purifying flames of righteous fury as he sent every last one of their souls straight to Satan's lake of fire.

And Adrian would do so by any means necessary.

THE END

A NOTE FROM MOI, THE AUTHOR

Firstly, I want to say a gigantic merci beaucoup for reading this book. Writing stories is my passion, and I hope this one transported you to a world to which you can't wait to return.

If you found it impossible to put down, that makes me feel incredible because that's exactly the experience I strived to create. But even if it didn't completely land for you, I truly appreciate you spending your time here.

You could have been doing anything else, but you chose to step into my imagination, and I'm grateful for that. Now, you probably have one or two questions buzzing in your brain, namely:

- Who da heck is Preeta, the little Indian girl?
- What da hell is Kalizar?

So let's get to addressing them.

WHO DA HECK IS PREETA?

Preeta Patel was inspired by stories my first girlfriend told me about her childhood. I promised her I'd one day write a character based on her, and said promise gave birth to Preeta. We lost touch about a decade ago, so I don't even know if she knows I actually did it.

But I like to think she does. I imagine her sitting in a penthouse in Singapore or Tokyo, balancing an infant on her knee as she reads this, and smiling with the realisation that I'm talking about her.

Seeing Preeta grow into such a pivotal figure in my fictional universe (the Addassaverse) has been one of the most rewarding parts of my journey as a writer. She's far more than just a little girl, and trust me when I say I have massive plans for her in the future.

If you want to know more about Preeta and the larger forces at play in the Addassaverse, I'd love for you to dive into Preeta's Web of Chaos and Start A Revolution. They'll give you a glimpse into the web of chaos, magic, and wonder that surrounds her.

WHAT DA HELL IS KALIZAR?

Ah, Kalizar! That trio of malevolently feminine demons Their identity and purpose will finally come to light in my next book, When Women Were Worshipped. I won't spoil the surprise, but let's just say they're central to the Addassaverse in ways you've only begun to glimpse. For instance, they've been in other books, not just N-Word.

Anyway, as Preeta herself said to Antonia, "All will be revealed soon." So, sit tight and brace yourself because the best is yet to come.

That said, what I will say is this, usually stories with a female heroine have her go up against a man to 'prove something' against evil masculinity but I wanted to flip that on its head. Why not have a female hero go up against female villains?

All will be revealed soon.

THE TIMELINE OF MY BOOKS

You know how Episode IV of Star Wars came out in the '70s, but Episode I didn't release until 1999? My books are kinda like that.

Here's the in-universe chronological timeline:

- When Women Were Worshipped (my next novel)

- Preeta's Web of Chaos
- Future Preeta's Web of Chaos Sequel (currently unnamed)
- N-Word
- Start A Revolution
- Future Start A Revolution Sequel (currently unnamed)

While each book stands on its own, they all come together to form an epic saga the likes of which the world has never seen. So, if you're feeling curious, go back and check out the others, you might catch connections you missed the first time around.

BEHIND THE SCENES

Fun fact: Preeta Patel wasn't originally going to appear in this book, but I couldn't resist weaving her into the story. Watching her evolve into such a vital part of this universe has been one of my favorite parts of writing.

Also, if you caught any subtle references, perhaps a Spider-Man nod here or a Malcolm X quote there then bravo! I love layering these little surprises for my eagle -eyed readers. Keep your eyes peeled because the Addassaverse is literally jam packed with them.

GOODBYE TO KARA AND ANTONIA

Don't think this is the last you're going to see of Kara and Antonia, because it isn't. They'll be back at some point.

"But Kieren, Antonia's dead, so how the hell will we ever see her again?"

In the Addassaverse, death is never the end. Keep reading, and you'll find out.

All will be revealed soon.

CIAO FOR NOW

This story may be over, but our journey together is just beginning. If this book resonated with you, I'd love it if you left a review or recommended it to a friend or even a mortal enemy. Your support helps bring these stories to more readers and puts a huge smile on my chocolatey skinned face.

If you've enjoyed the cut of my gib, follow me on Instagram for updates on new releases, sneak peeks, and behind-the-scenes glimpses into my world:

instagram.com/kierenpaulbrown

Once again, merci beaucoup for joining me on this adventure. Stay curious, stay connected, and get ready for what's next.

Like I said before my next book will be called When Women Were Worshipped and if that title intrigues thee I promise the finished book will be just as eye opening. I promise you an unforgettable story unlike anything you've ever seen. Follow me on Instagram to be notified when it's released.

Anyway, take care.

Excelsior!

P.S. I've got a big, fat, massive No-Prize waiting for the first person to DM me the origin of that reference!

Printed in Great Britain
by Amazon

57342635R00255